CH00321394

Lauretta Ngcobo was born in South Africa. After the 1960s political upheavals, she went into exile, with three of her children, eventually settling in London, where she works as a teacher and continues to write. She has written one other novel, *Cross of Gold*, published in 1981, and has co-edited a collection of essays by Black women writers in Britain, *Let It Be Told* (Virago 1988).

And They Didn't Die is Lauretta Ngcobo's second novel, a turbulent saga of survival in South Africa of the fifties and sixties. It tells the harsh story of a deprived rural community driven by the laws of apartheid to live off land, once poor, now altogether barren. Jezile, young and eager for change, is caught up in the relentless crush of history, but is determined to plot the trajectory of her own life. Through a conspiracy of events she finds herself caught up in the cross-fire of blatantly racist policy and coercive traditional values fighting for a place among the dispossessed.

AND THEY DIDN'T DIE

Lauretta Ngcobo

VIRAGO

Published by VIRAGO PRESS Limited 1990
20–23 Mandela Street, Camden Town, London NW1 0HQ

*A CIP catalogue for this title is
available from the British Library*

Printed in Great Britain
by Cox & Wyman Ltd, Reading, Berkshire

To my mother, Rosa Gwina (née Cele),
who by example taught me to cope
and to straddle contradictions, and who,
above all, believes in me

1

*T*he dipping tank was empty. The dip mixture lay green, drying in trickles and splashes on the grey clay soil. A lone white man stood planted like a spear in the earth of Sigageni. Mr Pienaar, the dipping officer – the only white person whose duties brought him regularly to the black reserve of Sigageni – the only one who was thought to know the pulse of the people. Yet, he knew that he did not understand anything about the place or its people or its problems. Anger and loathing raced inside Mr Pienaar, pounding through his veins.

'How could they? How *could* they?' He heard himself growl. There was not a herdboy in sight and no cattle for miles around. And this was a Thursday, a dipping day. For the fourth successive week the women of Sigageni had emptied the tank in spite of the threats.

'Senseless, unthinking creatures!' he hissed looking at his feet. He raised his voice and threw his head back as he shouted again. 'Senseless, unthinking creatures!' And he stamped hard on his right foot. Then he slowly walked around in circles, in an attempt to stay his rage. What more was he to report to the authorities at Ixopo; he had assured them that it was nothing serious – childish pranks perhaps or some lunatic wandering free – anything but an act of rebellion on the part of these unpredictable creatures. He wanted nothing to tamper with his job; he didn't want trouble. 'What do dipping tanks have to do with clinics and doctors and starving children; what have they to do with schools and beer halls?' Sitting on a rock he continued to muse, 'The government is doing everything for them, and they deliberately wreck it – they accept nothing that is done for their own good, no appreciation, no understanding at all – how can anyone teach them to think!' Then he saw them. A group of about seven women approaching non-chalantly, with hoes slung over their shoulders. They were going to pass him by as though they had not seen him. He could hear the rhythmic muffled sound of the earth under their measured steps. The women looked away from the slippery contents of the tank spewed everywhere around it. He stood up quickly, flushed and furious at the sight of them. He could have stopped them, but he did not – he went on cursing inside. 'These women, this strange breed of womanhood, thin and ragged and not like women at all – they think they rule the world, they spill men's beers, they herd cattle, they plough fields, they run this community. That's what it is; that's why this defiance – they've lost respect for manhood, for all author-ity, but they haven't got the sense to do it properly. In the absence of their husbands they've lost the need for men, if nobody stops them, they're going to ruin this country. In spite of what others think, it is these women we have got to deal with, not those far away men in the cities.' He paced up and down. Then he wheeled round to look at their retreating backs. A few strides and he was behind the wheel of his fifteen-year-old car – it rattled and bellowed and shook and he drove straight at them, following them from behind, if only to filch away the apparent calm. And he succeeded. They screamed and scattered in spite of themselves. He sped off at a grinding speed, with a cloud of dust shielding his car up and beyond the hill, to his world – the world of roads and safety. He was determined that the people of Sigageni should be brought to their senses, if only to safeguard his job.

The women's screams and the screeching car wheels brought out a number of people from their midday meal. In the ensuing hubbub they called out the name of MaMapanga and gathered around her.

'MaMapanga, MaMapanga, it's worked, it's working, they're getting scared! You were right, you were right.'

Jezile, one of the very young women, became the centre of the excitement. They shouted and shook her hand and danced in a medley. She had suggested the whole idea at one of the Thursday prayer meetings.

'There goes god,' they shouted.

'There he is in his dust cloud.'

2

'He's gone to call the army – they'll be back in hordes today.'

'Let them do their worst, let them find the culprit.' And so went on the many voices. One last voice was Jezile's.

'Let them come, then perhaps they'll listen to what we have to say – we must tell them—' Jezile did not finish, and in the excitement, no one noticed that she had not. Nor did they notice what had passed between her and MaBiyela, her mother-in-law. It was nothing more than a cautionary look and one or two barbed words in Jezile's ear. Jezile raised a phlegmy cough and turned silently towards her house. So ended the celebration prematurely but it did not destroy the sense of victory all around. In a community that knew very few victories the feeling lasted quite some time.

But for Jezile it was over. Mortified and angry she went straight home and flung the kitchen door wide open. The ashes lay white and cold in the brazier from the previous night. She slammed the door to shut out the voices of the other women. She sat down and stuffed her apron into her mouth to stifle a scream and allowed herself a good cry.

No one really knew how deeply affected Jezile was by her failure to have a baby. Up until she got married she had believed that one night with a man was enough to make her pregnant; Siyalo had left a week after the wedding and she had soon discovered that she was not pregnant. She would now have to wait another long year for him to come back home on leave from Durban – a whole long year of waiting before she could gamble another chance. She had recognised then that it was a game of chance. A couple of months after Siyalo had left home MaBiyela, his mother, had confronted her with the question that Jezile had seen forming on her lips several times before:

'Is there anything yet?'

'Anything?'

MaBiyela had fixed her eyes below Jezile's waist and had repeated, 'Anything?' Jezile had stared back at her mother-in-law and had shook her head silently. That almost silent exchange was to mark the nature of their relationship for a long time. That day Jezile had cried and cried. The episode was the start of a relentless persecution. MaBiyela would not stop. She talked about children, she talked about childless women and she wondered aloud often, to all and sundry, what would

3

happen if Jezile was barren, for Siyalo, an only son, simply had to have children. The year was long and anxious and as it drew to a close Jezile began to twitch with anxiety – if only she could tune and time her body this time; her heart was filled with anticipation and renewed hope.

When Siyalo came home there never was so much love between two people in a hurry to squander the year's store in a couple of weeks. It bubbled like a spring and filled their house with noisy chatter and their silences with meaning. Given a chance they could have spent every moment of the first few days together, piecing broken intervals into one memorable stretch of time. But by the end of the first week there were frequent interruptions from different people. They were teased for consuming each other like that; they were gently but firmly pulled apart. MaBiyela turned up at their door three or four times a day. At first the young couple thought it was understandable, for she too had missed her son while he was away. But what became remarkable was the regularity with which she found chores for Jezile to do; duties that would take her away from Siyalo for hours. Soon other members of the family came to 'take Siyalo out' – 'other people had missed him, too, while he was away'. If their love hadn't been so all-enveloping she would have entertained a little bitterness at this social conspiracy. But the nights were too full to give room, even a little way, to petty interferences. As things were, she mildly wondered when social custom would alter to suit the new industrial practices.

Time flew by like a whirlwind. She was left cradling a feeling of expectancy and joy. There was even a defiant look in her eye when she encountered MaBiyela's searching eyes. But a few weeks later Jezile knew that nothing she had done had bent nature her way. She was not pregnant. She wept for days and she could not look anyone in the eyes. She fled back to Luve to be with her mother for several weeks. She was engulfed with a sense of failure. It took her weeks to write back to Siyalo, to break the news of their disappointment. The year ahead was very long. Nothing her mother said to comfort her could give her hope. She spent hours before her mother's bruised mirror scanning her shape – the scourge of barrenness. How to hold it in your hand – was it some tangible predisposition, some frailty, some constitutional failure, where was it – had Siyalo lied to her when he had said she was full and round, ripe, complete and bursting with womanhood. Siyalo wrote back, a letter full of reassurances – next time they would not fail – they needed more time together – no need for a doctor yet – he knew for certain she was not barren – he felt it each time they were together – nature takes its course – nature takes its time – before long he would arrange for her to come to him in the city. That whole year was agony and it discoloured all those wonderful feelings she had had when he first left. Anxiety is a corroding feeling; and couples living apart cannot escape anxiety.

That year MaBiyela had the upper hand. She did not say much, except once, a couple of months after Jezile's return from Luve. She chose her moment well, and in her most caustic voice she asked, 'Is there anything to tell us MaMapanga?' A gripe caught Jezile in the abdomen and once more all she could manage was to shake her head in silence and walk away.

Socially, Jezile began to keep a low profile, and even in political matters she became silent, which slowed things down quite a lot at Sigageni. She spent more time with her childhood friend, Zenzile, who was married to that good-for-nothing Mthebe. For a while their friendship had cooled off, for seeing Zenzile who, in the six years of marriage, had four children was painful for Jezile. Each time Mthebe came home from leave he found a new baby, and he left another growing, ready to find on his next visit. But, Zenzile was a captive in her house, with children who whimpered and hung around her skirts. Everything around was drab and Zenzile looked haggard and despondent. On occasion Jezile wondered if her friend was not somehow to blame for her own decline, but she would chide away this thought as soon as it intruded out of loyalty to her friend. She visited Zenzile regularly, at least once a week, to take her the current gossip of the community, to help her around the house – in short, to cheer up her friend for old times' sake. She washed the children when she could, fed them, put them to sleep, but she tried not to wonder at their dried-up tears, or their thin withered legs. She needed Zenzile and her tumble-down family life. She needed to get away from her life as a water carrier, a wood gatherer, a road mender, from her life in the fields, ploughing, sowing, weeding and reaping. She hated running after cows that invariably broke through fences. It was a hard, unremitting life, which left her unfulfilled. So she looked forward to those days when she could manage a visit to Zenzile where all she could do was glaze over her friend's predicament. From this daze of superficiality she was jolted upright one day by the news that one of Zenzile's children had died suddenly. One of the ones she had washed just two days earlier – she could not even remember its name. She was there, helping with the funeral arrangements; she stayed with Zenzile for many days after. When the others tailed off to go back to their families, she had no reason to hurry back. She hung on and kept her friend company.

Jezile came back each night and helped to cook, wash the children and slowly to cheer her friend. She came to love the children – the more she knew them and played with them, the more she missed not having her own children. Zenzile was utterly disillusioned on the one hand and Jezile was full of hope and promise on the other. They differed heatedly. Jezile did not see motherhood as a bind, a fulfilment of other people's expectations of her. All she knew was that she needed children to love, to secure her, to help her with some jobs that threatened to break her life. She saw far into the future; she would bring them up healthy and strong, which was to her, Zenzile's greatest failure. She would love them and present them a perfect gift to Siyalo. Above all, they would fulfil her life and save her from social torment.

When things had slowly returned to normal for Zenzile, Jezile went back to her routine and waited. The year was long. Essentially, life constituted long periods of waiting; all that the women of Sigageni ever did was wait. Then one day she got a letter from Siyalo. Her heart raced as always, and she read it greedily. But then she let it fall from her hands on to the table. She stared at the letter without seeing it. She could not believe it – wild apprehension stung her – in two weeks' time he would be home. And that's when her next period was due – the 15th of December, that's when he was due home . . . it couldn't be! It was obvious, she wouldn't make it again this time. She spun round and round, babbling to herself, 'Just why, just why did he always choose the wrong date? Why couldn't he plan the time of his leave in advance with her? He said it all depended on his employer; but what did his employer know about her, or her body or their need for a baby? How could he plan their life without them? Surely Siyalo must have a say about his leave. There must be a way I can intervene; I must influence things somehow. It is all about me; it is not true that I'm barren . . . it is just not true . . . I need time . . . I've never had a proper chance . . . chance, chance, chance . . . malignant fate is always against me. And that woman, she'll have a field day – she's so happy to call me barren; it's as if it didn't concern her son as well – as though she wished him as much pain as she inflicts on me. Perhaps she wants him to leave me for someone else. I wait a whole year for his leave – to clinch that trick of nature – conception. What is it? Why is it so completely out of my control; why is it that something that affects my whole life should be outside of me. Have I ever had any power to influence anything in my life? Once I swore that if Siyalo married me he would have changed the course of my life for ever; that I would long for nothing and would fall into the pattern of what was expected of me accordingly. Now this.' She leapt to the mirror as though the problem was sitting on her body like a mole. She whisked her dress up in one movement, right above her rounded breasts. For the hundredth time she looked at her shape critically, caressed her breasts and turned round to look at the body that had let her down each time.

On the night of the fourteenth, the day before Siyalo arrived she lay awake curled up in bed and waiting. She felt cold. When the fifteenth finally crept slowly through the cracks of the ill-fitting door she woke up and stretched. She could actually feel her body snap and creak, so tight was the tension that gripped her. She felt she would not even be able to smile at Siyalo without her face seizing up altogether. She had a hot bath to relax her body, to ease it for the welcome. She was half-way through her ablution when she heard the high-pitched laughter of her youngest sister-in-law Simo and her cousin-in-law Jabu. Their excitement quivered in the air. She knew how happy they were. This was a yearly celebration – if waiting was hard for adults, children did not know it – they lived in anticipation – to see fathers and uncles and brothers come and go. They lived for the festivities at the time of home-coming and the dreams filled the emptiness in between. Jezile tried to smile for their sake, but it was hard to whip her sluggish heart even to a pretence of joy. It was hard to recall and will herself into the passionate anticipation of his first return from the city exactly two years before. She felt completely alienated from the young woman she had been, and a complete stranger to the girl that accompanied him on his first tour after their marriage – just three years before. There had been so much hope between them then, on that dawn when she first saw him off. So many hopes had died. He too had faltered on a few promises. He no longer wrote her letters every week, his letters were much shorter than before and less amusing. Then there had been that time when he hadn't written at all for two whole months. What had he been up to? Had he really been ill? The thought of their love cheered her up a little. She chided herself, for, in the two weeks of waiting, since his letter she had morbidly dwelt on their aborted hopes and not once on their great love for each other. Perhaps, in the final analysis, nothing else mattered. If babies would not come, all the more reason why she should give him greater love.

An hour later, at the bus stop, she sat waiting, more cheerful than she had felt for several days. They saw the bus two miles away, winding its way down the hills, now behind them, now appearing. As it drew nearer her heart bit violently and per-fidious joy filled her whole body and she trembled at the thought that he might not be inside the bus; what if he had missed the bus. She shared the tense, silent anticipation with the girls as the bus came hurtling on as though it had no reason to stop. But it did, and she saw him first as he stood up. He was home; he had come back to her; he had left the city attractions for her. She flushed all over; beads of perspiration on her forehead and a hot flood somewhere deep in her loins. She burst into tears and people thought they were tears of joy. Siyalo held her hand; the magic was gone. He knew they were not tears of joy.

The days that followed were marred, full of empty talk when there were people around and flatulent silences when they were on their own. They had waited for eleven and a half months for this holiday and all it had brought was disappointment. At first Siyalo was determined to retrieve the happy times that they had had in the past. He knew he needed wholesome home-brewed love to anchor his heart in the long months of loneliness ahead in the city. But try as he might there was a sag in the middle, a hollowness that nothing would fill. He knew that this time their marriage could not survive the long separation and the inevitable taunts that she would receive. Other men did it – they resisted the city and came back to their wives, but they had children. For the first time he admitted to himself that they needed a child to hold their marriage together.

2

*T*hree weeks later Jezile received a short letter from Siyalo.
It had a far-away feel about it. She was shocked, but she
did not cry. It was her will, strong and unbending even when it
hurt her, coupled with anger. She walked around the house
restlessly yet noiselessly. Then she lay down but could not fall
asleep. She got up and pottered around the house. Then,
suddenly, it rose like a burp – a thought-burp. She stopped
pacing; something was resolved inside her, had fallen into
place. She, Jezile, would wait no longer for other people to do
things to make decisions about her life; she would make them
herself. Why, it did not even need thinking about. It was the
most natural thing in the world; to stand up and prepare to go
to her husband herself and sort out their life – if he could not
come and live with her and give her babies, it was for her to
stand up and go to him. She would not wait for him to say it or
do something about it. She was going to go to the doctor, tell
him what letter she wanted and why she wanted it. Next, she
was going to write the letter that her husband ought to have
written a long time ago, asking her to go to Durban for a
medical for her failure to conceive. She was going to sign it in
his name and take the letters to BAD – the Bantu Affairs
Department – , present the two letters and stand there waiting
for her written authority to spend a month with her husband in
Durban. Easy, no magic in it! She was ecstatic. She darted to
her suitcase with all the family papers. First she wrote a short
letter to Siyalo; almost curt in its instruction. She informed him
that she had resolved to get to Durban to see him; that he need
not worry about the fare for she still had some money left over
from what he had given her when he left the month before. He
was not to worry about the intricacies of obtaining permission;

she would see to that. All he was to do was to wait for her in exactly two weeks' time from the date of the letter unless she wrote and informed him otherwise. Her letter had a decisiveness about it that thrilled her. It felt wonderful taking charge of her own destiny, she had never done it before. She stopped for a moment as an encroaching doubt about Siyalo reared to intimidate her. She dismissed it as instantly as it had come – he would have to live with a changed wife just as she was coping with a fast-changing husband.

She then sat a long time composing a letter that a husband might write his wife – a letter of concern about her medical condition; a letter instructing her to get a medical note from her doctor and for her to proceed with the letter to the Bantu Affairs Department. She tore up the first draft and the second and the third. She could feel her exasperation mounting. But nothing would stop her now; she knew she had taken a decision that she should have taken ages before. Nobody would ever take that power away from her – not his mother, not her own mother, not anyone. Both mothers had had such a hold on her precisely because they had never had that power over their own lives – they had both sat and waited for their husbands; both had lost them in the waiting. She looked at Siyalo's weightless letter still staring her in the face and she concluded that he too would go the way of both their fathers if she did not do something immediately.

The visit to the doctor was surprisingly easy. He asked so few questions, it almost seemed as if he had foreknowledge of her problem. He asked why she had not been to see him before, as he wrote his letter to BAD instructing them to let her go to Durban to seek further medical attention. Within moments she was out of the surgery, elated. It had been so easy, it almost felt like a let-down. And if things were this easy there was no sense in going back home and returning to the village of Ixopo another day. So she went straight down to the Department. She knew she would have to wait a long time. The queues were long – perhaps at the end of the day she would have to go home and come again the next day to join the queue where she had left off the day before. That place, the burial ground of all human dignity. The faces of all those people standing there, sweating in the sun, but parched at the mouth drained all her excitement.

It was as if they did not know why they were there, as though they had always stood there, half their lives in that queue. Before long she felt the ache in her legs. The queue did not move. She changed the weight of her body from one leg to the other, but she did not move forward. The line stood still. She thought of going to the shade under the jacaranda trees, but she knew she would lose her place when the queue did finally inch its way forward. The sun beat down. She complained audibly and people responded with guttural sounds beyond curse words . . . nxe, arhrr . . . mfth . . . . Even if there was only one person to attend that queue snaking its way round the block, it should have moved faster. Strangely enough, it was there that she began to feel guilty about her lies; she had lied to everybody to get her own way. Why she should have felt any moral compunction when these people valued her life and those of others so little she could not understand. All day she sat at the end of that tortuous queue watching women return from the interior of those offices looking ashen grey. Some would stop to explain their shattering experiences in there; others would look the other way, unable to put their rejection into words. All in all, she realised that she was not the only liar, and that out of necessity they had to cover lies with more lies till they could stand firm like the truth. She racked her brains trying to anticipate the ordeal. What else would they want to know? What else was there to say to justify the need to be with one's own husband? In the end, only the truth could stand against the humiliations suffered inside those offices. If they had a job to do, she had a life to lead; and she was resolved to lie or cheat, if need be, to live that life. To help her resolution stick she got angry. Once her anger surfaced it flared up in spite of herself; it was all-consuming. She herself had never known how angry she was. Her anger needed no object.

As the queue inched its way little by little, her anger inched its way up her throat. By the time she walked in there, she did not trust herself to talk, not coherently in a subdued voice, the way she was expected to talk to white people who hold people's lives to make or destroy. Her nostrils were flared and her eyes raised ready to will the officer and scare him into action without questions. In silence she handed over the letters, from her 'husband' and the doctor. He picked up her husband's letter first. She did not know what she should have expected, but she lost all composure when after reading it the officer burst out laughing without even looking at her. At the end of his outburst he looked round as though his question was meant for someone else, not her.

'So when you want a fuck you pretend you're ill. Why can't these people think up something original? Why do they all say the same thing?' Turning to her at last he asked, 'Are there no men around your village; must you leave everything and lie your way to Durban?' She trembled in humiliation. Her eyes dropped, she felt her anger hissing out through her ears, making them unbearably hot. Silence.

'You want a fuck maan, you look for a man here.' After leafing through some files he took out a card. Shouting from the centre of that vast room he asked why she was 'burning' that much, for her husband had just been home a month before. He came towards her still studying the card. 'I don't think I can allow you to go to Durban, your husband has just been home.'

'I'm not going to my husband as such, I'm visiting the hospital,' she ventured to say. She was surprised at her voice, her grovelling tone. Then he remembered the other letter. Again, talking loudly to no one in particular he raised his voice.

'So you've been to that lying doctor; if he had his way that man would let all these women go away from their villages and live in the cities. You can't live in the cities, you hear me – cities are for white people. This doctor . . . I don't believe all these women are ill and barren – some ask to go down because they're pregnant – he lets them go; others want to go because they're not pregnant, still he lets them go – why doesn't he cure them? He's a doctor! He's a man too! Give them what they want!' She began to shake with mortification. At this point she thought she heard another voice shouting other obscenities somewhere along the passage, but she couldn't hear properly; her ears were filled with whirring noises. Then he bent down and wrote, all the time muttering under his breath. She wondered what he was writing. 'Your pass,' he barked without raising his eyes. At first she did not think she had heard it properly. 'My pass?' she repeated, trying to grasp the meaning of the question.

'Yes, your pass. Haven't you got a pass yet? How can you travel to Durban without a pass? Every woman in this district should have a pass by now or are you one of those who won't have one. They were giving them at Nondaba, why didn't you go?' It was a crowded moment for Jezile. Was he giving her permission to go to Durban – but for the book? Would he have given her permission if she had the book – the book? How could she, when one of the most burning issues at Sigageni was the fight against the passes. She was sworn not to take the pass, like all the women. She went cold, her ears drained of all that heat of a few moments before. All the while staring at him without blinking and her thoughts running parallel to his so that she could not hear what he was actually saying to her. He looked intently at her. There was a decided change of mood. Did he sense reluctance in her eyes? For the first time he lowered his voice – she did not know why. 'Well, if you and your doctor want you to go to Durban, you'll have to have a pass, won't you?' There was a twist of triumph in his voice. An air of efficiency suddenly animated all his movements. He wrote something fast and boldly. 'There, you can go to Durban if you have a pass.' Jezile had a feeling of being cornered and bribed. She was on treacherous ground. She went past the last woman in the queue, still waiting her gruelling turn. She looked through her, just like some of the others who had come out through those doors had done. The pass. Now it stood between her and Durban; no, between her and Siyalo; yes, and the baby. Shouldn't a mother brave all obstacles for the sake of her child, even her unborn child. Only, it's the pass this time. 'God, I'm weak. This is an impossible choice. Only last Thursday I talked heatedly against taking the passes – how can I face the other women this Thursday, tomorrow. While my friends are talking and swearing against the pass at the weekly meeting, I will be queueing for the same pass – God, why are women so trapped? – are there ever any choices? If I go quietly to the pass office tomorrow, soon they will all know, for they must all know, and had known all along, except me, that one can't go to Durban without a pass. If I flout all authority, refuse to take the pass, that's only a temporary victory – hardly anyone will know of my noble sacrifice; sooner or later, everyone in the Sabelo will end up taking the pass. Like the women in Zeerust we've sworn to go to prison for this. Prison, yes, and what next, what happens when we come back? Another prison sentence – for how long? In the end it will be passes; we will take the passes. What will we have achieved then? And my baby? And Siyalo?

Perhaps it was her need for comfort that made her go to her mother-in-law's that evening. Perhaps it was a sense of guilt. But when they were done with each other that evening, she wished she had not gone to see her at all. As she entered MaBiyela looked at her feet rather than at her face – a cutting look that slide and went past her, and, then, silence. Jezile could not tell exactly what was bothering MaBiyela. It could be any of the reasons that were always smouldering. The two women seemed ready to ignite at any moment. Jezile had had enough for one day. She wished she had told MaBiyela of her plans before going to Ixopo; but she herself had not known what was going to happen until the night before. She felt under attack on all fronts. This was certainly not the time to talk about the possible visit to Durban and all the preparations. Perhaps she should have asked for her permission to pay a visit to Siyalo first. She hadn't. Telling her now would simply inflame her. Jezile hedged. Anything to calm her now. She stood up to have a drink of water. She moaned about the hot sun.

'Ugh . . . the hot sun?'

'Don't you think it was hot today?'

'In the fields, yeah; but you were not in the fields.'

'Oh, yes, it was hot everywhere mother – Ixopo was very hot.'

'Ixopo? Is that where you were. At this busy time of the year you go jaunting off to Ixopo like a trollop.'

'Like a trollop? Mother, like a trollop?'

'What else do you call it, off to Ixopo like a woman with no cares and no husband.'

'Mother! What do you mean – what are you implying? You're insulting me.'

'I mean, if you have any worthwhile business in town, you would say something to me – yes, to me – in the absence of Siyalo, you should tell me – I'm here to look after his interests.'

'You're accusing me, you know that – you're suggesting that I'm unfaithful to Siyalo—'

'What else is there to conclude?'

Irritation came riding over Jezile. The hot exchange incited Jezile to tell MaBiyela that she was in fact preparing to go and see Siyalo in Durban. That was like a bomb – it blew up and engulfed the two women. Such an explosion could never be countenanced, never between mother-in-law and daughter-in-law. Custom had prescribed that, no matter how bitter the scorn, each had to go along in churlish compliance. But not that night – they were unsparing in their attack on each other. When it had died down, in the silence that followed, Jezile could not believe it was her virulent voice that floated down and echoed in her ears from the walls all around her. She had never exchanged harsh words with her own mother – it was not at all like her. She had said everything, but she did not feel purged, she did not feel sorry either. The little kitchen hut was suffocatingly hot and she had the strongest desire to get out of there. She looked round at all the faces of her young nieces and nephews – they all read the same – she was on trial. She had the urge to go and see Zenzile. She wondered what they would make of it if she walked out into the night. They already thought the worst; if she got up and left they would assume she had a tryst to keep – perhaps with the same young man she was supposed to have spent the long day with. But she was in no mood to conform – let them think the worst. She did not care. She was changing so fast she couldn't even understand herself, but she had no time to speculate about it. So she walked out into the night – she would go anywhere to cool her inner furnace.

MaBiyela had so much power. She was permanently vigilant, armed with authority and custom. Her vigilance was born of her own embittered life, soured by her own outgrown relationship with her own mother-in-law in her own past. It was the bitterness of generations, from mother-in-law to daughter-in-law. It was the way she perceived her role, the guardian of morality in the absence of the men. Embittered by her own lonely life when she was younger she had to cope with the long absences of her husband. So she often exercised her new-found power with an element of retaliation against some malignant social order. When life had been harsh and she had had so little money to run the home; when she had been left to bring up the children single-handed, tend the stock, plough the fields to raise the crops, mend broken fences, father the growing children, she had secretly attributed her agonising existence to her

16

weakling of a husband. She had sworn then that her son would grow up strong and capable. He would grow up to show the world what a fine upbringing he had had under her authority; she had not failed. Conscious of her power, not only within the family, but in the community as well, she had to set an example – her daughter-in-law simply had to toe the line. She had exerted as much authority over Siyalo when he was growing up and he had turned out gentle like his father, and frightened of failure.

The women of the village were in many ways like MaBiyela. They were capable, they were strong. They had to be. They were lonely and afraid, therefore suspicious and prone to gossip about each other's failures and misfortunes. Outwardly, they shared a lot in common – they talked and laughed loudly, and prayed and cried loudly in church or at their prayer meetings. On Sundays, in the early morning bible classes and at the prayer meetings on Thursday afternoons they gathered and shared their troubles in loud prayers. They poured out their loneliness to God, and vicariously to each other. That was one way they came to know what burdened each one. And there were many burdens – the children were ill or dying, the women were childless, the husbands or sons were away in the cities and were jobless, or so they said when they wrote occasionally, or did not send any more money. Sometimes the women prayed about communal needs when there was little rain and the crops were failing because the merciless sun had scorched everything. Sometimes God would send pests of all kinds to destroy the crops, or would send them devastating storms, instead of gentle rain, that poured scorn on all their labours. Perhaps they had sinned and offended him and this was their punishment. Then there were things they could not even pray about, not at prayer meetings, but perhaps in the secrecy of their bedsides. Fears about their sexual needs – the dangers that lay under the surface – the daily longings and the ever-present temptations and attendant disgrace. The worst misfortune that could befall a woman was to be caught in adultery, or worse still, to be pregnant in the absence of her itinerant husband. It was around this furtive aspect of their lives that gossip arose – lurid gossip about possibilities, and ghastly fantasies concerning other people's lives. They projected their own secret needs, fears and desires on their neighbours and friends. They, who could be so supportive in other ways, were malicious and even inventive when it came to these matters. They were all essentially afraid – afraid of failing in the burdensome task of harnessing their human needs. If they failed, their husbands would have good enough reasons to send them back in shame to their own people. But, above all, the women were afraid of losing their husbands to women in the cities. They felt insecure in their ragged clothes, their emaciated bodies and their barefoot lifestyle. They felt they were no match for those 'wild' city women.

Jezile thought again of those few scribbled and meaningless lines that Siyalo had written in the letter of the day before. She felt a shiver running through her in the gathering darkness. She quickened her step. She was very afraid at that moment, not of the dark, but afraid of losing Siyalo. She thought to herself, the only thing that secured women a position in society were husbands, and the only thing that secured husbands were children. Children were the insurance; mothers used them to keep the memory of home alive in their husbands, and husbands used them to fill the lonely existence of the wives they left behind. In this vicious circle many wives were trapped. Their husbands made certain they bore a child with each yearly visit, like an insurance premium that had to be paid each year, lest the policy lapsed. But the women withered under the strain – they grew thinner and more ill with each baby. The children they bore grew weaker and less able to withstand the rigours of their impoverished lives. God, where was the escape? Look at Zenzile herself. This sudden flash of thought stopped Jezile in her tracks – Zenzile – she had so much to carry on her shoulders – she was ill, her children were ill, she was poor, Mthebe was a good-for-nothing and her mother-in-law was no help at all. God, show us the way! Her train of thought stopped – she was at Zenzile's door. She could hear a child crying, and she had to shout at the door for Zenzile to hear her.

There was a wildness about Zenzile's look. Her stark eyes looked larger than usual, the only feature that seemed undiminished on that haggard face. Jezile felt a surge of shame wash over her when she saw her friend. Compared with Zenzile she still looked and felt as she did before marriage; if anything, she felt stronger and clearer about what she wanted from life. A flickering doubt reared its head in her mind about babies – were they the answer; was it all she wanted out of life or was it an excuse for something else? But a louder voice affirmed that for her, babies were what she wanted most of all; even one baby would be better than none; even one that died was better than one that never was. They both stood looking at the howling child. Without a word Jezile took the baby from the mother into her arms. Contact with the baby brought hot stinging tears to her eyes. She squeezed rather than cuddled the little mite. Something akin to love gushed out of her. Zenzile could not understand why her friend was crying. She was preoccupied with her own problems. 'To think I'm going to have another one Jezile; I heard this morning from the doctor's – there's another one coming.' She broke out into sobs. So did Jezile – they both cried hot searing tears for very different reasons. Jezile wanted babies, Zenzile had more than she wanted. When they had wrung their hearts dry they both sniffed their way to the two chairs in the room. Zenzile waited for Jezile to speak; to say what had brought her out so late in the day. Jezile wanted to tell her friend about her new resolve, about the day's events at the doctor's, the blitz at BAD, and the row with her mother-in-law, but it seemed so futile now. She stared back at her friend until Zenzile coughed. When she finally spoke her words sounded dry and almost meaningless. 'I'm going to Durban soon,' she said, and flickering smiles lit up both faces. 'Perhaps this time Jezile.' They both understood the web they were caught in in such different ways. Finally, to dissolve the knot of tension they both began to talk generally. It was only then that the mother-in-law episode cropped up, and even then it had lost most of its intensity.

All the way home Jezile thought deeply about her friend's predicament – babies solved some problems, but others remained; there were other battles to be fought if life was to have a meaning. Among other things, she had a mother-in-law to appease. An unchecked quarrel with MaBiyela had the potential to spoil everything, including the visit to Siyalo. One word from her could turn Siyalo very sour. No self-respecting son would let his mother lose her battles with her daughter-in-law. So, the first thing Jezile did the next morning before dawn was to go down to the stream to fetch water and fill the water barrel for MaBiyela – she went three times before it was full. When she saw that MaBiyela was up she went to her, and in the most pleasant of voices, told her that she intended going to the white man's farm, to work in his fields for the day, so that she could be allowed to collect firewood as they were all running low. She intended going with Simo and Jabu, the little sister-in-law and cousin-in-law. She rattled off her intentions standing at the door, speaking into the dark silent vault of MaBiyela's kitchen. It was a stilted, hollow monologue that left Jezile waiting uncomfortably at the door, afraid to transgress beyond that threshold before the gesture of peace from MaBiyela. But there was an interminable stretch of silence. Jezile knew it was not going to be easy. She shouted rather than talked.

'Are you there – is there anybody in?' Then she saw the two girls silently emerging.

Mr Collett's lands were expansive, lush and green. They had to be there by seven o'clock, in time to start work with all his labourers. It was a long day with three short intervals for drinks in the morning and afternoon, and a half-an-hour stop at lunch time. After five o'clock they were allowed into the woods to collect firewood. It was dark before they got back and piled the heavy bundles of wood outside MaBiyela's house. Jezile's neck creaked and ached with stiffness from carrying the extra-heavy load to compensate for the little bundles of the children. When MaBiyela heard the clatter of wood outside her door she came out to receive the peace offering. Although her voice was subdued, it sounded pleasant enough. She invited them in for the evening meal. And so blew over the terrible storm of the previous night. There was relief all round, for MaBiyela was as anxious to stamp out the tide of disobedience as Jezile was to appease her. Her reputation and that of all mothers-in-law in the community had to be protected – it would not do for Jezile to flout that authority and to set a bad example to all young daughters-in-law. So it made sense to let matters rest as soon as possible.

3

*I*n a fortnight's time, with a burning conscience and very few words to her neighbours, Jezile caught the early morning bus to Durban, arriving there late in the afternoon. She was tired and apprehensive. The bus was full and people talked loudly as country people always do. They talked of the things that they knew were of common interest. They were country people stepping out into the city. There was no mistaking the air of anticipation, at once apprehensive and full of delight. They were leaving the securities and certainties of country life to face the hazards of police harassment and the brutality of young thugs. But they looked forward to days of ease if not leisure, away from toil and endless physical work. The other passengers worked on her the whole day with their 'tales' of the city – in the end she did not know what to expect. Anxiously, she willed Siyalo to be there when she arrived, before any of those ravenous city hoodlums whisked her off. In her anxiety she had lost her appetite and somehow lost her earlier confidence. She felt timid in the face of the unknown. She depended entirely on Siyalo and his resources. If his reaction to her visit was negative – well, she wondered what had possessed her in the first place to take so much into her own hands.

The journey along the south coast of Natal was spectacular. Now and again her mind would be diverted from her thoughts – taken breathless by the beautiful scenery, such as when she saw the sea for the first time at Kelso Junction. The difference between the grasslands and the sub-tropical coast – what a glorious wonder. The vegetation had changed altogether from the treeless savannah of Ixopo; the greenness, the lushness, the over-abundance of trees and flowers of every kind that nature had to offer. But all these were temporary distractions.

Late that afternoon, when the bus stopped, she reared her head and cautiously looked out of the window rather than join the other passengers' stampede to get out. In that milling crowd, that sea of human faces, she was frightened. Where was Siyalo? How would she spot him? How different it was from the lonely mound where she often waited for him on his visits back home. Just then she saw a head peering through the door – Siyalo. She was the last passenger and he was checking to see if there were any left inside. For a moment she seemed not to recognise him. 'Are you lost or something?,' his voice rang cheerfully. She was taken aback by the jollity in his voice. She could not believe he was happy to see her. She had worked herself into such a state of anxiety that she had expected him to have changed, to be aggressive with her for confronting the situation the way she had done. Instead he looked happy and proud. He teased her and nudged her in their first moments standing by the side of the bus.

'Who's been coaching you?' She smiled and looked at him for reassurance. But, as if to avoid her searching look he quickly picked up the bags and turned to go. She followed, as in the children's game, 'follow-the-leader'. She virtually saw nothing all the way, but people and more people, circumscribed by huge buildings. The city, that hotch-potch of human experience, that patchwork of human endeavour. It was at once elevating and shattering; vast yet constricting. The streets were wide but with limited views, tall buildings that dwarfed human stature, intent faces that vaguely acknowledged your presence. Jezile and Siyalo pushed and zigzagged their way through the crowds – people's faces varied in every way, black people, white people, Indian people, smartly dressed people, and people in rags, clean and dirty people; people with loads on their heads lumbering along and some swaggering with not a care in the world; but one thing in common – they all seemed in a hurry to get somewhere. She herself could not keep up with Siyalo who carried her heavy bags in both hands and jostled as though to catch a last train or bus. He hardly spoke even when they found standing room in the bus, crammed awkwardly with her luggage between their legs.

He seemed very distant when they got off the bus. Somehow on the walk from the bus station in town to the gates of the hostel, where, apparently, they were going to stay, he seemed to have undergone a change. He wore a worried look, perhaps angry even. On his face there was a crease of concern that had not been there before. He seemed to be mumbling to himself.

'You're saying something?'

Vaguely he turned to her, showing reluctance to say it, 'You see Jezile, you gave me little notice that you were coming to stay with me here. As you know, I live in a hostel, a bachelor hostel. I could not smuggle you in there – it's only for men, and we are strictly guarded.' He paused and she urged him on.

'How do others . . . ?'

'There are a few houses set aside on the borders of the location . . .'

'Which location?'

'KwaMashu. These are rented out to the men when their wives come for short visits, just as you have. As you can imagine, they are fully booked throughout the year – twenty-five thousand residents we have in the hostel. Many people never get a turn. But last year, I did book a turn, but I never pursued it because we had no definite plans. However, when your letter came I went back to them. By a sheer stroke of luck I got it. In fact someone else's plans fell through and I was given his place. Only, when I went there this morning, to pick up the key, the room had gone. There's been bribery some-where, but I intend to fight this one. I'll go to the white man himself, the superintendant; I'll fix them, those corrupt officials.' His eyes turned to her at last, softer, though still anxious. 'I can't do anything tonight though.' He hated having to say this – he felt he was failing her, after she had moved mountains for them to be together. He mulled over this with a sense of shame. Then he continued, 'I've spoken to our cousin, Mavela, who lives in this terribly old hostel; it's worse than our new KwaMashu hostels . . . it's a . . . in these hostels we share with several men in the same room . . . he's given us his bed; no privacy, but I promise you it will be only for tonight. You see, conditions are less stringent here, and people can come in and out without being detected. It's a question of talking to the guard at the gate. This is a city, with no place to hide.'

She looked him straight in the eye, listening intently, trying to make sense of his world. After a long pause she repeated slowly, 'His bed . . . in a shared room . . . with men.'

He did not answer, but picked up the bags and walked to the gate. They stood in front of the gate of a high red brick enclosure. Beyond the railings and above that high wall, she could see the tall buildings, honeycombed with a thousand windows. A large man stood at the gate, armed with a large knob-kerrie that he leaned on, rather than carried like a weapon. Nonetheless, there was still something threatening about the man. He boomed with authority, questioning every other man about his business in the place, exchanging words with those he knew and laughing loudly with those who humoured him. Except for the free flow of the people, in and out of that gate, the place was so austere and grim it could have been a prison. It gave the feeling of prohibition, a feeling of trespassing that made Jezile's heart beat faster. Siyalo drew close to the big man at the gate and spoke conspiratorially, while the man violently nodded his head – no doubt to some pre-arrangement.

Beyond that gate there were people and more people; a bustling stream of activity, loud voices, echoes of laughter and a brashness which seemed to betray a conscious effort to bear up.

Once beyond those walls, Siyalo walked more confidently as though he had accomplished something worthwhile, while all that Jezile could feel was the assault of serious doubts about Durban as a place worth visiting. Then she stood inside the great building, along a passage that was littered with beds. They were beds flimsily curtained off from each other in a great effort to preserve territory and afford some privacy. The place was crowded, with hardly a space for a chair. Siyalo crept with stooped shoulders towards one of the cubicles. He lifted the make-shift calico curtain and disappeared behind it as though they were back in childhood, playing hide and seek. She watched his jostling movements behind the curtain that further enhanced the feeling of play. With confused emotions she joined him behind the curtain. She felt something drop inside her, like a shutter, and heard herself whisper instead of talk normally. There was hardly any standing room. Pots and dishes lay under the bed, and a whole wardrobe hung on a string stretching across two nails on the wall above the bed. He turned and looked at her with a smile, intimacy creeping in as though they were behind some closed door at last. He was sweating profusely in the confined space and the sticky heat of Durban clung to his skin; his hand touched her arm and it felt clammy. She felt her face muscles twitch as though they would give way to a spontaneous heart-rending cry. He saw that look and he laughed nervously.

'This is Durban,' he commented uselessly for the second time that afternoon, as though this explained it all. He took her gently in his arms and rocked her like a child and slowly she began to grasp the reality of Durban – very different from the Durban of her fantasies. People came in and went out, talking loudly and whistling and she could hear one or two settling on their beds with acknowledging creaks. She tried to envisage what the night would be like when everyone was in, in that communal bedroom. Siyalo stood up, embarrassed to see the Durban of their dreams, and his life in it, under scrutiny. He pulled out the pans and dishes from under the bed. He was going to cook at some communal kitchen.

'Can I help?' she heard herself asking. He silently ignored her, and started humming a tune instead. She wanted to go to the toilet, and that posed a problem. In the end he accompanied her and stood right outside the door.

As the night gathered the men came in, in ones and twos, invariably talking loudly, louder than their average country voices of authority ever were. Then they would quieten down, as though subdued by the confining nature of the room. Late in the night the lights went off and rumbling soft voices could be heard from here and there. She realised that she was not the only woman there – two or three others were scattered about the long room. As the silence slowly fell around, their whispers could be heard. The stragglers came in, on and off for another hour. In the end it was dark and silent. She lay stiff and immobile, hoping Siyalo would not try anything. But she felt him stirring and snuggling closer, but nothing stirred in her.

Then she heard a creaking bed somewhere nearby. At first she thought somebody had turned in his bed, but it grew louder and unmistakable. She stiffened and turned cold like a corpse. Then the woman screamed, oblivious to where she was, a scream that suddenly tore the silence, 'Take me, take me,

25

Dlamini!' He must have stifled her cries of ecstasy, an ecstasy that would not wait, for they heard her muffled cries subside. There was a deadly silence in the room; the rhythmic breathing was suspended for a brief minute, but was soon followed by a restlessness, a commotion in every bed. Something stirred, then heaved like a wave assaulting everyone in the room, except for Jezile who was chilled to the depths of her soul and body. Siyalo gave two instinctive thrusts, but Jezile sank deeper into the mattress, as if willing it to swallow her. Then that final cry again, from throes of delight, 'Fuck me, fuck me, Dlamini!' The scream filled the room long after she was silent. Jezile wanted to cry; she didn't know why. She had never known that some people were transported that far – far beyond self-control or awareness. Did it mean that their pleasure was greater, far in excess of what she, Jezile, had ever experienced. Feelings of inadequacy mingled with all others under the blankets. She was certain that she had never reached those limits of human thrill. Perhaps she had never given Siyalo as much pleasure; perhaps this was the clue to their childlessness. She ignored Siyalo's fumbling hands and she vowed she would not let him make a public spectacle of her. She lay stiff and cold through that sweltering stickiness under the blankets and hissed, 'No, no, never – not here – tomorrow, away from here.' In the end he gave up.

They were up and out of that place before dawn. By eight o'clock they were at the KwaMashu Hostel Administration offices. She sat on a bench outside and waited for him and didn't know what battles he fought inside those offices. She only knew it took him half the day. When he came out he was smiling. He had triumphed at last. This one victory did a lot to restore his morale. It showed in his walk. He searched Jezile's face to see if her estimation of him had risen. She smiled and he felt reassured. Their joy, although pale and diminished, warmed up a little like the winter sunshine. They lugged her bags yet again, now to one of those holiday houses. She felt as though she had been travelling for days.

KwaMashu sprawled out like a barrack. The little houses stuck on the green hills like scabs. Her eyes flitted restlessly over the innumerable streets of houses on all the surrounding hills, as far as the eye could see and all along the crowded streets. Wherever she walked there were women hawkers sitting behind their mounds of fruits and green vegetables, the kind that was impossible to find not only in Sigageni, but in the whole of Isabelo. With her eyes wide open she stopped to admire the food and remarked, 'Food, so much food! Where does such food grow?'

'You have to have pots of money to live here,' he answered vaguely as if to kill off her excitement. 'This is a terrible place. People are poor, food is expensive, the houses are small and crowded and the Tsotsis have a field day.' She gave him an icy look, almost hating him for blunting her enthusiasm. She did not believe him. She thought he was trying to extinguish any ideas that she might have entertained about the life of luxury she was going to enjoy in the city. She slowly fell behind him, taking in the city in gulps and trying to enjoy it. She noticed ditches in the middle of the road, deep pot-holes that rocked the taxi-vans that carried people up and down the streets. There were deep gullies on either side of the road with the cars fighting for the middle of the road, speeding dangerously and swerving and sometimes skidding to a stop to avoid a collision. She looked up again in an effort to shake off the feelings of gloom that were fast engulfing her. She wanted to like the city and keep intact all her dreams of it. She saw the two-roomed houses interspersed among the four-roomed ones which looked even smaller and more comical. In spite of her sulk, she was forced to admit that KwaMashu fell short of her dreams. 'Those houses,' she asked, 'what are they? Are they for single people?'

Siyalo was silent for a while. 'Which ones do you mean? They're all small houses. Besides, single people don't ever have houses here. They live with their parents in their family homes, no matter how old they are. That is, if they don't live in women's hostels. That's why the little houses are so crowded. Ten, fifteen, or even eighteen people live in each house – mothers, fathers, grown children and their children. And if you have problems trying to have children, you don't share it with these city girls. Sometimes, even married young people have to continue living in a crowded family home because housing is a serious problem. They are moving people from all over Durban to come and live here. There's no room here. Some go to Umlazi

– a safe distance away from the centre of the city, and further away from the white suburbs.'

Everything he said shattered her illusions and she resented it. She turned her head and fixed her gaze in the distance in an effort to cut out Siyalo and the city. Nothing seemed right about this place. She was not sure whether it was the place or Siyalo. But she was determined that she was not going to rub Siyalo up the wrong way; she was not going to make this visit as difficult as his last visit home. She was here for one reason only – to conceive her baby. The whole world knew that, and she was going to do nothing to jeopardise the chance. If it meant going round blindfolded, she was going to do it; even if it meant a blurring of all her senses, she would do it. Out of that tumult of resolves she heard him blurt out with faked excitement, 'This is it!' She jerked back and saw that he had stopped. They stood in front of one house in a row of houses. She breathed deeply and coughed slightly. Something very much like a scream fought its way up her throat. A sudden spasm of will and muscle forced it back into the gut. It made her throat ache. She shuddered. The houses looked as though no one lived in them. More than half the window panes were boarded up. The walls on the outside looked greasy somehow, sticky perhaps. The little yards were all overgrown with grass that grew on the rubble from old building work.

'People live here?' She spoke as if to herself. 'You're not going to complain!' He sounded exasperated. 'Of course, people live here, people like us who are here for a week or two.' So saying, he led the way with a determined step over the grass that was knee high. He knocked at the door, and a woman opened it. Two young children bounded out past them. Some perverse part of Jezile wanted to push the woman out of the way and tell her she was trespassing. Muttering a few inaudible words, the woman pointed to one of the rooms. At last they had found their 'holiday home' – bare and dirty, but nothing that strong hands would not put right, she told herself. It had four walls and a door to shut out the whole world. Once behind that door, Siyalo put down the luggage and gently turned to her and for the first time he gave her a warm, tender hug and a kiss. They were alone at last. She warmed to his embrace and the suppressed tears flowed freely.

'I just had no idea, Siyalo. You never told me.'

'What's happening to my tigress then, what's the city doing to her? Please understand, I've done everything. This is the best and the only accommodation there is in the whole city.'

'Siyalo, don't tease me, I'm serious. Can't they keep it clean – the windows are broken and boarded, it's like nobody lives here.'

'In a sense nobody lives here. Nobody owns this place. You're here today, you're gone tomorrow. There's never enough time for anyone to clean the place. If the council won't do it, then nobody can. But then the council don't care.' His gentle voice soothed her ruffled feelings and restored her balance.

Once she had accepted the place for what it was, and in spite of the couple next door, she found she could relax. Their first night was wild – they lashed and loved each other as they had never done before. Away in the city, distanced from the strictures of custom, the inhibiting do's and don'ts, they felt free like children – free to explore – to go to bed when they wished – to lie in till late in the afterglow of their love when they could – this was all new. There were no fears of being found in bed in broad daylight. She was going to give him till it hurt, till it exploded in his head, till he cried like the woman at the hostel. It was a scorching love. For hours and days they were saturated in each other. Some nights they lay awake talking for hours. She felt revived and full of vitality. For the first time she was aware of how hard she worked back home in Sabelweni; how permanently tired she always was; and how they had hardly any time to talk about their lives. But now that they could talk the whole night through, she realised how much they had needed to talk to each other all along. There were questions that had lain dormant in their minds. Now they asked them of each other and groped for the answers. They guessed at the reasons and they searched each other's souls.

At the weekend they shopped at the market and at the Indian shops along Queen Street and Grey Street. The sheer abundance of things was exhilarating. He spoilt her with presents. They went to the seaside and then to the cinema, things she had never done in her life. The days were drenched with love and joy and abundance. During the day time moved slowly.

She was lonely waiting for Siyalo's return from work. She cleaned the little room, turned it upside down, looked at the grimy walls more than once, wondering what she could do to wash them clean. What an irony that there was so much clear sparkling water and only so much that one could do with it. How different from Sigageni. Finally she sat down to clip her nails and watched the hordes of people going up and down, some to the shops, others to the trains and the buses that raced past regularly to the centre of the city. She watched KwaMashu empty itself from the security of those matchbox houses. The coombies screeched, passing each other at breakneck speed, loaded beyond capacity with passengers in and out of Kwa-Mashu. The men strode hurriedly and the women jostled along on their precarious high-heeled shoes. People hurried along as though they shared the weightlessness of waste paper scraps that blew and flew and billowed in the streets every time the cars sped by. It looked like a mass exodus that made her feel she was being left behind, that nobody else but her would be left at KwaMashu for the day. But there were people – there were schoolchildren who soon followed and filled the roads in their different school uniforms much like their parents had done earlier in the morning. It was hard to believe that this was the daily picture of KwaMashu which grew to serve the big city next door. KwaMashu was not part of that city – it was the human reservoir of Durban, no different from the water reservoir on Reservoir Hill that Siyalo had pointed out to her. People were in the white man's city to work – to work in the city they did not live in.

In one such idle moment she picked up the previous day's newspaper *Ilanga Lase Natal*. Spread on the front page was a picture of a crowd of women, wielding heavy sticks and chasing after some men. It did not seem possible; yet there it was before her eyes, the men running helter skelter in different directions. She read on, 'Clinics, not beer halls' the headline read. A group of women had gone to the beer hall in the centre of the city, soon after work and had assaulted a whole crowd of men drinking beer, causing chaos inside and outside the beer hall. They had carried big sticks, and knob-kerries to frighten the men away. Jezile laughed to herself, at once feeling a bond with these city women – how similar their situations were.

In the evening, she could not get much out of Siyalo concerning the amusing spectacle of men under assault. But he talked at length about the conditions of life for the general mass of the people in the city.

'Drink is the greatest cause of family problems. In every family, there are quarrels every Friday night, which is our pay day; quarrels over what should be paid this week, and what was outstanding last week. The list of debts grows longer as the weeks go by with no hope of ever paying them back, or meeting all their family needs. The problems are compounded each week. And for many of these men, coming home from work is no joy. Many of the four-roomed houses have more than one family living in them; even though they look hardly big enough for one family. To increase the family income, many have had to sublet to other stranded families. The one-roomed houses, which were once built for young childless couples in the old days, are now full of children and grandchildren. Fifteen people stay in one room! The mind boggles at how anyone could have conceived of those one-roomed structures. KwaMashu is supposed to be an improvement on the Cato Manor slums. There life is raw, completely stripped of all conventions. Cato Manor is a sprawling festering eyesore that slithers down the hills below Howard College, part of the University of Natal, threatening to engulf the city itself and lick the waters of the ocean, judging by its determination to grow in spite of all the council efforts. It encroaches on Chesterville Location on one side, trampling Ecabazini and flaring up beyond Esinyameni on the other side. God knows where it will stop. There are people and structures everywhere – that place has a will of its own. It is willed by the people who live there; nothing will stop the people. That rusty place is the bold inscription on the wall; a brave warning of our determination to move on, to move on, to get what we want; to let nothing stop us.'

Siyalo's voice was loud and resounding; he was no longer sitting beside her, holding her hand. He was striding up and down in the short space between the two walls. Jezile gaped, wondering how Siyalo had become part of the slum on the hill. She no longer doubted the legitimacy of belonging to the hills and being one with them all. She was so enthralled she had not noticed the audience that stood listening intently from the other room – the man nodding seriously with his wife and child standing just behind him. But when Siyalo turned, spreading his arms wide like a preacher, facing his wider audience, she saw them and she stood up as if to obey a command. He wheeled round to face her and paused. Looking her straight in the eye, he continued:

'These women are right; and our women in the country are right to fight back. Something has to be done to stop the crippling of our lives. They build us beer halls, not clinics; they build us churches, not houses to live in. People are drinking themselves to death; children are sharing the same concoctions as their parents, for lack of milk and they are dying like flies.'

Jezile was moved. She had never known that Siyalo was one with the women of Sigageni. The barriers were down between the two families. They settled down on the floor in the utterly bare room. They introduced themselves afresh, smiling and shaking hands. They talked animatedly. They were fired. There were no more territorial barriers. That night they shared a common meal. They talked about their own reserves, Sigageni and Etholeni. They talked late into the night. Fakazile came from Etholeni, a place bordered on all sides by white men's farms. Somehow the outside world never seemed to penetrate that enclosure. She was thirsty for news of what other women were doing. Yet, she would acknowledge despairingly, in the same breath, that it could never happen in Etholeni. She was one of three wives. Although the other women had been to Durban to visit their husbands, she had never had a valid excuse. She was the first wife and children came easily to her. Each time he came he left her pregnant. The second wife miscarried each time when she was six months pregnant so she came to Durban regularly for medical care. And the last and youngest of the wives was the favourite. She never seemed to run out of excuses and he never refused her anything she asked for. Jezile listened with great interest to all the juggling that went on among women who shared a man for she came from Sigageni where every man had one wife. It sounded very complicated to her – life was difficult enough without the added complication of worrying about other wives.

*

For the next few weeks, the women in Durban were on the rampage, fighting, marching and making representations. After a couple of days of this Jezile and Fakazile decided to go and join one of the marches. Reluctant at first, their husbands could do nothing to stop them. Their nightly discussions had gone too far to stop them seeing for themselves what women could do to influence the thinking of white authority. Authority itself seemed nervous and uncertain in the face of this unlikely challenge.

Jezile and Fakazile got on a train for the first time on their own. The trains and the buses were full of it. The city women, large and loud, talked, fearless of opposition from any quarter. They were prepared to take on anyone in their fight for better living standards. If the men continued to drink at the municipal beer halls, that meant they were against the women, it meant that they stood with the enemy, and it was therefore right that they should be the target of aggression. They would continue to beat them out of those beer halls. Making people drink was an act of aggression; paying people little money for food was an act of aggression against the community of black people; women and children were the community, and therefore they had a right to defend themselves aggressively. The women heckled and silenced any doubts on the trains and on the buses. They commanded a following without stopping to enlist anyone. Individual men sank into silence and where there were two or more of them they preferred to engage in quiet mumbling conversation – quiet because there was no way they could drown the ping-pong exchanges that raged across the train compartment. Quiet also because it was best not to seem to oppose the women, lest one became the target of abuse if not physical violence. Jezile and Fakazile sat in a corner listening in silent awe, taking note of any valid points. When they got to Cabazini, they joined the milling crowds of other women.

Soon they realised that there were many men among the women as well. But the two friends had agreed not to lose sight of one woman in particular – they had marked her as one of the leaders. When she stood up on a rock, to silence the crowds, they knew they were right. In a husky voice, from days of loud speaking, and a wave of her ample arms, she hushed them all. In a few words that encapsulated their struggles and their demands, she gripped the crowd. One thunderous response from the crowd and she swung swiftly on her heels and led them. It was the first time Jezile and Fakazile had had some of their own grievances so well articulated. They followed the march all the way down towards the centre of the city on foot. But they did not reach the city, for half-way down they were surrounded by the police. Their columns were deftly broken up and little clusters were sent scurrying along the side streets, up and down those dusty hills. The police, although restrained that day, showed every sign of growing impatience.

In the days that followed, the police were everywhere in Cato Manor, day and night. They harassed every woman, man and child, asking for this, looking for that, and demanding every sort of paper. In a community that had been allowed for years to exist extra-legally, in spite of the law, they arrested scores of people. The very existence of Cato Manor put it outside the law. It was not the people who were illegal, it was the Council itself that could not house its own workforce. The Council had closed its eyes as Cato Manor grew over the years. And now this demand for law and order incensed the inhabitants.

One mid-morning a posse of police appeared from nowhere, poked around the shacks, leaving gaping holes in those flimsy cardboard and iron walls, spitting foul authority, cursing and calling every woman and child a whore. For a moment the place was hushed. Then one familiar shrill warning: 'Umeleko – the police are here.' The policemen grinned, their horses pranced waiting to see the scurrying women who lived in fear of the law. For one long moment nothing happened; the next, there was a stampede of flat feet, running to meet the police. For once they were not running away from them. Within moments, nine policemen lay dead.

No one knew for certain what had happened. The whole country rocked with shock. They could no longer ignore the women or their demands. Durban was caught in a frenzy. Jezile and Fakazile were petrified. Needless to say, a number of those women they had seen at the march were swept into prison in large numbers. Jezile collected clippings from all the papers that she could lay her hands on. She had a story to tell and the papers would do that best for her. She no longer had any illusions about the course that the women of Sigageni were taking; challenging the system was deadly serious business. But she was also aware, as never before, that they were not alone. The whole country was in a ferment.

The following Friday night Siyalo came home much later than usual, and he was quiet but restless. He slept fitfully that night and seemed agitated about something. Finally he woke her up and told her she had to go back home soon because there was so much trouble in the city, and he did not want her involved. Although she saw no reason why she should be implicated, and they still had a few days left before her time was up in the city, there was something in his voice and manner that made her consent. Although he seemed happy the next day, Jezile had a feeling that there was something he was holding back.

She owed it to Zenzile to see Mthebe while in Durban. Zenzile had not asked her to see him but she had understood that she must. Mthebe was a goodlooking man who enhanced his looks with fine clothes. He laughed often and radiated vitality. It was hard to associate him with sadness and despair. What Zenzile required of him, she could never find for he did not have it in him to give; what his neglect had done to her life he would not acknowledge for he could not associate himself with depression, ill health and poverty. There was no doubt in Jezile's mind that the marriage was over; but that it would only really be over with Zenzile's death. Divorce was never the solution. In these parts, marriage was for ever – unto death. Besides, a divorce would never solve Zenzile's problems. Jezile tensed with a palpitating heart. Zenzile with all her frailty, stood above her children like a tower of strength; the one who shielded them from great suffering. There was an urgency in Jezile's voice when she asked Siyalo again if they might see Mthebe before she went back home. Again Siyalo dithered. He knew how his one-time friend had changed. They no longer had much in common. As children and teenagers they had been inseparable. But for a reason that was hard to understand, Mthebe had remained a teenager in his mind – frozen at that stage. It was not that Mthebe did not love Zenzile – but that he could not cope with the demands of their changed relationship. He looked for, but failed to find, that young, pretty, intelligent girl who had laughed joyously at every prank he played before they were married. Zenzile no longer laughed at anything – only a smile, when she could summon it, would play on her joyless face.

Jezile met Mthebe on her last Saturday in Durban. He excelled himself entertaining her around the city. He hired or borrowed a car from a friend – he was not going to do things by half measures. This was his chance to broadcast to the people of Sigageni what a fine city man he was. Dressed immaculately, he would step nimbly from the front seat next to his friend, to open the door for Jezile, just the way he saw it done by his boss's chauffeur when he arrived at the factory. Such showmanship. He took her for a two-hour drive round the Durban Esplanade, round the South Coast – those fine houses, those spectacular views, that clean air! The sea boomed alongside the road and the air revitalised his fantasy. You could have thought he lived in one of those fine houses. The commentary never stopped. 'Look at those fine houses, the ones on the hill, the sprawling gardens.' One day he would build himself one of those. 'Where?' wondered Jezile, 'In Sigageni perhaps!' The unreality of it all was disconcerting. Mthebe was on the run, to escape from something, or himself. It pained Jezile. They went to the Shah Jehan for lunch – a fine exclusive Indian hotel that intimidated Jezile. There were not many people there for lunch, for they had a selective policy and many black people did not pass the test. The few Indian people and fewer white men looked the right sort of people in the right sort of place – opulent in their fine suits. Jezile had never been in such a splashy Indian restaurant. They had a fine hot curry and then went back to the city to try and see a film at the Avalon. Only, no blacks were allowed. They saw the coloureds and the Indians going in. There were no whites around, for they had cinemas of their own where no blacks or Indians or coloureds were allowed. But on this day, blacks and children were not allowed at the Avalon. 'Goodness gracious!' Mthebe cried loudly, reeling in surprise from the disappointing news. It galled him that anybody should think him inferior. For a brief moment, Jezile saw this man's crest falling. But this interruption would last for only a minute. In the next five minutes they were entering another, not as popular, cinema – but that did not matter to Jezile who knew nothing of the fine differences.

At the end of the whizzing day, he gave her £5 as a parting gift. She accepted the money graciously, but her hand remained half-extended. He looked at it and for the first time there was a pause between them; a pause when the Mthebe machine stopped whirring and for a brief moment he was a human mind puzzling over what she was waiting for. Then she dared him, 'What about money for Zenzile and the children?' There was a quick hollow laugh. He dug into his pocket again and gave her another ten rand for his wife and children. Her questioning look brought his eyes down, and he left in a hurry after that. Mthebe was determined to escape his countrified image. He felt that if he lived like city people – white people even – he would emerge a different man, acceptable in the white world, a man of fine tastes, fine manners, a respectable citizen who could live anywhere and enjoy any privilege he wanted, his company constantly sought after. Rejection hurt too much. He consumed his life in the pursuit of this dream.

The bus for Sigageni would leave at ten o'clock on Monday morning. But Jezile and Siyalo were at the market by seven o'clock to buy provisions for home. They bought meat and bags full of fruits and vegetables of all kinds. When Siyalo thought they were done, Jezile insisted on going back to buy some more meat and vegetables and fruits for Zenzile. They argued about whether Zenzile would want the money itself rather than the shopping, until Jezile confessed that she was going to use the £5 that Mthebe had given her to buy his children the good food they needed, and she would save the other £5 from Mthebe to give to Zenzile.

4

W hen the sun was red on the hills, the bus came to a stop
at Cromwell again. The hills and the grasslands lay in
utter peace. The silence hit Jezile as much as the hubbub of
Durban had hit her a few weeks earlier. It thrilled through her
veins, not like the absence of clamour but the presence of peace,
this condition of tranquillity. She was back home again. The old
faithfuls were there – Simo and Jabu – and one other woman
whom MaBiyela had asked to go and meet Jezile. All the way
home they talked and laughed and their voices echoed in the
hills, reverberating against the evening silence of Sigageni.
Finally, they stood on the brow of Sigageni and looked into the
darkening valley below. It had been a hot day and the dry heat
rose from the fields below and hit them on their faces. And
Jezile did not need the light of day to know that the crops were
scorched and dying in the grip of another drought. Sigageni
was in the hold of a slow death – each year worse than the last.
But for that night they could sweep aside such menacing
thoughts. There was more than enough to eat. She led the
procession to MaBiyela's main house, not to her own. There
was no disguising MaBiyela's pleasure at this gesture. It was a
warm welcome home. After separating Zenzile's provisions,
Jezile put all the food baskets in front of MaBiyela. Ordinarily it
would have been too late to start cooking dinner. But the air of
celebration filled the house and they were not going to let it slip
by. So they had a big late dinner with piles of food and meat.
The vegetables were saved for the next day while the fruits
were carefully rationed to last a few more days. And there were
little gifts of clothes and trinkets for everyone.

And so passed Jezile's homecoming. The next day things
were virtually back to normal except for the endless questions

about what Durban was like. She answered them all in detail, save telling them that she had actually been to some of the marches herself. MaBiyela would not have approved – all that mixing with city women, what had she in common with them? What did she understand of the city?

The following afternoon, Jezile took Zenzile the gifts she had brought back. She wanted to be there to witness for herself the joy in Zenzile's eyes. And she was well rewarded. Zenzile was enlivened – she darted about as she prepared to cook right there and then. She smiled broadly and kept repeating:

'He's never done this before. It's never happened before. Are you sure he bought all this himself?'

The children sank their teeth deep into fruit and for the first hour they had little time for the cheap little toys that Jezile had bought at the last minute.

'Perhaps he's maturing after all, Jezile.'

There was a new hope in Zenzile's voice, and Jezile was not sure if what she had done was worth it for one day's joy and a few days' hope.

Jezile talked fleetingly about Durban, the sights, the people and even about Siyalo's changing outlook. But just as she was about to leave, Zenzile started to ask her about Mthebe. Her voice dropped as though to persuade Jezile to impart something confidential, to let her into some secret knowledge: how was Mthebe? What sort of job did he really do? Where did he live? With whom? Why was he not in the hostel like other men from Sigageni? The questions were searching and to some of them Jezile had no answers. Zenzile pinned Jezile down with her eyes, without blinking, like a snake. It was the most uncomfortable time between the friends – that searching look that begged while it commanded Jezile to tell the truth. It was in this tug of minds that Jezile saw how haggard Zenzile really was. The pain deep in those eyes was fathomless. It was a dry, cold, enduring pain. Jezile felt a surge of hot tears and as she wept Zenzile loosened the grip of her prying eyes on Jezile and turned them away slowly. After a long silence Jezile asked almost irrelevantly:

'Are you sick Zenzile – how is your baby?'

'The baby . . . this one is not quick, Jezile. She sits heavy like a stone in me – I don't feel well at all.'

Jezile waited for a few empty minutes then turned and went away.

Life resumed its dusty mantle again and the Durban days merged into a beautiful memory. At first Jezile was bashful when she met the local women, in case they not only talked about the visit to Durban but made reference to the question of the passes. So, each time she met some of them she talked excitedly about the city giving them news of the women in Durban, and she would hurriedly promise to tell more at the next meeting. But when the following Thursday came, the day of the meeting, she could not bring herself to go. She waited until the next Thursday when she heard Dr Nosizwe Morena would be there. Nosizwe's presence would take the focus off her – the women would want to hear more from Nosizwe rather than plague her with questions. She could cash in on that and bring all her clippings to the meeting. Besides, if anyone were to say anything about her 'betrayal', she would rather it were Nosizwe herself. Nosizwe was so openminded that the whole matter would not deteriorate to an abuse – she would stand censured but not abused. While she accepted that she had broken the pact among the women, she felt trapped between the impositions of customary law, state law and migratory practices. And she, the physical creature in between, somehow had to manoeuvre successfully among the threads of the web woven around her by all these. Within such confines there was little room for capricious fate. Although all the women lived this reality, few could articulate it for themselves. They suffered it and with this sting in their lives they could be merciless to those who failed somewhere along the line.

Nosizwe was their political leader, the guiding spirit in the whole district of Ixopo, not just at Sigageni. They hero-worshipped her. She took turns visiting various women's groups from week to week. She understood not only the harsh extremes of their lives, but also the merciless system of white oppression that left them cruelly exploited and defenceless.

The women came from all over, in ones and twos and threes. They wore their unmistakable uniform of red blouses, black skirts and white hats. On his day, a Thursday afternoon, they knew that they were keeping a tryst with a large number of other women from the length and breadth of the country. Few things could bring together so many women at one time of day throughout the country, every week of every year, as the women's prayer meeting did. They took courage in knowing that they shared these moments with other women at the same time – helping to concentrate the mind of God on their needs and their struggles. Only, in some parts, prayer had assumed a much wider meaning over and above the strictly religious intention. They still sang and prayed and cried, but they also talked and discussed the causes behind their beset lives.

School was over for the day. The women met their children all along the pathways as they went home and the mothers came to pray. The building had, in the few moments after school, changed both its name and purpose. It was no longer a school but a church building. The older boys had helped to refashion the school into a church hall. A little wooden structure was immediately rearranged to serve as a pulpit at the end of the long hall, and the benches were rearranged to face the pulpit. The 'church' was complete and ready for the service. But when the women arrived they did not go inside. They went to nestle row upon row in the shade of the building itself. There was not a tree around to give shade in that blistering heat. The earlier efforts to plant trees around the school/church had long been given up for the cattle invariably came along and destroyed the saplings each year. So the women sat, leaning against the building, on the dusty hard-baked earth, loosening their babies from their backs, fanning the heat away from their tiny sweaty faces. They breastfed them and talked and drank from the bottles of water that they carried. Some had walked for miles from other reserves to hear Nosizwe. They could have gathered in the building itself where they held most of their prayer meeting. But somehow, as though by consensus, they could not bring themselves to spit the venom of their hearts on the same church floor where they prayed.

Jezile was among the first to arrive, for she wanted to make her confession to Nosizwe before the start of the meeting. Aside, in an intense conversation, Nosizwe was unexpectedly hard on Jezile. She was angry and disappointed and Jezile tried hopelessly to justify her decision. Before she could finish her tangled web of excuses Nosizwe interrupted:

'In fighting against the passes, can we allow exceptions? Did we ever talk of individual cases? Is that not what sacrifice means – personal needs sacrificed for the common good? Believe me, there are as many special cases as there are these women. We all need our men, but we live without them. I tell you, there is nothing to explain here – you've let us down, you have let everybody down. *You, you* of all people, who had so much to say last time. You're inviting the anger of all these people – they're ruthless once they know they're betrayed.'

Jezile was hurt, afraid and confused. She was no longer certain if she was going to be allowed to continue as a member of this group. When she thought the tirade was at an end, she silently extended the little pile of her cuttings. Nosizwe almost snatched them from her, and Jezile disappeared behind the building for she did not want the other women to see her upset. When she had composed herself she came back and sat down inconspicuously among a group of women she did not know very well. The meeting started and Jezile's heart throbbed with guilt and pain and conflict. Nosizwe started with a short prayer and one hymn. Then she spoke to the women.

'Today we have a lot of matters to cover. There are times when I feel that many of us suffer and fight back without the full understanding of what is going on, why it is going on, and where it is taking us to. We, the women in the rural areas, need to know why we are here when our husbands are there; why we starve when South Africa is such a large and wealthy country, and what might happen to us if we keep on asking these questions.

'We live in the reserves. The reserves are the creation of the government to provide a source of cheap labour for white people's agriculture, mining and industry. To force our men to go to these places, it is necessary that we should starve; that means we should have less land to cultivate and that they should go out and work for food. Also, the government has imposed a number of taxes of various kinds to force the men to work to pay these taxes: poll tax, quit-rent or hut-tax. So, we here, as women, serve to produce migrant labour – our children are the labour resource of this government. We work hard and suffer to raise these children, without any form of assistance from the government, so that one day they will go to the city and help to create wealth for them in the cities, where we are not allowed to go, and the wealth that we are not allowed to enjoy. And when these men are injured in their work or get too old to work, they are sent back here for us to care for them and feed them and bury them. They do not bring back to us any compensation for their injuries and they have no pensions.

'We are the dumping ground. We live all our lives without the help of our men and when they are useless we must receive them back and care for them. Our men earn very little for the jobs they do out there, often just enough for a single man. This government has never taken us into account when employing and paying our men. Even the most loyal of our men can only send back a pittance to support their families. And many fail even to do that – we blame them, but really it is the government that is to blame. When our men get lonely out there they meet other women and new families grow and we are forgotten. When our men have failed to provide for us, they have taken their frustration out on us; when they have been put into prisons for a thousand possible infringements of the law, we have suffered.

'The sole support for us and the children is the land. Seeing these reserves were never meant to provide enough food, it is clear that they have always been overcrowded – children are born, men are returned from the city and the land gets poorer with every passing year. Not only does it fail to produce food, but it cannot support the livestock which we use to till this land, and to provide us with milk, and which we can sell in times of hardship. The grazing lands are down to the grass roots and the animals are dying. Wind and rain sweep the good earth away. And as though God cannot hear our prayers, the drought scorches everything and things get worse and worse.

'The truth is, there are just too many people on too little land. But the government chooses not to see it that way – they say we have too many cattle. But most of our families have no more than six animals, just enough to plough the land, and that is too much they say. Many of us harvest each year less than the seed we planted. Few of us are able to get one bag from each acre we plough. This is not our fault – given the same con- ditions, any other farmers in the world would be just as poor and the land just as exhausted. The white man over there, with all the advantages and support of the government, gets three times as much. Also, he has ten times more land under cultivation than any of us can have. Dividing the land into small overworked strips makes it poor and unyielding. It is not our fault. The poor-white problem of this country was once caused in the same way by sub-dividing the farms into uneconomic units. In the end, to stop the vicious circle of their poverty, they were absorbed into the industries of the cities. But for us, the government is not prepared to solve the problem in the same way – they advocate the back-to-the-reserves policy – and this, without giving us more land. This is a policy that is bringing back more and more poor people to us.

'To cope with these problems, the government is introducing schemes without consulting us, schemes that will not work, for no matter how you cut the cloth, if it is not enough, it is not enough. They recommend reducing our stock, and moving the landless people into enclosures, fencing them in and limiting their right to own animal stock. These measures, we can see, are intended to further impoverish the people, if not the land. Those who are landless must also have no stock and they must be moved to work colonies for the landless.

'There's a lot of work in these Betterment Schemes. There are dams to be built and barbed-wire fencing to be erected. One would think that this would provide some kind of employment for some people, but one could not be further from the truth. What the government is doing is forcing people to work for nothing; what they call Compulsory Unpaid Labour. In other words, these people, who are for various reasons not allowed to work in the industrial areas, people who have been dumped in the reserves here, are being drafted into digging holes for the fencing poles, erecting barbed-wire fences and constructing dams, all without pay, while their white supervisors are paid. There is a whole list of jobs which, strictly speaking, fall under the Public Works Department – the list is growing every day. But they are done under forced labour, for no pay at all. Whole communities are being harnessed to build roads, make contours, remove noxious weeds, repair dipping tanks, and build houses for chiefs – the chiefs who no longer serve the people but who are the tools of the government. The women too are forced not only to carry the fencing poles and rolls of barbed wire from the depots to the working teams, but are forced to cook for the work teams, all for no pay. They are not even given any food to cook for these teams. They have to provide their own food when their turn comes. If one should fail to do so, she is punished because it is said she is defying authority. Any complaints against any of these impositions are punished as incitements to disobedience.

'In many areas the implementation of these schemes is causing chaos in our villages. People are up in arms against these injustices, and the government often finds it difficult to apportion blame to any one person in this resistance. Once in our history, kings and chiefs were influential people, leaders who were highly respected and loved by our people. The government is violating this age-old relationship between the people and their leaders. They are using our chiefs against us. The chiefs are no longer ordained by the will of the people; most of them now are appointed by the government to serve their interests. And slowly a deadly confrontation has developed between the people and their chiefs under the Bantu Authorities Act. The chiefs, without whose support the whole Apartheid plan cannot work have become conscious of their role and power. They are demanding tangible material gains in the form of more land and higher pay for themselves from the government. But the government insists that they can only qualify for such privileges if they also deliver, making sure that their people accept the soil reclamation measures as prescribed against the people, which are to reduce the number of people dependent on the small-scale farming, and to remove from the land all those who have no land allotments and have them placed in special settlements for the landless and dispossessed.

'The main aim here is to divide our people, not only from their chiefs, but to create a division of the few privileged land owners and the landless mass. First they took the great mass of our land and gave it to white people; now they must use the pittance they left to us to bribe our chiefs to favour a few and to discard the majority of our people in these landless colonies – the ultimate dispossession. And our chiefs agree! Great new powers have been given to the chiefs to persuade and to deceive and to force people into accepting the government's Apartheid schemes. They have power to try a large number of cases – and where there are fines, the complainant shares the fine with the chief. Tell me what this means for justice in our communities!

They tax us, the poorest of the poor, so that they can benefit from the government – they want to benefit from our extreme poverty! For all these reasons, we do not want Bantu Authorities Tribunals, we do not want all the schemes for the rehabilitation and reallocation of land, we do not want to carry passes, we do not want cattle culling and the dipping of our cattle to poison them and cull them indirectly – our cattle are dying, not from the insects, but from starvation – insects live on high grass, not on dead grass roots. On the other hand, we want the land to live on and cultivate to raise food crops for our children; we want clinics for our sick children, not beer halls to kill off our men. Not only do our children die in their numbers, but our men die young because they drink all these concoctions. These whites mean to kill us all off.

'You see, there's a lot for us to learn. We have to understand why we are in this position, what the government is doing and what we must do to frustrate their corruption and their evil plans for us and our children. I want us to know what other people in other parts of South Africa are doing, what they suffer as a result, and what we can learn from them. The war against Apartheid has started and our people are fighting back heroically. When I finish here, two women will give brief reports of what women are doing in different parts of the country. But before I sit down I want to warn you of the seriousness of the decisions you are about to make when you reject the passes and you protest by emptying the dipping tanks and spilling their brew. You may be assaulted, you may end up in prison, you may lose what little land you have and be dispersed, and be forced to live away from here with strangers in these new colonies or townships: all intended to weaken your resolve to fight this government. You may lose your cattle – everything. There are women who have been slashed and kicked all over their bodies by the police, women who have sustained fractures. The lucky ones are in hospitals – for many suffer without any medical care.'

The women were getting agitated and restless. Nosizwe, for a moment, wondered if she had gone too far and frightened them off. She sat down. The air was sombre. There was no applause on this occasion. After a few moments, the air grew still but distended. She saw faces that strained far into the distance with their heads held high as if to reach out. She knew that it was not the face of fear that she saw. Rather, it was a sorting out, an accommodation of new factors and of strange possibilities. The incision was deep. No one stirred. Then she remembered that she had promised that two people would give reports. She stood up to announce:

'The two women who will give us reports are Tokozile Zulu and Jezile Majola. Jezile as you know has been to Durban recently and seen the women's uprising there. Some of you may have heard about it. But to begin with we will hear from Tokozile. As you know she is one of our bright young women who has spent a lot of time working for the newspaper *Ezomhlaba* while she lived in Durban. She has often brought us news from the outside world and she occasionally wrote things about us in the paper. She is back with us now, but she still gets the paper and we hope she has some news for us in these troubled times.'

While Nosizwe talked, Jezile was trying to recover her surprise, for she had not known that she would be asked to speak; in fact she was still reeling from Nosizwe's words just before the start of the meeting. She felt so confused that she missed the first few words of Tokozile's speech.

'. . . living through a turbulent period. The spirit of the continent is rumbling and surging from the depths like molten rock. This is marked, among other things, by the revolutionary struggles of the people of Algeria against French rule. Those of you who get the papers will have heard of the Mau Mau of Kenya where people are united in their fight for their land and for their freedom from British rule. In Central Africa the people of Nyasaland and of Northern and Southern Rhodesia are working together to disrupt British Colonial rule there, committing brave acts of insubordination. In the Congo people have united behind their great leader Patrice Lumumba who is fighting the machinations of the Belgian Colonial powers and their puppets in their efforts to keep the Congolese people in subjection. So are the people of Nigeria and Sierra Leone demanding their self-determination. President Kwame Nkrumah of Ghana opened the way for us all when he won freedom for his people. These are historic times, God-given times for breaking all the shackles that have kept the whole continent in subjugation. People are ready to die for their freedom. It is not surprising therefore that we, the people of South Africa who are among the most oppressed, should rise and demand our own freedom in response to the call of that spirit of freedom that is raging through our continent. Different political groups are fighting various impositions from the repressive government of our country. Early this year you all heard of the defenceless people at Sharpeville and Langa. The government forces killed them in cold blood. But I tell you, as the prophet Ezekiel once prophesied, the dried bones of these men and women who have died will yet live. The God of Abraham and the God of our ancestors will breathe life into our nation and raise a new army which will arise and fight the evil on this land. Many of our leaders are in jail and others have gone into exile. Many young people are being arrested in large numbers, emptying classrooms to fill the jails. But I tell you, a new leadership will arise and take us to freedom. We and our children will fight on and on; if it takes a thousand years, we will win in the end.

'Women in many parts of the country are rising up against the issue of the passes. While men are away in the cities the government officials sneak up on the women, hoping they will find them alone, weak and defenceless. But the women of Tzaneen have engaged the enemy for months and are not about to give in. People all over the country are rising up against the imposition of Bantu Authorities, the schemes for the rehabilitation and reallocation of land as well as the extension of passes to women. Places as far apart as Witzieshoek on the borders of Lesotho; Marico, South of Botswana; Sekhukhuneland in the North West Transvaal; Ethokazi in Zululand on the South Coast and in many parts of the Transkei and Pondoland are resisting, choosing imprisonment and banishment and even death. The time has come for us to choose. We too, the people of Sabelweni, have got to make a choice. It is up to us to resist or be crushed.'

As she sat down a slow numbness seemed to creep among the crowd. They looked at one another like strangers. They knew vaguely about the rest of the world and yet Tokozile had brought that unreal world and laid it at their feet. She had even implied that they had a lot in common with that world. It was a dimension that they had hitherto found hard to grasp. While they sighed and whispered, Jezile could not find it in her to affirm loudly, for the talk and the reports had further confirmed her sense of shame. She felt that if people were dying for their principled stand against Apartheid, perhaps her baby should have waited, perhaps her need was not of paramount importance. She stood up on weak knees to give her report of what she had seen in Durban. No matter how hard she tried to bring back the fire of the events in Durban, her words sounded flat. Her loyalty had been severed in two; it was hard to be inspired.

As she sat down, she heard a strong voice singing 'Malibongwe Igama Lama khosikazi' (Let the name of Woman be praised). The women picked it up with gusto and the overwhelming feeling of helplessness left them and they sang on and on until they felt strong and equal to any task. When they stopped one woman rose – Jezile looked up – it was MaBiyela. Perhaps she had risen to speak in order not to be outdone by her daughter-in-law. Her voice was strong but strained. She praised the strength of the suffering men and women all over the country and she pledged their own determination to suffer to the end too, if need be. There was no eloquence in her words, only the strength of affirmation. Nosizwe then asked the crowd to pray for the alleviation of suffering in general and for the courage to go through with whatever it was that they might bring on themselves by protesting. They knelt on the red soil and Nosizwe prayed softly, imploring God, the God of their fathers, to be with them on that mound of earth that he gave to them at the beginning of time – the only place on earth that they could claim as their own. In a moment, she could not hear herself praying for, as if by some unseen signal, all at once, the women began to pray. Their prayer rose in a crescendo, high above, into screams or incoherent cries, a confrontation between God and women. They cried as they prayed. Then gradually their voices fell into moans and grunts and sniffs and into a silence. One by one they got up to go. As they did, they saw at the back of the crowd, behind Nosizwe, a line of men. One or two were in police uniforms, but the rest were in ordinary clothes. There were about ten of them. No one knew who they were. Somehow, their purpose seemed foiled, as they stood there, watching people praying to their God. The women had won the first round of confrontation. The police turned to go without saying a word and the women in silence, as if all had been said, stood up and dispersed in twos and threes, as they had come, back to the different parts of Sabelweni where they lived. But they took away a new insight. They also knew that the fuse had been lit and the moment of detonation was not far off.

From that day on, there was a qualitative change in Sigageni. People met on the pathways, stopped to greet each other, and to ask after their health as always – and lately, to inquire with their looks and gestures. What was it they wanted to know? Were they suspicious of each other or were they genuinely curious about each other's views? Was it a concern about the future? In all their daily chat, for years now, they had concerned themselves only about the past and the present – never asked about the future; it was as though the security of the past ensured the certainty of the future. And never having asked about the future, they now did not know how to. On the surface, up until these troubled times, things had been what they had always been. Authority had been well-established, powerful, deaf, and beyond questioning. Authority had had nothing to do with the people. Its power had not been derived from the gift of consent. There had therefore never been any mutual agreement between the governed and the government. As the people put it, 'A King is only a King if the people make him King.' So far, people had acquiesced, waiting for change in the fullness of time. At some point in their long wait something had stirred, something deep down – ever so imperceptibly at first, but there had been no mistaking it. Everywhere you had turned there had been a new sense of direction. It reached out so that those who had not felt it the day before, had woken up to it the day after. It was as though it had generated itself from the pit of the earth and had slowly kindled people's awareness from under their very sleeping mats. It had always been there, waiting to surface. News travelled on the high wind from one corner of the country to another, from the Bafurutsi of the North to the Pondos of the South. And lately, it had woken the Bacas of Umzimkulu and Ixopo. They had heard it first like a moan in the wind, but they had turned away from it and had gone about pottering and scratching the barren soil. Yet, none of them could pretend that they had not heard it, for it had murmured echoes of their own fears about their land and stock, their children's education and their women's right of movement. It had blown gusts of threats, whose full meaning had not always been understood, but whose importance could not be mistaken. There were the rehabilitation schemes, the resettlement schemes, the Bantu Authorities Act, the Betterment Schemes and many such fine-sounding terms that, nonetheless, had aroused awesome premonitions in the hearts and minds of all rural people. They had questioned and prodded and nudged and there had been a restlessness that had pervaded their existence. Things in the country moved at a snail's pace, but they did arrive in the end, and when they did they would crash in fury over people's heads.

5

*J*ezile was never more aware of her body than in the weeks and months that followed. That singular awareness, known only to women with child. As more and more people stopped her to greet her, to inquire about the state of her health and to inquire about her future – she answered broadly with a smile. Her future was assured. She could not tell them she was pregnant; one never does. At a time of seething communal uncertainty Jezile was filled with certainty. A hard worker at the best of times, she seemed more lively than usual. In the piercing heat of autumn she was down in the fields among the razor-sharp dry maize reaping the bean crop. She thrashed it, collected every bean and stored it in the common granary. Before MaBiyela could stop to thank her, she was out and away cutting the tall grass to repair the thatched roofs of the whole homestead. For days she carried home bundle after bundle and stopped only at sunset. When MaBiyela thought she had piled up enough, Jezile declared she would go on for a few more days to cut and carry thatching grass for MaBiyela's repairs as well. It was a time of great family concord. They shared their meals at the end of the day. There was laughter and harmony. MaBiyela knew without being told; but she asked her anyhow, when they were particularly happy one evening. With a smile that quivered all over her face, Jezile told her mother-in-law that she was two months pregnant. She had been to Nosizwe who had confirmed that she was in her third month. The excitement caught MaBiyela as well, who cautioned her against too much work. Jezile could not believe it, for she had never thought that her mother-in-law could have her welfare at heart. The following weeks and months were full of expectation.

Siyalo wrote regularly and sent more money than he had ever done before.

Meanwhile, Jezile had not seen Zenzile for weeks. Zenzile was rarely seen outside these days. She rarely attended the Thursday meetings, nor did anyone see her going down to the stream to fetch her drinking water. What was even more puzzling was that she no longer joined the Saturday washing team who picnicked with their children on the rocks of the great river Umzimkulu two miles away to do their weekday washing on those rocks in the plentiful clean supplies of water. It was the highlight of the week, a communal outing. Although no one was expected to attend every week, it became noticeable that Zenzile came less and less frequently and so one Sunday afternoon Jezile walked the distance to see her and tell her all her news.

When she arrived Zenzile was lying on the floor in her kitchen. Her eyes lit up when she saw Jezile. She sat up immediately with the baby playing at her feet. She looked very tired, but then she was about seven months pregnant by now. She cheered up listening to her friend and seemed happy to hear all the news and the joys and fears of the community. Then Jezile suddenly stopped. She asked where the children were. Zenzile was quiet for a moment – there was a decided change in the air.

'My mother came and took them.'

'What for? You mean, she's taken them all the way to Malukazi.'

'Yes, they're at Malukazi.'

'When – but that's so far away? When are they coming back?'

A long pause. Then suddenly Zenzile seemed to wilt before Jezile's eyes. The cheerful expression died on her lips and Jezile noticed for the first time how large Zenzile's eyes and teeth sat on that face. She was not just thin, she was ill.

'I'm ill, Jezile. I can't cope with the children. And because I'm not well myself, I can't look after them properly; they get ill too. My mother is going to look after them except for this one, Dumazile. They'll be there until my time comes. I'll soon be going to Malukazi myself, next month. We have arranged that I'll be better off with her when my time comes because I think I'll need a bit of care.'

Jezile hesitated.

'Zenzile, wouldn't it be better to go down to Durban for your delivery? In fact, wouldn't it be best if you went there now? If your mother had the children, surely Mthebe can look after you there until you have the baby. You'd attend the hospital clinic and have your baby there.' Jezile's voice trailed slowly as she watched the stony look on Zenzile's face.

'Don't talk to me about Mthebe. I want to forget he exists.'

They carried on their punctured conversation looking for alternatives where few were possible.

'Surely, Nosizwe can arrange to have you admitted now at the hospital at Clydesdale. It's not the best, but at least you'll have a rest.'

'What for? You see, I'm pregnant. I'm not ill as such. Pregnancy is not an illness, is it?'

'What on earth are you talking about? Pregnancy is a condition of the body, other than your normal. And you're not just pregnant, you're ill.'

'You know what I mean Jezile. This hospital takes people who are dying. I'll go again to Nosizwe. She says my body is in very poor condition. She's given me tonics and all that. She has ordered a rest and she wants to see me every two weeks from now on.'

'The baby, how does it feel now – does it move about? I can't wait to have mine moving, Zenzile,' she added thoughtlessly.

'Well, it started moving very late and even then it's very slow. It's not like the others – it feels heavy like a stone. And of course, I can't see Nosizwe every two weeks – there's simply no money for that.'

'And Mthebe? What does he say? You say you don't . . .'

'I said I don't want to talk about him . . . I've not heard from him since you came back, Jezile. In fact his last letter was way before you left for Durban.'

'You don't say it . . .'

Jezile felt a shudder of pain. She stopped prodding any further. As she said goodbye to the baby she put a pound in Dumazile's little hand, 'To buy some sweets Dumazile.' Zenzile smiled, her upper lip trembling, and her eyes filled up at the same time. Seeing her friend in her condition had sobered Jezile somehow. It was all so very complex; nothing was pure joy – everything depended on so much else.

The following weekend Jezile went off to Luve, to see her mother. She had not seen her since her return from Durban. Her visits home were few and far between, but they were always happy, not only for her and her mother, but for ali her mother's friends and neighbours. There was nothing like being home again where she was her old childhood self. She walked bare headed and laughed as loudly as she liked. She had come home to show off her success as a woman. She had been born to be a mother; every little girl was born to be a mother. Throughout her childhood she had been made aware that although she was well loved by her family, her place was with another family – unknown yet, but that was where she belonged, at her in-laws. She trained hard for the role, learning to do all the chores and to take responsibility for a lot of things. Marriage, complex as it was, was meant to make this possible. The fulfilment of her life depended on a successful marriage and the success of that marriage depended on hard work – work to produce food for those children. Marriage depended on hard work. Marriage was not just a relationship between two people, but a relationship between two families. And it was not the marriage itself, for its own sake – it was the children of the marriage who were of paramount importance. It was not the companionship, the love, the friendship and not the mutual emotional satisfaction of the couple. Yes, of course these mattered where they could survive, but marriage stood or fell on the question of children. And where the expression of emotional love and friendship had been hampered by the long-term absence of men on contractual labour mutual love and friendship died easily, but the marriage survived because the children were there.

What was difficult to understand was that despite the formidable position of power that being a mother implied, in reality young mothers were truly powerless. Being a mother did not put a woman centrally at the home of her in-laws. She could decide nothing about her life; where to live, where to go, with whom and when. Her position of power as a mother could only be exercised from the outside. Essentially, she was in a permanent state of dependency and estrangement – always under suspicion should anything go wrong. The fear of betraying her in-laws was always there. Not only was she placed in this isolated position, but there was a conscious effort to distance her from her husband as well. He was encouraged to keep the company of other men and she the company of other women. From the day she arrived at her husband's home, no one called her by her name. She would be called MaMapanga, MaMajola, MaDuma or MaSibiya – her father's name. Losing her name isolated a young married woman emotionally, further confirming her alienation. Her position would only change when she had her first child; she would then be known by her child's name – NakaJezile (Mother of Jezile), NakaDumazile, Naka-Zenzile – thus living her life through the identity of her father or her child. Her adult identity derived directly from her capacity to be a mother. To reinforce her isolation there was a string of taboos that she had to observe. She had, always, to have her head covered in front of her senior in-laws. She could call none of them by their names, except the very young. Sometimes she could not even call her husband by his first name but would have to identify him as a younger brother's brother or younger sister's brother. After the birth of their first child she could then designate him the title, father of so-and-so. And there were foods she could not eat because she was not a full member of the family.

Now at her parents' home Jezile threw all care to the winds – she was with *her* people and free to call anyone by their names, and to be called by her name and to eat any food she liked. The talk was endless and she could join in any conversation. People came in to see her and she took them half-way out when they left. Others met her and stopped to talk. She was herself again. Gifts of food came in from all the relations and for days she feasted on the choicest of her favourite dishes. Her mother was flushed with pride. No one asked her about her pregnancy for no one would be so indiscreet, but they could tell from the air of celebration that pervaded the whole home; it was good news all round.

Two weeks was soon over and she was back with the Majolas. The air was clear and MaBiyela was happy to see Jezile back. Winter had started in earnest and it was time to start harvesting the crops. They worked from early morning to sunset at this time of the year because the sun was not too hot. But it was hard work, carrying bags of maize and fighting one's way through all those sharp dry stalks of maize. Jezile hated it, but she was in perfect health and like everyone she pushed herself hard to try and finish gathering the harvest in order to enjoy the warm winter days in a more leisurely way by the fireside.

They were very nearly through with harvesting when one cold frosty morning, before dawn, Jezile heard a pounding noise at her door. It was Pumapi, Zenzile's teenage brother-in-law. Jezile woke with a start and she heard MaBiyela's voice reassuring her from the outside. It was all right, nothing to worry about, Zenzile was in labour, a little prematurely, but nothing unusual. In a few moments Jezile opened the door wrapped up in scarves and jumpers and an old rug. MaBiyela went back to her house while Jezile walked in silence, behind Pumapi. Somehow she found it hard to talk to him, to ask him why Zenzile had asked for her, not MaBiyela who was one of the local midwives. Somewhere at the back of her mind she identified him with Mthebe; somehow, she felt, the whole family was to blame for Zenzile's condition. No one seemed concerned about her life, the hard work she had to do, Mthebe's irresponsibility or even about those babies that came one after another every year. Jezile knew she was being unreasonable, but she could not change how she felt. They arrived at Zenzile's door just before sunrise. She heard a faint moan as she came in. MaGoba who was Zenzile's mother-in-law and the chief mid-wife was there and two assistants. Zenzile had been in labour for about twenty-four hours. She looked very weak but immediately beckoned to Jezile when she saw her.

'Get me a car, take me to the hospital.'

'She wants the hospital now,' interjected MaGoba, 'Whatever for, I ask. Where will all that money come from – money for the car, money for the hospital – and where can we get a car at this time of day?' Then there was another silence. Jezile did not feel equal to answer MaGoba back. She had no right to intervene in the affairs of this home.

'People seem to think,' MaGoba went on, 'it is the hospital itself, the doctors or the nurses who do the job. It's the woman who bears the child – she can do it anywhere; in her house, out in the fields, or if she wants to be fancy, she can go to hospital.'

The other two women did not concur – they looked at

MaGoba in silence and the weight of dissent was in the air. MaGoba fumbled a bit.

'I know she hasn't got a bridge – there is nothing there to stop that baby coming when the time is up.'

Then Zenzile called again, with her eyes fixed on Jezile's:

'Take me to the doctor.'

Jezile, with her eyes and voice lowered, said slowly:

'I have some money. We will look for a car and there is enough to pay for the hospital as well. Mthebe can pay that money back to Siyalo when he can, back in Durban.'

That seemed to silence MaGoba. As soon as Jezile said it one of the assistants darted outside and called Pumapi to rush away to Hongo who had an old van. Suddenly there was urgency in the air. Jezile held Zenzile tightly in an embrace and laid her down carefully. She felt Zenzile's body sagging, but she quickly wiped her damp body and changed her clothes. She chose her nice clean night-dress which looked hardly worn. Perhaps she had bought it when she first got married. She helped her put it on and Zenzile seemed hardly able to lift her arms. When her pains seized her, she gave one long wailing cry. They took a mattress out and laid her carefully on it, and covering her warmly, they waited for the van. Waiting, the test of human endurance, was familiar to these women, but they failed it that day. Impatience was inscribed on every face and time stood still as they waited for Hongo's van.

At first the morning was severely cold and the frost bit their bare toes. Even Jezile, in her shoes, could not control her chattering teeth. They made some tea and gave some to Zenzile as they drank it in gulps themselves. Then they waited some more. Finally, they lifted the mattress and put Zenzile back indoors. Perhaps it was the hot tea, perhaps the time had come. She gave one piercing shriek and they knew the moment had come. Within a few moments Zenzile sighed deeply and the baby was born – she was relieved of her heavy stone at last – it was a girl, stillborn. Jezile looked at the baby and began to cry – she did not know whether she was crying for the lost baby or with relief that Zenzile was free at last. While the others fussed over the manifold details that attend even a stillbirth, Jezile concentrated on Zenzile; she mopped her face, she mumbled words of comfort and she told her in the gentlest way possible that the baby was born dead. Zenzile looked up once to acknowledge the news and then she closed her eyes. She seemed to fall asleep immediately. Jezile held her tenderly while the others tidied up. After a little while Jezile slipped out her arm of support and Zenzile's head rolled off. In one convulsive moment Zenzile died. The whole place was thrown into utter confusion. There seemed nothing that could have caused her death – no evidence of excessive bleeding. Jezile looked at her face – there was such utter peace on it, but Jezile was petrified. How could it be, childbirth should be natural, it should not kill both mother and child, it was such a waste, so unnecessary. She felt that it could have been avoided. She was frightened for herself. She wept like a child. She wanted to chide MaGoba who was just as distressed – was it guilt or the sudden realisation that she would have to look after all those four children herself? Jezile was certain of one thing – it was not love or pain of loss.

Later the church bell was rung in the customary way, to inform the community of the death – two rings, and a minute's pause, then another two rings. It went on for about ten minutes. People in the fields laid down their half-full bags of maize and stopped work for the day to honour the dead, whoever it was. Soon, they all converged towards the Shabalala homestead. The community was stunned – a woman's death in childbirth is always such a tragedy. The waste of a young life, but more than that it was the reversal of nature's order; it was nature mockingly withdrawing her gift. There are those left behind, the man who loses a partner, companion, provider or whatever else she stood for in his life. There are also the children who drift around silently, hardly aware of the immensity of their loss, taciturnly accepting the abounding cuddles that everyone mutely offers with their tears.

And on this day people sat around repeating over and over again what had been said before as if to somehow extract the meaning of it all. After midday, the Zondis, Zenzile's family, arrived dejectedly. It was hard for Zenzile's mother to have to pay deference to that woman, MaGoba, who had made her child's married life such a misery. Yet, this was the custom. MaGoba was the chief mourner – Zenzile could have been her mother's child a hundred times over, but she was married into the Shabalalas and she had died a Shabalala. Not that there was time to think of that when they first entered the room where Zenzile lay with her stone-cold bundle on her chest. The sight of her three children clambering off people's backs, peering at every face, as if to look for someone familiar, brought uncontrollable sobs around the whole place. Some of the relatives must have wondered which family would swell up overnight with those motherless children.

The din made by the mourners' sobs was suddenly interrupted by a loud rumbling noise. Many got to their feet. Was it Mthebe? they wondered. It was common knowledge that Mthebe had not written nor sent any money for months. Morbid curiosity was aroused even at this dense moment of sorrow. But it was not Mthebe, it was Nosizwe. She joined the people on their knees and the cries rose to another crescendo. But many had spent themselves and the chorus soon died down. This doctor, this woman, this friend, this political leader, she seemed all encompassing, sharing with the community every form of adversity that befell them. When she rose from her knees and put on her white doctor's coat she was, in an instant, distanced from them, a professional who knew more than they would ever know. She gave them one sweeping look and, wordlessly, the mourners walked out one after the other until only two women, Zenzile's mother and Mthebe's mother, remained, weeping silently. Nosizwe turned the two bodies over, unwrapped them and examined them to establish the cause of death. Zenzile, she said, had died of internal bleeding – possibly, a ruptured uterus. After this discovery, she seemed more resigned to the tragedy – it had not been anything she could have foreseen. If she had known earlier of the premature labour, perhaps she could have saved both mother and baby – but she had not been told. She was exasperated, though powerless to change things. This sort of thing happened all the time. She always insisted on being informed at the first sign of difficulty, but many continued to think that childbirth was not only natural to woman, but was a test of her accomplishment as a woman – the greater the suffering, the more it enhanced her womanhood.

The next day as the sun warmed up and the procession was

about to start for the cemetery, they saw a big shiny black car lurching slowly down the uneven road, swaying from side to side until it stopped right in front of the house. Mthebe emerged in an immaculate black suit. He looked groomed and stylish and everything about him stood out in stark contrast. He wore dark glasses as if to disguise his feelings. No one could guess how he felt. People were torn between their need to cry at such a moment and the curiosity of the spectacle. Many came out and stood watching him silently. He paused in his flurry and looked around as if to ask why such awkwardness. He strode towards his humble grassy house. Zenzile lay in her flimsy coffin which was draped in black ready for her final rest. Mthebe looked at her, turned and staggered to a low stool. And he wept. He took a spotless handkerchief out of his pocket and continued to sob into it. People were surprised into joining him, first in quiet sniffles, then in one collective full-bodied cry. Jezile remained dry and stony-eyed, with one wish – to blow Mthebe apart. The preparations for the immediate departure to the cemetery were halted. Zenzile was buried with her baby later that afternoon.

6

*A*bout four weeks after Zenzile's death, on a Thursday morning, Jezile crouched behind a crevasse, grateful for once for the fissure on that scarred land. It just about stopped the gusts of the morning winter winds. Sigageni lay exposed in a corridor that stretched far into the snow-capped Drakensberg mountains many miles away. The biting cold winds blew on the path to Sigageni with a vengeful ferocity every morning and evening in those winter months. Jezile was carefully wrapped up in layers of jumpers and scarves and a coat on top. But all around her, she could see a number of men, women and children with nothing to warm them but billowing cotton wrappers. They were all waiting. For many months now they had religiously emptied the dipping tank some time between Tuesday night and Thursday morning of every week. It was to the credit of the community that not once had anybody revealed the identity of the 'culprits'; so high was the spirit of solidarity. The white officials remained none the wiser about the community's most guarded secret. Finally, the Sunday before, an official announcement from Ixopo had been read in church. The officials from Ixopo would come the following Thursday to discuss certain matters pertaining to the whole community – all families had to be represented by at least one member. At last something was stirring; the whole village was in a flutter for those few days after the announcement and before the Thursday.

Almost everyone who could make it was there. MaBiyela had indicated that she was not very well. And Jezile was secretly pleased for she felt she had to go because they could not trust the two young girls, Simo and Jabu, to listen carefully and to convey everything that would be said at the meeting. Too much was at stake to be left to children. But they came too, out of curiosity. There was a mixture of excitement, if not anxiety, in the air. People came early, at sunrise, as if to speed up preliminaries and hasten the hour of the meeting which could only take place after dipping the cattle. The cattle were actually going to be dipped after months of evasion. For once the dipping tank was full. From all directions of the village could be seen long or short bovine processions and their herders shivering in the early morning light. Being in a sheltered place, the sun would take another hour to reach Sigageni and warm the shivering herds and herdswomen and children. As the numbers grew around the dipping area, the cattle grew restive and lowed constantly, intermingling, so that it became hard to tell which cow belonged to which herd.

Jezile would have been in difficulty at this stage, if it had not been for the two young girls. It turned out they knew all the ten cattle in their herd, not only by sight but by name as well. It surprised her to find that cattle responded to their names almost as well as dogs do. Once she knew that her herd was in capable hands, she grew less anxious and she withdrew. Once more she reminded herself that she had to be careful in her condition, as MaBiyela was always reminding her. As the sun rose higher, reaching the dipping tank at last, feeling its way into all the nooks and crannies of those fissured donga walls, the ravages of erosion, it stilled the cold wind, and people rose up to stretch, and to talk to one another as they waited patiently. Some sat like lizards taking in the warmth of the sun. Soon, very soon, Mr Pienaar should arrive. But it was another long while before they heard the slow distant rumble of his car. As it grew louder and nearer, the waiting crowds realised that there were two cars. They looked curiously, not at his car but at the other car. Suddenly there was a feeling of being besieged. To further enhance this feeling of occupation the men in the big car behind stopped a distance away from the dipping area but did not get out of the car.

Pienaar got out of his wreck of a car with an air of triumph, but the people did not look at him. They stood transfixed, watching and waiting for someone to emerge out of the other car. Pienaar looked round in disbelief at the dry earth surrounding the tank. So, he *had* succeeded in getting them to dip their cattle. Pienaar ordered them to drive their cattle into the enclosure behind the dipping tank. Once inside the cattle jostled in discomfort in the overcrowded space. And as if to cause their herders similar discomfort, the four white officials in the other car got out quickly and more or less surrounded the people pushing them against the fence. Four burly men in heavy coats and gloves against a cold, huddled mass of peasants – largely women and children. They felt like their herds. It was strange how quickly and how easily the scales can be tipped. It looked as though the debate was won and the arguments dispensed with even before they had started. One of the men, who seemed to be the leader, began to speak when he was convinced they were securely penned.

'As you have been told, we are officials from the Bantu Affairs Department. We have come to meet you and to discuss with you a number of issues. We feel that there are certain areas of misunderstanding and certain matters for discussion with your community. We have been very patient with you when some people in your community have gone on for a long time spilling the dipping mixture. I don't need to tell you that this is criminal behaviour and a serious matter. But before we find out who these people are, we want to know why. We are convinced it is not just one person doing it and we believe you know who these people are. But why do they do it?'

Then there was a pause. The four men cast darting glances around and no one stirred. The man continued threateningly:

'Remember, we can find these people without your help, and we will find them if this continues.

'We are concerned about the question of the passes as well. Except for a handful, very few women have done what the government has asked them to do. Every woman should have a pass by now. We have been to Ndawonde and Magaba to give out passes, but none of you turned up there. To make it easy for you we are arranging that the next issue of passes will be here at Sigageni, and your chief will tell you exactly when. This is another very serious matter and from now on we will expect all the women here to have passes.' He ended with an emphatic bite of his lower lip as he looked at the women who stared obstinately at the ground. Another of his company stepped forward.

'One other matter of great concern to the government is the condition of the land around here. Right where we are sitting, we can see the deep dongas. These dongas mean that all the good earth has been swept away every time you have had a storm. Perhaps you think you cannot stop the storms sweeping away your good earth; but in fact, it is partly because of your own ignorance that the storms sweep away your good earth. It is the way you plough your fields; the way you graze your cattle and the way you have all these footpaths criss-crossing all over the place. It is what you do.'

There was so much heat and accusation in his voice that it aroused the people, and one could feel them arching their backs in anger. They all looked up and squinting their eyes against the bright sun, the few men who were there shook their heads and the women made clicking noises in a staccato. He reacted to this with a raised voice.

'It is your own stupidity. You've been told to divide your land into strips, so that one piece can lie fallow once every three years – but you won't do it; you've been told to make contours when ploughing on these steep slopes, but you don't. You've been told not to keep so many cattle because cattle destroy the land . . .' He was in full swing, his arms gesticulating and his coat flapping in the wind when he heard a clear question stopping him in his tracks.

'But that is not true – why is Mr Collett's land next door covered with all that grass and he has thousands of cattle on his land?' It was Jezile.

There was a hiccup. He stammered the next few words trying to finish off what he was going to say. Colour gathered quickly on his ears and his voice shrieked:

'You, you, who are you? You are a trouble-maker. Mr Collett knows how to look after his land – if you had any sense you should learn some lessons from him.'

If Jezile had been white, she would have been red herself – her whole face was burning – she did not know what had come over her. Everyone was looking at her – some in stunned admiration and the others in a way that pointed a finger at her. The official having been deflated stepped back and the first one came forward. His voice was calm but his eyes flicked towards Jezile frequently. The cattle behind them seemed to have settled down quietly and they stood lean and languid-eyed as though confounded by it all.

'We know you have encountered some difficulties in these measures. The government has plans to step in and help. Of course, you too will have to step in and help the government to help you. It is your work, you will have to do it yourselves. The government is providing the barbed wire and the poles to build fences around the plots. It is prepared to build a dam to help you along. And for those of you who have no land to plough, you will have to move to other places that are being provided where you will live more comfortably. And to those of you who remain, you will have to reduce your cattle to a maximum of six per family. That is all that this land can graze without ruining it.'

There was another silence as the ghost of Jezile's question went past through people's minds. But then again the official's voice rose, hollow, distant but threatening: 'You can see your cattle are lean and poor. They yield little milk and they die in cold weather. But more than that, they ruin the grazing lands, making furrows and laying the earth bare so that it is carried away in the summer storms. It is a vicious circle – because the earth is gone, the grass fails to grow the following season and your cattle get poorer and more of them die . . .' He sensed that the people were no longer listening, more preoccupied with the flies that pestered them in the hot sun.

As soon as the third official sensed the apparent loss of interest, he darted forward and waved furiously; in the same gesture he beckoned towards the car. Much to the surprise of everybody, they saw their own Chief Siyoka emerging out of the car. They watched in complete silence as he slowly came towards them, stopping right next to the speaker, who seemed to enjoy their puzzlement.

'Today we have come to ask for your co-operation in implementing this all important policy of the Bantu Authorities. The key to all the problems in this area is in this policy. We have had a long talk with Chief Siyoka and he understands what he and you, his people, should do to achieve your own freedom. Getting that freedom, of course, means you have to take responsibility for a lot of things in this area, and have to work hard for it. All good things come the hard way. If you are to have your own little allotments they have to be fenced in. No one else will do that for you, but yourselves. You will help each other and no one knows better than you how to organise work parties in your communities. Not too much beer though, otherwise there won't be much work done.'

But the people were not listening any longer; they fixed their gaze on Chief Siyoka's face as if to prise it open and see what deals he had made with the white people. Siyoka stood transfixed, looking straight ahead, his eyes on the horizon.

'. . . will explain to you exactly what each person in the community has to do to assist in this matter of freedom. Chief Siyoka.'

A silence followed. A long silence, in which nothing moved except Siyoka's grinding jaws and his fists that clenched and unclenched. The white official gave him a fleeting side-long look and repeated, this time urgently, under his breath, 'Chief Siyoka!' Siyoka slowly shifted his whole weight on to one leg and cleared his throat. But his eyes did not move from the far away hills.

'Two days ago I was called to the Bantu Affairs Department at Ixopo.' He paused and licked his lips. 'There they explained to me what Bantu Authorities means and what you have to do under this policy. They have asked me to explain to you what my role in this is and that I should persuade you to do your share.' There was a slight cough from the white official. And Siyoka looking like the soul of distress continued in a monotone, 'Some of you – those who have no plots to cultivate will have to leave Sigageni, to enable those who remain to live better on their allotted plots. They will be settled in rural locations together with others like them from other districts. I was told to tell you that this is good for you and that therefore you should give no trouble. Those of us who remain will have to work hard to make this place green and fertile and productive again. The government officials will come and divide the land and we shall fence it in. We shall build a dam, but we shall work for the Department of Public Works for the creation of this government's policy for no pay at all.' A shudder went through the crowd, but Siyoka went on like an automaton without blinking or varying his tone.

'The women will carry the barbed wire rolls and poles and

other building materials from the end of the road, where the lorries will off-load these, to all the corners of Sigageni. I was told to tell you that the women will also take it in turns to cook for the men at work. They will cook their own food because BAD will not supply any. The men will do all the work – fencing the allotments, digging the dam – for no pay. I was told to tell you that all this is good for you . . .'

The white official gasped to speak as the crowd broke up and started talking loudly, gesticulating among themselves and the mood suddenly becoming very ugly. The officials turned to each other and closed in on Chief Siyoka, talking to him threateningly, wagging their fingers in his face. They whisked him off to their waiting car. The meeting ended in chaos with the old man Godide shouting above everyone else, 'Ingene! The enemy is within the gates!' To those who heard him, that was a declaration of war. Some raced to surround Godide, but for others the significance of the war cry was lost. They raced round Jezile instead as if to congratulate her for her impertinent intervention during the meeting. But she did not acknowledge them. She was angry with them for failing to support her or to say anything in reply to those officials. That, then, was the end of the meeting, but not the end of the matter.

Soon after Chief Siyoka was deposed by the government the community rose up in arms to demand his reinstatement. They sold their cattle, sheep, goats and chickens to get money to fight in the courts of law. It was a time of high drama, with the people playing for stakes they knew they could never win and the government shamming that they could lose – a cat and mouse game. In court the chief won the first round against his deposition. The government then sought and found another loophole. And in the last round Chief Siyoka and two of his counsellors were sentenced to live in exile many hundreds of miles away. The people could not believe what was happening. How long would the exile be? Was it for the short-term, till the trouble died down, or was it for life? Ever since their great grandfathers' days, this family had ruled, and defended the people of this community. And now they were gone. As Chief Siyoka, his counsellors and their families were driven away one morning, no longer leaders or figures of authority but bewildered, powerless ordinary people cowed with defeat. The whole community came out flocking after them forming a long sad procession following behind the police vans. As the vans sped faster, the crowds fell back and slowly, one by one, they gave up the pursuit.

After the dismissal and exile of Chief Siyoka there was an open rift between the people and the government. On a few occasions officials called Counsellor Duma up to Ixopo, in the effort to groom him as the next chief. This caused Duma great embarrassment. Being the chief would fully identify him with the forces of government. He did not want this as it would isolate him from his community and set him up as a target; whereas remaining a counsellor left him some veneer of acceptability among his people. Privileges of such a position may not have been as high as those of a chief, but the danger and responsibilities involved were also correspondingly less. He preferred to be comfortable and safe. So when at Ixopo he could not bring himself to accept the promotion the government decided that he was not a man they could trust very far. On the other hand they realised that they could not get rid of him so soon after they had deposed Siyoka. Besides they needed some continuity, they needed someone who knew the community and what had gone on before. So they kept him in his office, as chief counsellor to the next chief. And to close the gap quickly, they decided to install a new chief altogether.

The 'crowning' of the new chief was a subdued affair. The invitation to the next dipping day meeting was given through Chief Counsellor Duma who was anxious not to betray any enthusiasm for the event. There was one announcement after church service one Sunday, and there was little publicity among the non-church-going members of the public. As a result, a much smaller crowd was there to greet the officials on the day of the meeting. And similarly, on the side of the government there was much less pomp and show of power. The chief spokesman from the last meeting was there. He was accompanied by a policeman, which added a new dimension and lent a different tone to the meeting. And, of course, there was the new chief. A burly man like his white counterpart, he came forward with a stride of confidence. He was not a man of Sigageni, but some people knew him from his days as a policeman. There was a hush and people held their breath, looking at this man dressed in the cloak of their lost tradition. He was all that stood between them and the vulturous government. A smile played around his eyes, if not his lips, as he nodded all round with an air of power. When the people and their herds had been forced back against the fence in the usual manner the official stepped forward. He dispensed with all pleasantries and preliminaries, and in a voice steeled with authority he began.

'We have come here today to introduce you to your new chief, a wise man, who knows what is good for you. He is prepared to work with the government. In fact he has been working for the government for many years as a policeman. Today he is a retired man, a wise man and a man who loves his people. This man knows the law and he will deal with all your cases fairly. He will also deal with those criminals who work against the interests of the whole community. Paramount Chief Siyapi lives in Ndawonde, which as you know is not far from here. But from now on he will be coming here regularly to see if your needs are met; and those of you with serious matters to discuss can either wait for his visits here or go straight to the Great Place in Ndawonde. Plans are afoot to build him a house here in Sigageni before very long to enable him to attend to your problems more efficiently. But that is in the future.'

The people stared at the new chief silently without blinking.

'Have you anything now to say to your new chief?'

Silence.

'Remember, he is the man to give you land if you want land.'

There was a quick shuffle in the silent crowd and one man piped up, 'What land? I've not had land to plough for the last four years – since I was removed from the last white farm where I lived before and was brought to this place. I was told there was no more land to allocate . . .'

Before he could finish, the white man cut in, 'This is your man, you can see him after this.'

After this there was an air of foreboding in the whole of Sabelweni. Strange people came and went and people betrayed no curiosity as though they all knew what was being mooted. It was at this stage that a couple of them went past Jezile's home.

MaBiyela was there too and Jezile was very near her time of delivery. They brought a package that they said Siyalo had given them. It was packed full of the prettiest little clothes for the baby. MaBiyela was angry. She did not know whether to be angry with Siyalo's friends or with Siyalo himself.

'Who ever heard of anyone buying things for an unborn child – it is just an omen, a bad omen – things do happen to unborn babies and they do not get born.'

She betrayed her feelings of anxiety which were just as strong as Jezile's as the time drew near. While MaBiyela went on ranting Jezile had other questions ticking in her head. Who were these men? How did they come to know Siyalo? She felt there were areas of his life in the city that remained unexplained to her, but she could not exactly put her finger on anything. She switched her mind to the beautiful things the men had brought. It meant one thing, that Siyalo was still as loving and faithful to her and their unborn child as ever. There was no cause for worry on that score. How different it had been for Zenzile. She told herself to enjoy her good fortune and stop worrying about things she could not change.

7

*A*fter Zenzile's death, and perhaps because of it, Jezile had taken every precaution to see that she and the baby were healthy. She went to see Nosizwe regularly; she asked her to book her a bed at Clydesdale hospital. She even booked Hongo's van, and he laughed heartily saying no one had ever booked his van so far in advance, simply because no one knew the day or the time when the baby would choose to come. Good humouredly he promised to be ready any time she called on him, day or night. All this, of course, behind MaBiyela's back. She was so tense by now, she did not want any references made to the baby at all. Which is why, when that baby did indicate its intention to come, Jezile sent Simo and Jabu to call Hongo even before she told MaBiyela. When MaBiyela was finally told, she was cold and detached, but not hostile. She seemed relieved that Jezile was going into hospital. She went in the van with her, but chose to wait outside while Jezile went to the labour room. She seemed prepared to wait for as long as it took. To her relief it took a mere three hours; the baby was a girl. As soon as MaBiyela heard, she called out: 'Wo, S'naye, S'naye nathi umtwana' – (We have her, we too have a baby) – and so the baby was named S'naye – 'We have her.'

On the next day, with a heart welling with joy and hope MaBiyela walked into the little sterile, clean ward to see her new grandchild. It was like no hospital ward that she had ever been to – there was no smell of pain and medicine. This ward was full of laughter and hope. For MaBiyela the urge to take the baby in her arms was strong, but there was reluctance in Jezile's eyes. Each time Jezile saw that imperceptible move of MaBiyela's hands to pick up the baby, her eyes darted towards the passing nurses with something akin to servility, seeking their consent, as if unsure of the right they had to that baby. MaBiyela sensed this and hated it. The baby was theirs, was it not? Yet, there was something constricting about the place. The nurses were pleasant enough, but somehow, in their absolute efficiency they had usurped her own authority. They were dealing with Jezile and herself and the baby as though they owned them. Soon it became very obvious to them that a bubble of tension had developed. Their voices became softer and MaBiyela became curious about a number of things.

'How was it, did you kneel on the bed or did they allow you on the floor?' she whispered.

'Not on the floor, mother; no, not in this room either,' Jezile whispered back.

After a silence, in which MaBiyela sensed reluctance again, she asked, 'Where then?'

'In the labour room.' Silence. 'Strangely, the nurses call it the slaughter house,' Jezile added.

'Who does? . . . why such a name?'

'I suppose it's all that blood.'

'It's a horrid name.' Silence. 'Were there other women who had their babies at the same time?'

'There were three others.'

'If you didn't kneel down, how did you do it then? What's done in these hospitals?'

'We all lay flat on our backs.'

'How strange! But how is it possible? On your back?'

'Well, that's what they tell you to do – they insist you do nothing else.'

A long silence.

'And the placenta? What have they done with it?' Jezile looked up in surprise. Then she quickly cast her eyes down again.

'I don't know. I forgot all about it.'

'Forgot? But you should have asked for that. That's very important. Nobody parts with the placenta just like that. Nobody leaves it to strangers to dispose of.' MaBiyela became agitated.

'You didn't say, mother,' Jezile ventured.

'But I didn't know you were coming into hospital. Remember? This was *your* decision.'

'But you could have said something in the van, on our way to this place.'

'What? In the presence of Hongo? Besides, that was not the time to think about such things.'

In the silence that followed, they both seemed to admit that the fault lay on both sides.

'The placenta is the bond between you and the baby and the earth. It will always draw you together. It should be buried in a secret spot, known only to members of the family. Otherwise, it leaves you and the child vulnerable . . . And, for the baby, it is the tie that binds her firmly to her place of birth. It will always draw her back to her home, no matter how far she travels. This is the belief and the custom.' And touching S'naye gently on her forehead, she wondered loudly what would happen to her now. She looked back at Jezile and asked what she thought the hospital did with such private personal things. Jezile shook her head again.

'Burn them I suppose . . . I see no placenta burial ground here,' MaBiyela went on in a kind of monologue.

In reply Jezile opened her eyes wide again in wonder.

'Burn it?'

'Yes, they burn everything here – they even burn dead people.'

Jezile shuddered visibly. It was her turn now to look disturbed. It was as though the hospital had deprived her of a prized possession; a bequest to her child; an affinity so abstract, yet so binding to her and to the land – the place of her birth.

'If you submit yourself to these people they destroy you. Give them a little chance and you're never the same again. They're butchers!'

'Butchers mother! They've just safely delivered our baby.' Jezile sounded angry and confused.

'Yes, it is for these small tokens they give us that we exchange the most basic and indispensable aspects of our lives, our beliefs . . . It leaves us with no people at all. We're starting this child off like a waif. Our whole nation is that of waifs and strays now. They ignore all our beliefs and all our pleas. It would not have cost them anything to keep the placenta for us.' MaBiyela's anger was gathering new strength. The subject simply refused to die and was getting Jezile quite agitated, and it was spoiling the whole visit.

'They could not make us the exception, mother.'

'I'm not asking to be made the exception. I'm talking of a general rule. All these women, and others besides, have had to lose this birthright. Surely the hospital could keep all placentas for all mothers, for the whole nation, in deference to our beliefs. That's if they had any respect for us.'

Ten days later, when Jezile was back home, the baby's umbilicus shrivelled and dropped off. MaBiyela held on, reverently, to this stump of a superseded relationship between mother and child. It was buried with due ceremony and when all else had failed it became the anchor between S'naye and her place, the land. And no one else ever knew where the ngalati (umbilicus) was buried, but they all knew that it would always beckon to her, no matter how far she went, and bring her back to her place of birth.

According to custom Jezile was taken to the Mapangas to be with her mother for some weeks. She was fussed over and she did not have to do anything for herself or for the baby.

When she felt stronger she returned to her own home, to prepare for Siyalo's annual leave. He was due back in about five weeks. MaBiyela was flushed with pride although she was not very demonstrative. Siyalo arrived in December in a whirlwind of joy; and the house was a beehive of activity, in a way that it had never been before. They all felt fulfilled. Siyalo seemed to spend more time away from home, which at first made Jezile think he wanted to be out of the way. If she had been less involved in her own life, she would have noticed that there were several strangers from the city in the area. She would have also known that Siyalo was constantly in their company. Being Christmas time, there were a lot more men of Sigageni back home for their annual leave too. She knew vaguely that a meeting was called one Sunday afternoon to discuss the points that had been raised at the dipping tank a few months earlier. It was a men's meeting that no women attended. It was like that at Sigageni. When the men were there, they attended their own meetings to which they did not invite the women. They did not have to say it; it was simply understood that a men's meeting was a men's meeting. In the course of time, women would come to make their own decisions. But for the moment it was men who decided.

Preoccupied though Jezile was with the baby and the Christmas whirl, she did notice a remark from Siyalo which seemed to puzzle her. 'Don't worry, everything is under control; we'll fix these Boers in time.' It was vague, but it was loaded. Who was 'we'? How? He seemed preoccupied most of the time. Was Siyalo changing somehow? He was as loving as ever. But there was no denying that he was holding something back. She thought back to that time in Durban, when in the midst of a good time, instead of enjoying to the full their last few days together in Durban, he had simply sent her packing back to Sigageni. There were times when it seemed like he was holding back. There was an air of secret assurance about him which, of course, might have had something to do with being a father; only, was it? The days went by and after a brief fortnight, Siyalo had gone back to Durban, and Jezile pottered about as usual, but with an added air of accomplishment.

She waited for Siyalo's first letter. It took long to come. When it did, it was dry, hurried and brief. It disturbed Jezile a little, but in the climate of things, there was no room for doubt. He had proved himself a loving father and faithful husband. Her next letter was warm, gushing with domestic news. But there was no reply to it. There was silence. It went on for several weeks. Jezile was at her wits' end. She would have been stranded for money if she had not saved from the time when he had sent her so much money before the birth of S'naye.

S'naye was about four months old now and was beginning to go up and down the countryside on her mother's back. Jezile decided to take her to the first Thursday prayer meeting she had attended in months. It was wonderful to be back with the crowds and to think again about the burning issues of Sigageni. This one, however, was more of a prayer meeting than a political one. Nosizwe was not there. They sang and witnessed, drawing their inspiration from the story of Ruth and her mother-in-law, Naomi: 'Where you go, I will go – your people shall be my people . . .' This passage was always so rich in its interpretation, and the women excelled themselves in eloquence; each viewed it from her own vantage point; all affirmed their loyalty – that highly prized value in their often trying lives. Just as they were winding up, before the final prayer, they saw Nosizwe coming in, followed by MaNgidi, the wife of Duma, the Chief's Counsellor.

They tiptoed their way towards the front and they sat down reverently, indicating that the prayer meeting should go on in spite of the interruption. Premonition fluttered in the room but people went on praying.

As far as the people of Sigageni were concerned MaNgidi was an old faithful and so was her husband. He had been the old Chief's Counsellor before he was banished. There was no doubting their loyalty to the community. Nosizwe stood up to tell the women that MaNgidi had some news to pass on to the women at this meeting, even though they would hear it again on Sunday. Nosizwe felt that it was best brought to the prayer meeting to give the women a chance to discuss it. Duma, MaNgidi's husband, had received a letter, which he would read in Church the following Sunday. The letter came from the new Chief, Siyapi, telling him to announce that exactly three weeks from that Thursday, there would be officials visiting Sigageni to give passes to all the women. They would pitch their tent on the school grounds. There would be no school that day, nor would there be a women's prayer meeting. The women exclaimed in a chorus, 'No prayer meeting! Why do they choose a Thursday?'

After this, there was a heated discussion; they went over the same points that they had debated many times before, but they had never meant them more than on this occasion. Their conclusion was the same as it had ever been – that they would definitely not take the passes. Then Nosizwe mentioned some names that were new to Jezile, names of people who would be there to assist them and to warn all the women of the area, including the non-church members, not to take the passes. In fact, they would organise a meeting, perhaps in a week's time, for all the women to meet. No one would take the passes, they agreed. Jezile was silent, stricken with a bad conscience. She fidgeted and murmured to the woman next to her.

'What about those few who have taken them already?' In the heat of the moment, the woman took up the question in a hurry.

'Oh, yes,' answered Nosizwe. 'What about the women who have them already?' She bounced the question back to the women. There was an abrupt silence. They looked up to Nosizwe to answer that one.

'Well, it will depend on them. If they want to join the other women, they will have to give them back to BAD, give them back to the officials.' There was a silence. 'Better still, we will burn the passes – if they give them back to us, we will all come together and make a fire – burn them to ashes.'

There was loud applause and the women parted on that high note. They carried their tense excitement back to their own homes. Jezile was perhaps the happiest of the women – at last she stood a chance to appease her conscience and to be reconciled with the other women.

In the following weeks there was a flurry of activity and there was no longer any doubt that the men who came from outside, more than give anyone new advice, gave the people courage to stick by the decisions they had made. They killed off any needling doubts – there was safety in numbers – the people of Sigageni were not alone.

In the early morning of the 15th of April, the appointed Thursday, big vans started to arrive and within a short time, the tents were pitched. As the sun rose higher, the officials could be seen walking up and down between the tents, or standing in groups of twos and threes, talking and generally surveying the area. The footpaths looked quite deserted – there were no people going up and down to Umzimkulu or Ixopo or to their fields. There was a silence that felt like a presence. The hours crawled by and people continued to observe the scene from the shelter of their pondokies. Then they saw a cavalcade of cars rocking their way down towards the church. Sigageni held its breath as the people watched a string of armed police-men get out of the cars. This was about lunch-time, and no one had gone anywhere near the tents to obtain passes. As if obeying a signal everyone emerged from their houses and walked towards the dipping tank. When they got there, they settled down and talked among themselves. The children played all around.

At this point, the officials up at the school came out to watch what the women were up to. For a while they looked puzzled.

Then the policemen who had come along with the officials started walking towards the houses. The women watched them and waited. Then the police, finding no one in their homes, converged towards the dipping tank where the women sat. As the police waited for the last of their number, the women drew closer and formed a ring around Jezile. A group of about twenty women quietly dropped their pass books at her feet and sat around shielding her. Jezile, facing away from the assembly of policemen, stealthily set the pile of books alight. The police watched unable to observe exactly what was happening at first. Then there was a sudden cry of triumph from the women who were mingling and dancing, some ululating and others shouting slogans. The police were thrown into total confusion, and it was quite some time before they realised that the women were burning their passes. Although they had seen the women forming a ring round Jezile, they could not say exactly who had done what. It all happened so quickly. They charged forward quickly, but were intimidated by years of their own conditioning – how to charge at a screaming mob of black women and children? While dancing in celebration and hooting in joy, the women swooped and picked up their children and placed them on their backs and carried their water jars back along their narrow paths against the setting sun. That moment of confusion saved the situation. And so ended one more confrontation.

Darkness gathered quickly and shielded the homes and the women, but with the events of the day, peace had absconded for good from the valley of Sigageni, never to return. That night they went to sleep in the unreal peace of their quiet houses. But they could no longer ignore the flutter of forebodings that invaded their sleep and kept them awake. Jezile was still half awake when she heard pounding feet, now approaching her house, now at the window, now everywhere. Then there was a resounding pummelling noise at her door, threatening to break it in two, a bewildering command to open up. Petrified, she stood in her half-nakedness behind the door. She would have asked one of the many questions that came to her mind, if her voice would come out, but her throat was dry, and unreasoning fear compelled her to obey the command outside. She opened the door to stare into the dark mouth of a gun, and the blaze of a torch on her eyes. A towering shape loomed behind it all.

Somewhere in the darkness a voice boomed in Zulu, 'Liph'ipasi lakho?' (Where is your pass?). Again, Jezile's voice let her down. It was in the middle of this that Jezile heard MaBiyela's voice piping out from behind them.

'And who are you, desecrating this home of our ancestors? What is it you want that you won't find in the daytime without noise and without guns?'

In the stunned silence that followed, Jezile leaped for her baby and dashed out to join a crowd of grandchildren that had gathered in the dark behind MaBiyela. MaBiyela seemed to gather courage with every passing moment, her voice rising and resounding as if to awaken everyone in the valley. She was screaming the names of all their ancestors without any regard for the five policemen, black and white. Slowly the people drew closer into the shadows of Jezile's little house, as if to watch the spectacle. Before long someone further down seemed to pick up the echoing voice and another and another, all around the valley. Voices echoed against the assault on the age-old village peace. The police seemed disarmed. They had never before been confronted with people who had no fear of their brutal force; people who owed allegiance to another order. They faced outrage, not fear. Confused once more they withdrew and left Sigageni enveloped in darkness, as they had found it. No one slept that night. They sat through the night trying to grasp the nature of power and intimidation that relentlessly sought to intrude into their quiet lives.

On the following Thursday there were milling crowds around the school building long before the women's meeting started. There were people from other reserves and the place tingled with outrage. The mood was dauntless. Nosizwe was there and she led the women in their fearlessness. The meeting went on for hours and it was agreed that it was time they took a decisive stand. They had a list of complaints against the government; they had done a lot to show their dissatisfaction in the past, but they had never actually gone up to BAD to present their complaints. They listed all their problems and Nosizwe wrote them down:

1. We do not want to live without our husbands all our lives.
2. We want the right to visit them in the cities when there is

need to do so; and those of us who want to go and live with our husbands in the cities should be allowed to do so.
3. We demand living wages for our husbands and our families.
4. We need more land to raise crops to feed our families.
5. We need more land to graze our livestock which are dying from lack of grass and water.
6. We do not want dipping cattle which have no food to eat.
7. We want clinics for our sick children and not dipping tanks for our dying cattle.
8. We do not want the Bantu Authorities Act which removes our chiefs and imposes government appointed authorities that only serve the government and not the community.
9. We do not want many of the terms of the rehabilitation scheme, especially those removing some members of the community who have no land for crops. It is land we want for the many people who are being settled in our communities from white farms and white cities. We want more land.
10. And we do not want passes. They have enslaved our men – and we do not want to carry them.

Some suggested that a delegation be sent, but the majority rejected the idea – they wanted no scapegoats. Besides, there was safety in numbers. If they all went, there would be no victims – it was time for a show of strength – the government had to know that none of their schemes was acceptable even to a few people in the reserves. It was agreed that they would all get up early on the morning of the following Thursday to assemble in their hundreds outside the offices of BAD at Ixopo, thirteen miles away. They would all get there early, whether they walked or travelled by buses. In the intervening days they would mobilise the other women who had not attended the meeting. Sigageni and all the other places in the Ixopo district bristled with determination and anticipation.

Something had changed – they could not say when it had changed. These women, who had, up until now, made decisions but had waited for their husbands to give them the final go ahead, were not talking any more about writing letters or the return of those far away men. They were making decisions and they were going to implement them. They were facing white intruders and screaming hell into their faces. This change had come over them slowly, not harshly in one exploding episode, but slowly like the weathering of rocks.

Their voices could be heard all along the pathways from the church building. Jezile approached her house with thoughts that buzzed like gnats around her head. She saw that her hut was lit but did not question why. It was when she fumbled with the lock at the door that she knew that not only was the house lit but the door was half open. She stopped and thought of the events of the week before. Could the police be waylaying her in her own house, she wondered. If the door had not slowly opened, she would have run screaming to MaBiyela again. But the door opened, and as though playing hide-and-seek again, Siyalo slowly revealed half his face.

'You! What is it? What brings you here today?'

'Come in; don't just stand there.'

She walked in slowly, not shifting her eyes from his face, even though she could not fully see it against the dim, crude paraffin lamp. Her foot landed uncertainly as though someone in her absence had dug out a deep hole in the floor. A silence followed as she slowly unfastened S'naye from her back. Siyalo was all patience as if to indicate that he had all the time in the world to tell his story and to delay further the moment of revelation. When he spoke at last, it was to say something inconsequential about how he had not minded waiting through the long afternoon for he knew their meetings took long. Jezile squashed the rising feelings of irritation and impatience. She curled herself defensively on the bench against the wall hugging S'naye close to her chest as if to fortify herself. He breathed a sigh, wishing hard that she would make it easy by asking some question – any awkward question, just so long as she gave him an opening. But he knew her well by now. If only he was able to think of something to say there and then, something that would provoke her. He felt afraid, as though he was guilty of some crime. Finally he took the plunge. It was best to start from the present and work his way backwards.

'I came this afternoon. I was brought back by the police . . . I've been "sent off" from Durban . . .'

'"Sent off"? What for?'

'Yes, "sent off" – you know, Section 10. It's a long story. I don't know when it really started. I could say, I became aware of some trouble around the time you were in Durban, over a year ago.' Suddenly he stopped mumbling with his face down; he sat up straight and looked her in the face.

'In fact, you should understand this case more than anyone.'

'I don't know what you're talking about . . . at least, not yet,' she said, looking at him fixedly.

'I mean, people throughout our country are oppressed in all sorts of ways. You women are facing great hardships here and we workers are oppressed in the cities and cannot live with our families – all that; I should not have to repeat it to you. All men . . . and women, can see the injustice of it and are fighting in every possible way. Perhaps part of it is to do with what you people are doing here.' She looked at him, as though to say, 'get on with it'.

'For a while now, I have been working with other men out there, mobilising people to stop killing themselves with liquor and to start fighting back. You will remember what I said to you . . . and to the Gumedes that night in KwaMashu.'

She gave him another look, more fierce than the last. He went on.

'I approved of everything you did when you were in Durban. I was happy when you joined the crowds on the march to the city.' Silence. 'In fact, I supported the women who organised it . . . I mean, not me alone – a whole group of us encouraged them . . . A group of us knew about the plot to fight the police back at Cato Manor – although I was not there on the 24th of February when the police were killed – I really did not know they were going to be killed. But somebody must have grassed on us; I'll never know who did. Sometimes I suspect Gumede himself – '

'Which Gumede?'

'Gumede in the house, Fakazile's husband. You remember him. I mean, I tried to recruit him – he seemed so interested in what was going on . . . I still wonder . . . I can't believe it . . . if he did, I think he did not really mean selling out; he just did not appreciate the danger, the security involved.'

'But how do you know it was him – did you tell him everything? It could have been any of the other people you worked with.' There was something in Jezile's voice that seemed to have eased. He gave her a sideways glance and he was encouraged.

'No, I'll never know if he did betray me; I'll never know who did. It could have been anyone . . . someone in the group who was a plant . . . perhaps someone who did not appreciate the danger. On that last Friday in Durban – the day I came back late and told you to leave – well, that's the day I first knew there was trouble. That afternoon at work I was called to the office. There was a man there I did not know. He seemed to know me well – a white man. He knew where I came from; he knew you were in Durban; he asked about that fateful day at Cato Manor. I knew he was from the Special Branch. I knew they were on to something. They did not know everything but they were on a trail. I was shocked but I denied everything. I didn't know what they were going to do next, but I felt you were safer out of Durban – that's why you had to go. At first my boss believed me. He dismissed the Special Branch man, because his case was loose and he could not make the right connections. He told him I was "a good boy", a hard worker, quiet and sensible. I lowered my eyes – I was angry, but it was not the time to show anger and rebellion. After that I lay low. I went back to the hostel and avoided all my friends. I sent them word of what was happening. I got word that several of my friends had also been visited. Soon, three of those who had been there when the police were attacked, were arrested. I don't think they squealed because there was a long silence. I almost forgot the whole affair.

'At Christmas time I came back here. I felt safe here in Sigageni, away from the prying eyes of everyone in the city. A couple of my comrades were here – they were here to mobilise – you should know them – Kunene and Dondo. It was unavoidable that I should work with them here – they were here to help us sort out the best way to handle all these matters. I spent a lot of time working with them – I felt safe here – this is my own home. But I was not all that safe – the police knew I was working with those men. Soon after my holiday, they came back again – two of them this time. My boss looked at me – and there was doubt in his eyes. They asked me about everything this time – not just about Cato Manor; they asked me about you, about the dipping mixture that you spilt every week, about your pass. I convinced them you had taken the pass, that's why you could be in Durban. That seemed to go down well – strengthen my case, I mean. I tell you I spent the whole day in that office. And my boss sat there, looking at me, throughout the interview. I knew I was in trouble. A week later they were back again. They took me away this time, back to the police station. They questioned me the whole day and most of the night. They hissed and they threatened and they beat me up. The whole of the next day they did not call me out of my cell. I sat in the dark waiting, but they did not come. On the third day they told me I could go. They did not charge me. I'll never know why they did not nor what they would have charged me with. I was detained for three days.

'When I went back to my job after that, I found a tidy parcel of my overalls and my envelope. The boss would not look me in the eye. All he said was, "Sorry, Siyalo, I don't care about your politics or whether or not you are a trouble-maker; that's none of my concern. All I want is people who come here and work. I don't want people who waste time sitting in this office, and me paying them for their politics. And I don't want these fellows thinking I'm shielding a skellem here at work. This country is good as long as you don't cause trouble. If you can't appreciate how lucky you are to have a job here, then I don't want you – what do you want, maan?" he asked me, almost in anger, "You have a good job and you got good money; what more do you want? You just cause trouble – you kill white men – you'll kill me next time!" There was fear in those penetrating blue eyes. I saw he was afraid. Those eyes can hide nothing – you see everything through those hollow blue eyes.' Siyalo was quiet for some time, as though reliving that harrowing experience. 'He snatched my pass off me and scribbled a discharge across at the bottom. Another silence. And that was it. I was jobless. I felt cold even though the sun was burning hot. I felt cold in the pit of my stomach.

'I walked out of that place feeling like a heap of refuse. I could not walk out of the front gate for fear of meeting fellow workers. I felt guilty as though I had been caught stealing – not just a car tyre, but the whole factory, the whole country even. I don't know how they manage to make one feel guilty when one has committed no crimes. I went out through the back past the garbage cans. Once out there in the street, I felt like a piece of paper blowing in the wind. I stood in the street not knowing which way to go. I did not even think of going to the hostel to have a rest. I felt compelled to go straight away looking for another job. Before the end of the day the police had stopped me twice. On each occasion they told me to go down to BAD to get a special pass to look for work. The second time it was late in the afternoon so I put it off. I drifted to the trains, went back to the hostel together with thousands of working people returning after their day's work. I was feeling sick with fatigue. All I wanted was to get on my bed and think about you and S'naye and another job. I walked into my cubicle. Something hit me at the door. There was an emptiness where there should have been my things – my clothes and my pots. I looked again and thought I was in a wrong dormitory. But I wasn't. All I could see was the bed frame and the bare mattress. My blankets, my clothes and my food basket were gone. I thought somebody was playing a joke on me. But no, they were not – three days' absence had been enough to justify stripping me of everything that I had – I felt obliterated – there was this eerie feeling that I had returned from the dead to find people sharing out my possessions. There was nothing where there should have been me. I looked around at the familiar faces who nodded in dim recognition or murmured, "So, you're back". I tried to ask about my things and the only response I got was vacant stares and shaking heads. I tell you, Jezile, if the police can't kill you, your own people will finish you off. People in the city are not the same people we know in these parts – they become vultures; they lose all moral sense.

'Late that night, I went back to the city, to our cousin Mavela, to the same hostel where we slept. As usual, he received me warmly. I had supper that night and again he gave me his bed.'

'Where did he sleep?'

'He has a girl in some location-in-the-sky.'

'Location-in-the-sky? What's that?'

'You know the big buildings where white people live in the flats. Well, on top they used to have small rooms for the servants who worked for them. The government stopped that because they want everyone in the locations or hostels. However, a few of them still have their servants living there. Those

86

poky rooms at the top of high buildings are called locations-in-the-sky. Nancy lives in one of those. Mavela is not allowed there at all, but in an emergency, what can we do? He spent quite some time sleeping there, stealing in and out of the commercial lifts at the back. Mind you, he could not have done it without the help of Zandi, the security man in the building. Mavela gets along with all kinds of people – that's his greatest gift.'

'Well?'

'Well, the next day and the many days after that, I went about looking for work . . . without success . . . At BAD they gave me the usual three days. I went back again, and each time I still believed I could get work before troubles started. But I did not. Days and weeks passed. I went on frantically trudging the streets of Durban but there was no work I could find; not any kind. Days rolled into weeks. My pass by then was long out of order. Then one day I found work.'

'Found it?'

'I actually found work. By then I didn't care what sort of work it was – as long as I worked and could remain employed in Durban. I dreaded being "sent off" – the way I've now been. I was going to work as a garden-boy . . .'

'You – a garden-boy?'

'What else? Work is work – I was desperate. What's the point – I couldn't even do that. My pass was out of order and we went through everything before this woman found out. She was not going to take me – no amount of begging her could change her mind. She said they would fine her £100 if they found her out. She was not prepared to take the risk.

'I feared anyone who looked at me twice in the street – they don't have to be dressed like police nowadays – they have this ghost squad who are black, like me, and dressed like anyone in the street. I tell you they are vicious. Then Jezile, one day after many weeks they got me . . . another three days in a cell. After the third day, I knew it would not work – they would define me as "idle" and send me off to any rural rehabilitation centre of their choice. As an "idle person" the commissioner could impose a permanent prohibition on me, which would mean I never went back to the city again. But I was wrong even there. That was before I knew there were other ways of dealing with people like me. Anyway, I still believed I could get work . . . They took me to the Aid Centre. You would think these centres helped you. This was simply a convenient place to keep me while they worked out where I fitted in. I was detained for a few days. That was the last week. On Monday, this week, I was told I was being "endorsed out" of the city for good. I was told that without a "call-in" card from my employer I would find it very difficult to return to Durban ever. The employer gives you one of these if he still wants you in his employment, but I know that my boss no longer needs me. If I still want to return, I will have to go back to the bureau here at Ixopo – I'll have to start from scratch and wait with the dusty crowds in the "labour pool". What chance is there, Jezile? This morning I was escorted by two policemen. They brought me right here to my doorstep, like a heap of city refuse. I feel broken. No work, no money, no clothes, no hope. I don't believe what's happened to us; it's as if I'm sleepwalking.'

Jezile started and turned to Siyalo with a surprised look. She had listened all this time to his strange story which she wished to believe had nothing to do with her life. But as the reality seeped in her blood chilled and her skin began to erupt in goose pimples. She shook her head to dislodge the attack of anxiety that gripped her. Yet when she spoke her voice betrayed nothing, as though she had not fully understood the meaning of it all. She told Siyalo to go and see his mother, MaBiyela and tell her all that had happened. She stood up; she had lost all appetite, but he must be hungry, she thought. Siyalo continued to sit, staring into space, as though he had not heard her speaking. This home-coming was so different from his visit four months earlier, at Christmas. He could not move himself to see his mother. He hated the thought of another confrontation after the gruelling time he had just had with Jezile. Perhaps she did not fully realise what it had cost him to tell her the long and painful saga.

After a while Siyalo stood up and followed Jezile to where she had put the baby to sleep. He looked at S'naye for a long time. His eyes filled with tears for the first time since all the trouble began. S'naye was growing beautiful, healthy and strong. She already showed signs of looking very much like her mother. Seeing Jezile in that tender little face flooded his heart with love for both of them; how much he loved Jezile; how much he wished to protect her from pain and inconvenience. But from now on they would endure the extremes of poverty; nothing stood between them and that prospect. Hot tears poured out without control. Jezile looked up, sensing his reluctance to go to his mother, and was shocked to see him crying. She felt a lump in her throat, but told him once more to go. Ignoring her, he prepared to lie on his bed, next to S'naye. It was then that she told him that all the women were going to Ixopo the next day to demonstrate. He rose with a jolt.

'To demonstrate? What for?'

'To demonstrate, Siyalo, about everything that's been happening here; about the passes and the rehabilitation schemes, and all that – you know.'

He sagged and sighed a long tired sigh. He did not know what he felt now about those campaigns. They had been the source of all his problems. She told him about the events of the last few months, for in the last three months he had not received any of the long letters that she had written to him at his hostel. She told him how they had burnt all their passes. He shuddered visibly. He knew then that he could not stop Jezile going where all the women were going. He felt weak inside, his courage and loyalty wavered. He was going down, not alone, but with all those he loved – his mother too – they were all he had.

As Jezile was preparing to leave early the next morning, a strange tingling feeling gripped Siyalo at the nape of his neck. It was not an anxiety but a premonition about something terrible that was going to happen. He lay back watching her flit from corner to corner, preparing the baby for the long day out in the sun in the crowded courtyard at Ixopo. In the darkness before dawn, he watched her shadow looming large in the dimly lit room, now bending low, now rising and towering above him; here and there, opening this case and packing that bag. She was all efficiency and determination. He coughed nervously to get her attention. Almost hesitantly, he told her she was not going to take the baby along with her to the demonstration. She stopped rushing about feverishly and swivelled to face him.

'Leave the baby? How can I? The baby needs me; she needs my milk – and . . . and she does not know you.'

'Precisely,' he went on, with a dry laugh, 'I want her to know me. Now that I'm back she may as well learn to know me. How else can she if you don't leave her with me. Today is as good as any day. Leave her some food ; I'll get some milk.'

'Where from?'

'Surely I could find milk somewhere in Sigageni.'

Jezile stopped and fidgeted with her fingers. 'If Jabu and Simo were not going to school they could help you – perhaps they would stay at home if I asked.'

'No, don't. I'll go down now – Mother should be awake now preparing to go – I'll go down and tell her I arrived late last night. Maybe I could persuade her not to go with you and tell her about my misfortune during the day. The baby knows her and together we can look after her.'

'Who? You mean Mother?'

'Yes.'

So saying, he got out of his blankets in one leap and he was dressed in seconds. Jezile waited for his return as she drank her morning cup of tea. Later, she left the house alone, leaving S'naye warmly cuddled in her father's arms. Her eye lingered on the unfamiliar scene as she gave her final instructions about the child's food and sleeping times half expecting S'naye to wake up and cry. But those two seemed locked in each other. She almost felt jealous, as though S'naye were betraying her by appearing so much at home in the arms of a father she hardly knew. Jezile chided herself and withdrew quickly into the darkness, feeling guilty. He was her father – not some stranger. Up until now she had had the baby all to herself, with no rival parental claim. She had not made any room for the father's role. She felt guilty and ashamed. She resolved that she would encourage Siyalo's role as a father, but she did not know how. She herself had never known what the role of father entailed. She had never lived with her father. She braced herself for the changes ahead in the family with Siyalo around the house all day for weeks and months. There were going to be adjustments. She silenced her crowding thoughts as she approached a cluster of women at Cromwell Station waiting for the bus at sunrise.

8

It was a typical autumn morning as the last of the stars shot across the sky, falling to nowhere. The sky was flushed pink and the nippy morning air swirled around their cotton skirts. The cold glistening dew that hung from the dry grass drenched their feet. They waited, shivering in the cold wind, wondering which would reach them first, the sun or the bus. It was the bus.

Two hours later, they stood in several clusters, some around the courtyard and some on the cold cement post office verandah, trying to catch the warm rays of the sun. Those who had a little money went to get some hot tea from the tea-room across the road – a privileged group, if such differences could be noted among these peasant women. Others compensated by eating their cold provisions and drinking their cold teas from glass bottles carried from home for breakfast.

The crowds grew by the minute as women arrived on foot and in carloads and busloads. The cold wind subsided and the sun hugged everything warmly. By nine o'clock when the courtyard was opened there were milling crowds everywhere. People talked animatedly, as though to still the tremulous apprehension below the surface. But the ones who could not hide their disquiet were the officials along the verandahs of the great building. There was a flurry of activity, but most women showed little concern for that – they were preoccupied with counting those of their number who had not turned up. They peered above the heads of others to find their friends and when they did they clasped each other to the sound of laughter and celebration filled the air. There was a feeling that the assembly itself was a victory. When Nosizwe's car approached, sending up clouds of dust all round, the women turned and swarmed after it hailing her in welcome. There were two other women with her in the car. She smiled and waved, but seemed in a hurry to get behind the building. Unknown to the demonstrators, there was a quieter more orderly line of women at the back. Nosizwe and her two companions went straight to the queue at the back. Jezile recognised two women from Sigageni standing in it who had burnt their passes at the dipping tank.

Nosizwe shouted, 'And here you are, you sell-outs – what do you want here in this line – didn't you burn your passes with the other women the other day? You have come to betray us all – you have come to replace your passes.' No one had ever heard Nosizwe raise her voice in that fashion before. The line broke up and most of the women ran off in different directions. One of them stood her ground, and argued that there was no point in fighting a losing battle – she knew they would never win the struggle. Before she could finish one of Nosizwe's companions landed a hot slap across the woman's face.

'You treacherous woman – by your actions you betray all these women!'

A fracas ensued and then there was pandemonium everywhere. Needless to say, the police were on the scene in minutes, and Nosizwe and her companions were detained immediately. With their spokesperson gone it was left to others to present the women's grievances. The rest of the women were told to break up the demonstration and go back to their villages peacefully and quickly. The vast majority of women heard but they took no notice. They could only take orders from one person, and she could no longer give any.

The day wore on, and it seemed they had reached a stalemate. There were no discussions – just a restlessness in the crowds and officers bustling up and down the verandahs. From their habitual sense of time rather than the hour of the clock, the women sensed that it was lunch-time. A sudden calm seemed to descend on the courtyard. The women sat down in groups and spread their food reverently. Each gave her contribution to a communal pool at the centre of each ring they had formed. They spoke in low voices, moving about on their knees. The officers inside became suddenly aware of the hush that had descended. One enterprising officer seized the opportunity to talk to the murmuring crowd. His voice boomed loud, and the women froze in mid-action: even their jaws stopped chewing. He told them nothing new; just another warning to go home peacefully. Then he said something that made them alert.

'If you go away after your meal, back to your villages, I shall stop the convoy of police vans from Pietermaritzburg. You will not be arrested.'

'Arrested?'

There was a flurry of shock and fear everywhere. Food forgotten, many of them stood up as if to leave; to run away, in fact. They argued, forgetting that they had made decisions knowing what risks were involved. Only a few appealed for calm and steadfastness. Jezile, for her part, bitter from Siyalo's return, was in no mood to retreat – she was ready for a fight to the finish, there was nothing to lose. Once or twice the thought of S'naye tugged at her, but she told herself it was for S'naye that she was fighting, and for all the children of South Africa. She knew there was no going back; having taken a pass once and burnt it later, there would be no more regrets and no more betrayals.

The authorities watched the bickering among the women with interest and hoped that one would lead the way out of the gate. The men coaxed and encouraged, but no one was listening, and no one was moving. If only one would lead the way out of that gate, many, many others would follow. The officers waited on tenterhooks, but nothing happened. Finally, a few women sat down and lowered their voices, a few more followed, and then a few more till they had all sat down. A couple of hours later a convoy of black police vans suddenly appeared round the bend from the valley below. They laboured up the hill, a whole procession of them, in funereal fashion. The women stood silently in a long line alongside the courtyard. Nothing moved except for a few officers who came rushing out with papers to meet the vans as they arrived. Jezile counted about ten.

'Ten? How many are we?'

'We're many, very many,' murmured another.

'Who will tell our families?' another voice crackled.

'They'll know when we don't return tonight, they'll know we've been arrested.'

'For how long?'

'How far away is Pietermaritzburg?'

'Why didn't they detain us here at Ixopo?'

'Or Umzimkulu?'

'How long will we be away?'

'My husband!'

'My children!'

'But we have to – there's no other way.'

'What's jail like?'

It was in the middle of this consternation that they heard a loud familiar voice – they turned as one woman – it was Nosizwe.

'Is somebody dead – are you mourning? Did they kill one of us?' She took her guards by surprise – they pushed and shoved her roughly and told her to be quiet.

'I thought you would sing or fight to get me out' – another push and a jostle. She stumbled, 'Come on, sing! This is our day of triumph; from now on they'll never ignore us. Sing! Sing! Sing!'

In the ensuing scuffle the women became threatening – 'Leave her alone' some of them shouted. But this was drowned in the song that the others started to sing. The police circled them, herding them one by one into the vans. By this time the mood of rebellion had caught. They sang their church songs and their political songs, one after another. The whole population of Ixopo seemed to have come out to watch the spectacle and some to give them a good send-off. They lined the opposite side of the road. Ixopo had not seen anything like this before. At sunset, the convoy snaked its way out of the village and the vans rocked from side to side with the women's song. It was not going to be an easy drive over the hills and down the deep winding descent, into the valley that cradled the Umkomaazi river, and up again on the ascent in the pitch darkness of a South African night. The sixty-mile journey took a good five hours and they finally stopped at about eleven o'clock, in front of what they guessed was their destination, the Pietermaritzburg prison. They were tired and many were shaken from their sleep. It had been a very long day for them. Now they shivered in the bitterly cold Pietermaritzburg air. Never had a group of prisoners hurried faster into their prison. It was only when they got inside that the realisation of their plight struck them afresh. For many, the sleep in the vans was all they got for the night.

They were filed into cells at random and perhaps, not altogether by chance, Jezile ended up in the same cell with Nosizwe. Those high grey cement cells were hard and chill and they were cowed into silence, feeling like they had been cast into a deep dungeon. When the prison lock clicked behind them they were left in semi-darkness fighting for a place in the queue that led to one bucket in the corner of the room. When the women pushed and jostled for the bucket, Nosizwe asked Jezile to help marshal all the other women into orderliness. Jezile knew then that she was expected to take a position of leadership among the women. And she, who had always expected so little from herself suddenly felt able and strong. Something deep down welled up and responded to the challenge. They lay side by side on the floor closely packed like sardines. The only warmth they shared was their own body heat.

The next day, outside the court where they had been taken, they shuffled together like the sheep they tended in the country. They seemed to have lost all purpose and were afraid to stand apart. Even those furthest from Nosizwe kept glancing over or craning their necks to see if they could still see her, envious of those who stood closer to her. They stood in the cold just as they had done the day before but the atmosphere was very different. This time there were men and women who seemed to come from nowhere, who buzzed round, coats flapping, exuding confidence, trying to whip up some cheerful air among the captive women. They kept relaying messages to them and interpreting what was being negotiated. Nosizwe was back in form laughing and talking intently to everyone. She was not intimidated by the surroundings.

At last they were ushered into the courtroom. They sat hardly listening to the rambling discussion which belied the gravity of the situation. Overwhelmed by the atmosphere, the room, the formalities and the uncertainty of their fate, they sat waiting. They were shocked by the total absence of any relationship between their demands and the court performance. How removed everything was from passes and fields and cows. The courtroom officials looked like they had never seen a cow, let alone visited Sigageni. How could they sit in judgement? And they were all white – what did they know about the lives of black women or about places like Sigageni?

Later that evening as they tumbled out of the vans, they were shepherded into a building where all their clothes were taken from them and they were given prison clothes. The new clothes were baggy and accommodating and had the instant effect of reducing them all to a shocking sameness. They wobbled in their shapeless drab mid-calf dresses feeling, not just stripped of their individuality, but debased. The air was heavy with despair; they had been sentenced to six months – a very long time for women with children and chickens and cows, and fields to plough, and crops to raise for the next year. Six months! Some of the women walked tight-lipped, holding back the sobs that pounded at the back of their throats like sea-tides. Others were stony-eyed, unblinking, fearing that one blink would open the floodgates. A few tried hard to marshal new courage, drawing on the resources of the support they had received from the demonstration in court. In court the crowds had shouted, calling them heroes, and had boosted their flagging determination with repeated slogans. But now in the evening only a few could take sustenance from the events of the day. For most of them the whole day remained a gulf that separated them from their quiet ordered lives. Their meetings at the church in Sigageni had always been meaningful and controlled, never the rebel-rousing, sloganeering of the day before. They felt ensnared and could not account for their wavering convictions; they felt betrayed, but could not accuse any women or friends of forcing them into their decisions. The whole experience had lost its excitement and was left with a rawness they had not anticipated. These women were accustomed to harsh conditions, so it was not the physical discomfort that affected them, but the devastation of both mind and spirit.

The morning was clear but frosty. After a quick breakfast they stood huddled outside with hundreds of other women, experienced old hands who strutted about in confidence. They wondered what crimes the others could possibly have committed. What did the word 'criminal' really mean? They too stood there like criminals. The word had lost its meaning. Criminals were no different from innocent people. The scales of justice were inverted. They were all dressed the same, shared the same conditions and the same sense of shame – and were waiting to do the same work. It was a matter of time before they too would be strutting around, confident, showing off to the new arrivals – the prison version of seniority and privilege. This was a levelling experience.

Later on when the squad drivers came to the yard some differences began to emerge. The prison guards, men and women, were allocated their day's squads. Women moved away in little groups until a core of about four hundred women stood waiting, self-consciously aware that they alone had not been allocated. Several guards who until then had stood around lazily suddenly closed in on the crowd. It was intimidating. Many of the women could not understand the caustic remarks that the commandant addressed to them, but they sensed the derision. Finally he started calling their names, sharing them out, in groups, among the guards. When he came to the end of the first list he paused, waiting for them to move – but no one moved. There was bewilderment all round – the guards looked alarmed, unable to believe that the amenable crowd of country women were staging a resistance. There was confusion among the women – the commandant barked at them in anger and the women became restless and began to talk among themselves as though in defiance of everyone. The scene turned uglier by the minute. It was in the midst of this that Nosizwe rushed to the forefront and started speaking in Afrikaans. She told the authorities that the women had not recognised any of the names that had been called out and therefore hadn't answered to them. There was further consternation among the guards, but Nosizwe was not to be put off; she insisted that the women had chosen her as their spokeswoman. She insisted that there were no Sarahs and Brendas among them. There was Mapungula Zibandlela and Masiqgobhela Qondeni, and other such names. The clerks who had registered them all, unaccustomed to the names, had written them all incorrectly – it didn't matter if the names were right or wrong, one kaffir maid was no different from another – that was always the attitude – any tag would do for any of them. It took half the morning to unscramble the mess and the women did not know whether to be grateful or not for the lost hours of work. Work held no terrors for these women, but they had never done 'hard labour'. They felt even more vulnerable as they walked away from each other in small groups, leaving an ever-diminishing crowd behind.

Out in the country, work had always been hard, but it had also been satisfying, accompanied by a sense of achievement. The only person that the other women had a concern for was Nosizwe; they knew that her work as a doctor had not prepared her for the kind of labour they were about to do. On her part Nosizwe displayed no qualms – she felt strong and friendly and equal to the others in every way.

When they got to the quarry they were shown their job – they were going to have to crush great big quarry rocks with steel hammers, and crush them fine. The women looked at the cavernous grey side of the hill and their hearts sank. It did not seem to make sense to them all – crushing stones seemed to them an exercise in futility, a waste of physical strength. What sense was there in that? The sheer size of the task was a challenge: to have to pitch themselves against the might of the earth, against nature, in conflict with the bedrock of life. Prison as a concept was not only alien to African thought but it was a reversal of the flow of life. They were accustomed to hard work in the fields – work that yielded fruit in the end – or at least carried the hope of fruition in it. They looked around and could see the other groups scattered on the scarred hillside; they could hear the echoes of the noisy clatter of rock and iron as the first groups started on the day's hard labour. And so they fell to their knees and started pounding – every blow echoed and reverberated far into the depths of the earth, followed by a ring that rose vibrating into the sky leaving a shudder inside their bodies. Now and again the hammer slipped from the head of a chisel and the blow fell with a thud. Before long, it struck Jezile that it was not just the rock that was being shattered; it was the substance of their lives. That had been the intention of putting them in prison – to crush them into timidity – what was that song again? – the women's song 'Pretoria – Verwoerd – you strike the women, you strike the rock! We are the rock!' How ironic – now they were forcing the women to strike the rock.

Two hours later it was lunch-time. When they stopped their hands trembled under the strain of the heavy work. Sweat poured down their faces in the piercing noonday heat. Their calloused hands had the shine of pressure against their hardened skin. But not Nosizwe's hands. They were blistered in the first hour. She hid them from the rest. When they talked about their hands, she looked the other way, filled with a sense of shame. Her eyes strayed to find their guard staring at her. He eyed her without blinking, a twisted smile playing around his mouth. She was jolted by that look – she knew then that she had been targeted. The stress and responsibility she had felt in the last few weeks of mobilising the women, and dragging them away from their families; the admission to herself that they had reached the ultimate in abuse, all culminated at this moment. Tears flooded her eyes and she wished she could cry more easily. Jezile saw her pain and began to talk loudly to draw the women's attention to herself. Nosizwe did not eat her lunch. But at the end, Jezile gave her a mugful of water. Within a short time, they were back at work. The sun was more intense because it beat to the rhythm of the hammer and the power of that watchful stare. The women around Nosizwe drew closer, so close that from a distance the watchful guard could not count her flagging strokes. In quick, deft movements Jezile dragged a mound of broken pieces in front of Nosizwe, a pile larger than any in front of the others. That evening, the women went back to prison happy that they had shielded her from the prison guard. As they entered the prison gates, he shouted gleefully:

'Doctor, what will you prescribe for those hands tonight?'

Nosizwe turned instinctively, as though he had called her by name.

'Doctor? Are you really a doctor? Ma se gat! I'll donner you; ek sal jou straf.' He flicked his sjambok threateningly and the evil menace in his face drove terror deep into the hearts of all the women as they turned in for the night. They were still standing in line, ready to file back into their cells, when another guard wagged a finger in front of Nosizwe's nose:

'You, you'll not sleep there – you'll sleep alone – away from the others.' So saying he snatched her and took her away. The other women stood stunned and their fear was palpable. For the rest of the time they were in Pietermaritzburg prison they would see her by day and she would disappear by night. They never asked her much about her isolation. Often she came to work in the mornings her face puffy as though she was recovering from long weeping sessions. No one knows to this day what went on in those dark hours in her prison cell. All the other women knew was that it was very small and she was all alone in there. At weekends, she was never let out.

On that first Sunday morning they had hoped they would be allowed to lie in a little longer, but there was no such luck. They woke up early and cleaned the cell as usual. Then they were shepherded out into the square. There were tin baths, full of water, scattered all around the yard. They were told to undress and to bathe. The women looked at each other, and then at the guards, in disbelief. Wash, in the open, in full view of all those people, including other prisoners! They looked at each other in horror. Among the Sabelo prisoners were a lot of young women, but there were quite a number of old ones as well. Back in the Sabelo where custom determines all forms of behaviour, these two groups would not and could not strip and wash together. Mothers-in-law and daughters-in-law were mutually exclusive. In fact they had well laid out patterns of avoidance on many aspects of day to day living. But the guards who seemed ready to quash any signs of resistance and trample on all tradition stood around ready with their sjamboks. The women took off their clothes and walked naked, with closed eyes, towards the baths. They did not have to whisper the word around – it was almost instinctive. The young carried their heads high and walked as in a march towards the baths, swinging their arms in defiance. But the older women – thin and emaciated – walked, half-stooped, with the hands clasped in front of them. They washed with their eyes shut and came back in the same manner. The hush was broken only by the splashing cold water and the sighing wind that sang in complicity. The guards watched with interest.

Having had their breakfast at six-thirty, they were given lunch at ten o'clock and supper at two o'clock. They were locked in for the night by three. This was an arrangement to allow as many warders as possible to spend time with their families on Sundays. Thus a pattern was set for all the Sundays they spent there, which spanned both the autumn and the winter months.

They spent most of that first Sunday locked in their cells. They sang their hymns, their voices crackling under the stress of their emotion. And the volume grew stronger as women in other cells joined in. They sang for hours till their voices fell and their emotions were spent. Then suddenly, somewhere in the deepest part of that jail, they heard a different kind of song. It pierced the prison air and shattered the silence of the vast corridors. The women in the cells listened for a few moments. Then they knew it was Nosizwe. They picked up her song and sang it with gusto. Her song was not a hymn, it was a political song that throbbed in the gut. Their voices returned to them full of strength and defiance. They grew strong and threw off the crippling feeling of inadequacy that had gripped them.

As weeks went by, the women grew accustomed to the Sunday ritual and it lost its terrors. But a new and more insidious fear crept in. Often, after the naked parades, some of the young women would be called out of their cells; sometimes for the rest of the day. No one dared speak out. But as with their nakedness in the yard, they all pretended it was not happening. They looked anywhere but into the eyes of those unfortunate women. The women most affected were the mothers-in-law. Back home it was their responsibility to see that order was maintained, and their duty to protect the younger women. But here, they were helpless. Jezile missed nothing. She had escaped so far, but she lived in fear, hoping and praying that no one would 'spot' her and pick on her. The added dread to this Sunday ordeal was the silent speculation: what if they went back home pregnant? They began to want to open their eyes to look at the women as they streaked naked across the yard, to see if any were showing any signs.

In the third month, Jezile, consumed by these preoccupations, realised that she had not had her periods since she had been in prison. Could it be the diet? She had not been 'called out', so she knew that if she was pregnant, it would be with Siyalo's baby. She thought of Siyalo and S'naye with an aching heart and quickly shut the thought out. She went to see the doctor on the pretext that she was ill. The examination confirmed that she was pregnant and it cheered her up enormously.

For some time she had been aware that there were mornings when she would feel sick and unable to pick herself up. She had not been able to account for those sudden spells. She had dragged herself to the quarry, and when the fatigue had grown worse each day, she had become ashamed of it, believing it to

101

be a sign of weakness. Each morning she had felt devastated and often she had not been able to eat those foul breakfasts – they were enough to make one sick. But now her secret joy would see her through the remaining days.

The women had to cope with frequent bouts of depression that would overtake them without warning. Jezile learned to discern the quality of their silences – the healthy silence that represented calm and the malignant silence which could destroy in minutes the store of courage and resistance they had built over some time. At such times Jezile would shake off her own feelings of misery and recount stories of interest from the past. She knew the kind of story that would ensure a lively exchange and possibly some laughter. She had noticed how eager they were to hear cruelly funny stories about the other women prisoners who were by and large city women. Jezile understood why the women behaved so unreasonably. The city women were their traditional rivals. They were the women who took their men when they went to work in the cities, or so they thought. Jezile, who had spent time with the city women in Durban, no matter how brief, saw them differently. She knew that they were really no different; yet she knew they thought they were superior. They were in their way just as narrow in their thinking. If Jezile had to take sides, she knew her loyalties were with the country women. There was a sense of strength in their numbers which was threatening to the others. As the tension between the two groups of women grew it could no longer be ignored. Jezile tried to reason with them without making a big issue of it. She knew they could not afford a split which the prison officers would take advantage of. Besides, all this animosity made no sense, and an open fight would be disastrous. Jezile spent sleepless nights, unable to confide her anxieties to Nosizwe during the day when they were slogging out in the quarry. After all, Nosizwe herself was a city woman, a fact which the others seemed to overlook. But soon it became obvious to Nosizwe that something was wrong. And she turned to Jezile to be enlightened. During the lunch break that day Jezile blurted it out to her. Nosizwe was visibly shaken. She had grown thin and pale, her high cheek-bones stood out of her once round face, leaving her eyes large in their sockets. But her eyes still sparkled with a deep fire that mirrored the power

102

within. If, in all her talks with the women, they had not grasped this fundamental lesson – the oneness of all suffering people and the need to unite – then perhaps the struggle was in vain. She charged Jezile with the duty of speaking to the women. There was no postponing it. It had to be done that night if trouble was to be avoided.

For Jezile this was a task more demanding than any she'd ever been asked to perform. It was one thing encouraging the women, it was quite another to criticise them, which they would see as tantamount to opposing them. All four hundred of them. After all, she was among the youngest in the group, and to have to lecture all those older women was more than she could handle. That evening as they sat down to eat, they could hear a commotion approaching their cells. There was a momentary stillness when they all stopped chewing and listened. Moments later they saw a crowd of women, some covered in blood, being driven in like cattle. The police were more ferocious than they had been for a long time; they seemed excited and afraid. The women tumbled in looking glazed and perplexed as though they could not take in the new reality of high walls and confinement. They blundered in confusion at the sound of each door as it shut to close them in, to rob them of their freedom and to contain their anger. They were driven into their own separate cells, and in the excitement that followed, and later from the shouts of the new arrivals, the rest gathered snippets of what was going on. There had been another riot, another confrontation between the people and the police and several people had been killed and many injured in Pietermaritzburg and other places. There had been a demonstration in many cities of South Africa. These women were the casualties of the local demonstrations. They were still heated after the day's events and it took a long time for them to settle in. They pounded the walls and shouted slogans. But as the night wore on, some began to cry, worried about loved ones, their children and their injured relatives. Luckily, as the women later gathered, none had died in the local uprising. But at the time the women feared the worst.

Needless to say, this was simply not the night for Jezile to talk to the women. She was partly relieved, although she did not know how to escape the responsibility altogether. The next morning they went out with their spans as usual leaving the new arrivals in prison awaiting their trial. When they got back that evening they found that the new city women were friendly and showed great interest in the country women. Because they were not allowed to mix and talk freely they communicated by passing secret messages and making coded gestures. The politicised new arrivals had known all along about the stand that the women of Sabelweni had taken. Their trial had been in the papers a few months before and they were heroes, they were loved and respected. Nothing could have raised their morale higher. That Sunday they all sang together through those thick walls. They sang longer than usual and they sang more political songs than hymns. These were political rallies that defied closed doors and high walls. Before long, a pattern of communication was established. The city women dispersed themselves among the other women, rather than kept to their own crowd. This had the effect of displacing the others who were a little uncomfortable at first. But soon the old divisions collapsed and the women of Sabelweni accepted that they were among friends. And without a single word from Jezile, but simply by example and the help of the other women, the 'them-and-us' attitude died a natural death. Rather, the politicised city women shared their ideas, indeed, targeted some of their talks at the non-political prisoners. They believed that they were all reacting to the same problem, but in different ways, and tried to show that it was better to fight politically than to engage in self-defeating crimes.

9

*T*hat fateful morning, when Jezile left home and did not return, Siyalo was left holding the baby and would have been completely out of his depth if MaBiyela had not taken over completely and mothered the baby herself. This marked the beginning of a very difficult time for MaBiyela in every way. That first day it became clearer with the passing of the hours that Jezile was not coming back that night, nor in the days that were to follow. How were they going to manage with S'naye? Although she was a peaceful, contented baby, she began to show restlessness by early evening, no longer interested in the bottle, but longing for her mother's breast. Siyalo rocked her, walking up and down, and his awkwardness and lack of familiarity with crying babies became more and more obvious. S'naye had patiently put up with those hands, but now she was demanding the familiar hands and the warmth and comfort of the body that she knew; above all, she was thirsty. She broke into full-throated cries that went on intermittently with short fitful periods of sleep. As the night wore on she cried continuously and MaBiyela began to panic. Weaning babies from the breast was difficult at the best of times, when they were cushioned by mother's love and enticed away with tempting alternatives. This time there was neither the mother nor the good things that they could give her instead.

By midnight S'naye was puffed and giving great concern to everyone around. No one could sleep. She had not eaten anything since the midday meal. So it was not just love that she needed, it was food as well. But by this time she had passed the point of knowing what she really wanted. She rejected all offers before they had touched her lips. When MaBiyela suggested slaughtering one of the young chickens to tempt her with some soup, Siyalo assented with a crackling voice and he leapt up and darted into the dark chicken coop. Simo followed him with a torch. Within the hour the unfortunate young chicken, roused from its sleep to die, was ready to tempt S'naye's appetite. Fortunately, the unexpectedness of the soup arrested her interest long enough for her to taste it. It passed the test and she drank it in gulps. In the early hours of the morning, she fell asleep, and so did everyone else. But when she woke up by mid-morning, the position reverted back to what it had been the night before. She whimpered and ate very little. But as the days went by, she seemed slowly to surrender her will resignedly to those around her. It was painful for both Siyalo and MaBiyela to watch their baby grieving.

As if all this had not been enough, about three weeks after Jezile's departure something that would have been a calamity under any circumstances befell the Majola family. For over a year their cattle, oxen and cows, were down to six, including the calf of their favourite cow, Nantshi. The calf was well over a year old: in fact, little stumps of horns were just peeping out indicating that he was well over the suckling stage. But the Majolas had gone on encouraging him to suckle so that they could manage a half-pint or so of milk for themselves. So long as Nantshi suckled her calf, she would produce some milk for them to share. But the milk began to turn yellow betraying the abnormally long lactation period. The milk boys reported the news to a dejected MaBiyela who hung her head and said, 'She will have to go on a little longer if S'naye is to survive. This cow is our only source of milk now.'

Three days later Nantshi could not get up to go to the fields. They coaxed and pushed and tried to raise her physically. She looked at them woefully trying to raise herself without success. They called her name many times, 'Nantshi', 'Nantshi', but she lay there completely still. By late afternoon, with tears in her eyes, MaBiyela said to Siyalo, 'We'll have to relieve her of her pain. Nantshi is not ill from disease. She is starved and too weak from loss of weight. There is nothing we can do for her.' Siyalo did not answer. It was too much for him to agree to kill off the only source of milk for S'naye. MaBiyela saw the conflict in his eyes. She went on. 'Siyalo, there's no point. They never rise up once they've fallen. This is the end. In the cold weather they just give up. If we had hay and good food to give her now . . .'

Suddenly Siyalo came alive and cut her short. 'Yes we have, we have. I'll cut all those useless maize stalks from the field and she will recover. There's a lot of good food in that.' So saying, he dashed off and left MaBiyela standing. Within a short time there were piles of dry stalks all around the sick cow. But she would eat nothing. She stared ahead with a drooping head and saw nothing. It was almost dark when Siyalo resolved to go down and kill Nantshi. By lantern light they skinned her, but her meat was not fit to eat. It was sticky to the touch and did not look like meat at all. MaBiyela insisted that it was inedible and that no one should eat ingcuba (an animal that dies of natural causes). So Nantshi was dragged to a great pit and buried in the dark. No dogs were allowed to eat her either, in case she had some infection that had not been detected. All they had was Nantshi's skin. They dried it and kept it in the barn. The whole family grieved for Nantshi as though she had been one of their number.

After these events life returned to its hum-drum rhythm with nothing to do but endure it. For Siyalo it quickly lost its attractive city variation. There was so little to do – yet this was not quite true. On the contrary, everything cried out to be done. The land lay flat and naked for the sun to scorch it dry. Nothing grew for miles around, except for that strange grass that grew in sporadic clumps. It was well adapted to the harsh conditions, dry and prickly, so that even the starving animals avoided it. If trees had ever grown in these parts they had been used to stoke the fires of the past and no one had thought of the future. For years now the land had lost its capacity to support life – trees, crops, grass, cattle or people. It was as though Siyalo had never experienced the curse of the Sabelweni dusty winters. He had left, when he was sixteen, to work in Durban and had always come home in the hot wet summer months. Winter was harsh in Sigageni – cold dry morning and evening winds and hot parched days. The combined effect was desolation. He missed Jezile terribly; she had become the focus of his life and he grieved her absence as though she was dead. He would wake up late, often panting and sweating from his nightmares. He would wake up in the glare of the hot morning sun. To have a reasonably comfortable day in these parts one woke up early to enjoy the cool, if frosty, morning air before the winter sun rose high and scorchingly hot on the dry plains of Sigageni. But Siyalo could not manage the early rising because he simply had not had proper sleep in the night. Often he lay awake till the small hours of the morning after which he would fall into fitful sleep towards dawn. When he woke up late he would drag himself shamefacedly to face his mother, daughter and the rest of the family. It never seemed to vary – bad nights followed by listless days.

By the beginning of July what was left of the crops was ready for harvesting. Siyalo gladly joined the harvesters; it would be a good distraction from his preoccupation with himself. They would get up early and face the blistering cold morning winds and crunch the thick morning frost. It was a bad year for crops and the puny ears of maize hung limp or clung tightly to the stalks and were very cold to the touch. Their hands would go numb and the sharp-edged leaves would cut cruelly with the cunning of a razor blade. Then the day would become menacingly hot in its intensity. But this did not last long. By the time he had yoked the cattle and carried the hefty bags to load them on the sleigh the sun would change. The shadows would lengthen and hang dramatically high, towering over everything. The departing day would look exquisitely beautiful but weak. And before Siyalo had off-loaded every bag into the barn the sun would retreat over the mountain, leaving a cold pool of darkness that must have lain skulking behind that brilliant red sunset all the while – so quickly did it pounce on the world all around.

After the flurry of the harvest days life fell back into the lazy flabby days again. For once there was nothing to do and no guilt that goes with that vacant feeling of indolence. It was the official time of rest for everyone. Siyalo tried to simmer down with the tempo of events, but the more he told himself that he was entitled to the rest, the more his subconscious fostered an anxiety that he could not suppress. He racked his brain trying to find something to do. Finally, one day, when he saw two men passing on horseback with torn tatty rags for saddles, he fell upon an idea. He would start a business – he would make saddles like his uncle had done. For hours and days and years as a child he had watched his uncle working. He would recover the skill from his memory. He had learned it so well from those strong hands. He looked at his own, which were not very convincing in their long delicate tapering shape. But he knew he could do it. He did not spend long looking for Nantshi's skin for he had recently moved it aside when he had put in the maize at harvest-time. The next day he sold it to the tanner's agent at Umzimkulu and he bought a block of wax, some needles and thread.

The first item in need of repair was an old bag that had lain in the barn for years. He did not know its origin but it had been there ever since he was a boy. As he turned it over and over he was surprised at its faded beauty. There was no doubt in his mind that it must have seen better days – the proud possession of some rich white woman. How it ended its days in dust and humility in his father's old barn could have made an interesting story if he had chosen to find out. But he set his mind to speculating upon its possibilities for the future. If he could repair it, it would make a beautiful present for Jezile when she came back. He was going to repair it and practise his new skill. Leather was not as hard to come by as other materials. He could make saddles, handbags and all durable goods from those animal skins that were to be found in every barn in Sigageni. The more he thought about it, the more his excitement grew. In the days that followed he sat, hour after hour, practising, slowly at first, till his stitches came faster, and tighter. He felt proud of his new skill, the sense of achievement and purpose was like a tonic. Soon he had repaired five saddles, but the shiny, neatly repaired pile lay collecting dust in a corner and the owners began to shy away when they saw him approaching. He was losing friends rather than collecting any money. The idea of repairing saddles was a good one, but there were no rewards to follow for people had no money to pay for the service. Some actually promised to pay him when they went on a labour tour in the cities, whenever that would be. As the pile grew, representing Siyalo's ambitious investment without returns, so did his disappointment. Slowly the dream grew dim and finally it died.

*

The end of harvest also meant winter was on its way. Cattle, sheep and goats were ushered on to the fields to feast on the sweet dry mealie stalks which they tackled with a voracity known only to the starving. They munched every dry leaf and stalk for hours on end. They would only stop chewing when the darkness of the night descended. Within a couple of weeks every field was bare to the ground, and what was left of them was trodden to a fine powder that swirled in the wind and prickled the eyes. The cattle, horses, sheep, donkeys and goats finally went back to lick the dust off the bare paddocks. By the end of winter they were on their knees with starvation.

The wind rose tauntingly in whirls as though it was possessed with evil intent. It flung the dust into people's eyes and drove them off course as it fought to topple their loads off their heads. When it did not succeed, it followed them into their houses and pursued them under their thin blankets, as it poured layers of dust, covering every dish, plate and cup. The wind and the sun dried away the last vestiges of natural oils on their bodies, and their skins stretched and cracked under the stress – a fine network of criss-crossing lines broke on their faces, arms and legs. Some people suffered more severely than others. In severe cases their lips cracked and bled and the soles of their feet hardened and shone like well-worked leather. Their fissured soles would bleed in the cold, sending shooting pains straight to the heart. With the shortage of money most people could not afford vaseline to salve their pains, let alone shoes to protect their feet. They could not afford meat and fat to insulate their bodies against the ravages of the cold winter. As with most afflictions, the community had concocted remedies to fight off the bitter weather. Often they were of doubtful effect. For most it was a choice between the concoction and light on those dark nights. For their feet they would melt a candle and mix its wax with the precious paraffin oil to make a warm soothing grease to spread over the gaping cracks on their feet. Then they would sit in the half darkness of a flickering fire until that too died for lack of firewood. They would curl up in sleep often under flimsy blankets. One effect of the concoction was that in the daytime it collected dust in thick layers that covered not only their feet, but their clothes as well.

When the August winds were finally over, and September

ushered in calm, clear, warm days that year, Siyalo had reason to believe that the pendulum had swung his way at last; that from then on nature would deal her temperate hand all round. He, on his part, was trying hard to grasp the drift of the tide and to follow its ebb and flow. But the harder he tried, the less he understood nature and man. Somehow he seemed in conflict with the whole of his world. It stood inimical to everything that was life-giving. It had spat him out. There was no deluding himself, he stood outside his world; it could no longer ingest him so that he became part of it.

10

*E*arly one morning the women were released from prison. Someone had bought every one of them bus tickets to cover their return journey home. It was a beautiful spring morning. But they wished it was a dark winter morning which would have shielded them from the public eye. Their clothes were creased and crumpled; they must have been stored in tightly packed bags throughout the five months they had been in jail. Many of them felt lost and afraid in the big city for they had never been out of Sabelweni all their lives. Sabelweni was their world and any city was like another country. They had often seen their men exit into the outer reaches of Johannesburg and Durban but they had never been there themselves. Their large number attracted a lot of attention as they filled the bus to capacity. They were returning home unannounced.

Jezile and a dozen other women got off the bus at the isolated Cromwell bus stop. They had known that they would not be met, for no one knew when they had been released. They said their last goodbyes to the others who were going further. At the bus door they huddled together as though they were afraid – afraid to part with those they had shared so much with – afraid to face the world again. And if the truth were to be told, they were ashamed as well. Prison does that, no matter how noble the cause, it leaves its stains on your mind; it leaves its shame on you. You know so much that you cannot share with those you know.

At first they walked slowly, breathing in the air of freedom, savouring a new realisation of their love for Sigageni. But soon their mood changed by the minute; they walked faster and talked excitedly – they were home, and the prison horrors were behind them, and their loved ones a mere two miles away. An hour later, they stood on the hill and with boundless joy they looked down on the familiar valley, their little homes silently huddled before them. The flaming aloe covered the Umkhwekazi hillside, a glowing crown of glory and a welcome in the red sunset. Jezile could not control the beating of her heart. She cried, standing there on the hillside, and the others followed. But they stopped as suddenly as they had started. With tear-stained faces they looked at each other with constricted smiles. They shook hands and held on to each other tightly as though they would not be together again the next day at the well, living their communal life, sharing and exchanging as they had always done. But this ceremonial parting marked the end of a shared experience that no one else in Sigageni would ever fully understand. It was like a conspiracy and they sealed it in their embrace as the sun set on the hillside.

Jezile stole into her house, listening and watchful. There was Siyalo lying on his back in the darkening shadow of his room alone and thoughtful. It took some moments before he reacted to Jezile standing at the door, her full height darkening the doorway deeper still. For a moment, fear tugged at her – where was the baby – where was S'naye? This was not as she had always imagined the two together, father and daughter alone in the little house. He caught her eye in its frantic search. He smiled and arrested that wandering look:

'She's all right. She's with mother.'

In the whirlwind of the next few moments she had no time to observe how thin he was and how shabby his clothes were. It was a blistering moment of love and tears and welcome. When the heat subsided, he walked out to pick up S'naye and to announce Jezile's arrival. MaBiyela had cared for S'naye most of the time that Jezile was away. Jezile would have wished it otherwise, but this was not the time to resume the vendetta. MaBiyela had a right to S'naye – she was her grandchild. While he was gone, Jezile stood outside the door, impatient to see everyone, especially her child. She saw them darting out and almost stumbling on top of each other – her mother-in-law, her young sister-in-law Simo and nieces- and nephews-in-law, people and more people. In that crowded moment she saw S'naye's little head, bobbing up and down as MaBiyela carried her cn the hip, half-running to meet Jezile. In the excitement and laughter, she almost snatched S'naye from her grand-mother's arms. Her eyes and smile and joy froze in an instant as she felt the weight of the baby in her arms. She set her eyes on the baby's face. She shook the baby as though to revive the spark that was gone from those eyes. When she finally dragged her eyes off S'naye, she looked at MaBiyela, she looked at Siyalo and back at her child. S'naye was not just thin; she was emaciated. Veins stood out distended and pulsing at the tem-ples. The bare head – where had all that thick crop of hair gone? – how had its colour and texture changed? – only sparse brown wisps remained. The large glassy eyes stared back at her – half-filled with copious tears that would not spill. The skin hung loose on the body except around the face and head. If it lay in folds on the belly, it hugged the facial bones tightly, but creased in folds around the permanently open mouth.

Jezile burst out crying, and the hubbub died down. The family drew closer to look at S'naye as though they had not realised how changed she was. The hush that followed killed off the laughter and joy in everyone. Slowly people drifted back to their houses until only MaBiyela and Jezile and Siyalo stood in the darkness that gathered quickly as if to cover the pain of reunion. Jezile could not accept that a mere five months could bring about such a change in a healthy child. When she had left S'naye at seven months, she had been a bouncing healthy baby. What could have happened? She looked at MaBiyela again and she was convinced that she had neglected her baby. And that she had done it out of spite. She screamed in excruciating pain and turned quickly to suffer her agony alone in her house. MaBiyela followed her daughter-in-law. She saw the accusation in those large brimful eyes under the flickering paraffin lamp and she choked with the effort to explain. She wanted to remind Jezile that when she left she had taken away with her, in her breast, the only supply of milk there had been for her baby; she wanted to tell her of the many sleepless nights they had spent with the baby crying day and night for her milk, so cruelly weaned away. She wanted to pour out the sad story of the death of Nantshi, the cow, but somehow the time did not seem appropriate. How there had been no money to buy any good food and no other source of milk for many miles around, except for Mr Collett's and Mr Hencock's farms that surrounded

Sigageni. She wanted to shout back and tell her of all their efforts to keep baby S'naye alive – how they had even dared approach both Collett and Hencock for their skimmed milk – and that both had refused. They had said they needed it for their pigs – their pigs! But MaBiyela did not say all this to Jezile. Instead, she broke down and cried and could not even tell Jezile that she too loved S'naye as much as Jezile herself did – she was the only Majola grandchild that she had – her only son's daughter. None of this could come out of her lips. She stood there watching Jezile contorted with pain, until she slowly walked away into the darkness.

In the days and weeks that followed, Jezile was to learn and accept that in the absence of good food, children will fall ill and die. She slowly came to know and accept those words that MaBiyela had left unsaid that night. But she could not forgive or ask for forgiveness. The rift between the two women widened. MaBiyela despised Jezile for her ingratitude; Jezile could not find it in her heart to apologise. 'For what', she argued, 'for words she had not even said aloud – for thinking her thoughts?' Life went on, distended with the unspoken pain and hunger and poverty.

If the women hissed ceaselessly at each other, Siyalo choked with mortification. He reasoned that it was his failure to fulfil his duty as a provider that was at the bottom of the bitterness. Once his reasoning took him along this road, there seemed no point of return. Seeing himself as the cause of the family problems had the effect of cancelling him out. The two women he loved most were at loggerheads, and he was the cause of it by default. His physical or mental or emotional self no longer mattered. Being unable to provide for his child and wife and mother was the cause of all the acrimony. They suffered not only hunger and want but disharmony as well. He felt annulled, and wished that he were dead. If only he could do something. Jezile, who knew him well, saw this and sometimes wished she could extend the hand of friendship; a lever out of his purgatory. But every time she looked at the pining face of S'naye her heart would harden and she would look the other way. It was not as if she enjoyed the pain and anger all around. Only, they were all trapped in it. All she thought about was S'naye – she had to live. She robbed her hen's nests and fed her on the eggs.

For a few weeks S'naye showed signs of recovery. But when no more eggs remained, S'naye stalled and then took another plunge for the worse. Jezile frantically turned on her hens, killing them off one by one to keep S'naye alive.

But all these were short-term measures – only one thing was certain in the long term, there was no food to sustain S'naye. Day after day she was faced with that maize meal; the only thing that was available in sufficient quantities; but maize meal alone meant certain death for S'naye. That's what Nosizwe had said. It had been her idea to feed S'naye the eggs. Now they were finished – there seemed no point in going back to her. Besides Jezile began to feel a sense of shame as though it were her fault – her failure. She had run out of pride and was embarrassed about her baby. For the same reason she did not attend the next prayer meeting. Nor did she attend the great feast and ceremony that was held at the next village where thousands attended. It was the combined effort to welcome all the women back from prison and to find a new way forward in their fight for better conditions at Sabelweni. But for her it seemed that she had reached the end of the road. There seemed nothing more to fight for. Beyond a certain point of suffering, all struggles peter out – only the struggle for survival remains.

Secretly, she knew she needed as much good food as S'naye herself. It was ironic that she should starve as much at home as she had in prison. There was the baby in her that she had told no one about. When she had been in prison she had been happy to carry another child. She had thought Siyalo would be happy to have a playmate for S'naye. But now she knew that another child would be another burden; so soon after the first one too. A quick succession of babies was frowned upon: evidence of lack of self-control. The conclusion would be that she was so highly sexed, she could not keep away from her man – such a cruel inversion of the truth.

For several weeks after her return from prison she walked with a stoop and a battered look on her face. Siyalo would steal a puzzled look at her, and she would bend almost double then. He seemed suspicious, but he could not quite believe she could hide the truth from him – if she was pregnant, and he was the father, she had to tell him – she simply had to tell him. But she could not bridge the gulf that had opened between them; she could not open her most intimate self to the stranger that Siyalo had become. She suffered her shame alone – she was pregnant again. This time it was not childlessness that brought her shame, it was an untimely pregnancy. In her self-consciousness she would cringe at every look and wish she had a shell to hide in. In fact for quite some time, no one suspected anything – she was so thin that nothing showed to the casual observer. But MaBiyela was no casual observer. Rumours fluttered softly in the community about women who used to 'disappear' on Sundays in prison. People whispered and wondered – no names were mentioned, no betrayals among friends. But this only fanned the fire of speculation.

When MaBiyela looked at Jezile the day after she heard the rumour, she was no longer so casual. And, indeed, one knowing look confirmed it all. The next time she found Siyalo sitting alone in the shade of his house, she went and sat near him. She coughed and mumbled vaguely to attract his curiosity. Without raising her voice any higher, she mumbled her insinuations. When she heard that Jezile had not said anything about being pregnant, she was convinced that the baby that Jezile carried could not be Siyalo's. She babbled with excitement and went away from Siyalo's side ready to blow the horn to the whole community. She only became deflated when all the women who had been in prison with Jezile denied that she had ever been 'called out'. That was how the news got out and the people of Sigageni came to know that Jezile was pregnant. But for many others, nothing would stop the speculation. Needless to say, Siyalo was incensed when he finally came to know the truth – to think that his own wife could hide her pregnancy from him. Up until then he had trusted his wife implicitly, but now niggling doubts set in. He believed her reason for not telling him; they had known each other for years and deep down there was trust between them. But for reasons he could not explain he wanted to hold something against her – it was not his intention to be cruel, it just gave him a tangible reason to remain disgruntled. He was no longer entirely to blame for all the unpleasantness; he was a wronged husband and somehow he felt justified. In short, everything that happened helped to compound the unpleasantness in the home. But deep down he knew that there was only one cure for everything. If he could only find a job. He tried not to think about the next baby. At least it was safe in Jezile's body. It didn't ask anything of him.

The rains were late that spring. The sun got hotter by the day, the silvery clouds laced the horizon each clear day, but there was no rain. The blustery August winds tempered down, and gave way to dusty, hot, dry days. People sat and waited, chasing the shade round their houses round the clock. They watched the sun glowing on the mountain tops at sunrise, riding the sky at midday, now majestic, now malicious and malevolent, sucking in every whiff of air like some wilful supergod of the skies, and they watched and waited till it relaxed its cruel grip on the earth as it receded over the mountains. The sky lost its palpable blue depth of spring and waxed pale, glistening and forbidding. The fields lay fallow and bare, baking in it day by day. It licked the trickle of the previous year's rain in the stream. All that was left to share with their stock was the salt water pool near the dipping tank – that never dried up even when the drought was prolonged and severe. The cattle would stand huddled together after their drink, unwilling to leave the side of the pool. In the heat of the day people shied away from looking at each other's eyes, afraid to answer the silent questions and respond to the bewilderment they would see there.

On one such unforgiving day, Siyalo ventured to raise his eyes and he saw what were unmistakable storm clouds rising high up in the sky. He sat listlessly watching them building up, wondering if they had any rain in them or if it was yet another of nature's tantalising tricks. By early afternoon, there was generated an air of controlled excitement, people not daring to hope for the rain, but forced to prepare for the storm. He watched Jezile packing in her cow dung cakes for fuel – it wouldn't do if they got wet in the rain for then they would not burn at all. A mild wind rose, softly at first, and Siyalo wondered where it had hidden skulking all along. Jezile's steps quickened with each new gust, with S'naye's bobbing head on her back and the unborn baby raised high in front. Here and there she darted, collecting her washing from the rocks nearby, where she had laid it to dry. Now it was the washing, now it was the blankets that she had taken out to air in the morning.

Siyalo sat watching this pre-storm ritual that he had watched even as a child when it had not been Jezile but MaBiyela who covered every water bucket with a cloth and the mirror with a heavy blanket – as though the flimsy covers were anything to stop the violent lashes of lightning in the violent electric storms they knew. For his part, he had little to put away, for all the ploughing implements had not been unpacked since the last autumn. They lay in the barn waiting for the rains. Perhaps he would unpack them the next day – it all hung on that storm cloud above. For all he knew it might just be a wind-storm with nothing more than a few blistering drops that would sizzle on the hot earth.

When Jezile finished, she curled up near him at their special storm corner. The wind had risen powerfully and they could hear things rattling aimlessly away from the angry wind, without direction. The rumbling thunder began to crackle with mockery, threatening in its fury. Jezile drew closer to Siyalo, in spite of herself, in her fear of the forked lashes of the storm, now blazing red, now dazzling white hot. They sat in complete silence as the storm raged and the torrents of rain came down in sheets driven by the wind. It was deafening. Then the growing roar of the water as it collected in rivulets that grew by the minute. The storm went on longer than expected. It seemed as if it would go on for the rest of the day. But, in the end, at first imperceptibly, they sensed its wildness diminishing. The intervals between the lightning grew longer, the wind abated and the thunder more distant and less ferocious. All that could be heard was the loud roar of the waters as they dragged everything away, and every morsel of the good earth. The two stood up and went outside like all the people of the village, to savour the smell of the rain and the coolness and freshness of the earth. The dust in the air was gone and hope returned as they looked across the plain to see if the storm had claimed any homes. They rejoiced, for the rain seemed to have cleaned not only the earth but their heavy hearts as well.

Siyalo and Jezile had not talked to each other except in grunts and mutterings for weeks. But now they turned to each other and smiled and talked and raised their voices to talk to neighbours and friends. MaBiyela came out too and raised her voice to talk to Jezile directly – the air seemed to carry their voices even further. They moved closer, drawn to each other in friendship by the miracle of the storm and the rain. They had said very little to each other since the day Jezile arrived from prison; they had merely endured each other's malignant looks. But now all that was swept away with the rainstorm. Perhaps it was a recognition of how trifling their continued silences were against the elements which sought to divide and separate them. But on the other hand, they could have been thinking of the next day when they would have to rise up early and go to the fields needful of each other's co-operation in raising new crops for the new year. They met each other half-way along the short path that separated their houses and they talked, first about the severity of the storm; then about the possibilities it had brought them, and lastly about all the news they had not communicated in all those weeks; they had a lot to catch up on. They stood there for a long time. The clouds drifted away and the sun came out, tame, and shone brightly as though all was forgiven. There was even a rainbow, but those two did not see it. Siyalo watched them with a gush of joy welling in him; how good it was to see those two reconciled. He stood up tall and walked aimlessly around mulling over the mysterious bond between people and nature. He was buried in thought when his eye caught something glinting and shimmering against the sun. He looked again. For the first time since he came out he looked down at the earth below his feet. He stood right in the path of the stormy waters. The heavy dust and earth that had covered the stones had been swept away in the flood. The raw earth lay stripped and exposed in small ridges like the ribs of cattle that stood listlessly across on the paddock. The earth was bare. What he saw shining at his feet was Jezile's ring that had been lost long ago. It lay in the sparkling trickle of rain water. The sight of that ring tugged at the strings of his heart – that ring had once meant so much – a symbol of their completeness. Looking at it there, washed in the stormy waters, he wondered how it had survived the storms that had swept away so many heavier objects. When all else was carried away, it had survived. For him, this was more than a fortuituous happening – it was a promise that when all else was destroyed they would remain, like the promise of a rainbow. A new hope filled him, and with it, copious joy. He turned round and called Jezile, and so split up the cordial chit-chat between his mother and his wife. She came to him, her face smiling and looking him in the eye for a change. He smiled back and held the ring between his fingers and said nothing. She looked at him confused. She did not understand. He held her hand up in silence and slipped the ring on slowly like an offering – he made a new ceremony of it. Then he explained how he had found it there waiting for him – how it had been there all along waiting for them to discover it. Like their life, it had been lost, but it was there all the time, waiting for them to look carefully and find it. She smiled at it and wiggled it on, that sacred moment fleeting like a thought; she held on to it as if afraid to lose it. He stood right beside her and breathed hard by her side. They had not stood like this for a long time, breathing into each other's faces out in the open air.

'It's too late now Siyalo, I've lost a lot of weight, it does not fit any more.' She wiggled her finger again and he took her hand and turned the ring round and round her bony finger. And hand in hand they walked into the house.

'I fear I'll lose it again if I should wear it, Siyalo; I'll put it away carefully till it fits again.'

'Yes, keep it. Keep it carefully this time.' He slipped it off her finger and gave it to her to keep. He watched her drop it into a beautifully ornamented pottery jar that her mother had made and given to her when she got married. She dropped it slowly as though to preserve it for posterity, a relic to carry into the future. That night as he lay on his own as usual, but just before he fell asleep, he felt something stirring deep in his loins. He stirred uncomfortably, not trusting his own body – there it was again, something prodding deep inside him. He hesitated to call her – what if it was a false alarm; if it died down and left him cold as it had done in many weeks. He could not cope if he failed her. But there it was, persisting, heating every part of his body, riding, riding. He did not want to call her – what if she dithered. He darted over to her bed. She was almost asleep. She jumped with surprise, but did not pull back. To his joy, she yielded, murmuring, 'Gently, gently, Siyalo, mind the baby.' Not that he needed a reminder – he was always gentle. He held her like a fragile thing while he caressed the baby inside as well.

121

They fell apart into a dreamless sleep which they had not had in a long time.

Early the next morning, before dawn, Siyalo got up and slipped out of the house. He went straight towards the cattle kraal. Already he could see the shadows of his young nephews pulling open the poles that barred the gateway to the kraal. There were only five cattle and they let themselves be led out in obedience to years of conditioning. Siyalo almost tripped on the pile of strops and chains and yokes at his feet. He stopped and waited. The young boys drove the cattle straight at him. Without any instruction they proceeded to inspan the cattle fast and efficiently. The cattle bent their heads low to level with the height of the young boys who puffed hard as they lifted the heavy yokes on to the willing backs of the cattle. Except for the soft murmur, 'Yoke, yoke,' from the boys, there were no spoken words and no resistance from the beasts. Such efficient co-operation between man and beast. Siyalo watched, entranced. He who had believed himself to be the only man around, found he was outdone by the young boys of ten and eleven. For a moment he felt redundant as though they had usurped his role as he watched the team ready to move with the plough to the fields. He was still dithering when he heard his mother's voice in the semi-darkness:

'Watch how you drive them, Siyalo; they are all very weak and the cow is carrying a calf. Look after her, she's too weak already. The boys drive them too hard. Watch out, for the heat of the sun.'

He felt revived: his mother had assigned him a role. The most important role – that of responsibility – she had restored his authority. He did not respond to her warning. Instead he walked slowly towards her.

'And you, Mother, what do you want here at this hour? We're going to plough, but it's not time for weeding yet.'

'I'm here on every day of the ploughing season, Siyalo. Do you suppose these boys rise up from their mats from instinct? No, never. I wake them up, I surprise them, I follow them to the fields year in and year out. But with you here, this is going to be a year of rest for me.' So saying, she swung round and left him to do his job. The boys stood waiting, one in front holding the lead, another flanking the team with a long thin leather strap and another holding the plough at the back. They followed the cattle spoor that led down the long slope to the valley, the fields and the river. A cool breeze wafted gently against their set faces. A brilliant silver cloud coursed down along what they knew was the river. Here and there the tall bushes broke through that silver cloud which gave the effect of magical trees that floated on a cushion of mist – a scene of incredible beauty that nature offered at the start of each perfect day. But there were no hearts to receive nature's offerings – things had gone wrong – life was not what nature intended.

By mid-morning they had taken a few turns and their achievement of the morning was clearly marked in a dark strip of upturned sods. There were spans similarly engaged all along the river bend. The sun rode the vast sky at speed. The team turned once more, twice, thrice and they were panting. The heat built up fast and was as intense as it had been for many days before, except that now the heat seemed to rise from below, rather than scorch from above. It was no longer dry, but it was the stifling humidity of the rain, steaming up and choking the breath out of both men and beasts. Siyalo wondered if it was his unaccustomed body reacting to hard work. He looked at the boys, and they seemed not to feel it. The gnats and flies came in droves like a pestilence; the oxen seemed more afflicted than the people – they twitched their heads and tails in agitation, but they drove on. The boys shed their coats. Suddenly they looked so fresh it seemed they could have gone on for hours. Siyalo looked across at the other teams to see what they were doing. He did not want to be the first to leave and so be branded the lazy townsman. After all, several of those teams had women and boys only and no men. He had to be stronger to prove himself; he had to do better. But when he looked at his team he knew it was time to stop. The cattle panted, frothing and dribbling at the mouth, a hissing belaboured effort that grated on his nerves. He was not going to overlook his mother's word for the sake of saving his face. She was always right. He had learned of her wisdom when he was a boy and her word was law to him. So he stopped the boys. 'Now, outspan!' he said. The boys looked at each other and stood looking at him, not daring to contradict him. But the boy at the lead coughed and one on the flank ventured, 'But it's still early; too early.'

'No matter, the cattle can't take the strain. When they're stronger, we can work long. Outspan!'

'It may not rain again for a long time,' the boy persisted.

'All the more reason then; why waste their effort if everything will die in the drought.' So they outspanned and Siyalo washed at the river and went home feeling purified, furthering the cleansing of the night before.

Jezile met him at the door and led him outside with a cool mahewu, a fermented maize-gruel drink. He drank hard and lay back waiting for food. He enjoyed being waited on, knowing he had earned it. There was still that warm glow of the night before between them. But somehow the actual conversation was not as easy as they had expected. It was as though in the grunting silence of the weeks following her long absence they had gone out of practice. He talked about the state of the fields, the rain of the day before which, though heavy, had done little to soften the earth beyond the top six inches of soil.

'Yes, storms are like that. They do little for the earth; in fact they are quite harmful. They take away the top soil and the earth below is not fertile. It's slow rain we need to soak deep into the earth,' Jezile stated the obvious in her effort to prolong the conversation.

'Now that the drought's been broken, let's hope we'll soon get soaking rains.' Then the conversation died down completely.

Beyond this, there seemed little to say. There was so much to avoid saying; so much that could hurt. Siyalo was dying to ask about the prison days, and deep down there was a curiosity about the baby that Jezile was carrying – till the previous night he had not had the chance to cuddle the baby in her, to love it and claim it as his own. He felt left out. She had somehow erected an impenetrable wall around herself; there had been an air of prohibition that had frozen his hand as he stretched to touch her each time. He never really doubted that it was his child; he knew Jezile enough not to think the worst of her – she would have told him – if only they could talk. How he longed to hear her tell him that she had never been 'called out' on those Sundays in prison. It would do a lot to strengthen his conviction and to squash his mother's 'knowing' look. But between them the subject had never arisen. He looked at her now – her blue dress was torn under the arm, and quite raised in front. He silently calculated how advanced her pregnancy was. The tear on the arm extended to the bulge on the side, almost revealing her now full breast. When her dinner was ready she brought him ujeqe, maize bread. His heart sank. This had never been his favourite dish even when he had had meat or vegetable to relish with it. It lay white and dry on the plate. The only taste it had was salt. There was a mug of black tea to go with it. He put four teaspoonfuls of sugar to sweeten it and as he reached for the fourth one, he saw Jezile's hand pull away, to stop him 'wasting' what little sugar was left. But there were no words. She eyed him silently and he knew why. He drank the tea first. He drank it in gulps and it seemed to fill him up.

'And you, aren't you eating anything? Where's your plate?'

'Not now, Siyalo, not now,' she said quickly with a whisper of impatience in her voice.

S'naye soon woke up from her sleep. They knew immediately when she was awake from her nagging cry. But it was not the full-bodied cry of the baby they had known. They looked at each other questioningly and Jezile rose to pick her up. That cry – it pained Jezile as much as it pained Siyalo. There seemed no remedy for it. She whined in the morning as she whined in the night. She was wasting away. Jezile came out of the house with S'naye who was drinking black tea from her bottle. Siyalo stopped chewing what was in his mouth and he followed the mother and child with his eyes as they sat down near him. He had visions of white milk that should have been in that bottle for S'naye to drink and he had difficulty swallowing his mouthful. When he did, he looked at Jezile's full breast again and he asked in a soft voice,

'Could she not drink any of that milk in your breast?' Silence.

'What would happen if she did?' he asked, looking at Jezile cautiously. Silence, a long silence.

'Siyalo, that's a childish question. There is no milk here – not yet. Besides, whatever there is here, it's not hers; it's for the other one. Her turn is passed. She should have milk, milk from a cow; that's what children live on. We haven't any and she is dying,' Jezile said with finality.

Siyalo pushed his half-eaten plate aside. He could sense the breakdown between them again and he did not know how to stop it. So they both chose silence – if all else failed, they had to remain together, one in spirit, one through suffering.

That night, he did not reach out to touch Jezile and the other baby, preferring to remain at the threshold of their relationship rather than risk possible rejection. The ache of his longing did not subside throughout that night, it remained there throbbing low below his wandering thoughts. The next day he went back to the fields, but the feeling of hope had ebbed and there was less talk. He did all he could to suppress a temper that did not wait to be provoked. The young nephews marked the crease of irritation on his forehead that would not go away. They in turn said very little to arouse his anger in any way. It was the same for several days that followed. And in the meantime there was little prospect of rain. It became as hot as it had been, the sun having licked the ground bone dry again. The plough failed to turn the sod, but would slip, and graze the surface with the metallic ring of iron against stone. Each time this happened, Siyalo started with an ache as though it was his flesh that the plough sought to scrape off. By the following Saturday his heart felt heavy. He was grateful that the next day was a Sunday, the day of rest. He was at his wits' end. He decided to go to church; he would do anything that might restore his hope – they did say God gave people hope, help and everything. A time had come to seek His help. But Siyalo sat through the service thinking his own thoughts. Once his eyes strayed and stayed with the group of young women who customarily sat separately on their own benches, somewhere near the pulpit. Was it by design they sat up there, so visibly, to draw attention to their beauty and availability for marriage – or just their availability. Why not? His thoughts wandered everywhere, and got no hope from the sermon. He was startled by the congregation as they turned on their knees to pray – that spiritual orgy when everybody prayed and cried loud to God for the relief of their suffering. Siyalo felt he too had a lot to pray about, but the weight of his suffering seemed to burden his tongue. He said very little to God, except stare at the image of God which materialised when he closed his eyes. He tried to speak to God as he visualised Him, but he ended up asking himself, 'Is this God I'm talking to?' The power of the image was cold and he withheld his plea. In his imagination, God looked angry and mischievous, moulding missiles to hurl against failures. When the service was finally over, Siyalo went out. He enjoyed the company of the congregation and the talk about the treacherous storm. There were many people from other areas who had travelled from far.

Once he got back home, his thoughts stayed with Jezile and S'naye. He could not forget them. At dusk he went to discuss with his mother the pointlessness of ploughing in the face of such a drought. They agreed it was best to wait until the weather, in its own time, changed and brought more substantial rains.

He lay awake through that night, wondering what he would do the next day now that he no longer had to go to the fields. Jezile slept soundly and only roused herself when S'naye woke up fitfully through the night. She always seemed to sleep. Perhaps it was her pregnancy – she was tired. She did work very hard. She always seemed to have alternative chores to do – when she was not cooking, she was fetching water; if not, she was trailing cattle wherever they were, looking for their dung, to make fuel – it dried easily in that sun. And believe it or not, she had even agreed to go with a working party to help build Duma's new house. He was building the house just to prove that there was money for those who supported the government. It was a fallacy to say that Duma was a good man, not tainted with corruption just because he said a few nasty things against the new chief behind his back. After all, wasn't he paid for his work as the Chief's counsellor? He did not reject the pay packet. It was strange how the subject of his payment never came up in conversation among the people of the community. The fact that he was paid less than the Chief did not alter the fact that he had regular money coming in. It was substantial as well, judging by the house he was building. Some might say his money came from his firewood business.

Duma regularly inspanned sixteen of his best cattle and drove them a good fifteen miles away to buy wood from the white forester who had thousands of acres of wattle plantations. After stripping the wood of all its bark, which is what he wanted in the first place, the forester sold the wood to the few who could afford it. Duma could afford that wood. He carried on a roaring business, not so much in money as in human labour – it was a form of barter. Few could afford to buy his wood. But the whole community could trade their labour for that wood. They did everything for him. They ploughed his fields, and again, he had more land to plough than everyone else in the area – a reward from the government for his services. The only thing he could not control was the sun, cause it to go away and bring rain on his fields instead. However, when the weather relented, people weeded his fields, harvested his crops, plastered and whitewashed his big house, so that it shone like a white pebble from a long way off. Now he was building an even bigger house, with mud bricks and big windows and iron tiles! In this tormenting heat, with little water nearby, he inspanned the same cattle down to the big river Umzimkulu to fetch water in great big barrels, to make the mud into bricks. The truth is, he did nothing, other people did it for him. Nor did MaNgidi, his wife, ever venture outside her house to weed or to mix the mud. Other people worked on it with their feet until it congealed. Other people's wives pounded it for hours, so that when evening came they could hardly walk for fatigue, and they would ache for days in their groins. MaNgidi was always clean and fresh and smiling as she served interesting meals to the people who serviced their growing business. But Duma did nothing – he just went round supervising the work teams, throwing in a malicious joke or two here or there against the new chief Siyapi. And because he laughed and he said the right things and he gave them beer at the end of the day, they did not see how phoney he was, how he was subverting all the old customs. It was hard for people to see their old neighbour in any other light – neighbourly trust died hard even in the changing times. Work parties were never organised for payment. They were given by anybody, regardless of their social standing. They were community gatherings first and foremost designed to help out in cases of need – the public offering their help to one another with no strings attached. But now it was the other way round – it was Duma helping the community by employing them. How was he any different from the white employers in the city, or for that matter Mr Collett, and Mr Hencock and all those other white farmers around . . . what was there to say about them? So much, but where to begin?

Our neighbours, Siyalo thought, why did they choose to be our neighbours? What is in it for them? Given a choice, who would live in these parts? But living here did not seem to affect those farmers; it was as if they lived in another part of the world. It was as if it rained on their farms by night – yes it did; they drew water from the Umzimkulu river and sprinkled their farms day and night. It was not for lack of water that the land was dry and the people starving. It was from lack of means to draw the abundant waters of the river to turn the parched land into green fields. Why could the government not irrigate the land – let the waters flow, turn the nightmare into a dream.

Every time Siyalo looked on the white farmers' lands his eyes ached, and the contrast between the fields of Sigageni and the lush expansive green of the white farms destroyed his spirit. If the government cared, if only they cared enough to save the land and the people.

Siyalo gave up thinking about the white farmers, as though to shelve the idea for another day. His thoughts went back to his wife. Now Jezile wanted to go to work for Duma and MaNgidi – and in her condition. In two months' time she would have the baby; and if he did not intervene, she would lose it. Duma and MaNgidi wanted labour for their wood business, not smiles and gentle care. She argued she needed the wood for when the baby came – a lay-by in preparation for her confinement.

'I argue, if we have lived all along on mealie stocks and cow dung why must we have wood now? She counters that the smoke and stink of the dung fuel is too strong for a newly born baby. I can't say much, but if that baby is to live under these conditions why not start the way she is to live?' Siyalo went on talking to himself. After all there was no choice in the matter; not for Jezile, not for S'naye and not for him.

Towards dawn Siyalo resolved to marshal the help of MaBiyela to use her authority to stop Jezile going to work for firewood. MaBiyela did not see the point of stopping Jezile, but under persuasion she agreed to talk to her. But when the two women met later the next day, it was MaBiyela who was persuaded to go with Jezile to work for firewood. MaNgidi was flattered to see the well-respected MaBiyela attending her party. She did not send either of the two women out to do the mixing, the loading, the carrying or even the plastering. She gave that to the able-bodied young women. The two women joined the cooking team. As usual in the early part of the day there was a party feeling about the place. Women talked loudly and joked and gossiped. When the meal arrived it was a feast; but many women looked tired already.

That afternoon MaBiyela and Jezile joined the other women plastering the walls with their bare hands. They were all accustomed to the job, but Jezile was particularly fast and neat. She earned MaNgidi's approval and open praise. If it irritated the other women, it did wonders for Jezile in restoring her self-confidence. These women lived for their capabilities – they were chosen to be wives mainly on this score.

The afternoon dragged on endlessly, the women plodded patiently waiting for the sun to deflect its rays away towards the mountains in the west. When it finally did they all stood in a cluster, with their eyes on the biggest logs of wood as they lay long and straight. MaNgidi stood clean and different and separate as though she was not one of them, thinking that she did her best to be fair, paying her squad, making sure that the logs she gave them were all equal in size. But there were those who noticed that Jezile's was thicker than the rest. Not that this was of any consequence beyond a few murmured grumbles. At sunset the women left, dispersing in all directions, balancing their logs on their heads.

Siyalo stood at a far distance and watched the women spreading fuel fires in their many homes in the community. Ironically, he thought, the ultimate source of that warmth and comfort came from the government itself. And that was as it should be – warmth and comfort should emanate from a good government. But he heard himself shouting to no one in particular, 'But no, not in this way – not by undermining our dignity, our existence, turning sister against sister, brother against brother, subverting our common morality. This is a negation of all that is good.'

He hated that log as it landed with a thump, hitting a rock in the yard. For once Jezile seemed happy and unconcerned and Siyalo's grouchy mood did not affect her. The heady atmosphere at the work party had revitalised her and the knowledge that there was good wood for the fire for the next few days.

When his sullen company became intolerable Jezile slipped out into the evening to be with her mother-in-law.

For the next four days Jezile went out each morning to the Dumas'. And for Siyalo it began to seem like a nine-to-five job just like any other. That was not how work parties usually were. They were a one-off thing. He was getting more angry by the day, unable to reason with Jezile or even to try. By the fifth day, Jezile had a respectable pile of wood, but she was beginning to feel the strain. S'naye continued to nag and whimper. In fact she looked decidedly ill, but no one could say what was wrong with her. The week at work might have been a release for Jezile, but it had certainly marked a deterioration for S'naye, who was left in the care of the younger girls, Simo and Jabu. That cry had a corroding effect on Siyalo's mind. It was driving him mad and it certainly drove him out of the house, more often than not. The weekend was foul for the family. On Sunday night he came back late. He stood in front of his door, listening, hesitating to open it. There it was, that faint cry, that was a complaint, an indictment against himself. When he did open the door, he did not look into his wife's eyes. He shouted angrily, more at the whining child than at anyone else – how she never stopped; how she would not sleep; what sort of child was she . . . he went on and on. His eyes grew fiery and his voice strained, shouting incoherently until Jezile shouted back to shut him up. There was a short exchange of sharp words.

'It's not her fault, Siyalo; it's not her fault at all. The child is dying, while other babies grow, ours is dying. She'll die soon; she's shrivelling up and she's dying.' Jezile screamed the unmentionable words. 'We are the problem; we are her problem. There's no food. All she needs is milk and meat – food, food, Siyalo; that's what babies grow on. That's how you give them flesh and health and smiles!'

Her voice was like a thunderclap. He stopped and saw how desperation filled her large eyes with tears. He stopped and looked straight into her eyes. He looked at his wife's ragged body and saw how emaciated her arms were. The realisation struck again that everything around him was slowly diminishing; his wife, his child, his love, his peace of mind, and now the peace around the home. The year before, she would not have talked to him with such vehemence; she would not have

131

shouted with that bitter edge in her voice. After a long pause, he asked softly:

'Do you think I could go to the labour bureau tomorrow – do you think I stand any chance at all of entering Durban and finding another job?'

She did not answer, but silently took out his last good shirt and trousers and laid them next to his bed. He mused quietly:

'Before dawn, I'll rise before dawn, and walk the thirteen miles to Ixopo. I've got to be the first person in the line at the Labour Bureau. Long before the buses arrive with the hundreds that fill the place every day. I can't afford the bus fare. But I've got to be there.' He was spent. The heated exchange had drained him of all that tension and the resolve to go again lulled his anxiety, as though he had been promised a job already. For once in many weeks, he fell asleep straight off, and S'naye did not cry that night or he was too deep in sleep to hear her.

The dusty town of Ixopo was just awakening when Siyalo approached it slowly, with the crunching gravel under his feet marking every deliberate step. He must have risen soon after midnight to be there at that time of the morning. He was tired and hungry. Being the first in the queue he congratulated himself as he sat down to have his breakfast of black tea and mealie bread. He ate it without thinking about it for his mind was full of thoughts and his heart full of hope. Before he was through with his meal, the next man came and sat next to him and the stream of endless job seekers had started for the day. They came in ones and twos and threes, until they were just hordes of men and women. They sat everywhere, in front and behind Siyalo, until there was no queue at all.

As the sun warmed up, the officials began to arrive. To his surprise, one came with a heavy iron chain and he strung it all along in front of the job seekers. People talked softly, aware of the ripples of tension and anxiety that coursed through and among the crowds. Siyalo stared vacantly ahead as the street filled up with cars that raced past in rapid succession, sending clouds of red dust up against the waiting job seekers. All those people, where were they going up and down the streets? There were women in shabby long skirts with black head scarves and babies on their backs. Often they stopped and talked loudly to one another among the drifting waste papers of the previous day's litter bugs sweeping along at the slightest breeze; young women precariously and self-consciously balanced on half-worn high-heeled shoes in short country fashions, and knobble-kneed boys idly hanging about pillars and waiting – for what? Siyalo half-registered the country-town scene with fresh wonder – there was a general feeling of weariness about the place, a sense of waste pervading everything. Its air of despair was palpable.

He was jolted out of his reverie by the sudden hubbub that rose like a swarm of flies all around him. The first of the vans from Durban had arrived. It was a big one. Everyone assumed that the employer must have needed a whole squad of people. Hope fluttered among the crowd and people stood up and surged forward. Siyalo understood then why they had a chain in front of them. It was to contain them. Employers came from the cities to hire people from the Labour Bureau, in the outlying rural areas. This made certain that the city was free of drifting job seekers. Only those with actual jobs went there, while the unemployed were confined to the rural areas. There had never been any need for a queue, for the employer would simply hand-pick those he wanted, regardless of who had come first. The white man walked into the office and stayed there for some time. But this did not calm the waiting crowds – they pushed and quarrelled for space in the front row. When the white employer finally came out in the company of one of the local officials, Siyalo felt his throat go dry and a burning feeling in his stomach. He stood tall and, compared to the others, he was clean and tidy. His eyes burned the man's profile; he willed him to turn his way, but his voice would not emerge. People screamed and bellowed on all sides but all that Siyalo could do was stretch his arm, his index finger charged with mental energy, pointing directly at the base of the man's head, now turned the other way completely. At last he heard himself grunt with his deep heavy voice and his sharp eyes burning the spot his finger was pointing at. Suddenly the white man swivelled round and his blue eyes gripped Siyalo's. Almost involuntarily the man's arm was raised and he pointed his own finger at Siyalo, two men pointing at each other.

'You!' he said, and Siyalo leaped over the chain. He beamed and then he shut his eyes as though he was praying. He would have, if he remembered how to. There was a feeling of self-worthiness, something akin to triumph – how long had it been since he had last felt he could influence people, let alone events. But there he was, the first of many people, to be chosen that day. He heard the echoes of the man's voice calling others who followed him, 'You, you, you . . .' Siyalo stood beside the man, unable to contain the rush of joy that coursed through his veins. He kept repeating to himself, 'He chose me, he chose me first.' He felt redeemed – the man had given him his selfhood back. When the white man turned, he did not go into his van, he beckoned the men to follow him into the offices, the pass office this time. Siyalo stood transfixed, unwilling to follow the man in through the door. But there was no choice. He was the last to enter and by this time all the men had their passes out ready for the stamp that opened the way back to the city. Siyalo had the urge to turn back and run out of that door. When he did open his the officials' stamp stopped half-way down, poised in the air.

'Ngh, ngh,' he told himself. 'No, you can't,' he told Siyalo. The white employer turned and looked him in the face.

'Why, but why old chap? You've been endorsed out of Durban; what did you do? What offence? No you can't – I can't take you there.'

'I . . . I . . .' Siyalo went quiet. How could he explain that he was politically involved? He had almost forgotten that his real crime was political. He had never committed any other crime; he had merely held some views and spoken them. He would have been a dead man not to have views on a matter that occupied every thinking person in the country.

'You're wasting my time,' the man replied impatiently. He seemed to be getting angrier by the second, and Siyalo felt guilty. As though he had been caught stealing, stealing the man's time.

Siyalo turned and rushed out of the office unable to bear the upheavals that caused him to feel disoriented by the minute. Once he was outside he ran at full speed, past the crowds who still waited despondently near the gate. He was off and away along the road, unable to bear the disappointment. The worst moment was when the van passed him on its way out to Durban, with its load of passengers packed like sardines, swaying from side to side. One or two waved him a sad goodbye. He cried copious tears. Grateful that he was all alone on the road, he sat by the roadside under a scraggy bush and cried. He felt a little better, but he knew he could not bear to face Jezile that day; how to tell her of his painful rejection. He sat there a long time in the noonday heat, before he realised he was facing a white man's farm. The grass was knee high and lush green. Before long, some cows came by parading their full udders that were obviously too heavy for them. They swung from side to side and the teats stood out tumescent in their fullness.

'Milk, there's milk in there!' he heard himself say aloud. And he cried again. S'naye was dying for lack of milk, and the cows went about on every farm with milk ready to burst out of every teat. The cows stopped and stared at him as though they understood, as though they pleaded for relief. Gripped with fatigue Siyalo lay down and fell asleep. Late that afternoon he woke up with a start and scrambled to his feet. He still had twelve miles to walk back home.

It wasn't long before the sun set gloriously, blazing red in the west. The darkness gathered fast. It was a moonless warm night. Somehow, he felt better inside. Was it the evening air or was it the tears he had shed? He walked slowly with the slight wind washing over him, gently caressing his face. The fireflies flashed in groups in every direction and the trillions of stars winked mischievously from their safe distance. Such nights were familiar now. He was spending more and more time away from home in the evenings. The pitch blackness of the night had the effect of stopping him thinking. The darkness depicted nothingness, except for those fireflies there was nothing. They danced and jostled gracefully, disembodied sparks of life, of freedom. Those fireflies, dissipating their brilliant light in heat-less burning that left the valley dark and cold. How very much like his own life they were; they tossed and threw themselves and finally fell down in cold burning. He recalled that once as a boy he had captured one stray firefly and had held its secret in the cup of his hand; yet even there it had withheld its spark of freedom from him. By the light of the paraffin tin lamp he had looked closely into the secret of its tail, but the light had faded, and died in his hands. Here in the dark, like them, he could dream. He could reach out and dash away and escape; like them he could fade and in a trice come to life again. Heady thoughts swirled about in his mind – fireflies that played hide-and-seek and yet lived on to appear yet again. No one could say how many there were, or how often one flashed and hid and danced again. Then a thought-seed hatched out in the darkness. A thought no more than the spark of a firefly. If little acorns grow into big oak trees, none grow bigger and faster than thought-seeds. A thought-seed should not be thrown away for they are not easy to find. He reached forward with his hand and grasped at nothingness. He cupped his hand in the darkness and looked at it unseeingly as he had once held the spark of a firefly: will it grow, will it die?

'There, I've got it; I've got the idea. My child will live. We will all live; we will survive. One pint a day will save the life of my child; two will save us all. I'll go, I'll go tomorrow morning. Why didn't I think of it before?' He worked himself into a frenzy; he pranced around and shouted for joy. 'Each day I'll relieve some cow of two pints of its sixteen-pint load of milk. I'll milk them. No one need know; no one will be any the wiser. Masadubana, Mr Collett, himself wouldn't know if I took a whole cow, he has so many. No, just two pints a day; that will do. Why didn't I think of it before?' He leaped with excitement, 'Why not, why not?' He gambolled like a young calf, full of life. He ran all the way home.

The baby was at last falling asleep on Jezile's shoulder. Jezile turned round, petrified. When he had not arrived earlier she had half concluded that he had managed to get away to Durban. Perhaps he was now employed. She had dared to hope. She was beginning to believe she would next hear of him from Durban. His dramatic entrance was not only a shock, but a disappointment.

'You're still here?' she gasped. But Siyalo had no time to answer. He grabbed the child and held it up above his head. He looked into her face as she strained yet again into another long breathless wail. He danced round and round, not listening to her cries – and not looking into her wide open glassy eyes, nor to Jezile's bewildered calls. Was he going mad? Was he drunk? Things were bad enough without having to cope with a demented man as well. She burst out crying. It was a truly mad scene. He danced on and on, and S'naye cried on and on. Finally Siyalo sent Jezile to bed and promised that he would stay up and look after his child that night.

When at last S'naye fell asleep, he put her on his bed and he lay next to her. He pillowed her on his forearm and gathered the little mite to him. Her tiny form lay there awkwardly. He drew her closer still till she lay on his bare chest and shared his warmth and his breath. The two lay still in utter exhaustion. He from his excitement and she from her deprivation. But Jezile could not sleep; she lay awake, seeing them both go their own ways, away from her; one to her grave, the other into the safety of his insanity.

When S'naye stirred for a while in the early hours of the morning, he took her to Jezile. Because he did not want to risk falling asleep again, he sat up in his corner, his knees raised to his chin and a thin blanket wrapped round his thin legs. Jezile and S'naye fell into short fitful bouts of sleep and he watched them till dawn broke. He threw the blanket aside and leapt up to take the old jam tin that Jezile used to put drinking water in. He put it in his grass basket and slung it over his shoulder. One last look at his wife and he saw her questioning eyes, but he did not stop to explain anything.

He had heard that cows were milked twice a day. Once early in the morning at about six and again in the early evening, at about five. Only, he knew nothing about where they were kept overnight and whether his plan would work in the early hours of the morning. Besides, this was late spring and the sun rose early, so that it was in full blast by six o'clock in the morning. It was not going to be easy at all. He crossed barbed wire fences not daring to walk through any gates and risk being seen. This was another world. The farmhouse nestled deep among the trees. The jacarandas were in their last throes of bloom and the ground was covered with a thick purple carpet where they had shed their blossoms. The grass was high, soft and damp where he walked. It seemed all the birds for miles around chose to come and nest in this ideal surround. Naturally, there were trees here. They loved it. They sang in a chorus, to outdo each other. He was about to go into another reverie, wondering why there were two worlds . . . but he stopped himself in time. This was no time to question the differences. This was a time to accept them and to act accordingly. He was here to bridge the differences. So he walked almost crouched, alert with his every sense. Finally, he smelt rather than saw the milking pen. Warm smells depicting abundance. Then he heard the cows mooing and somehow he felt energised. Here was life in plenty, not the death spectacle of Sigageni. Now he was close enough to see the men working. There was no white man there, only black men draped in plastic aprons and wellingtons. They walked briskly, efficiently, pouring pints of milk in great big barrels – the milk landing with a splash each time. He spotted one or two that he thought he knew. This alerted him once more to the danger of being found out. Suddenly, he felt a spark of fear coursing its way down his spine and he darted away. He went deep among the surrounding trees, past the farmhouse, where he was assaulted by the wonderful smell of bacon frying as it wafted in the air. He felt faint with hunger – he had not eaten since breakfast time, the day before.

In spite of himself, he drew closer to the house. Now he could see the 'girl' through the open window, cooking the enticing breakfast. He went up to her to ask for some water, hoping that he might get more than just that. When she brought him a mug of water he looked her in the face and told her in a husky voice how hungry he was and how far he had travelled. She stood with the cup in her hand and looked at him. His eyes did not waver. Turning without a word, she spilt the mug's contents among the flowers in the back garden and walked back through her kitchen door. He waited hopefully for her return. He reasoned that she would have to serve the master's family their breakfast first, and perhaps while they ate in the inner recesses of the house she would slip him something. He was no longer afraid. Now that he had come out into the open, he had a reasonable excuse and no one could suspect him of any sinister intent. In fact he began to see the whole morning's exercise as a necessary reconnaissance. But, when the 'girl' finally reappeared with two crusts of bread and jam and a steaming hot creamy cup of coffee, he was so assailed by the inner need for food that he forgot to ask some of the vital questions that he had thought he would ask the kindly woman. She warned him to drink his coffee quickly and go away. She did not want them to find him eating their food in the back garden. She did not like answering questions. She said all this without a smile and she swung round with a touch of urgency in her voice. Jam and coffee with rich milk! Oh God, that all-consuming need! How he wished he had time to sit and savour slowly such a breakfast. Thoughts of Jezile and S'naye flashed through his mind, but he had to drink fast. He never enjoyed anything without giving a thought to Jezile. This love of his was deep and he could never fathom why she occupied the whole of his heart. He never had room for other stray thoughts. It was always Jezile for him. Though lately it was sometimes in anger and sometimes in sorrow. Jezile, for a brief moment, and the world was shut away and he was there with his need gulping that hot cup of coffee. He almost slung away the empty cup of coffee as he turned to rush off with the bread in his hand. He walked a good distance from the house and he sat down to eat his bread slowly.

Food! To think others have food such as this any time they chose. He could still see the big farmhouse through the trees. After a while he saw the farmer go to his car and drive away towards the fields. From a safe distance Siyalo followed the cows as they were driven away from the homestead. Later still he saw the cows being divided into two lots and driven to two different paddocks. His plan began to unfold. Now that he had had his breakfast he could hang around and stalk the cows and study their routine. That would do, he thought. Later in the day, the cows will have replenished the supply of milk in their udders. They all looked tame and he would persuade one to give him some milk.

The cows showed little interest in the grass. They lacked the need for food – they had never gone without. They seemed more concerned about the sun on their backs. By ten o'clock they headed for the huge water tanks and they drank and splashed, making a mud puddle at their feet. Siyalo looked on, amazed. These cows, these beasts, did not even know the rigours of a drought; they had water replenished from some unfathomable depth every day, while humans on the other side of the fence had to travel for miles to get drinking water. After their drink they went and lay under the scraggy bushes near their drinking tanks. Slowly he approached the same shady patch and he sat down. When he became thirsty he drank the same water from the tank. He was all attention, sitting and watching for anyone approaching. But it was all clear. At about noon, he thought his moment had come. Slowly he uncoiled his thin rope from his basket. In one swift movement he threw the lasso around the backlegs of one cow standing near him. He threw it as deftly as he had done when he was a boy. She lashed out in great surprise but he was ready. He knew how to handle her. He was well practised and so was she. She calmed down when she realised what he was doing and let him milk her. Once he had got his skilful hands moving, the milk rained into that tin with a familiar rhythm that deepened with each squirt. He was enjoying this. If he hadn't had to keep a look out for any intruders, he would have been whistling his favourite tune. Once or twice he squirted warm liquid arrows straight into his mouth, just as he had done as a boy. In no time at all, the tin was full. He covered it carefully and put it down. Then he took a long drink. The life-giving drink seeped through his every fibre – he felt its smooth rich taste. Then he hurriedly loosened the rope and left in a hurry.

Jezile was at home with S'naye on her back. She turned and looked at him apprehensively, no doubt convinced that he was losing his mind. And when he laughed with boyish glee and came straight to her, tickling her unexpectedly on her side, her fears were confirmed. All she managed to do was call his name.

'Siyalo . . .' He did not let her finish. His happiness bubbled out of him in many words that made little sense to her.

'She won't die, no she won't. And where is our old calabash? Bring it out, bring it out and we'll start to make her some amasi today.'

'Wait, Siyalo, wait. Sit down.'

'No! You sit down, and I'll tell you something. Then you can have a little yourself; no, have some in your tea.'

'Have what?'

It was all so incoherent that Jezile burst out crying.

'No, Jezile, no. I'm not going mad. Listen. Look.' She went on crying, her face averted. 'Look, Jezile.' He opened the tin and forced her hand off her face. She saw the milk, and she stopped breathless, her tear-stained face agape.

'Siyalo, what is the meaning of all this!' she asked when she could get her voice back.

'If you sit down calmly and let me explain, I'll tell you. The whole story.' When he finished she made as if to rise, but she remained kneeling, shaking her head and her hands, violently repelling the very thought of what he was telling her.

'Siyalo, that's stealing, that's stolen food.'

'Stolen food! Did you say stolen food? I want to know who's doing the stealing in this country . . .'

'I'm not talking of this country, Siyalo, I'm talking of this house. Our child. I've never eaten stolen food.'

'Neither have I.' His voice had risen to match hers. 'But I'm not going to let my child die simply because all odds are loaded against me. I want my child to live. My child will not wait for that long-awaited freedom. She's dying now. All right, so it's not Masadubana himself who's responsible for the chaos in our country, here in Sigageni and in this very house, but he benefits from this unfair system; he supports this system. This government would not remain one day longer if it wasn't for people like him.' Siyalo had not spoken like this in many many months. He was getting carried away. He did not realise that Jezile was no longer listening. S'naye was stirring on her back and Jezile loosened her shawl. She sat down with S'naye in her lap and looked at the milk with all kinds of thoughts rushing through her mind. While Siyalo went on ranting and justifying his actions, Jezile took the milk and began pouring it into the bottle. S'naye sucked furiously a few times and stopped, then she sucked again gulping fast. Within seconds she had emptied the bottle. Only then did Siyalo seem to realise what had happened.

'What?'

'Yes, what do you think? Did you think I would throw it out now that it's here? Of course she must drink it.' She was going to give another bottle but Siyalo stopped her.

'Hey, be careful. It will give her diarrhoea if you give her too much. Not all at once. A little at a time. Besides, we want to make amasi. From now on I'll do what I can to get her some every day.'

'Be careful now. This is very dangerous business. I don't want anyone knowing about this. I don't want you getting arrested. I never thought – I never thought this could happen to us.'

'Me, never. I'm very careful. I've studied the whole situation,'

Siyalo said, ignoring her anxiety. 'It's easy. Just promise me that you won't tell anyone. Not even my mother. I don't want her thinking we are eating stolen food.'

'It is stolen food, Siyalo. How are we going to live with this?'

'What can we do? Things are bad, Jezile. Things are bad. You know, about yesterday. I actually got the job within the first hour of the day. I was the first person chosen . . .'

Then Jezile stood up and prepared their usual uputu, maize dry porridge, and tea. Only, this time it was a milky cup of tea that she gave him. They celebrated in the silence of their house that afternoon. They all lay down. S'naye fell asleep again, almost immediately, as though she had not had a day's sleep already. Siyalo took Jezile in his arms and they made love. It was prolonged and passionate and very loving, such as it had not been in a long time. They slept throughout the afternoon. With their door securely shut, no one thought they were in and no one disturbed them. And so they sealed their secret in love.

From that day on Siyalo woke up every morning knowing that he had a job to do. At first his conscience gnawed at him but as days went by he learned to cope with it – he became less guilty and less afraid. Each day he looked at Jezile and S'naye and he would murmur, 'I owe it to them. I must, for in a strange way I owe my life to them. Without them my life has no meaning.'

Within a week, S'naye began to smile. She slept soundly by day and by night. And her whining cry was replaced by her old full-throated cry and an occasional smile. Siyalo talked more cheerfully and some of his boldness returned. Jezile told him all about her prison days. They mulled over the events of the past months and sometimes they even laughed. S'naye was fast recovering and from that point of view Jezile argued what they were doing was worth every discomfort, if it saved their child. What a choice – one's child or one's moral beliefs: which to sacrifice? Within a short time S'naye could be heard gurgling happily. Neighbours told Jezile how well she and S'naye looked. But somehow these normal village remarks embarrassed her. She wanted no awkward questions asked. The worst thing was having to hide the food from MaBiyela and visitors. Amasi gives its own secret away, for it has its own aroma. MaBiyela asked suspiciously about the flies that buzzed around. Jezile began to meet her half-way if she saw her coming towards their home. It was all very uncomfortable. Jezile suffered the guilt terribly and wondered many times each day how Siyalo's solution would end. One day she resolved to tell him to stop for this was no solution at all. People knew what the witches did at night in the dark. People had more than just five or six senses – they had a seventh sense as well.

For Siyalo the farm became a familiar place. He began to wonder if he might work his way into being employed on the farm, no matter how menial the job. Anything to buy Jezile some new clothes. Her time was very near – any day in fact. One mid-morning, preoccupied with such possibilities, he walked among his now familiar herd. He lay low as usual, but his mind was not on the job, his vigilance worn thin by the routine. At midday, he went about as usual, a tuneless whistle on his lips. He marked the rhythm of the milk squirting into the empty tin as it gradually filled up between his knees. It was a bigger tin than he started off with. Then he heard him cough, right behind his back. Siyalo froze and coughed back in reply. His body stiffened, his head bent low; he was petrified. He half expected a bullet to go zing past his ear, or thud into the back of his head. It was the white man himself – Masadubana in person.

'Ufunani lapha? (What do you want here?)' he asked him in awkward Zulu. 'Izinkomo zakho yini kanti lezi? (Are these your own cattle?)'

Siyalo turned slowly, 'No master. These are your cattle. But you don't need this can of milk as much as I do. My child is dying. She's starving. I came to you for your skimmed milk a while ago; the kind you give to your pigs. I wanted to buy it from you but your servants said you would not let me.' He would have gone on babbling anything, if only to stop the white man asking any more questions. But Masadubana interrupted.

'So you felt you would take it anyhow, regardless of my wishes? You know that I don't want to sell the milk, but you're stealing it from me.' Siyalo looked past him and he saw a black man standing a distance away.

'Awu, Mfowethu (Oh, brother),' Siyalo heard himself shout to the man, who had obviously betrayed him. But before there were any more words, two policemen appeared from nowhere and Siyalo was arrested.

By early afternoon Jezile guessed what had happened, when Siyalo did not return. She had sat at the door the whole afternoon, looking far into the distance to where Siyalo would appear if he was coming back. She had sat there, not daring to move, willing Siyalo to come back home as hard as she could. But at sunset Siyalo had not returned. She sat there even when it became dark. She sat there when her labour pains started. She would not tell anyone she was in labour, lest they found out her secret. When it became unbearable she put S'naye to bed and prepared a little corner for herself, laying her necessities within easy reach. The dogs barked and once or twice she thought someone was coming right up her garden path, but it was not Siyalo. It was after midnight when the baby was born – a girl whom she called Ndondo. Jezile, in her agitation had given birth all on her own. What to tell the village mid-wife now? What to tell MaBiyela? At dawn Jezile cradled her baby in an embrace of apprehension. Where would she go from here?

Before sunrise MaBiyela woke up to get drinking water from the spring. She preferred to get the water at this time when the water was clean and cold and before the animals had dirtied it. She was picking her way slowly in the half-light when she became aware of quickening footsteps. It was Fuziwe, the village gossip.

'Oh, that's you MaBiyela. That's you. I knew it would be you, no one else wakes up this early for water.'

'You do. Here you are. I'm not alone in it, am I?'

'Oh, occasionally. I've got a journey to Ixopo today, and I thought I must see you before I go for I wanted so much to tell you how sorry I am.'

'About what? What are you sorry about, Fuziwe?'

'Well, your son of course.'

'What's wrong with my son, you mean Siyalo, don't you – what's wrong with him?'

'You mean . . . you mean you don't know he was arrested yesterday?'

'Arrested? What for?' By now they stood facing each other, MaBiyela intrigued; not wanting to believe a word.

144

'Oh, Fuziwe, you and your strange stories . . . you spend your life snooping around . . .'

'It is true though. He was arrested on Masadubana's farm stealing milk from the cows . . .'

'Hew, . . . that woman, that wife of his. I've known all along that she would be the ruin of that home . . . Where do you get all this? . . . Did Jezile tell you all this?'

'I said it's Siyalo that's been arrested; not Jezile.'

MaBiyela turned right there and then and went to Siyalo's house. She almost drove the door in, pounding on it, not waiting to be invited.

'Where's Siyalo? Where?' And when she saw that Jezile had a baby in her arms she screamed. 'And you deliver yourself, alone, in his absence. You don't call me or anyone. You're a criminal, you are. You drove him to this, you wanted him imprisoned – I've got to get to the bottom of this,' MaBiyela pranced about feeling buffeted from all sides. 'I think I can guess why; in fact I know why. You wanted him out of the way when you had that child because that's not his child now, is it? I've known all along that when you were in prison you slept with all the policemen; this is your policeman's child. I bet you don't know which policeman . . .' She was mad, hopping mad. She would have gone on if Jezile had not suddenly uttered a shattering scream. This calmed MaBiyela somewhat, although she went on grunting and heaving. Then she began to shout abuse at Fuziwe whom she left standing in the half-light on the way to the river. 'And that snake; that forked tongue. To think I must hear about my son from her! The news is over the mountains by now. She's worse than the wind for carrying news. She's full of poison. Oh Siyalo, oh Siyalo . . .' She broke into heaving sobs. Jezile got up from her bed and she drew close to MaBiyela.

'Sit down Mama, sit down.' Seeing MaBiyela in a state of collapse strengthened Jezile. 'I'll tell you. I'll tell you everything.' Jezile's voice remained calm, even when MaBiyela tried to shake her off. 'It's a long story Mama, but it's not what you think. This is Siyalo's baby. I've never been unfaithful to Siyalo. Siyalo knows that.'

'How does he know it? He was not in prison with you, was

he? When you left here for prison you were not pregnant, were you?'

'Yes I was – only we did not know it then.'

'Oh never mind – what do I care. But I do care about him,' she started sobbing violently again.

'About the milk. This was never my idea . . .'

'What idea? You talk as though I know what got him arrested. What story can one get from Fuziwe, eh?'

'How does Fuziwe know about this whole matter?'

'Go on, Fuziwe knows. That's all. She knows. Go on.'

'As I was saying, when S'naye looked as though she was going to die, Siyalo had an idea; he was going to save her life; he couldn't bear to watch her dying.'

'Go on, so what did he do?' MaBiyela said, choking between her sobs.

'So, he has been going to milk one of the cows every day to get some milk for her. That's what saved S'naye – the milk from Masadubana's cows.'

'And you hid that from me – you wouldn't even tell me that you had food while we starved. I asked you, I asked you, didn't I? About those flies and the smell of amasi. You wouldn't tell me. Ah, the whole idea doesn't sound like Siyalo. It sounds more like you! You think I've forgotten how you blamed me for the baby's condition when you came back from prison. If this was his idea, why didn't he do it then? S'naye has been dying a long time – why didn't he do it then? If you had had your way, even then, you'd have had me stealing food from the shops to save her. Why do you suppose your child is more valuable than all the children who die in this village. Countless children die here; their parents see them die for lack of good food. That is the fate of all children here, they live with the threat of death and there's nothing anyone can do. But you figure out that yours is the exception!'

'What do you mean, mother? Does it not upset you that our baby was dying – must she die, just like that – because others die, must we let her die! Pity no one has had Siyalo's resourcefulness; food is all around us and children are dying. I'm proud of Siyalo, proud of him in jail. It's high time somebody did something to save the children.'

'Steal, is that what you mean by doing something?'

'If that is all one can do, yes even stealing is an act justifiable in moral terms; that is not stealing; moral laws are not blind. If I take what's not needed that's not stealing.' She argued the way Siyalo had taught her to.

'That's how you were brought up. You have brought your father's . . ., no your mother's occupation into this house. My children live on stolen food. Awu, awu, awu!'

Jezile felt faint and she collapsed back on her bed. As MaBiyela slammed the door, Jezile was left wondering about Fuziwe; how had she come to know what had happened to Siyalo. She longed to see her. She broke into loud sobs and she wondered about what had actually happened to Siyalo, and how it had happened. She felt friendless and completely alone. Lately, she had been haunted by the memory of her dear friend, Zenzile. If only she were here now. She had fallen lower than Zenzile now, for Zenzile had never been accused of stealing.

By midday, she saw two women coming in. Both had no husbands. Gaba's husband had died in Johannesburg and Nomawa's had simply disappeared, again in Johannesburg. Some said he was now in prison, but no one knew what he had done to be there. Not that it mattered now. The reality was that all these young women were on their own, left exposed to all the callous talk reserved for women bereft of husbands. As soon as they entered Jezile cast a quick look at them to ascertain if they came as friends or enemies. She knew in an instant that they came in sympathy when they burst into tears. She joined them in sheer relief. And anyone who heard them might have thought there was a death in the house. They told Jezile what they had heard from Thubi. Apparently, Thubi's husband worked for Masadubana. It was he who milked the cows. It was he who had spotted Siyalo, but he had not realised it was someone he knew, for he had seen him at a distance. They had heard MaBiyela that morning crying and telling all those who cared to listen what an evil woman Jezile was for having caused the arrest of her husband. From that moment Gaba and Nomawa had known that Jezile was in trouble.

'When a mother-in-law blames you for any catastrophe, then you're in trouble,' said Nomawa.

'It is not usual for a mother-in-law to talk about matters of her household to all and sundry. If she does and people believe her there is trouble. Who is going to listen to your side of the story?' Gaba added.

The two women spent several hours with Jezile. They washed the baby and warmed some water for Jezile's own bath. They cooked some gruel for her to drink and keep her warm. Thus Jezile was adopted into the unofficial women's league of the lonely, the deserted and the widowed; those who were left at the mercy of their mothers-in-law without recourse to male protection. Up until then, Jezile had not been fully aware that these young women led such exposed and vulnerable lives. And that, without any formal structure, they had such vast inner resources with which to support each other. From that day she knew she could depend on these women. Whenever they ran short of supplies, they appealed to each other for help; when one was in difficulty, they rallied in her support. They made friends and tended to go out together even on public occasions.

When they left, Gaba promised to send Ndeya, her eldest daughter of ten, to help and carry messages for Jezile while she was in confinement. They promised to send a message to her mother at Luve. If she came, she could find out more about Siyalo, pay him a visit in jail if necessary.

Jezile spent the rest of the day alone. She kept hoping that MaBiyela would send Simo and Jabu over to keep her company and help her out, even if she did not come herself. In the gathering darkness she heard a soft knock at the door. Half hoping that it was Simo and Jabu at last, she told them to open the door. But no one came in. Another soft knock and Jezile stood up to find Ndeya instead. She came in cautiously and knelt by the door. Jezile made her welcome and invited her to her bedside. She had met the child a few times before, but they knew very little of each other. However, within a short time Ndeya was efficiently warming the gruel, giving S'naye her last dish of amasi and putting her to sleep. Jezile was amazed at the maturity of the young girl. She showed a competence far beyond her age. But then children of single mothers learned a lot in their early years, for they had to stand by their mother's side, in the absence of any other helpers. Jezile felt a liking for the quiet, able girl. As for MaBiyela, Jezile thought this would mark a breaking point between her and Jezile. Their stormy relationship could not survive this episode, especially in the absence of Siyalo.

In two days' time MaSibiya, Jezile's mother, arrived. She came accompanied by two other young women who carried baskets filled with every kind of food. The stream at the bottom of MaSibiya's garden had watered all kinds of food: tomatoes, cabbages, sweet potatoes, amadumbe and other vegetables. Her neighbours, on hearing what had befallen Jezile, had sent gifts of food and money for Jezile and the new-born baby. It was a feast day. Jezile cried for joy when she saw the mounds of food and the little money that her mother had brought her. She secured the money in a knot in her doek (head scarf) and tucked it under her pillow.

Soon word got round that MaSibiya had arrived, bringing baskets of food. At first two women came trailing each other 'to see the baby' they said. Jezile could not make out whether this was genuine or whether they had other reasons – perhaps to see her mother or to share in the feast. But she gave them the benefit of the doubt. Perhaps her mother's arrival had given them a good excuse to bypass MaBiyela's authority and override her wishes. Before they were through drinking the tea, two more came in. After the third couple, Jezile knew that their reasons were not as honourable, and she withheld her cups of tea. She gave them amahewu, a maize drink, instead.

Next door, MaBiyela was in a quandary about what to do next. She had done all she could to influence the community against Jezile, but they were going over her head to see Jezile, her mother and the baby. Finally, she went round and greeted MaSibiya ingratiatingly. But the rift was too wide and deep.

When MaSibiya invited MaBiyela to go with her to see Siyalo MaBiyela became defensive. What had MaSibiya to do with Siyalo? However, she soon gave in. Early the next morning, the two women could be seen waiting for the bus to Ixopo. When they got there, both of them felt strange to be asking passers-by where the prison was. They had never had reason to visit the place before. They walked in silence, not out of malice for each other, but because they were afraid and ashamed. It was not until the early afternoon that they were allowed to see him. There were several other people there who had come to visit relatives. MaBiyela in particular felt very much out of place. She looked at the other visitors and assessed that they were not Christian at all; in fact they looked like criminals. If you were to ask her how criminals looked, she would not have been able to answer. She was going through a difficult time trying to reconcile her moral judgement of others and the position that Siyalo had placed her in. She had waited for the moment when those massive doors would finally open and Siyalo would come out and they could talk to him quietly and she would finally know the whole truth and perhaps MaSibiya would know what a conspiring evil daughter she had. Instead of the prison door opening wide for him to come out or for them to walk in, it was a little window on the side that dropped behind strong bars and a face loomed behind them, asking them to come to the window to say who they wanted. The other visitors who knew the routine, rushed ahead and were there before the two women. They shuffled at the back of the line, too daunted to argue with anyone. Everyone seemed in such a hurry. The voice of the face behind the bars shouted disrespectfully:

'Hurry, hurry, Mama; whom do you want; Yisho! (say it).' She whispered back, anxious that the others did not catch Siyalo's name, in case they knew him.

'Yisho Mama, Yisho, memeza ngikuzwe (say it Mama, say it – shout so that I can hear you).'

It was all so intimidating. Finally they were ushered into the dark corridors, and were led to a room with a fine strong wire mesh that divided them from the prisoners. All that was left of their relatives, the prisoners, were piercing whites of the eye and mouths that babbled like puppets. MaBiyela was very distressed. That quiet procession of visitors that had been so subdued as they entered, suddenly broke into a din of babbling voices as though they were all praying at once as they did in their Thursday prayer meetings. MaBiyela finally caught sight of Siyalo and was further distressed that all he wanted to know about was Jezile and the baby. The last straw was to see his joy when he was told that Jezile had a baby girl.

'Tell her, tell her Mkhwekazi wami (mother-in-law) that as soon as she can manage, she must get to Nosizwe and tell her to organise a defence for me. She has to hurry because I have no idea when the case is coming up. I need a lawyer. The doctor knows all the good lawyers and how to contact them. If she can, she should come up and see me. I know the doctor comes to Ixopo often.' MaBiyela could not get everything he said, but MaSibiya seemed to have got it all. Before MaBiyela could ask any questions about the whys and wherefores of Siyalo's arrest, a loud voice boomed over the hubbub and the noise died down as the men were being led away into some hidden recess on the other side of the screen.

'Remember to tell Nosizwe,' Siyalo's voice trailed after him as he disappeared.

MaBiyela shuffled out in a daze. It had been a frustrating experience and she hated the fact that she had to suffer this humiliation in the presence of someone else – an in-law, and Jezile's own mother of all people.

In spite of the gravity of the whole matter Jezile laughed when her mother told her how MaBiyela was put out. In a few days Jezile found the strength to go with the baby to see Nosizwe. She went in the company of her mother and MaBiyela. Somehow MaBiyela did not want to miss out, especially while MaSibiya was around. It was an emotional meeting between the two friends, peppered by some words of complaint from Nosizwe. Why had Jezile not been to see her for so long? She wondered about the struggle, the meetings on Thursdays. She wondered why Jezile looked so cowed – was she ill? Was the baby ill? Could it be because they had failed in their fight against the passes?

'Well, yes. All the women accepted the passes when we came back. Yes, we failed. We suffered for nothing.'

'The struggle goes on Jezile. Don't lose heart. There's a lot we have to fight for.' But Jezile was self-conscious. First on account of not having come back to see her doctor friend throughout the last few months of her pregnancy, and also because her mother and mother-in-law were there. She kept trying to gloss over the questions that Nosizwe kept asking, but Nosizwe would not let her. She pressed her until she had to confess that she had kept away because she could not afford the fee for consultation and for S'naye.

'The fee? You mean to pay me?'

Jezile nodded.

'Oh Jezile, I thought we had passed that stage. I thought

when you crushed those stones for me in jail we had cemented a friendship that nothing would break. Pay? No, never.'

'That was prison, Nosizwe.'

'That was our life, Jezile. Now tell me, have you got the money now? Is life any easier? Has your husband found a job? What's wrong with the baby?'

She asked endless questions as she loosened the cloth around the baby.

'No, the baby is fine so far. She's only eight days old.'

'Eight days old? And she's fine? Then why have you come all this way?'

Jezile did not answer. She burst into tears instead.

'Something wrong, Jezile? I should have guessed. What's the matter?'

'It's Siyalo. He . . . he . . .'

Nosizwe led her gently to her surgery.

'Come inside. Tell me. You are in trouble. Tell me.'

Jezile calmed down, once they were alone. She told Nosizwe everything, including Siyalo's message.

'Remember next time, if the children are ill; or even yourself, please come straight here. I'm not here to make money. I'm here to help.' Those were Nosizwe's last words as she left the surgery. 'Take these and they'll keep you strong while you're breastfeeding.' Jezile cried again as she left the surgery. The meeting had brought back the memory of her former self, when she was strong and self-confident and unafraid. She was aware of the change in herself and a tinge of self-pity crept in.

They got the best lawyer they could for Siyalo. He was charged under the old Stock Theft Act. This seemed incongruous as stealing milk could not be equated with stealing a whole cow. But, in court, the case went very badly against him. The very name of the lawyer who represented him, Mr Ginsberg, a friendly Jewish lawyer, was anathema to the court. He was known for the political stand he took and the kind of cases he always defended. He did his best to argue the moral question involved, how desperation had driven Siyalo. He also argued that the heartless farmer who would not extend his compassion to save the life of a dying child did not even miss those two pints a day – he was talking of those who had so much against those who had so little; against the human instinct to save one's child on the one hand, and the heartlessness of society, personified in Mr Collett, Masadubana. He tried to invoke the principle under Roman Dutch law, that theft is theft only if there is a complainant – who was the complainant in the case – was it Mr Collett or was it the cow? Neither Mr Collett nor the cow had suffered any loss as such. In fact he had helped to relieve the cow of its heavy burden. He tried his best to soften the case, pointing out mitigating circumstances.

But the argument of the prosecution swayed the facts to show that Siyalo was in fact driven by his political views. In stealing the milk he was trying to throw the whole country into anarchy. He was dispossessing white people of things they worked hard to get. It was a case of envy and theft. Cattle rustling could never be tolerated. They brought into evidence his political views and actions which had resulted in him being endorsed out of Durban. They further argued that his political influence had caused the women of the whole area to resist the issuing of passes to women and to fight the Bantu Authorities Act. Siyalo's solicitor fought hard, much to the pleasure of the people, many whom Jezile did not know. If the magistrate did not pass an exemplary sentence the country would be thrown into chaos, with hordes of people feeling justified to plunder and pillage and rob white people simply because they were hungry. Under the Stock Theft Act sentences were very high in South Africa, dating from the early years in the Cape when the indigenous Xhosa sought to repossess their cattle that the white men had taken from them in the first place. And so, Siyalo was given a hefty ten-year sentence, a deterrent to others with similar ideas.

When the case was over and people left the court, they hailed and congratulated the solicitor on his hard fight. There was a celebratory air, reminiscent of the case at Pietermaritzburg when Jezile and others were the accused. There were arguments too, legal arguments, refuting both the nature of the charge and the judgement. People talked all at once. Jezile stood with the baby in her arms, stunned and aghast, feeling like a cold spit. She wondered why it was that invariably in such cases the next of kin were forgotten and the politicians worried about points of law and political questions, never about the human question. What was she going to do now? With Siyalo in jail – jail as she knew it – ten years: how monstrous! She felt cold from the inside. Just then, Nosizwe saw her and hurried towards her.

'Oh Jezile, he did his best. He is the best solicitor the Defence Fund could hire. And of course you don't have to worry about payment. The Fund will pay all his expenses. They always do when they defend political cases.'

'But this was not a political case. He might have stood a better chance if the whole argument had not gone political.'

'Of course it is, Jezile. You should know that. The reason why Siyalo took that brilliant stand was because it was a political stand. You have a brilliant man, Jezile, brilliant.'

She opened her mouth to speak, but Nosizwe was anxious to convince her that the best had been done by the best man for the best reasons.

'Look Jezile, it's straightforward. The reason why Siyalo has no job is political; the reason why he could not make use of the land to raise crops to feed his family is political; the reason why all your cows have died in the drought is political. We have no grass when Collett has so much – that is political; the reason why he has such a large farm and hundreds of cows is political – it's not because he's a brilliant man, it's because he buys the land for so little and he can occupy an area ten times the area of Sigageni; it's because the government gives him such high subsidies to maintain his crops and preferential treatment in marketing his produce – there's no magic in it – it's political.' Nosizwe stopped breathless to assess the impact of her words.

Jezile nodded and MaBiyela too. Encouraged, Nosizwe went on. 'Do you suppose all these people would have come here to Ixopo all the way from Durban and Pietermaritzburg if Siyalo was a common thief? Never! Siyalo is a hero. You should be proud of him.' She turned and beckoned to Mr Ginsberg, the solicitor. She introduced the family. The man was very friendly. He spoke English so fast that Jezile could not follow everything. She was not accustomed to fast English speakers. So, even though she was on the verge of crying, she gave a smile. Her only answers were, 'Thank you, thank you.' MaBiyela too thanked the man in Zulu, 'Siyabonga, siyabonga.' And just as Mr Ginsberg was about to go, he turned round and told her she would be allowed to visit Siyalo after the first four months after which she could write to him once a month and pay him a visit every month.

'Oh, what we don't know, of course, is how long they are going to keep him here. With such a long sentence, they are likely to take him away to a bigger, more secure prison. I'll let you know in good time.' Then Nosizwe took them back in her car. She dropped them on the hill, just above Sigageni before she proceeded to Umzimkulu, where she lived.

They watched her car as it sped away in a cloud of dust which enveloped them, two lonely figures on a hill cut off from the rest of humanity. Then the dust died down, and the two women emerged carrying their bags; defeat was written all over their faces. They did not talk to each other. They plodded heavily one behind the other as they descended into the valley below. Simo and Jabu saw them first and ran back inside to call the others. MaSibiya had come back to be with her daughter at the time of the hearing, even though she had chosen not to go to court. People rushed out to meet the women to find out what the verdict was. There were many people assembled at Jezile's house. There were Gaba and Nomawa as well. They stood in a silent cluster in the yard. The two women walked, their silence unbroken, passing the crowd into the house. When they went in, the others followed. A long sharp wail from Jezile broke the silence. The others joined in. It was as though Siyalo had died. Jezile could not be consoled. Ten years! Why, that was longer than she had known Siyalo. It was almost half her life. It had been bad enough without him when he worked in Durban. At least he came home at the end of every year; there was always that explosion of joy when he came on visits. But now, ten years – possibly without ever seeing each other. Life without Siyalo was impossible to visualise. What a pity that the only year they had been able to live together had been so full of pain and wranglings and poverty. She cried aloud again when she thought of this, 'But nothing, nothing has diminished our love!' She felt she loved him as much as she had done when she was a young girl.

When everyone had quietened down, MaBiyela gave a cough, a signal that she wished to talk. She felt weak and the sense of shame would not leave her. But she felt it was her duty to exonerate her son and the family in the eyes of the community, if not in the eyes of the law. If they were going to live in this community and keep their respect, she had to repeat, as best she could, the arguments that Nosizwe had put to them outside the courthouse. Siyalo was no common thief; he was a hero; a political prisoner like any other, and his imprisonment was no different from that of the women earlier that year. Her unwavering look met Fuziwe's shifty eyes and she felt a spasm of anger and became impassioned in her speech. Her voice rose higher and she could feel she was swaying the house her way with people assenting loudly. It was at this heated point that MaSibiya, who did not want to interfere in the matters of the Majolas gave her support by starting their favourite hymn. They sang fervently to purge the memory of Siyalo.

But for Jezile the problems that she was going to suffer in the next ten years were inscribed on every wall. She saw it in the eyes of Gaba and Nomawa and many women like them who had to fend for themselves without husbands. She would have to learn a lot from them. They shook hands with her as though to welcome her to the group. When her mother prepared to go back home the next day, Jezile cried again. She felt as though her life with the Majolas had ended. She wanted to go back to her people with her mother. But her mother, in tears herself, comforted her daughter and told her she was a Majola to the grave. She would remain with them with or without Siyalo, until they themselves broke the link.

'But without Siyalo, I've no home.'

'Remember my child, you're not just married to Siyalo; you're married to all the Majolas. If Siyalo should desert you, you remain a Majola. Stay here and bring up your children. Siyalo will thank you for it. This also means you have to make peace with your mother-in-law. MaBiyela is the pillar of this home and you have to lean on her. You can have friends outside, but MaBiyela is the law and your support. With her by your side, few people will try to exploit you.'

'Exploit me, mother?'

'Yes, exploit you. You don't need to know what exploitation means – you don't have to learn from experience. It's not worth it.'

Jezile turned to enter the house. The house seemed darker, and she could not face it – it was suffocating her. She took the

156

baby in her arms and went out into the sunshine. She felt she had to escape. It was the hopelessness that was hardest to cope with. As long as Siyalo had been free and around there had been hope that something would turn up. She thought she had suffered every affliction and could cope with many things, but hopelessness was destructive. It consumed her. She sat outside for a while and felt cold in spite of the hot sun. Then she saw MaBiyela shuffling out of her house, her head bent low. She looked like a picture of depression. She was actually wearing black as though Siyalo had died. Jezile felt a tug of pain within her for MaBiyela; she tightened her arms around her baby and she knew what MaBiyela was going through. She stood up without a thought and walked towards MaBiyela. Although she was conscious of MaSibiya's words, it was her need that moved her. It was pain and compassion that drew them together. If they did not like each other much, they had something they shared intensely which drew them closer. No two people had so little love for each other and yet had so much in common. They both recognised this. They sat down in silence for a long time.

Just as Jezile was about to go, MaBiyela said to her, 'You'll have to find a way to live somehow. You have very young children. They must live through this and survive.'

In silence Jezile walked away. She was to hear those words many times, from many people. In their effort to comfort her they told her how to face her new life. At first, their words had little meaning; mere words that grazed her pain. But their repetition slowly convinced her – she had to live through this and survive with her children.

11

*T*he little money that MaSibiya had given her before she left was soon gone. There was no salt, no sugar, no candles, no paraffin, and she was now on her last bar of soap when she heard cheerful voices outside. Even without laughter, she could tell they were happy voices. She dashed out of her house as though in pursuit of that happiness. As soon as she stepped out, Gaba raised not only her voice but her beckoning arm as well.

'Hey Jezile, are you so fond of your house – why don't you get out and meet people?' she said as she quickened her step to meet Jezile. Jezile stood still and that radiant voice coursed through her blood, tingling like an electric current.

'Just what do you think you're doing, burying yourself in that house like a mole. A house is the death of a woman, don't you know?' Jezile smiled but she could find no words to answer. At that precise moment she was too busy sensing the unfolding of her own mind, opening to air and sun like a flower. Gaba was standing before her and staring into Jezile's eyes, her own eyes dancing knowingly.

'You'll kill yourself worrying about men. You have a life to live and children to keep happy.' She turned to S'naye who stood with her head raised at her mother's side, searching the face with the happy voice. Gaba picked her up and talked baby words into that questioning face, until S'naye smiled shyly. 'But seriously, I came to tell you that we heard that MaNgidi needs people to weed her field. Her maize is choking with the weeds, and she is paying money this time.'

'MaNgidi? You know Siyalo didn't want me to work for MaNgidi.'

'Well, well. That's the funniest thing I've heard in a long

time. When Siyalo was around you defied him. Now that he's not here, you intend to obey his every wish. That's ridiculous. He won't even know that you were such an "obedient" wife – not ever. Don't let your love ever enslave you to a man. Siyalo is where he is because he obeyed his own conscience, not because he loved you more or less or considered your wishes paramount. Can't you see this as a kind of release? From now on you use your own judgement, and there's a lot of sense in you; there has always been a lot of sense in you. This is the time to use it.'

'Yes, I understand, but do you think MaBiyela will let me – the baby is so young . . .'

'MaBiyela, footsek! Since when has she been concerned about you and this baby? Does she now acknowledge it's Siyalo's child? Look, from now on it's you and you alone that you need to consider, whatever decision you're making. Are you well enough to work in the fields for a whole day? That's what's important. MaBiyela has no money to give you and MaBiyela must shut up. Are you or are you not coming tomorrow?'

'How much is she paying?'

'As always, a pittance. But you and I have no choice. We take whatever she gives us. And about the children – if MaBiyela won't let Simo and Jabu look after them, remember Ndeya is there. She looks small, but she can cope with anything, that girl of mine. She's a match for any woman, I can bet on that. She's seen me through the hardest times. If you bring the two children along, Ndeya will sit with them and mind them on the border of the field. Now and again you can go and feed them and see if all is well. As for MaNgidi, she can lump it.'

Jezile suddenly turned with a firm voice, her eyes looking straight into Gaba's, 'Yes, I'll come with you tomorrow.' They woke up early at sunrise, kicking the glistening dew along the pathway.

The days were hot and long and Jezile was not yet strong. But she kept up with the others. In spite of the hot sun and the buzzing insects, the children were reasonably comfortable. Ndeya made a little canopy for shelter. MaNgidi showed great consideration to Jezile in those early days, often murmuring in her ear to take it easy, not to try and keep up with the stronger women. She might have been Duma's wife whose social

159

position remained ambivalent in the community, but the women would work for her anytime rather than go off to work for Masadubana. When the sun became unbearably hot at midday, they all got away to the big shed where MaNgidi sat them down to rest until the afternoon sun had cooled off. She made concessions here and there such as a four-hour break in the middle of the day, roughly between eleven-thirty and three-thirty. But then, neither did she look at the clock at the end of the day. This made very long working days. Jezile valued the little money this earned her and at such times she pushed aside the disapproving image of Siyalo that invariably flashed across her mind.

What she valued most in the summer of that year was the company of the other women. Many of the women were young and hardened through bitter experiences of every kind. They had been trained from childhood to expect little from life and when disillusionment had come they had given each other support. They had little to hide in their lives for there were hardly any secrets in the community. They talked with ease about their personal lives and had come to terms with many misfortunes by learning to laugh at themselves. They were generous in giving each other advice, and often took the advice that was offered. Jezile slowly eased into this company. She spent more time listening and laughing than thinking about herself.

Soon the seasonal job was over. Before all else Jezile bought a big tin of powdered milk for S'naye and Ndondo. It cost her more than half her pay from MaNgidi. She would have bought it if it had cost her all of it. The life of S'naye had cost them everything they could afford. It was on her account that Siyalo was in prison. She swore to herself that whatever else she went without, milk for S'naye would come first. And she did go without many things. So, in a few days' time, she had nothing left. For many weeks she had not done any washing, having spent all the hours of daylight weeding MaNgidi's fields. So one day she and a few friends collected every scrap of clothing in their houses and went two miles down to the Umzimkulu river to do their washing. It was to be a whole day's job. There was a picnic feeling in the air. Ndeya was there and so were Simo and Jabu. MaBiyela was slowly relenting, seeing that Jezile was not only coping but apparently enjoying herself. The vast waters of the great Umzimkulu gurgled cheerfully over the big rocks and this alone added its own excitement to the crowd. First they soaked their washing and spread it on the rocks. In these parts there was no better bleach than the sun. This also helped the women to use their soap sparingly. Their voices rose high chatting and laughing in competition with the clamour of the river. Nomawa was narrating an episode in her rocky marriage about how she had gone in search of her 'lost' husband in Durban; how she had found him well and happy in the company of a hefty woman who met her at the door and looked down at her as though she was a lost child.

'Mama, I am looking for Timba, Timba Mayekiso. The last address he gave us was this one. Do you know where he lives?' The woman stood squarely in the doorway blocking it altogether.

'And who are you my child?'

'I am MaS'kosana, Timba's wife.'

'What? What did you say? What Timba's wife? You slut . . .'

The women rocked with laughter and merriment which was suddenly broken by a screeching yell which rose above every voice – they turned round, but for a moment they saw nothing. Then a flurry of arms and bubbles. It was little S'naye struggling to surface in the rocky pool. One moment she had been toddling some distance away, and the next she had slipped into the water. Jezile leapt up and plunged into the river. In one swoop she surfaced with S'naye in her arms. Both gulped and spluttered, but they were neither the worse for it. It was a crowded moment that left everyone shaken. For a while they all sat comforting each other. When Jezile had recovered sufficiently, she went back to the washing. S'naye was securely tied on Ndeya's back.

It was then that Jezile found that the only piece of soap she had was gone. At first she looked silently all around, ferreting among the dirty washing, looking silently and frantically, burrowing through this pile and that until her agitation was written all over her face. The conversation which had resumed died down and the women looked at her questioningly.

'My soap, my soap, who's taken my soap – it's the only piece I've got.' The tone of accusation in her voice shocked them.

'Jezile,' said Nomawa, in a cool, subdued voice, 'Jezile, nobody's taken your soap; we don't steal from each other; we share things instead. We are friends who suffer together.' They all stood up and searched for the lost soap among all the piles of clothes and in the grass beside the slabs of rocks; they looked everywhere.

'It must have slipped into the water when S'naye fell in,' Jezile whimpered. She was crying silently now – a confluence of emotions: at first the shock of her child, followed so soon after by the lost soap and the mortification brought on by her accusation of friends and the recognition of the depth of the friendship they were offering her – everything – the fear of offending, if not losing, that friendship, and perhaps worst of all, the predicament of carrying that wet pile of unwashed clothes back home. She sobbed and sobbed, filled with a general sense of self-pity. Nomawa sat down beside her and again, in her gentle, subdued voice she told her:

'Now come and do your washing; there's no question of you going home with dirty clothes. I told you we all share. We will all share and if necessary we'll go home with half-done washing, and the sun will do the rest. After all, between our hands and the sun we've often done the washing when there has been no weeding at MaNgidi's, and no money anywhere.'

Jezile quietened down. She looked around at them and she tried to smile back, but could not. She nodded instead and they all went back to the rocks. They worked hard to recreate the spirit of jollity trying not to waste the day in depression. They had enough of that when they were alone in their homes facing all sorts of problems on their own. By early afternoon even Jezile had fully recovered, and she went home with a clean pile of washing, like everyone else.

For a change the dry days of spring gave way to a good wet summer. The crops grew lush and green. There were cabbages and tomatoes and for once people had enough to eat. In the autumn, the maize crop ripened and there was a lot of green maize and marrows. Even MaBiyela had a successful yield of potatoes which made for variety. They had vegetable stews and mealie bread and there was a feeling of well-being all round.

When Ndondo was about four months old, MaBiyela suggested that she be baptised. There was a reluctance in Jezile's eyes.

'Will they allow her to be baptised? Well, I mean, with Siyalo in jail, I mean; what will the minister say? I haven't seen him since Siyalo went to jail.'

'But, what's Ndondo's baptism got to do with Siyalo? Besides, there is no sin in what Siyalo did – he saved his child from death – you told me that yourself. He didn't seem to mind when you women went to jail.'

'That was different. We had committed no crime.'

'Neither has Siyalo. That child will be baptised if I say so myself. So many people go to prison; that's never stopped any child from being baptised. I hear the minister will be coming to Sigageni to administer Communion in two weeks' time.'

That Saturday Jezile dug out the beautiful frilly dress that had been bought for S'naye two years before. It was still dazzling white, more pretty than she remembered and had been well preserved in mothballs. The strong smell and its dazzling whiteness transported her back to another world, to the days of plenty that were gone. The memory stung her and her eyes filled with tears as she remembered the pride and the love that Siyalo had had and had given so freely. It had all gone. The Siyalo of the past year had been a broken man. When her eyes were dry, she took the dress outdoors and aired it. She ironed it with pride, careful not to burn it. MaBiyela joined in the spirit and gave Ndondo a chicken to celebrate the day. They cooked samp and the chicken to eat when they came back from church the next day.

The church was full to capacity as it always was on the Sundays when the minister came which was once every three months. The Ixopo circuit was wide and he could barely make the rounds in three months. In the past, he had always come the night before and stayed with Cele, the Deacon. But this time he had a car and was to arrive on the Sunday morning. This meant that the service did not have to start very early to give him enough time to get to the next village for their afternoon Communion. He could now make the distance easily in his car. The service started by half-past ten in the tin-roofed church–school building. People came from far and wide: hot, dusty and sweaty. They fanned themselves vigorously with hands and handkerchiefs. In the crowded church this was a great distraction, but it was familiar. People sang with gusto and seemed to enjoy themselves. They all seemed extra smartly turned out on this day. Most women wore their red, black and white Thursday uniforms. It gave the congregation a military look, indicating a kind of resolve in the heart of the community. Mothers sat by the door through which they frequently escaped with their children when they got too noisy. The older children sat a little distance away looking very perplexed. People prayed but, perhaps in deference to the minister, did not have their usual ululating prayer session. It was a subdued prayer that left everyone feeling slightly deprived. After the prayer the minister came forward. There were the young and old with babies in their arms. Among them was old Magasa. She had spent her younger days living 'riotously', drinking and sleeping with anybody's husband who was available. It angered some in the community that in her old age she should seek solace from the church in preparation for the next world. But Magasa did not seem to notice the resentful looks. She turned around frequently, flashing her broad, toothless smiles at all those behind her.

'What is your Christian name?' the minister asked in his most dignified voice, seeing that she was the cause of such distraction.

'I'm . . . I'm . . . I've forgotten.' Again turning for assistance from those behind she asked, 'What do they call me now? What is my Christian name?' The women stared at her like a wall of stone. She turned to the men.

'Who am I?'

Two voices boomed at once, 'You are Celestina.' The two old men turned to look at each other in accusation. But Magasa was smiling at the minister by now.

'Ah, ya, I'm Cerestina, Cerestina.'

The minister smiled, but Jezile burst out laughing. The minister turned swiftly to look at her, perhaps to silence her. He did not want anything to destroy the solemnity of the hour. But it was too late. Her laughter triggered many other outbursts and for a few moments the atmosphere of sanctity was shattered. MaBiyela, who was standing beside Jezile, was very annoyed with her and to salvage the situation she started up a hymn which the others took up with vigour. The minister

164

welcomed this, even though it prolonged the interruption. At the end of the service the minister looked accusingly at Jezile as though to mark her for the future.

The rest of the day went beautifully and Ndondo was christened Barbara Ndondo Majola. The good dinner after the service restored harmony again. The whole family were together at Jezile's. MaBiyela played with the baby, and Jezile saw that she no longer was in any doubt about Siyalo being the father.

The autumn days quickened and that cold morning and evening air was back in force. The maize in the fields dried up quickly and so did the vegetables in the garden and once more the people of Sigageni resorted to the bitter wild herbs for their food. But there was not the same despair as there had been in other years as the crop in the fields, waiting to be harvested, was promising.

It was late June. The cold drizzle of the past few days had been no ordinary drizzle high up on the mountains. It had snowed up there. The winter winds blew icily along the three-hundred-mile corridor from the Drakensberg mountains. The frost lay thick on the ground and Jezile took the brunt of it when she woke up to fetch water from the spring. Her hands and feet were numb even before she got there. The flimsy floral wrapper that she used to tie up Ndondo on her back was no match for the penetrating cold. She got home aching and numb. She longed for a cup of tea to warm herself, but there was none; so she cooked porridge instead. But maize porridge was unappetising without sugar. She could feel the depression descending on her like a menacing bird of prey. The dung fire smoked furiously and their eyes stung from its fumes. Ndondo's eyes discharged great big blobs of rheum and Jezile did not know whether it was an eye infection or the acrid smoke. Little S'naye's skin was dry and parched and her lips had deep dry cracks with traces of blood in them. But over and above these distressing signs, Jezile felt afraid. She was alone again and she feared for her children. The weather isolated people, driving them back indoors. Friends were shut out and problems grew large and menacing with no one to share them with. The end of harvesting and threshing ushered in what was to others a time of rest and beer parties, but what was a time of loneliness for single women like Jezile. She would have gone anywhere in search of company. Anything to escape her own company. The hours of darkness were long and dreary and daylight brought no relief. The sun would rise pastel yellow and coyly slant across the sky, and in what seemed half the time it would scurry across and over the mountain in the west, red but devoid of its usual vigour. Then night would swoop down indecently to cover the land.

With the children asleep, the stillness brought an invasion of inner voices from her past with Siyalo, their joys, their laughter, and worst of all the regret for those wasted days and nights when they didn't talk to each other. She swept aside the reasons for her sadness of the year before and thought only of the love and the loss, suspending all reproach. At such times she had an itch to get out and visit friends; go anywhere in search of company; anything was preferable to her confinement in the little house. Only, spending too much time at other people's thresholds was strongly disapproved of. A woman had to learn to keep her own company and keep her private feelings to herself. Mulling over the changes in her life, Jezile had to admit that her life was empty, and on a downward trend. She was frittering away her time in the fulfilment of the most basic needs; food, fire and that craving for social acceptance. She was torn between the support of her new friends, desperate women like herself, and the security of old friends that she knew when she frequented the church and the meetings. What exhilarating days those were when they fought for the land and their rights on that land. Even prison days seemed wonderful in retrospect. Her life felt splintered. She had not thought for a long time about the enduring problems of the people and she had kept her distance from old friends like Nosizwe. She felt a strong urge to change all that – draw the separate strands of her life together. She didn't like the preoccupation with the personal. She had to renew contact, if she was not to end up like Zenzile. How stiflingly house-bound she had become before her death. Before Jezile fell asleep that night she resolved that the very next day she would start going to the Thursday meetings. She would meet her old friends and piece her life together again, perhaps even draw her new friends back to the church with its spiritual comforts and protection. Yet at this last thought her mind faltered. Why was it that the church judged these young women of the community so harshly – it drove them away. But quickly she shut her mind to this last thought, for it raised doubts about her own acceptance back to that church.

There was a sudden urgency about her need for the church; the Thursday meetings in particular – the companionship that allowed each and everyone some expression. Where young daughters-in-law had as much right as mothers-in-law; a place where each tumescent heart could pour out its vial of pain. It was a place of Christian equality in the true biblical sense. And it was the only place that she knew that brought their earthly suffering face to face with mercy. She had to admit also that since she stopped attending the meetings she did not get to hear much about the struggles of Sabelweni against the government.

Thursday morning dawned dry and bright with a biting cold wind. It blew straight through the cracks around Jezile's kitchen door, filching what little warmth came off the flickering fire. She and the children huddled close to the fire and the simmering pot of water. But by midday the wind had fallen back letting the sun warm the earth. Jezile waited until Simo and Jabu were back from school. She left her two young children in the care of the girls and went off to the church meeting. The meeting had started when she walked in. Either they were having a very short meeting or they had started much earlier than usual because they were on the last hymn. Everyone turned their heads when Jezile walked in, but she bore their surprised looks with courage and cast her eyes down. She was sorry to miss the prayer for she felt she needed it. She was still shamefaced when she suddenly heard a man's voice begin to speak. A man's voice! She looked up as if to make certain she was at the right meeting. Her eyes met MaNgidi's looking down at her with a kindly smile, as if in recognition of past confidences. But other faces in the room wore masks that gave away nothing. She saw Duma the Chief Counsellor standing uncomfortably right next to Nosizwe. He dithered and coughed allowing Jezile enough time to recover and assess the whole situation. She looked round and straight back at him. Where he stood the sun glared at him; he squinted and inclined his head this way and that way, but the sun pursued him. He finally spoke in a subdued voice; not at all the voice of the most important man in the community.

'Many of you will wonder why I asked to come and talk to you at this prayer meeting. I want to thank you for letting me, for I believe that together we can achieve a great deal. At such times co-operation between us is very important. I am a member of this community and have served it as a counsellor for many years. Together we have shared a lot. A little while ago we suffered the loss of our beloved leader, Chief Siyoka, when he was so ruthlessly taken away from us. I am not in a position to tell you what his absence means to me. But I believe you should understand what I feel and how difficult my position sometimes is. MaNgidi here suffers with me and is one of you. That is why at certain times it is not easy to know which way one's loyalties fall.'

The women looked at each other and fidgeted. There was a slight tension in the air. He noticed it and coughed slightly before he continued. Some of you will have received your letters about the culling of your stock, and many of you are resisting. Those of you who attended the meeting at Nondaba which was called by Chief Siyapi will remember how everyone resisted the question of dividing the land into fenced-in allotments. You all know I know that lately some of you have cut down the newly erected fences along the river's edge. Living here among you I know who are involved in this. And my superiors know that I know the people who are engaged in this practice. And if I will not tell who they are I take the blame. That is what I mean by split loyalties. I understand that you, the people of Sigageni, have requested the Chief for another meeting. I personally am very interested to know what further discussion you want with him after you have resisted every change that has so far been suggested. In a situation like this it is important that we have some kind of co-operation. It is embarrassing for me that I should not know what you want, and what you are planning, especially because it is well known that out of the whole of Sabelweni, you are the ringleaders; your influence is felt throughout the district. It puts me in a very bad light that I don't know your views, and that you discuss nothing with me.

'I've come to your meeting to ask you to share your views and I shall give you the benefit of my knowledge from the

168

inside. Chief Siyapi will attend that meeting in person, and we shall go into all these matters there. But I want to warn you, I can only do my best for you if I know what you want and what your plans are. Above everything else, I want to warn you that a time has come when we must be realistic and accept that the government means business. Resisting these changes is taking us nowhere . . .'

Before he could finish there was a sudden hubbub and his voice was drowned in the clamour that rose from the floor. Nosizwe had quite a time trying to silence the women. He could hear the many varied questions they were asking him.

'Is that what they've sent you to come and tell us, to soften us? Whose side are you on? Why don't you say openly that you are no longer on our side? When did you realise that our efforts are in vain?' Duma stood there quite shocked. He had never seen the women in such a mood before. When order was finally restored Nosizwe asked him to finish off what he had to say, and if, as one of them, he had any plan or strategy to suggest for the forthcoming meeting, and could tell them what the meeting was about. She turned to the group and warned them that if they were prepared to face up to the government they had to do better; they had to keep their calm, and above all remember not to split the people of Sigageni into 'them' and 'us'. If Chief Counsellor Duma came to consult with the women, that was wisdom which they had a right to refuse or accept, but not rudely, as though they had lost all control. And above everything, they had to remember this was God's house. The women sat down not looking chastened at all, just obedient to Nosizwe. She saw the anger rippling underneath and she added that they did not need to court prison this time. She then started a hymn, 'Sikuyo Indlela Yelizwe Lobomi – we're on the road of life'. The words struck home and the tune was catchy and soothing.

The women sat down and turned to listen, but Duma could not regain his stride. If it had been hard for him to start, it seemed impossible for him to continue. Jezile caught him looking towards his wife who had her index finger firmly planted down the middle of her mouth and her eyes down. With one quick turn to the right, away from the tormenting ray of the sun, he held his head high and thanked Nosizwe for the privilege she had afforded him, but he now thought it best to withhold the details of the meeting. The women were taken aback and Jezile could sense their anger surfacing again. Even Nosizwe began to look ruffled, but she did not know how to handle the situation. She let him go, and all he said as he reached the door was that the meeting would be at Nondaba at Chief Siyapi's nkundleni, the meeting place, in two weeks' time. The women clamoured after him angrily and they would have gone without another prayer if Nosizwe had not called them to order once more.

On the way home Jezile gathered from the many conversations that went on all at once just how angry people were with Chief Siyapi. Also, they were beginning to see through Counsellor Duma's double-dealing with the government, and were losing all loyalty and respect for him. At an earlier meeting that Siyapi had called the people had left him in no doubt about their determination to resist all aspects of the scheme, including the imposition of the exorbitant taxes. And he, being anxious to demonstrate his authority to both his masters and his subjects, had retaliated by threatening to refuse them the right to plough their arable allotments the following spring. This had been a frontal attack on the community's rights. And with the support of the South African government, Siyapi could do anything. But the people were not going to let it happen that easily.

Men who were able to leave the cities at short notice were called back to augment the numbers in the defence of their land and their rights. They came back in ever-growing numbers to stand side by side with the rest of the community who had for so long maintained a stand against the assaults on their families. Throughout the ploughing season the spans were accompanied by a contingent of armed men. Siyapi proved powerless to carry out his threat and stop the community from tilling their lands. At this point some members of the community requested Chief Siyapi for another meeting hoping to resolve the stalemate. But, mistaking this for a softening of attitude on the part of the community, he became arrogant and would not grant the people's request. There followed a long period of silence when nothing happened on either side. Some men went back to the cities, believing the trouble had abated. But this was not the end of the story. After a long time of bickering Siyapi finally acceded to their request. At the meeting that followed, with a false sense of triumph, he was haughty and uncompromising in his attitude. They then asked him if he was their chief or the government's stooge. The wrangling reached a crescendo, and it ended in disorder amidst widespread cries of 'Umazipate uyosebenza sifile' (Bantu Authorities will work over our dead bodies). One man called Ntonga, to show his disdain, turned round and exposed his bare backside to Siyapi, which was the ultimate insult. The rest of the people then booed the chief and his officials down.

In response to this episode a large contingent of police and the paramilitary entered the area in an attempt to intimidate the community. They arrived in their hundreds, driving those elephantine tanks slowly over the broken landscape. They descended in helicopters in thunderous clamour like birds of prey. It was enough to scare the rural community. The children quaked and the adults would have done so as well had there been time to stop and ponder the invasion. But there was none. It was then that Ntonga took a number of men with him and led them to the neighbouring hills. This was to be the core of an alternative authority to by-pass Siyapi and deal directly with the people and their problems. In the heat of these events, the Minister of Bantu Administration and Development, Mr de Wet Nel, along with Chief Siyapi came to Sigageni to sell the same policy that the people had long rejected. Without Ntonga and his core of men, they must have thought, they would get round the people and convince them. Once more they failed to appreciate the depth of feeling among the people of Sabelweni. The authorities focused their attention on Ntonga and his men, hoping that the troubles would die down and the people would comply with their wishes once they were left without leadership. At the meeting they regurgitated the same old vain promises about the changing status of the local courts and how they were going to make positive changes in the whole system of justice as it operated in the rural areas. Once the minister and his men left the area, the people were so disgruntled that they pressed Siyapi for another meeting without the minister. This was to try and bring him to his senses, for some believed that even he could see that the whole scheme would only bring destruction to their whole way of life, jeopardising his position of chief as well. No matter how elevated chiefs were, they still had to live in their own communities and sink or swim with them. After much persuasion Siyapi agreed to meet the people of Sabelweni.

So, early one clear morning, the people gathered at the meeting place to negotiate with Siyapi. They came from far and wide, men and women of all ages, many with young children on their backs. This was to be like no other meeting in the recent past. It had been agreed that everything would be calm and reasoned, reminiscent of the orderly traditional meetings which were always marked by consensus. Everyone looked forward to this meeting where they believed issues would be discussed point by point. The people waited as the sun rose higher and the cool morning air became parched and hot. Out of habit the women sat around on the periphery of the great gathering. Now and again, they passed drinks and mealie bread around. The men, out of habit, passed the beer pot around. The sun rose higher and higher and the heat grew intense; the people grew restless but they waited. The air grew still; only the heat waves shimmered blindingly for miles around. The crowd fell silent, speaking only in monotones. After what seemed an eternity, the sun rode past, and took a decided turn towards the west and slowly the people were roused from their stupor. There was still no sign of Siyapi and his men. The people of Sigageni looked out especially for Duma and he was not there. There was not a helicopter, nor a tank, nor a policeman in sight. This was evidently a conspiracy of silence on the part of the authorities intended to undermine the spirit of resistance by ignoring the masses of people. The realisation hit them all at once; not only was Siyapi not going to attend the meeting, but he had gone and reported this 'private' meeting to the authorities. Without declaring the meeting opened or closed, some men's voices in the heart of the gathering began to rise above the good-natured conversation in the crowd. There was an altercation. Some were for going up to the house on the incline and dragging Siyapi to the meeting place. Others contended that it was best to give up Siyapi for good as part of the solution to their problems. But before any decision could be reached the crowd surged forward, the common will initiating its own action. They rose up as one person, too tired of waiting in the hot sun and too tired of authority that cared so little for their suffering and their pleas. Siyapi had somehow escaped that suffering and the multitude of fears that stalked their lives. Having chosen a life across the power barrier he had never cowed in fear. And like all those who abuse power, he had learned to despise his victims, his neighbours. They moved fast towards the house. No one had a clear idea why they had to go to Siyapi's house; nothing had been discussed fully; each one knew one thing – that they had to vent their feelings each in their own way, and Siyapi had to know it once and for all. Against the glowing sunset, they set their eyes on the blinding light that reflected from the windows of the large house on the hill. As they surged up the incline, Siyapi's entire family and gaggle of servants came out to see advancing up the slope a heaving, rising human tide. As they came closer, Siyapi himself rushed out as if to stop the tide. But when he heard their fury that threatened to engulf him and all that he owned, he turned tail. With his braces hanging loosely and flapping at his sides and his snow-white vest suddenly wet with sweat, he raced back to the great house, gesturing frantically with his arms for his children and grandchildren to go into the big house, his fortress. Within minutes that house and all the surrounding barns had been set alight, and angry flames licked the sky. They killed the chickens that were drifting to their coop and the pigs in their sty and the calves that were tethered on the green grass behind the great house. The rage of the community could be seen from afar, billowing against the setting sun. The spirals of smoke and leaping flames pulsated against the darkening sky. The shrieks from within were soon mingled with the baying chorus from without.

'Down with Siyapi, down with the traitor, down with the white man's stooge!'

The pungent smell of the burning flesh of dogs and cats and people inside told the story of anguish and death within. It drifted across the valley and beyond. As the sacrilegious glow rose the people stood facing the spectacle – a ring of guileless faces as though they could not comprehend the disaster. Their voices died down as they watched with feverish curiosity. Then one by one they straggled along into the darkness like tired pilgrims leaving the skeleton of the house bathed in a red hot glow, looking like a temple of some unknown god.

After the evening's orgy the people from Sigageni, like the rest of the crowd, walked away wearily in groups feeling neither joy nor sorrow, but a fatal acceptance of what had to be. That night God had been rejected once and for all. And later that night Jezile's group came upon another flaming, crumbling temple – one that they themselves had helped to build. They could not tell who exactly had done it, but they knew it was one of their own number. Duma's house burnt so furiously as though they had built it out of tinder and petrol, instead of mud and bricks and water. The flames leapt and blazed and lit up their faces like a thousand searchlights. They all stood compelled, straining to hear the voices they knew so well from that furnace. But all had been silenced in the crackling flames. Jezile could not reconcile the image of MaNgidi in her uniform on Thursday afternoons with her horrible death. She shut her eyes tight in an effort to banish the thought of God standing there watching. She had lit no fire herself. God knew that. But she felt dirty; God, how to get clean, how to clean the world, how to clean Sabelweni again? How to get rid of the government that poisoned the leaders, and now their people – was there nothing that was not tainted by the evil policies of the government?

The next day dawned clear and bright like the many days before it. People rose and stole out of their houses, looked at the rising sun, and furtively turned their heads to the hillside, as if to establish the reality of the previous day's events. There was a charred gaping space where the brick house had stood. Having seen the proof, the people averted their eyes, afraid of being caught staring at the scene of their crime, their guilt vying with their fear. But this was no time for remorse for even as they looked away the army moved in. Alarmed by the uproar of the approaching convoy of army tanks, helicopters and soldiers on foot aiming their bayonets at no one in particular, the people ran in and out of their houses like disturbed ants. The soldiers went up the hill and inspected the devastation. With something akin to respect for the dead, the police took out the bodies and laid them in a row on the hillside. They waited for the community to come and bury their dead as was the custom. No one came up to pay their respects or even to dig the graves. On a hot day like that, they ran the risk of putrefaction. The police waited anxiously and nothing happened.

Towards sunset, strange contraptions that had not been seen in Sigageni before came lumbering clumsily and headed straight for the cemetery. Within a short time a big digging machine had dug a big communal grave. The white people were burying 'their own'. They shovelled them into their grave with a great roaring scoop, people and animals together. That was the end of Siyapi. The same scene was repeated at Sigageni when his Chief Counsellor Duma and his wife MaNgidi were buried. This marked a turning point in the warring at Sabelweni. The whole area, covering many villages, was swarming with police and more soldiers. They patrolled day and night, flashing search-lights through the hours of darkness. All meetings were declared illegal. Large numbers of men were taken to prison summarily, and every member of the community, young and old was under suspicion. The authorities were on the war-path. The same police who had been brought in to stamp out crime began to commit atrocities against the community. Perhaps it was a form of intimidation or retaliation, no one could say. Whenever individuals were found in isolated areas they were bound to suffer some attack of one form or another. Women were particularly vulnerable. Their only safety lay in numbers, so that a lot of work was done in large groups. People spent nights in each other's houses for they were often raided in their sleep on the pretext of some search or other. Sometimes it was for weapons, at others for fugitives; on occasion the soldiers would demand food to eat or would impound any tools they found – even ploughing implements – claiming they were weapons. Many who had escaped the police dragnet retreated to the mountain hideout to join Ntonga's Mountain Committee. The villages were left denuded of men, and fear stalked the whole area. But in spite of everything, women still took food, without fail, to them. They showed great ingenuity and courage in the face of the enemy who were on surveillance day and night.

Soon the Mountain Committee set about creating their own administration in order to sever completely their connection with the whole white administration. They set up a popular justice system to herald in a more democratic way of life. To start with they called for the nonpayment of taxes to the chiefs. These were the rudiments of self-rule which were accompanied by in-depth discussions of the many strategies they were going to implement in their fight to overthrow white rule in their area. In a neighbouring district, where things had not progressed to the same extent as at Sabelweni, the people erected modern offices and conducted cases on the pattern of a magistrate's court. The courts had officers, docks, good recording systems of the proceedings and proper filing systems. But it wasn't long before they found out they were being infiltrated by government agents. Not all the people who came to 'join' the Mountain Committee were honest members of the community. It was disconcerting for the Committee to find that for every step they took the government was one step ahead. There were those among them who had no difficulty in deciding what should be done with the sell-outs. There was only one solution – the way of Siyapi. But others had qualms, arguing that killing one another could only benefit the enemy. There was only one enemy and that was the white government. All the others were victims of that government, even the 'sell-outs'. Besides, what sort of society were they fighting to create, if political problems could only be solved by killing those who held different views? What sort of future were they creating, where brother killed brother and children were taught through practical experience that murder was a solution? Such murders were no solution at all. They debated for hours wasting valuable time with their disagreements threatening to cause a split. It was while things were in this state of flux that something happened which resolved the question by default.

One morning, while the people were locked in discussion, they noticed two aircraft and a helicopter flying very low. Before they could scamper away, the aircraft began to drop tear-gas and smoke bombs. Trapped among the cliffs with no easy escape, the men raised a white flag to show that they were not armed. But just then, there emerged from behind a kopje, a group of armed police from behind the rocks who immediately fired at the gathering. They killed eleven people on the spot and a large number were arrested. The authorities had avenged their dead most effectively. Those who went down to the valley below to report the deaths called everyone to the church house. They rang the death knell which sent a chill throughout the area. The first tolling of the bells called out a few children who were instructed to tell everybody to assemble in the church house as soon as they could. The bells rang for almost an hour. By the time they stopped, there was a large gathering inside the church house where the news of the attack and the death of so many men was given. Silence descended like an omen. No one stirred or blinked. But more remarkably, no one uttered a cry. The men who brought the news looked at the women in astonishment. Falteringly they went on to say that obviously they would have to go up the mountain and bring the dead home. In the stunned silence that followed some women suggested that a collection be made so that they could buy wood for make-shift coffins. The men stood perplexed, watching the women take the initiative. In the next few hours, a group of women were seen entering the timber-yard in the dorp of Sibaya. The first three came out in a line balancing the wood on their heads and headed for the mountain. They were well away before they realised that some of the other women were still inside the timber-yard. They did not know that a new problem had arisen as they left the yard.

The people of Sabelweni should have known that things could not remain the same between them and the white community in the dorp and on the surrounding farms. That relationship had always been subject to the African people's taciturn acceptance of their subjugation, whether they acknowledged it or not. But for the Africans that dorp and those farms were part of the landscape, like hills and valleys and streams. Struggles break out everywhere in the world, but people never dream that they would alter the landscape. Somehow, in the minds of the Africans the white people in the dorp were not quite the same as the impersonal government officials out there, or the invading army who came to violate their existence. The local whites were traders; they sold merchandise to the people of Sabelweni and bought sheep and goats and cattle from them when they needed money. The Africans worked for them in their shops and in their houses and on their farms. They needed each other as each hand is useless without the other. But the people should have known that their revolt against white authority was an indirect declaration of hostilities against their neighbours. What the people of Sabelweni did not know was that in response to the uprising the local white population had formed themselves into the Civic Association through which they now acted. They did not know that their white neighbours had met and discussed them and passed resolutions against them. They did not know that they were buying guns and arming themselves against them, when they had no weapons but sticks and stones.

That day, when the white trader realised that the wood was being bought to make coffins for the dead men up on the mountain he flatly refused to sell any more wood to the women. At first he gave no reason for his refusal. But soon it became clear that he was on the side of the government, the police, and the army. The women shouted at him, questioning his loyalty to his neighbours and customers, the African community, the source of his livelihood and that of the whole white dorp. But he remained deaf to their arguments. Even when they threatened to boycott the shops and to withdraw their labour he did not take them seriously. But when he saw them turn all at once he calmed down and began to shift the blame on to others of his community who supported the government at whatever cost. In great anger the women left and headed for piles of wooden poles that had been stocked by Siyapi and the authorities for fences and enclosures. They loaded the poles on their heads and carried them up into the hills where they hacked them into crude coffins.

At sunrise, on the day after the funeral, the people of Sabelweni came out in a large demonstration against the white dorp. They had already confirmed that they were going to boycott the shops and abandon all jobs in the dorp. There were two thousand people from all the neighbouring villages on that silent march. Some women wore long black dresses. Others wore long skirts and black scarves. They carried a big black flag with no inscription of any kind. They walked silently for five miles into the town and the spectacle made a chilling sight. The white community watched fearfully through their windows and some came out cocking their guns. Others wished that the procession would voice their sorrow and their anger in some way, some gesture or song or disorder of some kind. In all their experience they had never associated 'their' blacks with such organisation. They had never attended any of their meetings where many could have learned basic lessons in consensus decision-making. The march ended in front of the timber-yard where they stood silently for about five minutes before they turned around to head for their village.

Later that night the timber-yard mysteriously went up in flames. The flames billowed and crackled and people at Nda-wonde and Luve and Sigageni and the surrounding villages watched the night sky glowing red in the darkness. No one saw the fire start despite the vigilance of the members of the Civic Association.

In retaliation, the authorities served a banning order on Mr Rubotsane, the lawyer who had been briefed to defend the members of the Mountain Committee who was effectively confined to the Durban Magisterial District. He could not therefore travel to Sabelweni eighty miles away. By this action the authorities successfully prevented him from appearing in court on behalf of his clients. There followed a period of bitter suffering for the people of Sabelweni. The place was virtually under siege. Villages would be encircled and searched hut by hut to ferret out those who were suspected of infringing the regulations. Often people were physically attacked. The auth-orities would carry out raids to confiscate everything that remotely resembled a weapon. This often occurred in the middle of the night; they would wake the sleeping villagers, turning everything upside down, spilling their food and often interfering with the women, and even raping them at times. All kinds of atrocities were committed in order to intimidate the people and to crush all manifestations of resistance. The army carried out a lot of what were in fact police duties such as collecting taxes, confiscating stock in lieu of cash and enforcing communal fines to pay for some of the damages that had occurred in the upheavals.

At the height of the struggle when the police and the army attacked people at random with tear-gas, smoke bombs and guns Jezile managed to send a message to Nosizwe to come over with help. It was difficult, but Nosizwe wasted no time. In a dark hideout, half-way up the rocky hillside there was a recess, nature's own cavern, that was known only to the local people. Nosizwe came in broad daylight with two women who were trained but unemployed nurses. Trained nurses often found it difficult to get employment after they were married – one of those odd practices in these rural parts where there was always so much medical need, but not the imagination to use the skills of those who had them for the benefit of their communities. However, this time Nosizwe brought those skills to use. Daylight hours were relatively safe, especially for women. It was hard even for the occupying army to stop every woman from their far-flung daily chores of fetching water, collecting wood and other innumerable jobs. Nosizwe and her team came in the garb of ordinary local women. They came on foot, carrying their medical kits in embroidered pillow cases, balanced on their heads like any other woman's shopping. They clawed their way up the steep hillside and disappeared into its entrails. Even before they reached the hideout they were assailed by a strong smell of festering wounds and the loud moans of people in agony. Some had lain there for more than a week with their gaping wounds. It was war as Nosizwe had never seen it before. Many would have died if Nosizwe had not spent the whole day and night with her team operating and dressing the wounds, teaching Jezile's group as she did so some simple first-aid measures. She left them a few illustrated medical pamphlets and some supplies. These would keep the women going until her next visit; they did not know when that would be. Nosizwe's presence that day revived their spirit of hope, and new ideas about how to get the injured out of that hole were devised.

To the casual observer the women of Sabelweni were at home looking after their children and their livestock. But beneath the surface, within the community, they formed a network of messengers relaying messages from one group to another. And whenever the police or soldiers came round, the women gave warning cries as signals to others in hiding. Throughout this time they dressed entirely in black to show that their area was in mourning – even those who normally wore their traditional 'red blankets'. Day by day their food supplies diminished but they remained undeterred and defiant.

12

*I*t was on one of those mornings when Jezile had just returned from the hideout and she was depressed that she heard Nomawa shouting from outside her house.

'Are you there, Jezile are you there?' She pushed the top half of the door open. 'I was passing and I thought I'd come in to share your tea and your warmth. Why do you always shut yourself indoors? I never do; I dread that house in these terrible times.' Nomawa opened the lower half of the door and saw immediately the fear in Jezile's wide unblinking eyes.

'What's the matter?' she asked, fearing the worst from the soldiers and the police. But Jezile shook her head slowly and continued to stare. It didn't take long for Nomawa to guess the cause of Jezile's fear. Jezile had no food for herself and the children. She knew the look well. Nomawa sat herself down in front of the fire, and they exchanged a few pleasantries. They could have gone on in this manner for a little longer, but Nomawa broke off suddenly.

'Jezile, why don't you ever come and ask for anything? Don't you ever need anything from anyone? I'm always asking my neighbours for tea, sugar, salt and things like that. Pride won't do you any good. We all ask of one another. Sometimes I ask even when I've got a little left, just so that my neighbours feel at ease to ask me when they need help. Our mothers made it easy for us to share, for they found out it was the only way to cope.'

'And if you need anything and everything, Nomawa, do you ask your neighbours for everything?'

'Yes, for everything Jezile; if people die of hunger among neighbours, that's the death of our community. In sharing we defend each other against the extremes of need. We owe each other that. And we in turn should make it easy for our neighbours to share what they have. We ask for what we need, and we show no sense of shame for that. That's what neighbours are there for.'

'What if you're always afraid, Nomawa – afraid of loneliness, afraid of the police, of murder, of neighbours killing neighbours, of white people's hate and all those things? I'm always afraid.'

'Again, you get out and share your fears with your neighbours; together, sharing our fears we're not so afraid. The police and the soldiers are more afraid of us when we're together, but when we're alone they pick on us. Share your fears, that's what friends are there for.'

'Well, then, now that you're here I'm no longer afraid, and I need sugar, tea, salt, soap and some meat for the children. They haven't had meat or beans for weeks.'

'I'm not joking, Jezile. I mean it when I say you must learn to ask for the things you need. I'll give you a little of some of the things you need. Ndeya will bring them to you later. But I've no meat my friend. To get meat you've got to be earning.' They both laughed. Nomawa could see the softening in Jezile's eyes.

'But where do you get these things from, Nomawa? I mean, you don't go anywhere to earn money, I don't earn any money either, but somehow you have a little of everything, and I have nothing. I can't understand it.'

'Don't ask . . . once I told you about the man from S'tobeleni. Well, he's working, isn't he? If women can't go and work in the cities it stands to reason that they've got to depend on some man that can. So when this man sends money to his wife he sends me a little too. He can't just get what he wants from me and give nothing in appreciation when he's in Johannesburg. He knows I've no husband. I'm not asking for a lot; just a little. I know he's got his wife and children to look after, and I don't expect him to look after Timba's children. Timba who can't be bothered about his own . . . I know, I know. I don't want to cause his wife any pain; I don't want her to know. I wouldn't wish any of my own pain on any woman I know. I'll never forget my own humiliation at the hands of that woman in Durban. She kicked me, Jezile, in front of all those people and called me names I'd never repeat. That's the day I gave up on him – for him to see me at his door being abused, kicked and punched and not to say a word. Not to even acknowledge that he knew me. That was the last straw. No. If it was possible I'd stay away from men. All I want from this man is a little fun on the side and a little money to keep me alive.'

Jezile laughed cheerfully without reserve.

'I can never not laugh at this story Nomawa, each time you tell it. It's a terrible story, but it's the way you tell it. Somehow you have come out stronger. Look at you, even now you're laughing at yourself. I've got to learn to laugh at myself . . . But I can't see myself having another man. It's always been Siyalo; I've never known another man.'

'Well, for you it's different. You're still married to Siyalo; he's never betrayed you and it's early days. No man with any decency would ask you for anything so soon after Siyalo's imprisonment. Maybe after some years. So far it's as if he was in Durban, as he always used to be. Besides, there are few men around these days. Times are bad, Jezile, times are bad. There's so much fear and trouble, people can't think of women and sex; neither can we really.'

As if to wipe away the thought, Nomawa quickly changed the subject. 'Look Jezile, did you know that there are road-works on the main road to Umzimkulu? I saw them yesterday.'

'Why, I went past there the other day, I didn't see them.'

'I believe they were only arriving because they were busy fixing those elephantine corrugated tents. You know the kind they had when they were here two years ago. I suspect they're going to be there for a long time. If that's the case there's got be some work going there.'

'What d'you mean "work"? Of course they've come here to work.'

'No, I mean there's bound to be work for us. Such isolated men on the road are bound to need something.' Jezile looked at her questioningly. 'Beer for one thing. They might even need good home-cooking especially at weekends.'

'It depends how far they've come.'

'Their white boss might also need a washer-woman if he's a long way from home. Let's go now and find out before the others get there ahead of us.'

'What? In these times who dares trust anybody? How d'you

know they're road menders, for a start? They could very well be soldiers in disguise for all we know, moving in here for good.'

'Oh no, they are road menders all right; I saw their gear; it's African labourers and one white man. Well, I can only say that things are easing a little here in Sabelweni; the authorities would not let them come anywhere near this place if things weren't changing for the better.'

'Not necessarily, Nomawa. This is a main road. It starts way out in the Cape and it goes all the way through Natal, up to Johannesburg and Pretoria. It must be kept in good order regardless of our problems here in Sabelweni.' But as she spoke thoughts were flashing through her mind; thoughts about Siyalo when he berated her for daring to think of brewing liquor and selling it. She was quiet for a moment, but dismissed them as fast as they had come.

'And the children? What do I do with the children?'

'What d'you mean?'

'I mean, if I should find some work with the road menders.'

'Maye, maye. Take them to MaBiyela, of course. They're hers, too. There's Simo and Jabu – they'll look after them; you're not their sole minder. You, you'll have to do better than this if you're going to take good care of these children. Stop dithering about every detail.'

'No, I'm not dithering, Nomawa. I'm making sure that every detail is taken good care of. I can't afford to slip up; I'm now the sole breadwinner – if I should find the bread. Jezile bit her lower lip hard to stop herself from saying it out aloud. Finally she blurted out: 'Right.'

Within a short time the two women were out on the main road. On the way Nomawa was busy coaching Jezile on how they were to behave with the men.

'Remember their wives are far away; they're looking for any stray woman. Make it clear you're not that stray woman. But of course that doesn't mean you stand there aloof like the Virgin Mary. You don't look wary. You allow a touch here and a touch there; but nothing more, Jezile. Be careful, it's harder to retreat once you've allowed men to go too far. Keep them talking. They can talk as much as they like, but keep it there – words, words, and more words; you laugh and tease them and keep it there.'

'It sounds tricky. I've never been good at this sort of thing.'

'Neither were we, Jezile. We've learned through hard experience. If you consider that I was only seventeen when I married Timba and he left me when Bonani was only a baby. She's ten now. Times are hard, we've got to live. Our children have got to live, hard times or not. Now here we are.' She lowered her voice as they got near the tents.

There was a fire burning outside the tents and the men looked chilled to the bone. At first they seemed not to notice the two women. But when they saw them heading for the prefabs they stopped and straightened up. One or two managed to make half-hearted wolf-whistles. The two women were just as cold. They went straight to the fire, and soon all the men were standing, warming themselves around that fire. They made tea from old teabags. If it had not been wet and hot, it would have tasted foul even to Jezile who had not had tea for two days. They talked and talked and became bolder by the minute. Jezile left the talking to Nomawa. The men agreed that whenever they needed something to be done, they would give it to no one else but the two women. It was nothing binding, but it was a working agreement.

As they were leaving they saw the white boss stretching himself outside his prefab looking at the women with interest. He looked as though he was just getting up. His idea of work!

'Where do you get women so early?' they heard him asking his men as they receded.

'They're looking for work, Bass.'

'I need a washer-woman myself; did you tell them?'

'No, you didn't say, Bass. Hey, hey, come back.' The two women went back. That is how Jezile came to brew beer for the squad and wash a few items a week for the white man.

By mid-morning, the sun had warmed up appreciably. The two women did not go straight home; they went to Sibaya to buy everything they needed for brewing and some soap. Jezile borrowed the money from Nomawa. A few days later, the two women went to the road-works balancing tins of frothing beer on their heads. The tins had wobbled and splashed beer on their newly washed clothes. Jezile hated the smell of beer on her but there was little choice. She needed the money. And before very long her children grew healthy, and plump and her anxiety about money grew less. She had relaxed a great deal with the men at the campsite which had become a hive of activity with several other women hanging about for no specific reason that Jezile could see.

As the weeks turned into months there was something Jezile could not ignore entirely – something in the white man's eyes that looked at her every time she went in to collect his washing on Friday mornings and when she returned it on Tuesday evenings. She tried every ploy she could think of to put him off. She stood outside his tent in the open to make the exchange of money for clothes. But he invariably found a reason to call her back into his tent – a lost sock, a torn sock, a loose button, anything, real or imagined. Sometimes she talked and laughed loudly with the workmen when she was meant to be talking and handing over his clothes to him. Anything to put him off. She flinched from his red face and the paper dry skin of his arms. The sun dealt harshly with his skin, even though he did no work at all in the sun. His main job was to stand or sit under an umbrella all day, making sure the workers did their job. That's what he got paid for, several times the money that the men who pitched themselves against the rocks like machines got. But that's where the comparison ended. The workmen sang and worked in unison, building and mending the network of roads all over the country. Jezile could identify with these men who earned the little they were given through honest hard work. She herself was a hard worker. As in everything she sought perfection in her work.

On a few occasions when the white man did not feel like going to the hotel at Umzimkulu for supper he requested Jezile to cook some food and bring it to him on the road. He approved of her home-cooking. And the washing she did for him could not be faulted. The men had commented on it. Some began to give her their own washing to do. So she was kept very busy and had few distracting thoughts. MaBiyela may not have been happy initially, but she could not ignore the advantages. There was enough food for everybody. Jezile was generous enough to share everything with her mother-in-law and to pay her a little in money as well for taking care of the children, even though she could not say the money given was payment for such services.

Wherever MaBiyela went she took the two children; one on her back, the other trailing behind. She talked endlessly to them, telling them a lot they did not understand. She relived the days of her own motherhood, and she loved it. The days of privation were over and this restored her confidence and standing in the community. To boost her morale further, there were no unsavoury reports about Jezile's behaviour with the men at the road-works. And so the days of winter and spring went by, free from apprehension. And the two women were thrown together again as they had never been before. Jezile had spent all her nights at MaBiyela's ever since the soldiers had invaded Sabelweni.

It was in the height of summer, six months after the road-works squad had first pitched their tents, when they told the women they were moving on at the end of the week. It was bad news for all the families concerned. Jezile took it very badly, and so did MaBiyela herself. They knew destitution and they dreaded it. That week they suffered deep depression about the future. On the last Friday, when she went to pick up the white man's last batch of washing, he stopped to talk to her. This time his eyes did not have the shifty look she hated in him. He talked to her directly and she stopped to listen. He told her he was sorry because she had done her work for him so honestly and so well. Then he put a proposition to her. Would she consider going to work for his family in Bloemfontein? It was a long way away, but with the efficient public transport system, no place was too far these days. It was a one day's train journey. He and his wife had six young children and for some time they had not had anybody reliable to help with the household chores. He was always away from home and he wanted to know that his wife could cope in his absence. He told her that his wife was a good woman. She had lived with Africans in the platteland. She knew 'girls' like Jezile well. In the six months that Jezile had worked for him she had proved that she was reliable, and just the kind of woman his wife needed for a servant. At first Jezile dismissed the idea outright. It was simply impossible. It was too far and she had very young children. And she had never worked for white people before. He told her clearly that she would have to leave the children with her mother-in-law. That was completely unthinkable, she told him.

But he told her to go along and think about it and tell him her answer when she brought the washing back the following Tuesday.

By the time she went round to the squad she was agitated and not herself at all. She had lost her cheerfulness altogether. When she was with Nomawa later that day she could not bring herself to tell her about the white man's proposition. (His name was Potgieter, Mr Potgieter he had told her.) All the while she had done his washing, it had not occurred to her to find out what his name was. But their short conversation had changed all that. He had materialised as a man with a name, and a wife and concerns that made him human. She knew then that her mind was not as made up as she thought it was. In fact she was very undecided. She thought Nomawa would laugh aloud and say the very idea was preposterous. Preposterous? Was it? That meant she wanted to go. She spent the whole afternoon rubbing the hard khakhi drill trousers furiously and tossing her indecision about. By the evening she thought she was falling ill, with a fever perhaps. She had not meant to tell MaBiyela anything. But somehow that night, without any forethought, she found she had blurted it out to her. MaBiyela was quiet for a long time. When she raised her head, she looked out through the window and with a voice that seemed to come from afar she said, 'You recall once I told you that you had a responsibility to raise these children. Well, responsibility, MaMapanga, takes you through many unforeseen byways. There is no virtue in staying with us here to preserve our way of life and reputation and to lose these children through starvation. That makes no sense to me. Many decent women nowadays are forced to do just this; leave their children to work in the cities. It is a pity that Bloemfontein is so far from us. But what does it matter where you are, as long as your children are not starving. Moreover, the man says it's barely a day away by train. I think you should tell the white man that you will go and work for his family. I shall accept the responsibility for that. I hope you can trust me this time to do everything I can to look after these children. These children are mine, MaMapanga. Given money, I can look after them as well as you can; just as I looked after and brought up Siyalo. I love them. Go to the city and we shall all survive.'

'If I am going it will be as early as next week because he will take me with him when he goes away. He is having a short break before he starts another job.'

There was no time to tell any of her friends; not even the Women's Union that met on Thursdays. She wrote them a letter to be read when she was gone, asking to be kept in their thoughts and in their prayers. She wrote another letter to inform her own mother. She promised to send MaBiyela money regularly and asked her to write often. It was a very distressing time of parting made worse by the suddenness of it. That last evening the two women cried bitterly and the young children, Jabu and Simo joined in as well. The next day Gaba and Nomawa took her to the Cromwell bus station from which they gave her a tearful send-off.

There was nothing memorable about the first lap of the journey to Pietermaritzburg from where she was to take the train to Bloemfontein that night. She cried all the way. She made no effort to chide herself, but gave in to the need. She was tired of being told to be strong. Strong while she was buffeted! She wallowed in self-pity for everything she had suffered in the twenty-seven years of her life, especially the last seven. Life was hard and bitter. When it did offer anything it tantalised and thwarted in every way possible. She saw her life speeding past the window of her mind as she watched the receding landscape. She did not touch the provisions in her bag. She was not hungry. Later that evening she waited for hours on end, hanging about the Pietermaritzburg station waiting-room for a train that would only arrive later that night from Durban. Only then did it dawn on her that the journey to Bloemfontein might be one day by train to Pietermaritzburg, but it was two days to Umzimkulu. And for a while she was agitated by this; it was as though Bloemfontein had actually moved further than it had been when she agreed to go.

Mr Potgieter came twice to check if she was all right in the African women's waiting-room. He looked shabby compared to the city whites. He was tall and imposing, but ungainly. In fact, his smile betrayed a lack of confidence, not the same masterful stride that paced up and down the road to Umzimkulu. He smiled at Jezile as though she was an old friend for whom he could not spare much time – a quick warm smile, soon wiped off as he avoided being seen to be friendly. He had been to some pub or restaurant and had brought her back a crumpled packet of sandwiches. She stuffed them in her bag together with everything she had not eaten that day. She felt spent inside and she wished for a hot drink, but she could not be bothered to go and look for a place that would serve Africans. So she drank cold water from the tap, and she waited.

At about ten o'clock, the train arrived. Just before she boarded the train Mr Potgieter rushed back to give her the ticket. She had expected a third-class ticket, but there was no third-class compartment on this long-distance train. This cheered her up for she knew she could sleep comfortably in a second-class compartment. Her travelling companions were a strange assortment of women; two bright-eyed young women who seemed to have no care in the world but their looks. Their faces were well powdered, their eyes made up and their nails well manicured and painted. They even had red lips. Their skins were so soft as though they had never walked in the sun. Nearest the women sat a large middle-aged woman who held her walking stick as though she was ready to walk out. She looked confident and assured, with no qualms about such train journeys; as though she had taken them all her life. She seemed to identify with the pretty 'butterflies' who fluttered in and out of the compartment – now to wash and cream their faces for the night and now to change into flimsy lacy see-through nightdresses and fluffy bedroom slippers. Jezile felt a wave of irritation swamping her. 'All for show,' she thought, 'have they no care in the world?' She cast a long sideways look at the woman at the other window with whom she identified. She had a young girl of about eight years of age beside her. They were simple country people judging by their clothes. The woman returned her look meaningfully. The people from Durban were ready to go to bed when there was a general air of restlessness in the compartment. The large woman with the stick suddenly spoke. She was saying something that Jezile could not follow. It was Sotho. It had completely slipped her mind that Africans in Bloemfontein spoke Sotho and she did not know any. The woman pointed her stick at the top bunk and looked Jezile in the eye. When she thought she understood, she pointed the other woman at the window to the opposite bunk. Jezile wondered from where she got the authority to direct the other passengers. 'Mother-in-law authority,' Jezile quickly surmised. But it felt rude all the same, and Jezile resented it. The 'butterflies' immediately got on the middle bunks as though the matter had been settled earlier and they already knew where they would sleep. Then the 'mother-in-law' pointed her stick at the child and spoke to her in Sotho again, pointing her to the opposite bottom bunk. Then she herself turned over, took off her dress and pulled a housecoat out of her suitcase and rolled on to the bottom bunk. In actual fact, Jezile was quite pleased to be right on top, as long as she had a bed to sleep on through the long night. She would escape all the commotion of people getting in and out, on and off, squeezing through all these pieces of luggage at the bottom. It was peaceful up there.

Very early the next morning she heard a commotion. She had slept soundly through the night, better than she did in her own bed with the baby at her side. The 'butterflies' were getting off. They were already in their day clothes. They were dressed like models. She could smell a choking scent rising up as they splashed themselves generously with perfume. She wondered where they worked, how much they earned and why they spent all of it on beautiful clothes. It was when they were saying their goodbyes to the 'mother-in-law' that she heard them talk about returning to St Martin's Hospital the following month and guessed that they were nurses.

No one entered their compartment at Ladysmith. Jezile watched the coming of dawn on the Drakensberg mountains as they were crossing from Natal to the Orange Free State. It was spectacular. Her view from the top bunk was limited, so she clambered down in a hurry and stood outside in the corridor. She peered to see the mountains that brought the winter frost to Sigageni, but there was no snow. It was all green and rocky. The rugged multi-faces of the mountain pointed majestically to the sky. As the train drew nearer the mountains, they seemed to confront her with their awesome beauty. The jagged tops were oppressively close. They stood there defiantly stressing their permanence against the transience all around. Jezile lost herself in the beauty, stretching her arms to touch, if not to pick, the blossoms of every description from every kind of shrub which grew profusely tantalisingly near, all along the railway line. Jezile smiled as though this dewy morning treat was prepared especially for her, a treat to welcome her to the Orange Free State. The sun rose suddenly, spilling on the mountainside like liquid gold and Jezile was breathless. She was still gasping when all of a sudden the train was swallowed by a long tunnel without warning.

They were in that tunnel for what seemed an age. When they emerged on the other side it was like another world. The mountains were behind them and ahead of them lay land flat as a plate. After passing the small town of Harrismith there was nothing more to see. No small towns, no African villages, just a wide expanse. They could see speckled on the landscape white farms, and dotted around them, beautiful willow trees. There would be water where they grew, for the rest it was acres and acres of fields of maize and grazing lands for sheep. The train snaked its way for miles with nothing but this terrain to see. Then there would be a hillock of rocks, great big boulders, standing there in the middle of nowhere as though someone had put them there overnight. The January sun was blazing hot with hardly a breeze to relieve it. It was early afternoon and Jezile was getting very tired. Earlier a few more people had joined them at the sleepy dorp of Bethlehem. They all spoke Sotho and she felt very isolated. She began to entertain more pangs of anxiety. Was this what it was going to be like? Would she have any friends at all? The nearer she drew to Bloemfontein, the more unpromising life seemed. For the first time she concerned herself with Bloemfontein and what the immediate future held for her. Bloemfontein, the very name, began to sound threatening, full of engulfing emotional privations, loneliness, namelessness, anonymity . . . She was getting herself worked up to a fever pitch when something quite minor distracted her. The train had stopped at a station and she saw large peaches being sold by frantic young women. She bought several of them for, beautiful as they were, they were going very cheaply. Where did those luscious yellow peaches come from in that dry place? From the farmers' orchards no doubt – but what access had these women to the farmers' peaches? They were large enough to fill the cup of her hand – the size of a good orange, and she found herself gently caressing them in their rich yellow fruitiness. Then a feeling that she had managed to banish deftly for months took hold of her. Her body throbbed and ached inwardly, awash with longing, while she sat there oblivious of the bustling scene on the railway platform. She turned her thoughts voraciously on her self, squeezing her body greedily as she wondered why she had not allowed herself the privilege of these deliciously painful and unfaithful thoughts. There was no guilt in her mind as she speculated what might happen – if it should happen – just by chance – that someone should arouse such wild uncontrollable feelings in her. It could happen right there in Bloemfontein – she tried to peer into the dark future. Released from communal supervision, she wondered what the future held. For once it was the future and not the present or the past. The throb galloped wildly within, her heart racing wildly and her thinking clouding over. She was alarmed by it all. In that crowded compartment! She darted out into the corridor, to escape her hungry thoughts and bring her body under control once more. At last, as the train pulled out, chugging its way out of that remote station, she felt her riotous blood cool down. She stood at the window watching the station receding and wondered what devil possessed that scorching patch of earth. Or was it the peaches? Then she looked ahead and it soon became quite evident where the women got the peaches from. All along the railway line there were rows and rows of peach trees. No man's land. It was surprising to see such succulent fruit growing where the land looked so dry and barren.

It was late afternoon and it began to feel as though they would be travelling for ever. She drew back into the compartment in despondency and closed her eyes for what she thought was a few minutes. She was suddenly awakened by the sound of squeaking brakes as the train came to a stop. It was Bloemfontein. Her heart fluttered excitedly and she scampered to her feet. Looking through the window she could see Potgieter looking around for her. Her heart stopped and she was almost pleased to see him. She had never thought she could be pleased just to see him. He helped her off the train. When she got down, she was amazed to hear him addressing her in Afrikaans. She was stunned. In all the six months she had known him, he had never spoken Afrikaans to anyone. It was either English to her or Fanakalo to the squad. Jezile felt tears stinging her eyes.

No one spoke anything she vaguely understood anywhere around that station. It was Afrikaans and Sotho all around. If she had had the choice, she would have gone back and hidden in that train to await its return journey home. But she was in Bloemfontein to stay, and, as long as she was there, she was in the hands of Mr Potgieter.

In that tower of Babel, he led the way to a taxi while she trotted mutely behind. In the gathering twilight, they stopped before a gate, in front of his nondescript house. It seemed he was not expected, for when the door opened a massive woman stood before them darkening the door, her arms akimbo. For a brief second it seemed she did not recognise him as he stood at his door waiting to be acknowledged. It gave Jezile a strange feeling of being lost – a man lost in front of his house. Her arms fell to her sides and she turned her head, calling. As she gave way for him to go in, a stampede of little feet came running to the door. With a peck on her mouth, he turned to the children who soon crowded around his legs jostling for his attention and babbling in many voices. His wife stood looking on, holding the door protectively, with a smile on her face, while Jezile stood forgotten outside. A confusion of emotions swept through her as she witnessed this family reunion. She noted a change in his voice when he turned to talk to his wife. Afrikaans, a deep guttural language, conveyed a certain degree of gruffness and a lack of friendliness to Jezile's unaccustomed ears. But even taking that into account, Jezile noted a lack of warmth between the two. He was about to push his way into the house when with a slight twist of her shoulder his wife gestured to stop him as she looked inquiringly at Jezile. They talked animatedly between themselves, their voices rising until they sounded quite heated. Jezile could not make out what they were saying, but she knew it was about her. She felt like a shard of old bone that the dog had dragged in. Finally, the woman turned to her and in Fanakalo told her to go to the back of the house.

Jezile stood at the back for quite some time before the door opened. Finally the woman came out and gestured her in. A second gesture told her to leave her suitcase outside. It sounded like they were going to have their evening meal judging by the clatter of cutlery that went on in the room next door. The woman busied herself in preparation for the meal and for a long while Jezile was a forgotten factor in the scheme of things. She could hear the children chattering competitively to their father in the inner room. Jezile watched Mrs Potgieter as she swung from one corner of the kitchen to another and from room to room. She had a great presence. She was almost as tall as her husband who was himself noticeably tall. In addition she had a great double chin that dominated her face and quivered when she talked. Two pale pools for eyes nestled under a shaggy pair of eyebrows. Her other facial features lost their importance to the great feature of the chin. Her arms and legs were massive, which had the effect of making her hands and feet look small. Having taken in the woman, the children as they flitted by, and the shabby kitchen, Jezile concluded that the household was of modest means. But all this was relative. When the food was dished out Jezile was assailed by its goodness and she had a sudden pang of hunger. Besides the smell of its goodness, she remembered she had not had a hot meal in three days.

After the meal she saw all the dishes coming back empty and knew there was little chance of her sharing any of the food. She was getting tired of standing near the door when Mrs Potgieter came to speak to her. Mr Potgieter had always spoken to her in English and there had been no time to ponder why he had switched to Afrikaans earlier that evening at the station and in the taxi. Those were the dynamics of the relationship which she could not fathom at the time. Mrs Potgieter addressed her in Fanakalo. And Mr Potgieter introduced his wife as though Jezile had not surmised who she was in the past two hours. At this point she expected a clear definition of her duties, but she was simply told she was going to help Mrs Potgieter in her work. She would wake the family up with cups of coffee at six in the morning and from then on she would do what Mrs Potgieter asked her to do. The end of the day was left open. She was about to be sent off when she asked about the pay. The wife told her £5 a month. But the husband, hot on her words, quickly added as though he had not heard her, that Jezile would be paid twenty-five. His wife looked at him for an instant and then she turned to Jezile, who was looking straight and without blinking at Mr Potgieter. She had looked at him many times in that fashion. She had never felt like an underling – she had simply felt different – a different kind of person offering a service. Mr Potgieter himself had not exerted his power over her in his minority status among the villagers. His whiteness had not seemed to matter much among his squad of men except that his job was to stand around and watch them work hard in the blazing hot sun for days on end. But Mrs Potgieter sensed the familiarity and she did not like it.

As Jezile was about to leave the room, Mrs Potgieter asked for her pass. This had a devastating effect on Jezile. She stood stock-still and for a moment she could not turn round to face the woman. She had forgotten about her pass altogether. Conflicting memories of the pass flashed through her mind – the day she burnt her pass so long ago at the dipping tank; the memory of that defiance before the police, the morale-boosting company of the women of Sigageni. She stood there and thought, 'But we have fought the pass, we have served our term of imprisonment for fighting it.' In the converging events of the past week, she had completely forgotten about the pass. She had not needed it for she had not needed to go to the Labour Bureau to look for work. She had never gone back to ask for another pass. People in the countryside never needed a pass to go anywhere, unless they were going to the cities. They did need the pass to go to redeem registered letters at the post office. But with Siyalo at home, and lately in prison, she had simply not needed the infernal book. But now she did. In an unruffled voice that did not betray the confusion inside her she said quietly that she did not have a pass. They looked at her as though she had not spoken. After a tense minute Mrs Potgieter asked disbelievingly, 'Did you say you don't have a pass? How is that?'

'I have just never needed one.'

'But . . . but you need one now. How is this possible?'

Mr Potgieter intervened. 'Perhaps it's my own fault – I should have taken her to the Labour Bureau. Never mind, I'll take you to the local offices tomorrow.'

'But you can't . . . that's not the way to do it, is it? I've had trouble with these people before; I know what I'm talking about.'

'Sh . . . sh . . . I'll deal with it myself. I'm the employer.' That seemed to mark the end of that problem. Jezile was evidently relieved. But Mrs Potgieter looked clearly annoyed by her husband's dismissive attitude and the way he was taking over in what was her domain. Hiring and firing servants was her responsibility. But it became quite clear that this was not going to be the same as in other cases. She was puzzled and irritated. Jezile saw it in her look as she turned to go again. She did not really know where she was going – to collect her suitcase perhaps. She did not know where she would sleep that night. She had assumed that maids always had little rooms, hidden from view, somewhere at the bottom of every white person's garden. She was almost at the door when Mr Potgieter said something to his wife. She called Jezile back and offered her some bread and jam and a big hot cup of coffee. Jezile was about to sit down and enjoy that hot cup of coffee; she was so conscious of her hunger and thirst that she immediately sat at the kitchen table to eat. She did not see Mrs Potgieter's hand shooing her off the table.

'Ayi khona lapha. Phuma, phuma. Not here, out, out.'

She picked up her food in a hurry not knowing where to go to eat it. Mrs Potgieter ushered her outside and pointed Jezile to a space near the hedge in the garden not far from the kitchen. She drank the coffee hurriedly in the dark. She needed its comforting warmth. It quickly filled the gap of anxiety that was yawning inside the pit of her stomach. When she brought back the utensils she stood at the door, hesitatingly, wondering if she would be allowed to enter the kitchen. The woman stood smoking, apparently waiting for her, gestured her to come in and put the things in the sink. She then led Jezile down the garden path to the room right next to the garage at the back. She could have found that room by herself. When the room was opened, to Jezile's surprise, Mrs Potgieter produced a candle and lit it for her. She was familiar with the candles back home at Sigageni – that's all they ever used there. But then that was rural South Africa and she had not expected candles in the city of Bloemfontein. Looking up she saw the socket where a light bulb should have been, but it hung open-mouthed and suspended from the ceiling. However, she could not give this detail any lengthy consideration for there was a lot to take in all at once. The room. She peered from behind the expansive back of Mrs Potgieter, her eyes struggling to adjust in the flickering candlelight. There was a bed, a chair and hooks on the wall for hanging her clothes. The floor was bare concrete. Even by Jezile's standards the room was sparsely furnished. She put her case down and was beginning to wonder about blankets, when Mrs Potgieter turned to her and told her she was not allowed any visitors. And that if she needed any water there was a tap at the back of the house next to the kitchen door. 'Well, what else? Come on up to the house,' she finished off. Jezile followed behind her once more.

When they got to the kitchen Mrs Potgieter asked her to wash up. It was a great pile of dishes, which made Jezile wonder how many people there were inside. She mused silently that Mrs Potgieter could not wait to start her off on the job. While she was washing up Mrs Potgieter brought her a pile of blankets, a pair of sheets and an alarm clock and left them on the table.

'Ah, one other thing. About your time off. You have an hour and a half off for your lunch every day, and on Sundays you can take time off from after lunch until Monday morning, all right?'

When Jezile finally crept into bed, she realised how very tired she was. She fell into a dreamless sleep. The next morning she was up at five o'clock, anxious to come to grips with her new routine and get the feel of the place. By six-thirty Mrs Potgieter was up, taking Jezile round the house, familiarising her with its geography and presenting her with a schedule for the day. Breakfast at seven-thirty; preparing the children for school at eight; washing up and cleaning the kitchen by eight-forty-five; making beds and dusting the bedrooms by nine-thirty; cleaning and polishing the living-room and dining-room floors by ten-thirty; doing the children's washing by eleven-thirty; preparing lunch in time for the children when they got back from school by twelve-thirty; washing up by two; taking her own lunch by two-thirty; back to do the ironing by four; helping with preparation for dinner by five; dinner by six-thirty or seven; putting the children to bed by eight; washing up after that and that would mark the end of the day. Jezile looked at her schedule in utter amazement. She coughed slightly and braced herself for a comment. Mrs Potgieter was looking at her intently all the while.

'But this means I have no time to do anything for myself,'

Jezile ventured to say in as controlled and humble a voice as she could. She had not realised that Mr Potgieter had walked into the kitchen and was watching her. When he heard this remark he quietly advanced and snatched the paper from her hands. He scanned it once or twice and without looking at his wife, he talked straight to Jezile.

'This, Jezile, is the routine of this house. My wife here is telling you everything that goes on in this house, but that does not mean that you do all the work. You help her as she requires, but you don't have to do everything. You help each other.' He turned and looked at his wife sharply, and Jezile did not know what to make of it. He turned to Jezile again, 'You wait, we're going to straighten it for you. And remember, today I'll take you to the pass office.' Jezile could see the resentment mounting between the couple and she was happy that Mr Potgieter was coming out strongly on her side.

After taking the children to school, he came straight to pick her up and she dutifully climbed into the car leaving Mrs Potgieter to her own work for the morning. As usual, at that early hour of the morning, the pass queue was long and coiled right round the office block. But Mr Potgieter went straight ahead, side-stepping the long queue, into the office with Jezile trailing behind. In no time at all she had answered all the questions, had her photograph taken and affixed the prints of all her fingers on the pages of the pass-book. Within a very short time she had the pass-book in her hands. The petty official who gave it to her was so pleased, as though Jezile had done him a personal favour to come for the book. It was surprising how easily the whole problem had been sorted out. But all the way back to the car Jezile thought sadly how little those demonstrations back home had really achieved. She clutched the pass-book like a valuable possession. By eleven-thirty they were back in the house with Mr Potgieter's signature badly scrawled on the employment page.

She found her uniform carefully laid on the table – a blue dress, a white apron and a white cap. It was slightly big, but nothing that a few alterations would not put right. She immediately set to work alongside Mrs Potgieter preparing lunch. As the children arrived, Jezile heard Mrs Potgieter calling, 'Annie, Annie,' and Jezile thought she was calling one of her children.

It took some moments for her to realise that she was actually referring to her.

'Annie . . . me?' Jezile felt emptied of herself. 'What's wrong with Jezile, I wonder?' she thought to herself. Later that afternoon, Mrs Potgieter told Jezile to call her 'Nonna'. 'Nonna' was the generic name for most Afrikaaner women employers, just like 'Annie' was one of several generic names for female black servants. They were fast erecting barriers to map their relationship. By the next day their relationship had formalised into a distant if not hostile exchange. Everywhere Jezile turned, she encountered bars that marked the limits of her humanity in that household. Mrs Potgieter brought to the kitchen table what she called Jezile's rations – they were samp – crushed mealies – beans, mealie meal and tea and she was promised bread and jam every morning. She was told she would be given meat four times a week. She thought that very generous until she found out that it was the same bones that Mrs Potgieter put down on the order as dogs' meat. Her self-esteem plunged deeper. Mrs Potgieter went around with a jingling bunch of keys in her apron pocket. They were the keys to her food cupboards and other areas of the house where Jezile was not allowed. The implication was that she, Jezile, was a thief. One key was to the telephone. But this did not matter much as she had no need of a telephone. She had no one to telephone for hundreds of miles around.

As the days went by Jezile awaited the revised schedule of her daily work, but neither Mr nor Mrs Potgieter said any more about the matter. Instead, she was fast established as the maid-of-all-work in the house. Her work was varied but monotonous because it followed such a strict routine. She hated being asked to do one-hundred-and-one things a day, and being closely observed whatever she did. It was all so inhibiting. By the end of the second week, Mr Potgieter had successfully effaced himself and seemed not the least bit interested in Jezile and her work. Mrs Potgieter was effectively in control. It surprised Jezile that Mr Potgieter did not go away to his usual work on the roads. She understood that he was doing some correspondence course which he had started in his idle days on the road. Jezile felt hemmed in and every day brought new restrictions. She was not allowed to listen to the radio nor to use the carpet-sweeper. She hated asking for permission to do even trivial things like eating at the kitchen table on rainy days. She hated eating outside, leaning on that concrete stand every day. She hated being refused the use of electricity in her room. She hated entering by the back door. She felt powerless and vulnerable, trapped inside that home. She hated baking because she never ate the cakes. She hated cooking meat because she never ate the roast. She just lived to fulfil Mrs Potgieter's every wish – totally steeped in the life of this alien family and stripped of her life as she had known it. She had lost her name, her past, her friends and relatives, her language, her initiative, and she felt she was just a shell of her real self. But more than anything else, she felt lonely. Two months with this family and with no communication with anyone else was killing her. She saw the other woman who worked next door, but they could only nod to each other across the fence owing to the language barrier. On Sundays she went walking and window-shopping, but for the same reason it was hard for her to make friends with those she met on the road. She learned to knit and began to make warm jumpers for herself and her children; but it was human contact and recognition she longed for. She wrote long letters to everybody she could think of. Her life depended on those long letters that came back in reply to hers. The children were fine and from all reports they were well looked after. MaBiyela was keeping to her side of the bargain faithfully, and Jezile became even more determined to send as much money home as she could.

The six Potgieter children ranged from two years old to twelve years old. If they had not been so rude she would have been happy to make friends with them. The two eldest regarded her as the property of their parents and she resented that attitude. But the two youngest were lovely and she warmed to them a great deal because they reminded her of her own children. But she could only enjoy their company when she was baby-sitting, which she was asked to do increasingly as time went by. Mrs Potgieter had realised that Jezile had nowhere to go even when she was free and she began nibbling into that time little by little. This extended Jezile's working hours infinitely. But she did not resent it as much, for it brought her closer human intercourse. Slowly, the children got closer to her, especially the younger ones. She played with them and little by little she began to learn Afrikaans.

In the third month she saw a great deal more evidence of the unhappy relationship between the husband and the wife. There were frequent rows and once or twice Mrs Potgieter woke up with a black eye. Occasionally Mr Potgieter came in very drunk and created unpleasant scenes. On such occasions Jezile did not know how to react; a night of steaming angry scenes would be followed by frigid mornings. It was a strange relationship she had with the family, marked by intimate knowledge of their quarrels, drunken scenes of humiliation observed across the gulf of formality and rigidity. To relieve the tension inside her, she would polish the floor furiously from room to room with hardly a pause. Her arm would ache and she would change to the next until it ached too and she could feel the trickles of perspiration running in rivulets down her forehead, ending in drips down her nose. They would tickle the nape of her neck at the back and flow to wet the cleavage between her large breasts at the front. It was a race that she set herself every day, pitching her body against anything that would help to alleviate her inner frustrations. Only when she had finished this task would she stand and inhale deeply the smell of polish – and she would feel purged like the house itself. It was at such times that she wondered at the beauty and cleanliness of the white world, their houses and their neighbourhoods. The house was spotless – the floors and the walls glistened. No such clean water gushed cold and limitless from the taps at Sigageni. The washing billowed on the line, dazzling in its cleanness, bleached in the sun. The trees swayed green and large and the grass lay soft and green and thick. No such green trees and grass at Sigageni. Such abundance. Everything inexhaustible. The streets beyond the gate lay clean and dust free – no mud even on rainy days. She never tired of counting the sharp differences that marked Sigageni from the suburb of De Wit Pak where the Potgieters lived. In the hierarchy of white suburbs, De Wit Pak was quite mediocre, but for Jezile there were no such remarkable differences. It was a white suburb. It was not just the distance that separated Sigageni from such places, it was a whole lifestyle; they were a whole world away, like heaven and hell. But that was as far as the comparison went. In the same breath she would stop and wonder at the unhappiness that such beautiful places generated. People here seemed never to run out of ways and means of destroying each other's lives. It did not make sense. And judging by the loveless, begrudging air of the house, she knew that good living could not in itself ensure love and happiness, even in the midst of such extravagance.

One night, in the middle of this alienating existence, she heard Mr Potgieter's car arrive rather late. He drove into the garage next to her room to park his car. This woke her up. She heard him lock up. The next moment he tried her door. This was followed by a knock. When Jezile would not answer, he called her by her name, Jezile, not the anonymous Annie and told her to open the door because he had brought her a table. When she opened, she saw the table. There it was. 'I thought you needed a table – I've seen you writing letters on your knee and eating your food standing out there. It's not right. So, there you are.' Jezile was grateful, but she did not like the idea of him waking her up so late in the night when the table could have waited till morning.

The next morning she watched self-consciously for any change of manner on his part. But he was the same indifferent person of the last few weeks. She felt a twinge of self-reproach for her suspicions of the previous night. A few days later when Mrs Potgieter went out shopping, Mr Potgieter asked Jezile for the key to her room. When she raised her eyes questioningly he said casually that he wanted to fix the electric switch in her room, 'It makes no sense that you should use candles when there is electricity in the room.' He fiddled for a long time in her room while she worked her routine in the main house. It was early evening before he gave her back the key. When she finally retired that night she was thrilled to find her room flooding with electric light. This would change her life significantly – she could find a cheap electric iron; she could buy a radio and spend her spare time listening to all those programmes that would bring her nearer home. It was wonderful. But, to her surprise, the very next day, Mr Potgieter gave her a little pocket radio. She was happy, but that flicker of doubt swept across her mind again and when she raised her eyes, she thought she caught a glimpse of guilt in his averted look. Jezile hoped and prayed that this was not the start of something she could not handle. When she was back at Umzimkulu, she had been able to put him off easily. She had been in her territory, among her people within a structure that she knew and could handle. But now she was not so very sure of how to put him off. Her job made her powerless and so very vulnerable. She saw that she would have to depend more and more on his wife to protect her from his designs. But, by this time Mrs Potgieter was already beginning to ease her way out of the house and its drudgery. She was often out during the day. She looked happier for she had begun to feel she was having her way with Jezile, and her husband was interfering less and less. So, while Mrs Potgieter spent more and more time out, her husband spent more and more time in his study, wanting more and more cups of coffee and Jezile's general attention. But Jezile was all attention, prepared to fight off any of his attempts to get more familiar, should he try. But then, for a long time nothing happened and slowly Jezile began to relax.

Early one evening Jezile heard the Potgieters having a huge row. She closed the doors and drew the children into the kitchen. They heard Mr Potgieter rush out to his car and drive off, leaving his wife screaming in the bedroom. Jezile waited a while and then went to the bedroom. On the bedroom floor lay Mrs Potgieter crying disconsolately with blood all over her face. Jezile was horrified and for the first time she felt sorry for this insecure woman. She rushed to get some warm water and helped clean her face and change her clothes. She hustled the children off to another room and closed the door. Mrs Potgieter for once lost her reserve and did not bother to hide her unhappiness from Jezile, who worked till late that night putting the children to bed. It was about nine-thirty when she left the main house in darkness and walked to her room. Right there on her bed lay Mr Potgieter. For a moment she stood petrified, but without another word he was on his feet, and he shut her mouth.

'Now quiet. I'm not going to hurt you. I love you. I've loved you a long time and you know it. If you sit quietly down here we can have a lot of fun. I need you and I'm sure you need me.' Jezile wriggled in her attempt to get free. But his grip tightened 'I said I won't hurt you. You know I don't love her; I've neve loved her. Now calm down. I'll be good to you.'

Panic and horror seized her. He had her arm twisted and h

204

rolled her onto the bed and pinned her down. In the ensuing struggle she managed to loosen his grip on her mouth and she screamed. But in that isolated backyard it was like whistling against thunder. The only person who could have heard her and perhaps raised the alarm was the girl next door. But apparently she was not in, for no one came to Jezile's help. He had his way with her. Afterwards she curled up like a ball at the opposite end of the bed and winced and whimpered like a wounded animal. He did not leave the room when he had finished with her. He sat there and pleaded with her to understand. He was sorry it had happened that way, he said. For a long time he had had visions of a beautiful time with her. He sat up next to her trying to calm her down and to comfort her. 'If it wasn't for the law, I would love you openly; I would even marry you. I loved you when you were with your people at Umzimkulu. I brought you here because I love you; I could not bear not to see you ever again . . .' He went on and on babbling but Jezile was inconsolable. She was outraged and she felt completely alone. Finally, he left the room after midnight. She felt dirty and steeped in evil. The feel and the smell of his slimy emission filled her with so much revulsion. She had to wash it off; go out into the dark night to fetch some water, cold water, from the tap outside the house. She wished for the comfort of warm water to purge her whole body; but there was none. She willed her hand to touch the desecrated part, but it would not. Pain was etched on every muscle of her face; her body was in revolt against itself, against the outrage. She prayed to God to help her get clean. She had to be clean. Finally, she walked out to the tap and poured water over the top of her head letting it flow, bowl after bowl after bowl, until she felt cleansed. She then crept back into her room and she packed her things ready to leave the next morning. But as the dawn broke, the thought of telling her community back in Sigageni about her bitter experience filled her with shame. She was no longer so sure of their sympathy and understanding. Any other misfortune but this. They would never understand this. Something in her could not face it. Rape is a burden to its own victim. It was as though she had wished it on herself. She could predict all the lurid gossip. They would even suggest that she had followed him to Bloemfontein because she had had an affair with him. And what would Siyalo think when he came back and heard these stories? Would he believe her against all those rumours? And the children, where would she get another job? Going home would certainly not solve her problems, it would only complicate matters. She felt so alone.

She rose from her bed out of habit. She had not slept a wink. She drifted rather than walked purposefully to the house. She could not bring herself to take coffee up to the couple, but she prepared the children for school. When he heard her pottering about in the kitchen he came over and silently helped her with the children. But his presence brought on a relentless stream of tears. She could not stop crying. She was in tears when she finally took breakfast to Mrs Potgieter, who lay with a swollen face in bed. They were two women trapped under one roof, unable to escape and allied against their will. When she saw Jezile in tears she thought Jezile was crying because she was sorry for her. This heartened her a great deal and a bond of understanding grew between the two women. Jezile did not dare tell Mrs Potgieter what had happened and why she was crying.

Mr Potgieter continued to work silently alongside Jezile for the next few days trying to prove to her he was not a beast. But she could not bring herself to talk to him. Whenever he came closer to touch her, she recoiled. For days he followed her about the house like a shadow, and slowly that shadow became a familiar feature of her life. Whenever Mrs Potgieter was not in the house, he spent his time with Jezile. He touched her when he could. He spoke gently to her, and he continued to give her many little favours. It was like a scourge. Jezile was in an invidious position. How could she continue to live with the Potgieters and not encourage him by that very fact? Slowly she began to feel part of the complicity. The cause rather than the victim of the couple's unhappiness. Once again she thought she would go away. Awake or asleep her mind was a milling concourse of contradictions. There was never a single thought, a single decision without conflict.

As the weeks went by, Jezile no longer shook him off when he touched her; her eyes no longer filled up when he talked to her. But she continued to lock her door at night and push the bed against it to barricade herself. Once he knocked at her door, but she would not open it. He gave up and went away not wishing to alarm her or his wife. He was intent on never forcing her again, but he was not going to give up persuading her. She turned cold and stony-eyed. The house was like a tomb. She did not seem able to acknowledge even his wife's advances of friendship. She worked from morning till late at night and did not feel the need to get away. All the things she had hated about the house before, about Mrs Potgieter, about their treatment of her became matters of indifference. Her life ran on in neutral gear. When she noticed her waistline beginning to grow, it was as though it had been ordained since the beginning of the world. The only privilege she allowed herself was her Sunday outings when she would take the bus to the African location. Many Africans spoke English there and it was such joyous relief to meet and talk to them. She regretted the months she had spent in the isolation of the white suburb. In time she would have been happier in Bloemfontein, but now it was too late. She found a group of Zionist worshippers and joined in their hymns and sang and danced devoutly like the Zionists she had seen in Sabelweni and Durban. She herself was a Methodist. The Zionists sang and prayed loudly and literally commanded God to come down and save them. That was what she needed – a God who was at her command. She sang loudly, her own words to the tunes and she screamed to be saved. By the end of the service her heart felt lighter. From that week on she survived for her weekly Sunday absolution.

When it was no longer mistakable that Jezile was pregnant Mrs Potgieter became quite mollified. She was no longer restrained about her offers of friendship to Jezile. However, Jezile remained cold and aloof. Somewhere at the back of her mind, she blamed Mrs Potgieter. If she had not treated her so harshly Jezile would have been less well disposed towards Mr Potgieter. She would not have unwittingly encouraged him by her openness and willingness to serve him. However, the more unresponsive Jezile was, the more friendly Mrs Potgieter became. She improved Jezile's rations and included in them fruit and vegetables, even though they were usually the more jaded ones that had not been eaten by the family that week. She also gave Jezile some of her children's old clothes, hand-me-downs, some of which had seen their best days. But on the whole most still had a lot of wear in them. She even gave Jezile some of her own clothes although these seemed useless to Jezile as they were far too big for her even when she was very big.

It seemed odd to Jezile that Mrs Potgieter should be thinking about preparing for the arrival of her baby when she herself could hardly believe in its existence inside her or contemplate the day when it would be born. Nor could she anticipate the day when she would have to tell MaBiyela or her mother, MaSibiya, about it. She knew one thing, that the baby had no place among the Majolas nor among the Mapangas. Therefore it could not exist. She willed it out of existence and for her it was annulled. Therefore, she made no contingency plans with regard to her work, or MaBiyela, or MaSibiya or even Siyalo. She put up the shutters and lived from day to day. When Mr Potgieter tentatively asked what her plans were, she stared back at him in silence. Mrs Potgieter broached the subject by suggesting that she was thinking of giving her a few months maternity leave so that she could come back to her job. Jezile was silent. Mrs Potgieter went on to confess that she had come to like her very much as she had proved so trustworthy and hardworking. When pressed for an answer, Jezile nodded and looked away.

One Sunday soon after, on her way back from the Zionist meeting, Jezile suddenly caught her breath, for sitting in that bus she suddenly felt a hard long grip of abdominal pain. It was unmistakable. She opened her eyes wide as though it was only then that she knew there was a baby coming. It must have been the dancing that brought it on, she reasoned to herself. But it gave her no time to think again for this was followed by another spasm. After what seemed like an age the bus stopped. She rushed straight for the main house. Mrs Potgieter looked at her in some alarm.

'What is it?' she asked.

'I'm in pain, a lot of pain.'

Mrs Potgieter ran in and came back with her husband at her heels. They took her to the hospital immediately, and later that evening she gave birth to a baby boy. She was too tired to look at him that night. Early next morning, a white nurse wheeled the baby round to her bedside. Jezile lay back and would not turn to look at him. The nurse fixed her eyes on her and asked if she was not going to hold the baby. She then picked him up and gave him to Jezile.

'This is your baby, is it not?'

'Yes . . . it is.' Jezile looked at him for one fleeting moment and then stared abstractly across the ward.

'Are you going to feed him?' Jezile was quiet. 'Here, Jezile, i'll show you.' Finally, the baby was sucking away vigorously. It was only then Jezile sat up properly and began to look at him intently.

'He's yours,' said the nurse stating the obvious. 'Have you got other children besides him?'

'Yes.'

'How many? Girls or boys?'

'Girls.'

'Are they white too?' Jezile suddenly looked up and looked at the nurse straight in the eyes. But she did not answer the last question.

'Who is the father?' persisted the nurse. Jezile did not answer, and the nurse left her alone.

Later that morning the doctors came round. They were happy with her progress. But just as they were leaving her bedside, the senior doctor hung back and asked, 'This is your baby, is it?' Without looking at Jezile he went on, 'Who's the father?' Jezile remained silent. He looked at her medical sheet again, but it left him no wiser.

That afternoon Mr and Mrs Potgieter came to see her and the baby. They brought her the choicest fruits and sweets. Jezile looked cynically at the fruit thinking, they must want everyone in the ward to think they are wonderful employers. Mrs Potgieter stared at the baby all the time they were there and she grew very subdued, while Mr Potgieter hardly looked at the baby at all. But they were soon gone.

About ten o'clock the next morning, while the ward was buzzing with activity, Jezile had two white visitors, a man and a woman. They were followed by the same staff nurse who had quizzed her the day before. The man and woman asked to talk to her. They asked her who the father of the baby was. She stared at them without betraying her surprise. Then they told her she would have to answer their questions because they were the police. They had been told she had a white child. And, as this was a crime, they wanted to know the name of the father. She listened silently to everything they said. Then suddenly she looked past them. They followed her gaze and turned to find Mr Potgieter just behind them. The man seemed to know Mr Potgieter. He nervously greeted the police and told them hurriedly that he had brought her the nightdress she had asked for, adding for the benefit of the police, 'We were here yesterday and she asked for it. She's our girl you know, a very good girl. Aren't you, Annie? How's your wife?' he quickly added, changing the subject.

With the subject successfully changed, they began to talk about a number of things to do with work. It turned out that Mr Potgieter had left the road-works altogether and he was now working at the prosecutor's office. Jezile had not known this. The policeman asked him about his studies and it turned out that he was doing law by correspondence with the University of South Africa. Towards the end, when Mr Potgieter had regained his composure, he asked them what they wanted from Jezile. They gestured to the baby in the cot and mumbled something. He nodded violently and laughed aloud, 'Ah, well, so it is, so it is. To be honest with you, I didn't look at it much yesterday.' They turned to go without another word to Jezile. But soon after lunch that day, Mr Potgieter rushed in again looking very harassed. He talked fast looking around furtively.

'You must go back home to Umzimkulu tomorrow. I've arranged for your ticket . . . Mrs Potgieter doesn't want you back at work . . . at least, not yet. She'll pack your things and we'll bring them along when we come to pick you up . . . oh, she likes your baby. The train leaves at six o'clock. Ya, is that all right? . . .' He had become accustomed to his monologues with her. He turned to go but swiftly turned back again. 'Don't worry about money. She'll pay you for everything . . . Eh, eh, if the police come back again, don't tell them who the father is. Ya, is that clear?' He left her in a hurry, without expecting an answer.

On the third day after her delivery at about four o'clock, Jezile carried her baby out of the hospital into the car. Mr Potgieter was on his own. He told her he had sent on all her luggage, except for the baby's things. He knew she could not manage the luggage on her own with the baby. At the station he gave her a bag full of nappies and some provisions, and a lot more money than was due to her. 'Right. Ask anyone to help you into the train with that bag. I've booked you a bed. So you should be all right. Look after yourself and the baby.'

So Jezile left Bloemfontein. She had been there exactly a year.

13

MaSibiya was out in the fields weeding when she received a message that Jezile had arrived with a baby in her arms. She threw her implement aside and strode home with the little messenger at her heels. When they were some distance away and out of earshot she turned to the child, and lowering her voice she asked, 'What baby are you talking about? You don't mean Ndondo do you?'

'No, not Ndondo, Ndondo is big, I know her.'

'It's a small baby is it?'

'Yes, it's very, very small.'

'We Nkulumkulu wami, my God, what's going on?'

MaSibiya almost ran the rest of the way, leaving the child lagging behind.

MaSibiya collapsed on her knees right beside Jezile where she sat in the shade of the house.

'Jezile, Jezile, my child, what's that you've got in your arms? Where did you get it from? What shall I say to the Majolas? What shall I say? Have you come from there or straight from Bloemfontein?' Jezile shook her head, but said nothing.

'You mean MaBiyela does not know about this baby? Have you told them? It's yours, Jezile, is it? Bring it here.'

She took one look at the child and she screamed. 'Jezile, what child is this? This can't be your child. And it's so small, how old is it?' She began to show concern for Jezile. She looked her up and down.

'Jezile, my child, my child. What's been happening to you? Who's the father of this child?' she asked repeatedly with tears streaming down her face. 'But it's white Jezile, it's white!'

Jezile began to sob uncontrollably. With the child forgotten on the mat, mother and daughter clung to each other. By then a group of young children stood watching, confounded. Jezile wept on and on as though she would never stop and MaSibiya rocked her daughter as though she was the infant instead of the little bundle on the mat. Slowly Jezile's sobs became quieter, but more convulsive. MaSibiya put her head down gently on the mat and rushed to make some tea for her. When Jezile had recovered, MaSibiya concentrated on the baby and asked no further questions of Jezile. When friends and relations and neighbours came to see her they were all subdued. None of them rushed to see the baby. Others pretended there was no baby to speak about, while some talked discreetly about the inescapable temptations that face all young women without husbands, with God being the only protection. It did not escape some that MaSibiya sat with the baby carefully covered and facing the wall throughout the time of their visit. It was one thing to tell the people of Luve that Jezile had a baby, and it was quite another to tell them that it was a white man's child, which was not only a transgression of their own customs but a crime as well.

It was three days before MaSibiya summoned up enough courage to tackle the subject with Jezile again. She dreaded another scene, but she had to know; she simply had to know for the Majolas' sake, if for no one else's. She had a responsibility to let them know that their daughter-in-law was here, or better still to take her there herself, before the local gossips carried the news. To MaSibiya's surprise, Jezile seemed drained of all feeling and ready to talk. She sat her mother down quietly and in an even voice she told the story about how she first went to work for the men on the road, how MaBiyela had advised her to go to Bloemfontein, and about her unspeakable life there. When she had finished MaSibiya summoned all the relations that were within reach and asked Jezile to tell them the whole story over again. Calmly, Jezile did, and the whole place was thrown into utter confusion. Many believed her, but it was clear that there were those who doubted the details of the story. Nobody dared to ask too many questions. The matter stopped being MaSibiya's problem – it affected all the Mapangas. This child would be called a Mapanga, one of them; a white child among them; a child born in this unorthodox way, if Jezile was to be believed. Others said the child could not be a

Mapanga – it was a Majola child; Jezile was no longer a Mapanga herself – if she was unmarried, yes, it would be a Mapanga. But now, according to custom, the white child was a Majola. The older women treated Jezile with such tenderness as though she had only been raped the day before. MaSibiya, who was overwrought, told the gathering that she needed a few women to accompany her and Jezile to the Majolas within the next day or two for she daren't keep a Majola wife and child for too long without reporting her presence. But the general opinion was that Jezile should stay until she had fully recovered – after all, it was only a few days since she had had the baby, followed by the long journey from Bloemfontein. So, the next day, two men were sent to report to MaBiyela and all the Majolas that Jezile was with the Mapangas.

Two weeks later, when Jezile was a little stronger, she and MaSibiya accompanied by a group of six women travelled to Sigageni to the Majolas. Jezile dreaded facing her mother-in-law. But to her surprise MaBiyela looked a shadow of her former self. She sat them all down and in a quiet voice she sent the children to call the other Majola relations. The visitors were served tea in silence. When everyone had arrived, the two families sat facing each other. Jezile's eldest aunt on her father's side began to tell the whole story from the start while the others listened. Not a cough interrupted, and when she had finished the stunned silence was followed by a restless shuffle in the room. In an even voice MaBiyela asked to see the baby. When she opened the bundle and looked at its little face, she gave one deep groan. After some moments she asked one question of Jezile, a question directed more at destiny than her.

'Why didn't you just leave this child with the white man? The child does not belong here; it does not belong anywhere. This child will bring the white law on us. Who will face them when they come? This is not a Majola nor is it a Mapanga.'

It was no longer Jezile's misfortune that lay in front of them, it was a communal catastrophe. There was a long silence; then, the oldest man in the room told the Mapangas that the matter could not be discussed further because Siyalo was away in jail. It would have to wait until he came back. It would have to wait for seven long years. No one spoke after the old man. The Mapangas were served with a light meal and they left after that.

Then the Majolas left one by one mumbling their goodbyes softly with their heads bent low.

It was hard for Jezile to relate to the community as before. They received her back as they would any of their many unavoidable natural disasters. Her two friends, Gaba and Nomawa came to see her, but even they had little to say and less to laugh about. But at least they were openly sympathetic. They carried the baby, admiring it and expressing the usual 'oohs' and 'ahs'. Until that point everyone had treated him like a curse, a thing to be discarded, and she herself had not explored her true feelings towards the child. She had ministered to its needs mechanically, but now she knew that she cared. She wanted him to be loved, to belong. For the first time she told herself she loved him and so it did not matter that he had no second name. From that moment a new determination grew in her: she would face that community, she would live in it. She would give the child every chance to live normally. From that day she raised her head and talked normally to the people that she met along the pathways.

The baby was about two months old when the minister came to Sigageni to administer his quarterly Communion to his parish-ioners. As usual, the Deacon had to report to the minister about the state of the community. And Jezile was on his list. She and MaBiyela did not go to Church that Sunday to avoid the embarrassment of being discussed in the presence of the entire congregation. Later that afternoon, when the minister had left, the Deacon went to see MaBiyela. Within a few minutes of his entering MaBiyela's house Jezile heard the sound of weeping. She was curious but she thought it better to wait. When the Deacon had gone, Jezile went down to see MaBiyela. She was on her knees, sobbing and whimpering in a most pitiful way.

'What is it, Mother, what is it?'

'Oh MaMapanga, this is truly a curse . . . The minister has censured me for keeping you here. He has banned me from attending Service. He said I have condoned everything you have done; that I should have sent you back to your people. Oh, MaMapanga, I've been excommunicated. I wasn't there; I could not have stopped what happened to you . . . and I cannot do anything now, without Siyalo . . . He is hard, MaMapanga, God's ways are hard.'

Jezile was 'excommunicated' as well. She had broken a strict moral code. But at that point she was more deeply concerned about MaBiyela, and less about herself. She looked on compassionately, but she was stunned. She had never once thought that she stood condemned by the Church and by God. Surely God who saw everything knew that she had not sinned; she had been sinned against. Now he was punishing not only her but MaBiyela as well; it simply made no sense. She wanted to say something to the crumpled shape on the floor, but the words would not come. The life of the Church was a lifeline for everyone in this community. When life was hard to bear, that is where they all went. Other aspects of life in the community were channelled through the Church. That was why this judgement was like a death sentence.

Some members of the community were sympathetic and others cynical. Jezile could not bear to see MaBiyela suffering. They were both cast out and it was unbearable. By the end of the week, Jezile could bear it no longer. She picked up the baby and went with her other two children down to MaBiyela's house.

'Mother, I've decided, I'll have to go. I'll go back to my people until Siyalo comes back. I cannot bear to see you suffer for something you have so little to do with. God's ways are not easy to understand and cannot be argued with. If you let me, I'll go away tomorrow.'

'It is not for me to let you go. This is a matter for the Majolas. I hear you. I'll have to call them all back again to discuss this. If they let you go, then you will go. Tomorrow I'll call them. But for tonight go and sleep with the children.'

MaBiyela looked grey and thinner than when there was no food around. Jezile had not expected her to crumble in this way. Once she had seemed so strong and powerful. But all that power was gone now and seemed never to have been hers in the first place. Even Siyalo behind his prison walls had more power than MaBiyela.

At the meeting with the Majolas the following day it was agreed that Jezile should go back to her people to release MaBiyela from her remote responsibility. They allowed her to take the Majola children with her as well. But they were not unanimous on this point. Some argued that Jezile's children could not be taken away from the Majolas. But others said they were too young to be separated from their mother. MaBiyela cried bitterly to see them go. She had become attached to them in the year that Jezile was away. Besides, they were her grandchildren, Siyalo's own children, the only real link with him in his long absence and she loved them dearly.

By the beginning of the following week Jezile left Sigageni, her mind in torment and her loyalties deeply divided. The burden of shame was growing heavier with every decision and every decision was completely out of her control. She had always known she was weak; she had fought hard against this helplessness. Yet it seemed that all her efforts were in vain; she felt as if she was suspended in space, at the mercy of all nameless authorities. However, after a few days with her mother, she began to feel safe. In her house she learned to laugh again.

14

When Jezile had first arrived in Bloemfontein her thoughts had been full not only of her family but equally with the upheavals in Sabelweni that she had left behind. The distance robbed her of the sting of personal fear, but she could not shut out the terror that was locked into their life in the reserves. Thoughts of MaNgidi, Duma and Siyapi would often jolt her, in spite of her fatigue, out of that state of half-wakefulness, just before she fell asleep. Her first few letters home were full of questions about the situation, ever hopeful that things would change overnight. It was hard to reconcile her love for the place with the grim future it seemed to hold out. In the end the people of Sigageni would be the losers. Local uprisings could only chip at the granite power of South Africa; in the long-term they knew that they would overthrow that power, but in the short-term, people suffered and whole communities made enormous sacrifices.

Jezile wondered why the many questions in her letters were never answered. She did not know that many from the area were being censored and that people avoided any discussion about the goings-on in Sabelweni in their letters for fear of being picked on. As time passed, Jezile slowly shut her mind to the problems of Sabelweni. Instead, she allowed herself a selective memory that revelled only in the love of her family, the laughter of friends and the security of a known past.

Had Jezile not been so distressed when she arrived back in Sabelweni she would have seen that Sabelweni lay bleeding. But as it was, what she saw was no more than a thud on the shores of her own pain. In the days that followed she gathered, in dribs and drabs, and from the evidence of her own eyes the story of Sabelweni. Whole homesteads, where people she knew had lived, stood in ruins. She was told that the troubles had gone on through the summer and into the winter. Spring had followed and still the people had resisted. By then they had fully established an Appeal Court which they called the Sabelweni High Court on the Ingwe Hill and it became the headquarters of the African movement. The court was fully recognised by the people themselves. Those who had earlier co-operated with the chiefs in their corruption were fined and the money was used to pay the legal expenses of those who had cases which the government had brought against them. In the following November, the government declared a state of emergency covering the whole district of Sabelweni. Public meetings were prohibited; entry into the area could only be gained by written permission of the Bantu Commissioner; likewise, residents had to have permission to leave the area; anyone making a subversive statement, undermining the authority of the Bantu Commissioner or organising a boycott of any kind or treating the chiefs and counsellors with contempt was guilty of an offence. Chiefs were given powers to banish people and to do what they pleased with the immovable property of those they banished.

If the people of Sabelweni had thought that the earlier occupation had been intolerable, that was before they knew how arbitrary the situation could be under a state of emergency. People were certain of nothing. They could hardly go to relieve themselves in the open veldt without a second look over the shoulder for fear that some snooping, prying, ferreting eye was waiting and watching and ready to pounce. The place was swarming with young, bored soldiers. Some of them had participated in quashing urban uprisings, with the exciting tempo that crowded confined city spaces allow. They were not accustomed to the long-drawn-out rural campaigns that pinned down large numbers of soldiers in isolated places, often each man on his own. They were brutal and walked with an air of licence that allowed them to do as they pleased.

The emergency hit hard at the root of things. Thousands of men and women were detained in prison without trial. To scatter their influence and dissipate their revolutionary zeal they were flung into prisons in all corners of the province. According to the official figures 4,769 men and women were held in custody for indefinite periods during that year. Of this number 2,067 were eventually brought to trial. Some would be released for short periods, only to be rounded up again and thrown into jail for a second stint. All this was wearing the morale of the people down. Already about thirty people were sentenced to death for participating in the revolt in one way or another. The authorities had no secure way of gathering their own intelligence and had to depend largely on hearsay. This increased local rivalries, while frustration drove individuals and smaller groups to avenge their relatives by killing pro-government neighbours or suspects. They were caught up in a vicious circle.

As time went on the heat slowly went out of the struggle. Gradually, the road blocks became fewer as the police relaxed their vigilance along the highways and replaced them with more police support to the individual chiefs, increasing their striking capacity and mobility. Now and again, sporadic acts of intimidation occurred out of the blue, and mobile army spotter planes still landed almost on the threshold of people's houses. The people of Sabelweni were never altogether free to live without any intrusion.

It did not take Jezile long to settle back into her home community. She soon lost the stigma of transgressor. Her own people knew her better and were more willing to forgive her. Although she missed some of her friends like Nomawa, her old girlhood friends were still around. Besides, she was far too busy reordering her life and looking after her children to worry too much about other people. She lived in her mother's house and as the weeks went past she began to feel conscious of being a nuisance with her young children's constant crying and quarrelling. She began to want a small place of her own. At first, her mother was aggrieved, thinking that perhaps in some way she had made her daughter feel uncomfortable. She knew that part of the problem was that Jezile had no work and no plot of her own to raise food on. She feared that if they went to ask for a piece of land from the local chief Jezile might be sent to some distant rural part where all the landless were being dumped. In the end the Mapangas got together and decided they would build a small house for Jezile within the confines of her mother's homestead. And she would continue to share her mother's crops from the garden and the fields.

Jezile's house was soon up and she moved in within a month. To keep herself busy and to earn a little money she began to knit jerseys and sell them. But jerseys were a very seasonal business and so when the weather turned hot she switched to sewing and embroidering pillow cases and children's dresses. But so few people had money to buy them that it all went very slowly, and she made little profit. However, it kept her going. When she was not sewing she was in her mother's vegetable garden which she loved. It was green even in the dry winter months because of the little stream that passed through it. Working there gave her time to think. At times she felt agitated and trapped in a hopeless patchwork of effort, determination and failure.

The Easter season was approaching and that year the Easter festival was going to be held at Luve. It circulated among all the villages of the district of Sabelweni and, once every ten years, it came back to Luve. Long meetings were held after the church services and the Thursday meetings, discussing and planning and collecting funds. Some brought their chickens and their goats and so paid in kind when money could not be found. They concentrated their minds on the religious things and political problems took second place. They fussed about the food that they would serve the hundreds of people who would gather in their village for those three days. Each household would take as many people as they could accommodate, according to their means. They plastered and mended and whitewashed their little houses, praying hard that the late summer storms would not arrive and ruin the hard work before the Easter visitors came. The whole plain was speckled with white, blue and pink clusters of little houses. Water was going to be a problem. That was the only time that Jezile saw the local Chief Pungula using his new-found power to the advantage of the community. He inspanned his oxen and brought great big barrels of water from the great Umzimkulu river. They went up and down for days filling the barrels and lining them up impressively against the back of the church building. The whole village was enlivened with joy and expectancy. They woke up early and went to sleep late in the night. They could talk of nothing else wherever they met. Often the women ended up talking about what they would wear on the occasion. Some worried about their threadbare blouses, others about their faded hats or sailor collars. Others described the good heavy materials that they had brought, or had sent for, from Durban to make up their special black serge skirts. Many of the women asked Jezile to sew their clothes – they wanted to look smart and be noticed. They all betrayed their secret vanities as they chatted to Jezile. They could talk as much as they liked to her because she was no longer one of them – she was not in the running. They even betrayed their petty jealousies with unkind words about each other's appearances. While they walked in and out of her house, she listened and worked tirelessly day and night, sewing their hats, their collars, their blouses and their skirts. Money poured in and Jezile could not believe her good fortune. It was interesting seeing the women from her position as an outsider, for it revealed to her all those personal rivalries of which she had not been fully aware.

Time went by and gradually Jezile's heart ached less and less. Siyalo's return was nowhere near in sight, and except for an occasional chill down her spine when she thought of what his return would mean she carried on in much the same way as the other women whose husbands were away in the cities. With the help of one or two people, who knew the chief rather well, she was able to ask for and get a plot for her own home and a small garden for herself. So she moved away from her mother's, but close enough for them to still live almost communally. When the stream ran dry and there were no vegetables life was hard. But at such times she looked back to the difficult times in the past and told herself if she had survived those she would survive anything in the future. She learned to ask her friends and neighbours for what she did not have, knowing that she would pay them back in kind sooner or later. Just like Nomawa had advised her long ago. This way of life had systems built into it that made survival possible without the stigma of begging attached to it. Life was a shared experience, and those who did not share became isolated.

Jezile's white child grew bigger every day. He was tall for his age with a big frame; his skin remained remarkably white in spite of the long days in the sun, and his eyes were grey. His hair, though short and African in texture, was blond. He had his mother's full sensuous lips and like her, he was steady and deliberate in everything he did. Jezile had named him Mazwi but as he grew older he came to be known as Lungu, meaning white. When he was seven years old Ndondo was ten, and S'naye was going on twelve. They were a great source of pleasure to Jezile and all that she lived for. In a couple of years, she thought, Siyalo would be out of prison. The passage of time had made his return seem unreal. She tried to convince herself that all they needed was a long talk and things would be sorted out; Siyalo would understand that there was nothing to forgive and that she was as much his wife as she had been when he had left her to milk the cows that morning. She believed in Siyalo, she believed in their love for each other, she believed he could protect her against the worst pain and believed in his trust.

She was preoccupied with such thoughts one morning when Lungu suddenly burst through the door, an expression of infectious wonder in his eyes and full mouth. In his hands he balanced a bowl of hot meat stew. He made the offering, reverently, if not greedily as well. He could not wait – the smell of good steamy stew in the bowl aroused in him an obliterating craving for food. He could not remember the last time he had had meat. What was it about meat that made it so different from all the foods he had hungered for? His mouth watered, he swallowed another mouthful of saliva as he offered the bowl into his mother's hands. For months he had eaten that maize meal in all its many guises. The memory of good, tasty, nourishing food had slowly faded. His hands trembled, his mouth tightened and so did his grip on that bowl. He breathed hard, his eyes opening wider still. Gogo – Grandma – had sent the stew, only she could give things as rare as meat – all good things came from Gogo. His mother asked in surprise, 'Gogo?' Lungu nodded his head violently. He knelt beside her and she gave him the first spoonful of the heavenly stew. She had the next. She turned it round in her mouth and gave one long soft moan of delight. When she could speak again she told Lungu to go out and call his two sisters. Jezile carefully covered the rest of the stew as she swiftly rose to warm up the cold porridge for the second time – this time it would be different, the meat would transform it – it would go down well. The children trooped in silently, expectantly, and they sat still, on their haunches. She gave a spoonful to each wide open mouth in turn. Then they all waited. She told herself – it had to be done, they had to eat the stew with dignity so that it would leave them a respect for food that was so hard to have when all one ever felt was hunger, envy and greed. When they finally sat down, the meal was eaten in silence, broken only with sighs and the clanging of spoons that grew louder as the meal grew to a close with the scraping of every last morsel. Lungu finally threw the spoon aside and licked the plate clean. Jezile would have rebuked him, but she stopped short feeling that any correction at such a celebration would only serve to spoil things. The children played quietly for a while and soon fell asleep. Jezile lay awake till late as usual. Her thoughts were clear, peaceful and reconciled, and when she finally fell asleep, it was a deep, peaceful sleep.

The next morning, she was woken earlier than usual by the playful noises of the children on the grass mat on the other side of the hearth. A kind of liquid joy welled up inside her. The children were happy and she knew why. She watched them silently bouncing about in the half-light of the house. A shaft of light broke in through the wooden shutter at her window and played hide and seek with the jostling shapes of the children. She lay there, afraid to get up and startle away the ray of joy that had strayed into her home.

Later, in the sun-dappled shade of the tree in front of her house, she sat silently, her head bowed, afraid to think – thoughts shatter peace. When she looked up she saw someone emerging from between the houses of her mother's homestead, a quarter of a mile away. It was her nephew, Mafika, heading straight towards her place. From the urgency of his half-walk, half-run, she knew something had happened. She immediately drew in her legs and curled up defensively as though she had known all along that something would soon come to disturb her life again. She did not know whether to stand up and run away from whatever it was. Life had struck her from all sides and she had learned to stop fighting the odds that were stacked against her. Once Siyalo had said she was as sure-footed as a leopard; but this was no longer true, and she knew it. For a brief moment she slipped back in time and revelled in his image of her: a woman with something unconquerable about her, in her faraway look, in her walk and her slow deliberate speech. There had been a certainty he admired. But now, sitting there abjectly waiting for God knows what, she knew that she had changed; nowadays, she was weak and she could hear herself whimper, always anticipating the worst. She held the tide of probing thoughts at bay until Mafika stood panting before her. She wanted to jump up and gag his mouth – time stood still – she bade him sit down. He crouched on his haunches before her and averted his eyes as though he realised how difficult his message was.

'Gogo says to tell you . . . to tell you . . . to tell you that . . . that there are messengers from the Majolas.' Jezile shuddered visibly at the mention of the Majolas. After a moment of silence she asked without a flicker of eye or muscle, 'What do the Majolas want here now?' The question fell flat in spite of its poignancy.

'I don't know,' Mafika replied needlessly.

'You must have heard what they want – when did they arrive?' she went on, asking as though to stall for time.

'A little while ago.' He was determined to be noncommittal.

'What now . . . what more now? What more is there to say?' she asked, expecting no answers; her voice was cracking. Falteringly Mafika began to answer questions whose answers he had already disclaimed.

'I hear S'naye's father is back from prison. He's been back a week . . .' She let out a half-scream, quickly raising her hand to shut her mouth. She raised herself and knelt upright.

'What do they want here? What have I got to do with them now? Haven't they explained everything to him? Where is he? Where is he . . . ? Oh, where is Siyalo now? He's the only one who'd understand . . . oh, what's the point, it's all over now.' She was agitated and she expected no answers from Mafika or anyone else.

Mafika turned round to go – his eyes still cast down, afraid to look at his aunt's face. She turned round and looked at the children who were playing behind them. She stifled the wish to hide them, to run away with them, somehow to escape the present. She rose up instead and staggered after him, leaving them to continue their play in blissful ignorance. She was not going to drag them into that fractured world.

Arriving at her parents' home she stole behind two rondavels, hoping to catch her mother alone. Jezile looked fiercely at her mother whose eyes were red from crying and they instantly filled up again when she saw her. She sprang silently foward and clasped her mother's limp hands in hers. She fell on her in a tight embrace that fought to lock out all pain.

'They're here Jezile, they're here to take away the children – they've come for them – I knew they'd come for them some day . . .' crying and wringing her heart in heaving sobs. MaSibiya went on repeating the message as though neither of them had understood what was happening. Jezile stiffened and drew back. The message thrust its meaning through every tissue of her body. She knew that she had reached the final border of hope. She had hoped that Siyalo would understand. She shook her head as if to dislodge something in there, loudly denying what was happening, 'No, no, never, never – oh, why didn't he come . . . ?'

Her uncle spoke through the din, 'The Majolas are here. They've come for their children.'

It was as if God had spoken. The sentence had been passed. But after a moment, Jezile dared answer God. 'Their children? No, they're my children; these are my children,' she screeched, listening only to the pain in her heart. Frantic, she saw her children being led away by the two Majola men who walked past as though they had not seen her. They said not one word to her; they did not falter in any way: custom was their guiding code – unyielding primeval adjudicators, administering primordial laws. In her absence, her people, the Mapangas and his people, the Majolas had judged her, condemned her and disowned her. How was it that laws were so clear cut, when the lives they governed were so muddled; how was it that those laws could not order life protectively and mercifully? Where was the law when she was so mercilessly raped and so utterly alone? Where were the Majolas when she and her children had cruelly starved so that she had to leave her children and work in other people's houses and look after other people's children and be so exposed to abuse? She leaped forward, her arms open wide, as if to collect them in her arms and save them from some terrible fate. She looked straight into her children's eyes, and they looked back at her, their eyes pleading for her not to let them go with strangers. The children did not know the men. They remembered little of the Majolas – and they would not have known Siyalo, their father, if he had appeared in front of them. And she, Jezile, who had been a mere vessel, a vessel to carry humanity – to carry the Majolas and only the Majolas – was now unable to claim for herself her own flesh and blood. They were Majolas and she was a Mapanga. Pain raged beyond her control. Life seemed to recede like the setting sun leaving a pool of darkness behind. She had been emptied, turned inside out. She lay whimpering, huddled on the grass mat, covered in her dark grey, threadbare blanket. Doors of memories opened and shut as she raced back to the beginning. She shut herself away from the unbearable present, from her loss and her world. She heard rather than saw the other women surging round, a human wall to protect her. They seemed always to be there in times of crisis. They appeared from everywhere as though they had sniffed news in the air. They murmured, they caressed, they force-fed, insisting that life must go on, no matter what. They would not let anyone succumb for they each depended on the other. They kept vigil night and day, taking turns to give comfort to Jezile. They were always there. They accepted the harsh execution of custom without question. They were there to see her through.

After two weeks Jezile stirred one morning. She woke up and sat facing the women. It was no longer a frantic look in her eyes that sought an escape. She looked round at every face in turn, but she said nothing. She looked through the window and to everyone's surprise she shouted for Lungu. Her voice was loud and clear. She called twice and Lungu was at the door. The women looked at each other and then at her and smiled. He looked at the women and rushed to Jezile's side. 'She's awake, mother is awake, she's all right.'

Jezile rose from her mat, and new resolve filled her heart. She would discount the past and recreate her life afresh. Her daughters would always be hers. She nursed the hope that the wrench of their parting had not been as devastating for them as it had been for her; that their youth would give them the resilience that she had lacked. This she told herself over and over again. For ten years she had counted each passing year. Siyalo's return had been something to live for. But now that time had come and gone and taken with it her main reason for living – her children. How was she going to take command of her life again? She had done it all before; but now she was back where she started. What more was there to do?

For weeks and months after these events, Jezile lived in a state of suspension, waiting for nothing in particular. MaBiyela sent a message one day to reassure her of the children's happiness. This gave Jezile the encouragement to write to her and the girls, feeling that she had not been totally banished from their lives. And thus began a slow process of mending their abruptly ruptured relationship. It was hard to explain the causes that had disrupted their life. What woman could tell her daughters she had been violated? And so it was that MaBiyela undertook the task of bringing up the girls with love and understanding.

As for Lungu, Jezile squandered all her love on him. She felt deeply for the child and often wondered how he would bear the burden of his life. He was caught between two warring worlds. The rift in the family would certainly make that burden heavier when he came to understand. She sought to cushion that discovery with love, for there was no doubt that his little life, in spite of its innocence, bore the responsibility for the great pain that the family had suffered. Jezile was determined that she would teach him the importance of justice as a virtue, for he was one of those whose own life had known no justice. If he wanted it, he would have to fight for it in the community in which he lived and in the politics of his country that was South Africa. Life at Luve was a training ground for that fight for justice, for even before the dawn of understanding he felt it as he played with the other children, in the absence of a father, in the lonely struggles of his mother, and in the vexing references to his colour and apartness that gave him his nickname, Lungu. He soon learned that by virtue of his birth he had been disinherited from all sources of power – the white world, and his place in the African male structure. This soon opened his eyes to the needs of others who were oppressed by power.

An incident occurred one day, out in the veldt, which brought it squarely home to Lungu how much at variance he was with everything that he was part of. All the children at Sabelweni had grown up in the awareness of the upheavals that had taken place just before or just after they were born. They had spent their childhood in fear of their lives, if not in fear for their parents' lives. The legacy of the insurgency lived on and could not be forgotten for soldiers still appeared now and again in the villages. And when they did they stomped around insulting everyone and confiscating things. Up until then Lungu had hated the soldiers like all his playmates. But on this occasion when he was about nine, a white soldier appeared out in the fields where they were herding some cattle. He came straight over to them, and out of habit, they huddled together in fear. The soldier started to say something, but stopped as his eyes alighted on Lungu. He looked him up and down and muttered something. Then he lowered his voice and said something in English or Afrikaans. When he realised that Lungu did not understand, he switched to Fanakalo. He wanted to know who he was, what he was doing out there, and wondered if he would like to go away with him to live in town like all white children did. He took out from his rucksack a crumpled parcel of dried-up sandwiches and broken biscuits and gave it to him. The children did not see him leave because they were all jostling to get a share of the booty. Lungu asserted himself in the effort to create some order, saving himself the lion's share, explaining that it had been meant for him and he was going to share the rest with his mother. That is when the others began to tease him, saying he was not one of them, but a white like all others; one with the soldiers and all that was associated with them. By the next day the others had forgotten the incident and played with him as though it had never happened, but Lungu never forgot.

15

T wo years passed and Jezile seemed more resolute in everything she did. She went back and worked hard at her
knitting and sewing and her work in the fields. And even
against her instinct she took in some washing from a young
white couple in Umzimkulu to ensure that she had a more
regular income. It was a pittance, but it ensured that she and
Lungu never went hungry. And with strict budgeting she
managed to save some of the money that she got from selling
her knitting and sewing. The fact that there were only two
instead of four mouths to feed also helped. She was thinking of
the time when the children would have to go to boarding
schools as children in rural Sabelweni had to do. She would
need every penny then to pay for their school fees and their
books. She had heard that Siyalo had a job in Ixopo and he was
looking after the girls well. She knew she could rely on his love
for them and on his sense of responsibility towards them. But
she had learned in the past that life was unpredictable and that
things could turn upside down at the most unexpected
moments. She did not want to gamble with the children's
future. She was determined that they should never need to
work for the Potgieters of this world.

Siyalo kept his job at Ixopo working as a cook in a school for
coloured children. Coloured people as a whole, though powerless, enjoyed better privileges in the country than Africans. The
pupils at his school ate decent food and enjoyed a higher
standard of living. But above all they did not have to endure
the scourge of Bantu Education which was inflicted on African
children. However, in spite of that much reviled quality of
education in African schools, Siyalo worked hard to send his
daughters to what were considered better African schools,

when the time came for them to leave the Sigageni Combined School. He sent S'naye to Mnene School, a boarding school for girls about fifty miles away from home. There was an air of general excitement in the family about the school and S'naye was advised on several occasions to conduct herself with respect for authority and to work hard to pass her examinations. The school looked big and beautiful although the facilities were not as good as in the school for coloureds where he worked. But for an African school it was certainly among the best. It was with surprise then that towards the end of S'naye's first year Siyalo and MaBiyela got letters from her saying she was unhappy. She complained generally about the food and the school authorities. Her letters betrayed a restlessness they could not understand. The school had been recommended for its good discipline and for its high moral training. However, soon things stabilised and S'naye, being an amenable sort of person, settled down to her new environment.

Two years later it was Ndondo's turn to go to boarding school. She was excited about it, and being more outgoing than S'naye, she made it clear that she did not wish to go to Mnene School where her sister was. She said she had heard enough about the place and wanted to go to Zotheni School. She chose it because she liked their uniforms and she had heard that life there was much more exciting and the pupils were not as regimented as at Mnene. At seventeen she had blossomed into a pretty, vivacious girl and was very outspoken. There were times when Siyalo wished she had had a mother to bring her up. She had strong views on many things. Siyalo tried hard to curb her high spirits and forthrightness, but at times he found himself actually encouraging her, she, who in many other ways, was very much like her mother. For this reason he had a soft spot for her and would give in easily to her demands.

It was 1976. S'naye was nineteen and finishing off her matriculation at Mnene. If she passed she wanted to train as a nurse if she could find a hospital that would accept her. Ndondo was in her third year. There was news in all the papers about trouble in many schools throughout the country. Ever since the students' uprising against teaching school subjects in the medium of Afrikaans in far away Johannesburg, things had never really settled down. In some schools in the Transvaal and in the Cape, students no longer attended classes. What had started as a language issue had become a sweeping rebellion against all injustices, not only in the school system but in all aspects of life in South Africa. However, the violent clashes between the State and the African children in the schools had not reached this part of the country yet. Although Siyalo supported everything those students stood for, he was anxious that his own children's schooling should go on uninterrupted.

That same year, it was Lungu's turn to go to boarding school. Jezile agonised a great deal about finding him a 'safe' school. She would have done anything and everything to keep him from danger. The students' revolt was sweeping across the country, from the cities to the rural areas. Jezile continued her hopeless search until she stumbled on an idea. Technically, Lungu was a Coloured, she thought, although she had never registered him as such. So perhaps she should take him to the Coloured school at Ixopo. The Coloured schools and Coloured communities seemed peaceful and safe at the time, especially in the rural areas. The more she thought about it, the more it seemed like the obvious thing to do. But that was where Siyalo worked, and the thought filled her with new reservations. How would Lungu adjust? He knew no other lifestyle but rural African life. He knew no Afrikaans and had never attended a Coloured school before. But the more she thought about it, the more she felt it his right to be with his own kind at last, and to start learning to live like a Coloured, and above all to escape that infernal pass. But what if the new life created a rift between them, a son who would look with different eyes on his mother?

After days of agitating over the problem she managed to convince herself that the love they had known as mother and son, thrown together by forces they had no power over, would be strong enough to keep him from ever drifting away. But, Siyalo too had to decide. Could he bear to have the child in the same school as he was? Once she had reached this point she wrote MaBiyela a letter asking her to put the question to Siyalo. Ever since Siyalo's return she had never written him a letter. She did not want to do so now because she could not bear a negative answer directed straight at her. Unreasonable as this feeling was, she knew that, should he write her a letter rejecting the idea, she would take it as a rejection of herself. However, when MaBiyela's reply came, it brought a reasoned answer from Siyalo. He would accept that the child join the school because in spite of everything, Lungu was his child – according to custom any child she bore while still married to him was his child. As he had never divorced her she was still his wife and the child was his. It surprised Jezile that custom could be on her side as well. What surprised her more was to see what a creature of custom Siyalo was.

And so it was that Lungu went to Mansfield School for Boys the following year. The first term was particularly hard for him because of the cultural gap between him and the other boys. The teachers too were a little embarrassed by his ways that betrayed a part of themselves that they wished to forget – the African half. In the South African hierarchy of races, it made sense for many Coloureds to identify with the side that had the power to confer status and a little privilege. However, Lungu was a gifted child and his appearance did much to identify him with the source of power. He was bright and popular and happy. This gave him a new confidence and he began to read avidly. He was hungry for knowledge. The more he read, the more he learned about South Africa as a country, and his place in the society, and therefore his own identity. As a result he confronted his mother about the true circumstances of his birth and his mother felt that at the age of fifteen it was his right to know the truth. But when he knew the whole truth, it filled him with a burning pain and a great anger. From then on, although outwardly happy, there was a raging anger inside him, mingled with conflicting nameless emotions.

When Ndondo was in her final year and Lungu was sixteen, about to finish his second year at Mansfield, the students' uprisings reached Zotheni. There did not seem to be any particular issue that gave rise to the troubles at Zotheni. Some said it was over a trivial argument in class about the value of Bantu Education against the general background of oppression in South Africa. But tensions had been bubbling under the surface and the student body exploded without warning, causing great chaos in the school. Windows were broken, books and desks burned, and the teachers were torn between upholding order on the one hand and siding with the students' long-established grievances. The school's authorities though not directly to blame, were soft targets for a very angry army of young people; angry against a faceless, ruthless government and its racist policies. The teachers were implicated in a situation which was not of their own making. Many were guilty by default, if they were guilty at all. As soon as the troubles started the police were called in and among the student leaders was Ndondo, conspicuous by her height and her remarkable ability to mobilise the other students to the attack. When the police began to open fire she fought on fearlessly as though she had nothing to lose. The young people had never engaged in a confrontation with the police before. Several students were wounded and a couple of them died. The school was closed down. A hunt for the ringleaders was on. Ndondo was at the top of their list. Frightened to face her father, she chose to go to her mother until things cooled down. While she was at Luve she heard that the police had been at Sigageni looking for her. It seemed evident that they wanted to arrest her. Telling Jezile that it was important for her to be with MaBiyela at such a time rather than leaving her at the mercy of the police to hassle and intimidate her, Ndondo left Luve, ostensibly for Sigageni. For the next three weeks everyone assumed she was with the other half of the family: Jezile thought she was at Sigageni, and Siyalo thought she was at Luve. Every time the police came they were told a different story. It was only when the police caught on that Ndondo was at Luve with her mother that they went there to arrest her. Jezile realised then that in fact no one knew where Ndondo was. Later they heard that she had skipped the borders of South Africa into exile.

Her escape left the family stunned. But there was more to come a couple of months later. The events at Zotheni had an infectious effect on the whole region. The students' political movement had finally reached Mansfield. Siyalo, who was secretly agitating over his 'lost' daughter, had no way of knowing that problems were smouldering right under his feet. And there had been no one to tell him. Although Siyalo liked Lungu and admired his spirit the two had never had much chance to develop their relationship. Lungu had never really known how to accept his step-father. They treated each other with superficial politeness, although Siyalo had, on a deeper level, aroused emotions in Lungu that bewildered the boy.

The time had come when the Coloured students at Mansfield questioned their 'privileges' which they now saw as a strategy on the government's part to divide them from the majority mass of the African people. They abdicated their previous position and began to identify themselves with the mass of the struggling people. Lungu, whose life had straddled so many experiences of oppression, became at sixteen the leader of the Mansfield uprising. The atmosphere in the school was electric. There was a constant police presence, and at the slightest provocation they would open fire. They had already shot and killed close to a thousand students in various parts of the country.

The biggest demonstration at Mansfield was short-lived. The police moved in, and without a flicker of hesitation turned their guns on the students and watched them fall like autumn leaves. Lungu felt a hot sting somewhere in his hip; then a spreading numbness flowed down his legs. The demonstration had turned into a bloody riot which the police, through force and violence, finally brought under control.

Lungu was discovered among the injured in hospital by Jezile hours later. He was paralysed from the waist down.

Jezile found it very hard to see Lungu trapped at home day after day, being wheeled about by his friends on contraptions that they had spent days making so that they could carry him with them to the fields. Often she saw the contraptions break up before they were out of the yard. Things eased a little when S'naye saved enough money from her student nurse's pay to buy him a wheelchair. That gift brought great joy to the family and enabled Jezile to take him with her on long bumpy country walks and, once in a while, she would even load the wheelchair onto a local bus and go to the Umzimkulu dorp which was always crowded with young people. In the meantime Lungu continued to do very well in his studies at the private school for the disabled where he now was. The greatest day was when he won a scholarship to take him to university to undertake his studies in medicine. As the long years wore on S'naye, especially, was very proud of her brother's ability to remain ever witty, ever cheerful. But, for her the most exciting thing was that he was going to be a doctor. To think they were going to have a doctor in their own family, right there in Sabelweni – their own doctor! At one time this had seemed impossible. But there he was, a living proof that nothing was impossible.

After qualifying as a nurse S'naye came back from Durban to work nearer home at the Clydesdale Hospital. Perhaps it was for this reason that Lungu chose to come and serve his house-manship at this little hospital rather than in one of the big hospitals in Durban. Perhaps he needed his sister's support.

Meanwhile MaBiyela learned to believe in Jezile and constantly looked for ways in which to atone for her behaviour in their earlier life together. She felt guilty about the difficult relation-ship that existed between the family and Jezile and secretly felt that it was wrong that Jezile should have nothing to do with the upbringing of her own children. But she, like everyone else, knew she had to bow to the demands of custom. Whenever opportunities arose, she tried to make amends. She wrote to Jezile regularly about the girls' progress and their health. And when they did meet a few times at public gatherings they spent the whole time talking to each other like long-lost friends. She was also concerned for Siyalo. If he did see other women, his relationships remained casual and he made no move to divorce Jezile and remarry. Years ago, when the girls were younger, he had left the home he had shared with Jezile to live with his mother. It had seemed the most practical thing to do at the time. Without Jezile the place had seemed dead. The weeds were overgrown and the place had fallen to ruin. Sometimes in later years MaBiyela would catch him looking intently at the ruins of his old home with the fascination of a man looking at a temple.

As the years went by S'naye and Lungu talked less and less about their sister Ndondo, and their hopes of seeing her again began to fade. In the time she had been gone they had had only one letter from her. There had been no indication where she was when she wrote that letter. It had been posted by someone within South Africa. But for Jezile there was not a single day that went by without thinking of Ndondo. She no longer cried as frequently and as copiously as she used to. She had grown more religious with age, having been accepted back into the church. She had joined the Women's Union again and had gone back to attending the women's Thursday meetings. With Lungu away most of the time, first at university, and later in hospitals all over the country, she was often alone. She called Lungu's success 'her miracle'.

Jezile was sitting on a grass mat, weaving a basket, when S'naye came in late one afternoon. She was still wearing her hospital uniform. Jezile looked up with a broad, welcoming smile. She always looked forward to S'naye's surprise visits.

'Mother,' said S'naye, still on her feet.

'Yes,' replied Jezile looking up again. There was something in S'naye's voice that tugged at Jezile's insides. S'naye knelt down next to her mother, and not wishing to alarm her, she went on softly.

'You know what, Ndondo is back. She's around these parts.' Her eyes fastened on her mother's eyes and they both held their breath in silence. 'I've seen her.' Jezile stopped everything, and except for the thumping vein in her neck, nothing moved.

'Mother, calm down.' They embraced each other, locked in silence. When they both relaxed S'naye went on, 'It's true. She's being very careful about her movements, so she can't come straight here and see you. She came to see me at the hospital today. She was disguised as a doctor in a white coat with a stethoscope showing clearly from her coat pocket. She walked calmly towards me and I didn't recognise her at first. She actually talked to me, and I still didn't recognise her.'

'Why, is she very much changed then?' Jezile spoke for the first time, showing some anxiety. 'Are you sure it's her?'

'Sure as I am of my name. It's just that I didn't expect to see her. She looked familiar, very familiar. I thought she was one of the doctors I'd met somewhere. I wasn't being very observant, I suppose. She's grown; she's a woman now. Her hair is short and she looked very serious . . . she had to be – trying to pretend that all we were was a doctor and a nurse discussing patients.'

Jezile could feel physical pain building up in the pit of her stomach. S'naye continued, 'But it's her, it's her all right. She's in hiding. She says she's come to start her political work in these parts because she's the only one who knows this area well.'

'Political work! What, more political work? Hasn't she done enough? Haven't we given everything to politics?' Jezile asked, getting agitated.

'It's her life Mother, she's given her life to it . . . just like I've given mine to looking after the sick. Politics is her life.' Then they both went on talking, each to herself, exploring their own thoughts, and not listening to each other. 'She's not the only one, of course. They're under very strict instructions not to blow their cover; one false step and things could go wrong. But whatever her instructions are, she says she will see you. That's why she had to come to see me at the hospital, she had to take that risk. She's coming to see you tonight, mother! It's unbelievable!'

'Her political work. What is that?'

S'naye went on, her voice rising in excitement, reliving her meeting with her sister. 'You don't know how I felt when she stood there before me and looked at me. At first she called me casually. "Nurse," she said. "Nurse," she called again. Then she came across to me and stood really close to me.' But her mother was not listening any more.

'Then she called me, "S'naye, it's me, don't say anything; it's me." I stood there staring and shuddering, not believing my own senses. "C'mon," she said, "Don't shout, don't say a word. Just listen." I suppose I looked as though I was going to scream. "I want to see mother, I want to see you all, but I must see mother first, tonight. I came to see you because I want to see mother. I'm not allowed to see you or talk to anyone I know, but I have to see mother." She wears glasses now. Oh, Mother, believe me, I've seen her.'

Jezile continued muttering. 'Oh my child, my child.' She knelt on her mat. 'God, please protect my child, at least until I see her tonight; even if I never see her again; just until I see her tonight. Don't tell anyone S'naye, don't breathe a word.' Suddenly she felt as though the four walls of her little house would collapse on her and crush her down. She went outside and sat on her haunches, her knees tucked right under her chin. When she felt more secure in the cradle of her arms and knees, she asked, 'What time did she say she was coming?'

'Late. About eleven o'clock.'

'That late! Will she come alone that late?'

'I'm sure she can cope with anything like that these days. I'm sure she's a well-trained soldier – equal to any danger now.'

'Soldier, is that what she is? How long will she stay? D'you know? She can't stay the night, can she?'

'I've no idea, Mother.'

'We have to prepare her a meal; a meal for us together; I'll cook the meal myself tonight. You'll stay S'naye and help me. I'll need your help tonight; I couldn't do anything without help.'

'Yes, Mother. I'll be here tonight. I've arranged for all that.'

They killed a big chicken and cooked a little rice and the last greens in the house. The food was ready and waiting before seven o'clock. Time stood still. They waited. The hours crawled by slowly. By nine o'clock Jezile was trembling and cold with apprehension. Then they heard footsteps in the distance. They listened intently, holding their breath and doing all they could to stop their pounding hearts. They listened, and looked at each other, waiting breathlessly. They could hear the footsteps drawing closer and closer until they were certain that they were heading straight for their door. They were not the gentle, familiar crunching of bare feet but those of a person in heavy shoes or boots. Jezile stood up as if to open the door, but she stopped short, for just then the steps seemed to pass her door and in that measured step they slowly receded into the distance and stillness of the dark night. They looked at each other uneasily. Doubts began to flutter. Jezile shuddered and shook her head violently. Who was it that went past their door? And loudly she asked:

'Ndondo couldn't miss our door, could she?' They both sighed at the same time and the wind rose tremulously and filled every crevice in the room. They calmed down, reminding themselves that it was not yet eleven o'clock. So they waited. It was about a quarter to eleven when they both held their breath for a second time that night – they could hear muffled steps approaching. Jezile stood transfixed in the middle of the room.

The door swung open and Ndondo burst in with her arms wide open.

'Mother!' she cried and squashed Jezile in a tight embrace. Then she turned to her sister and hugged her and cried and laughed all at once. At last they all sat down, too excited to eat the food that had been so carefully and lovingly prepared. They wanted to know where she had been, which countries she had lived in. What had she done in the nine years she had been away? But each answer she gave brought home to them the gulf that yawned between the Ndondo of her childhood days, whom they knew and loved and had missed so much, and the Ndondo who sat before them now, a woman of unfathomable experiences. Lovingly, desperately, they pieced together the past and the present. If only there was time! Jezile hedged round the one question she wanted to ask; why had Ndondo chosen to come back home when she was still in danger? Ndondo herself was full of questions about the family and was shocked and distressed to hear about Lungu and the injuries that had left him crippled.

Jezile said light-heartedly, 'I thought you were a hardened soldier now; you've seen worse than that I'm sure.' Then she began to talk about Lungu's success and they were soon laughing and talking about him as a doctor – a doctor from Luve. There were so many questions that were left unasked, let alone unanswered. Before they knew it the time was two o'clock.

'I'll be leaving soon. I'll leave at three.' It was so strange to see her sitting there before them after so long and yet it also seemed like the day before. The intervening years melted away and they were surrounded by a warmth that went back to the days before they had been separated. Jezile could not stop staring into her daughter's face, studying every change – more than the other two, Ndondo resembled her most. And Ndondo marked the many lines that scarred Jezile's face. They were lines of sadness and pain, she thought. Aloud she said, 'Don't worry mother, everything will soon be over.'

'What will?'

'All our troubles and long separations. We'll soon be free; we'll see to that.' At exactly three o'clock, with military precision, Ndondo stood up to go.

'Mother, I must leave now,' she said.

'I know you have to go, my child. I don't want you to go, but you have to. I wouldn't want anyone to find you here. I know I'll treasure these few hours for the rest of my days.'

No one spoke. Jezile saw tears building up in Ndondo's eyes but she would not allow them to spill. To diffuse this terrible moment, Jezile took Ndondo's hand in hers and spoke almost casually.

'You know, the state of emergency of long ago is still in operation. Soldiers still come now and again and wake people up from their sleep, and make a general nuisance of themselves. They come when they suspect there's trouble in the air. Otherwise it has quietened down a lot.'

They went to the door hand in hand, casually, as though they were going nowhere in particular. S'naye, who was starting to cry, decided to remain behind.

'I'll show you a new path out of the village,' Jezile said to Ndondo. 'It's a short cut and not many people use it.' And they walked away. It was a warm black night.

Her spirit renewed, Jezile walked determinedly back into the house after she had seen Ndondo off.

Minutes after Jezile and Ndondo had left, there was a loud banging at the door. Terrified, S'naye made no move to open the door. The banging continued till the door swung open with the force of it. A soldier burst in brandishing a big gun.

'Where's she, where's she?' He pulled out a photograph from his pocket, looked at it, and looked at S'naye again.

'It's not you, is it? Where's she, what's her name? Ndondo, that's her name. What's your name? She's been here, hasn't she, hasn't she? C'mon speak, speak maan speak.' He poked her with the barrel of the gun. He saw the deadly fear on her face. That fear had sent him into a frenzy of anger and violence. He shouted and grabbing her by the shoulders shook her. In one movement, he pulled her close to him as if to embrace her. And chucking his gun aside he ripped the top of her uniform open. S'naye was too petrified to shout or do anything. All she could think of was that any noise she made would attract attention to Ndondo and her mother.

Jezile walked into her house and there before her eyes was a young man, pale as white paper, locked in a struggle with

S'naye. They did not see her. His trousers were down, and in his struggle to subdue S'naye, he shifted his position to one side, revealing a fully tumescent penis. He held S'naye in the grip of his arm as he pressed her hard with his knee against the wall. He was pushing and panting and grunting. Jezile recalled in an instant her own struggle with Potgieter and the memory stung her into action. Right there on the side, lying on the floor, was the mighty instrument, carelessly abandoned in a reckless moment of misplaced power. Another look at the gun and Jezile knew she could not use it. She had no clue how it worked. Her eyes landed on the knives on the table that had not been used for the meal that night and in an instant she had plunged the sharpest one deep into the left side of the depraved soldier. He staggered forward and gave one yell as he fell on S'naye, relaxing his grip as he twitched in his final moments. That towering symbol of power lay sprawled and dying on Jezile's floor. S'naye scrambled up not realising fully what had happened. Then she saw the knife in her mother's hand.

'Oh, God, I've killed him, I've killed him, my child.'

'What? What did you say, Mother?'

'Look, he's dead. It was bound to happen at some time or other; we have to fight back. I couldn't let him do it to you . . .' There was something so calm about her as she walked over and sat down on her old chair. Something akin to peace settled on her face. She sat dry-eyed, an air of achievement about her.

'Go and tell them,' she said. With another look at the dead man she stood up swiftly. 'No, don't tell them yet. Come with me. Help me through the night, S'naye, my child.' She leapt up, energised by a thought that S'naye could not fathom. 'Together we can face the dark night. We have to go now before they come. I have to see Siyalo before they pick me up.'

'See my father? You're going to see my father?' S'naye managed to ask between hysterical sobs.

'Yes, I've something to tell him before the end.'

'Mother, what's happening to us?' she asked like someone drowning.

'This is no time to cry, S'naye. You have a lot of crying to do, but this is not the time. Crying does not change a thing. God knows I've cried – all my life.'

'Are we walking all the way?'

'All the way? Yes, what else is there to take us there? We can't sit here with him lying on the floor like that. Besides, we're less likely to get caught now than if we waited for the buses in the morning. Here, change that uniform. Put on one of my dresses.'

They walked silently; the sky was pitch black. It was almost four o'clock and a lively morning breeze had risen. They walked briskly. For S'naye it seemed like a bad dream. They walked mechanically, feeling no fatigue or thirst, and they said very little to each other. Dawn came and lit their path, but they did not seem to notice it. They kept pace as they had done for the last three hours. They were more than half-way there already. For S'naye, the rising sun brought new terrors. She felt exposed. It was about eight-thirty when they saw the Ixopo village nestling among the wattle trees, dusty and complacent as ever. S'naye led the way for the last half mile. When they finally got to the school Siyalo was not at the men's quarters. He had been up and about for hours. His day started early in preparation for the boys' daily routine when they woke up at six-thirty. At nine o'clock, after breakfast and assembly, classes were about to start. Work was just beginning to ease off for the kitchen staff. The two women waited silently outside the door of Siyalo's room until someone else saw them. He promised to go and tell Siyalo that he had visitors.

When Siyalo saw Jezile he stood stock-still, his face expressionless for some moments. Then, with a kind of smile, he came forward hurriedly.

'Jezile, it's you, isn't it? What's brought you here after all these years, and so early in the morning?'

She looked him up and down. He was so close to her. They had not been so close for more than twenty years. In spite of the intervening years, and despite her many confused emotions, she felt a gush of something strong and familiar; something that coursed through her blood, draining her head of all thoughts. Slowly her face became contorted with pain, but her eyes remained dry. He raised his hand slowly as if to touch her, to iron out the creases on her face. S'naye looked at them feeling unnerved. She shuffled her feet slightly and that movement reminded Siyalo that they were not alone. He looked at S'naye and ventured, 'We three have not been together like this, a family, in a very long time.'

'Shall we go inside your room, Baba?' S'naye asked hurriedly.

Once they were inside Siyalo asked again, 'Why have you come now, Jezile? It's been so long.'

'Why didn't *you* ever come Siyalo, ever, ever?'

'Something has happened Baba – something very serious,' S'naye broke in.

'What is it? It must be serious to bring you here.'

'Siyalo, this time I want to tell you myself. I must, before it's too late. The last time I waited for you to come and ask me for the truth; you never came. This time I've come to tell you the truth, myself.'

'Jezile, what's happened? Tell me, tell me.' There was great urgency in his voice.

'It's happened again. Only, this time, he wanted to rape S'naye.'

'Who? What are you talking about?' He could see traces of dampness at the corners of her eyes. He stifled the wish to take her into his arms and rock her gently. Instead he played feverishly with the ring on his little finger.

'Tell me, tell me Jezile what has happened – '

When she saw the ring a tear began to trickle down from the corner of one eye. Then stubbornly, she looked back at him.

'Last night, Ndondo came home. Our Ndondo is back.'

'Our Ndondo?'

'She's back, Siyalo. She came to see us last night. Only for a couple of hours. Then I had to show her the safest route away from the house. It was this morning, in the dark, at about three o'clock. I don't know how long I was out. But when I came back I saw this man, this white man, a soldier, I believe. He had her – he was going to break her in two and he was going to rape her. Not again Siyalo. No, not again.' She grew incoherent and shook her head violently. 'Not again. I could not let it happen again. It's happened before. It happened to me. It poisoned my life. That man, long ago, broke my life. And you never came to ask me. You didn't want to know what had happened to me. You don't know how Lungu was born; not from me, you don't. That man, Potgieter, held me, and broke me, and raped me. That's how Lungu was born.'

244

There was a long silence. And Siyalo slowly drew close. Unable to trust his hands not to touch her he secured them in a link behind him and he asked her very softly, 'So, what happened last night?'

'I stabbed him, Siyalo, I killed him.'

Siyalo swiftly swung round with his hands tightly covering his face. 'Oh Jezile, oh Jezile, no, no, never. It can't have happened. Oh God, never. Why have my ancestors forsaken me and my family? Jezile what haven't I done to solicit their help? Oh God, oh God! You mean you've killed a white man this morning!'

'I had to kill him. They've destroyed us, Siyalo. They broke our marriage, they broke our life here at Sabelweni, and they've broken all our children's lives and killed many. He was raping our daughter. I had to defend her. We have to defend ourselves.'

He swung round to face her, carnage in his mind, and looked at her wordlessly, penetrating those eyes, mind to mind, heart to heart. Together they drifted back in reverse into a vortex beyond recovery, in a kind of falling away. In that silence he held her hands tightly in his and he whispered inaudibly, more to himself than to her, 'Jezile, life of my life.'

LET IT BE TOLD
Essays by Black Women Writers in Britain
Edited by Lauretta Ngcobo

'We are laying claim to our selfhood . . . as women: separate and equal with men, demanding recognition not only from the host society but from our own community' – *Lauretta Ngcobo*

In this engaging and dynamic collection of essays by ten Black women writers in Britain are personal stories, glimpses of history, discussions of the intentions and obligations of writing itself, and a powerful sense of resistance in the face of British racism. These essays are also about colonialism and slavery, male domination, the family and motherhood, work and sexuality. The contributors, some of whom were born in Britain, others originally from other countries, are Beverly Bryan, Stella Dadzie and Suzanne Scafe (writing about their collaboration on *The Heart of the Race: Black Women's Lives in Britain*), Valerie Bloom, Amryl Johnson, Grace Nichols, Marsha Prescod, Lauretta Ngcobo, Agnes Sam, and Maud Sulter. Poems, prose pieces, critical commentaries and a comprehensive introduction combine to offer a view of the rich and multi-faceted cultural tradition of this writing in the 1980s.

YOU CAN'T GET LOST IN CAPE TOWN
Zoë Wicomb

Frieda Shenton has returned to South Africa, a reluctant visitor to the land of her birth. She has put behind her the childhood years in rural Namaqualand and the later experiences of living and working in Cape Town: there was no reconciling the restrictions of apartheid and her father's vision of what her own bright potential might mean for his family and people.

Frieda knew that education, for a Black woman, meant neither freedom nor an end to personal insecurity. Now, years later, return brings a fresh perspective,not a vindication of her exile. Visiting family, talking with friends, in fleeting glimpses of the clandestine resistance movement, Frieda must confront the ambiguities of her exclusion and acknowledge the price of having strayed from the culture that shaped her.

Zoë Wicomb's first collection of connected stories is a superb portrayal of a woman coming to terms with her rejected racial inheritance. Marvellously vivid evocations of past and present, the stories intertwine as incidents recalled build up to give shape to Frieda's identity.

BIRD AT MY WINDOW
Rosa Guy

'She has translated into living terms Thoreau's inspired
phrase "quiet desperation". This is her triumph and it is by
no means a small one' – *Chicago Tribune*.

'A hauntingly vivid portrayal of the rigours of Harlem life in
the 50s' – *The Voice*.

Wade Williams wakes up in a New York hospital wearing a
strait-jacket and with ten minutes of his life blanked out. Ten
terrifying minutes from which his feckless brother, Willie Earl,
and loyal sister, Faith, would protect him, his mother and
themselves.

  In search of the key to his lost memory, Wade backtracks
through his whole life. Born in 1920s Harlem to a legacy of
deprivation where the only way out is in the teeth of racism, or
on the backs of family and friends, with just two real chances
of happiness in his life. Wade Williams is a tragic figure whose
glowering honesty contributes to his own destruction.

BROWN GIRL, BROWNSTONES
Paule Marshall

'This book, so rich in complexity, history and beauty, is of great importance to those of us who wish to affirm our connectedness to and understanding of the struggles of all women to emerge through their families, lovers, and societies, whole and free' – *Alice Walker*

This is the story of Selina Boyce, daughter of Barbadian immigrants, living in Brooklyn through the Depression and the Second World War. Passionate, stubborn, reflective, Selina is caught between the ambitions of her hardworking mother, and the fantasies of her charming, lazy father. But Selina wants independence and, above all, her own identity. As Selina grows to womanhood she comes to realise that only by accepting the great dreams of both her parents can she take her life into her own hands.

    Brown Girl, Brownstones is Paule Marshall's first novel; written with pride, anger and a fierce generosity, it is both a moving account of the efforts of immigrants to surmount poverty and racism and a beautiful, powerful evocation of what it is like to grow up black and female.